THE FORGOTTEN GEMSTONE

A Xiinisi Novel

by

KIT DAVEN

THE FORGOTTEN GEMSTONE
© 2013 by Kit Daven

All rights reserved. No part of this book may be reproduced in any matter whatsoever without permission in writing from the author, except by a reviewer, who may quote brief passages in a review or critical article.

First Print Edition: November 2013 (US)
ISBN: 978-0-9919827-1-4

This is a work of fiction. All characters, events, situations, and references portrayed in this story are either fictitious or are used fictitiously.

Written by Kit Daven (www.KitDaven.com)
Cover Art by Sean Chappell (www.SeanChappell.com)

KIT DAVEN is a fiction writer who enjoys blending science fiction, fantasy, and horror. Keenly interested in social dynamics and understanding the world through her senses, Kit's writing is partially autobiographical but mostly fantastical in nature.

She grew up in Petawawa, Boucherville QC, North Bay, Borden, Germany, and returned to Toronto and eventually settled in Cambridge, where she continues to grow up really, really slowly.

ACKNOWLEDGMENTS

My deepest thanks and appreciation to—

Sean Chappell, for being supportive, encouraging, and staying sane throughout this crazy process; for being a sounding board, an editor, a cover art illustrator, and the most patient man I've ever known.

Kelly Mero and Monica Montague for reading an earlier draft and providing their first impressions; their feedback helped clarify the direction I needed to take with the story.

Donna Stewart for her editorial input and eagle eyes; who, shortly after introducing herself at the Riverside Print Group, agreed to be a Betareader.

Visit Kit's website to learn more about her and her work.
www.KitDaven.com

For

Monica
Moni
Mo

— 1 —

A YOUNG WOMAN crawled from the center of a megalithic lily. She stood upright, her heels resisting the hard coldness of a thick petal which had once been pliant and warm. Scanning the desert, she winced at the horizon where the rising sun kissed a waking world, making the sand blush. How disgusting, she thought, that something inanimate could express such intimation.

She looked to the flower beneath her. "Elishevera?"

Ossified petals sprawled in rigid curls over the wasteland. The woman felt as though she stood on a grand marine beast floating in a tawny sea, the bulk of its body hidden far beneath glittering waves. Stiff and frozen, the bleached flower's face gazed upward. All around tiny, spiny, crooked cactuses bobbed in the sand.

The woman glanced over her shoulder, toward the place she had crawled from. A stale gentle wind issued from the crevice at the center of the flower. Within the narrow gap, located just beneath the surface of the ground, a receptacle existed—a tiny round chamber with walls which should have rippled and flowed with breath. Beyond that, a hollow stem with rows of tiny teeth descended deep, very deep into the ground. For all its similarities to a plant, Elishevera fed like an animal, grinding flesh and swallowing with a gullet that extended to the center of the world.

Flower beast: the only one of its kind the woman had created in any of her worlds. It had nursed a land of lush gardens and rolling plains dotted with copses of trees. It was a playmate, companion, and confidante during the woman's adolescence. It was a sacred being.

"Elishevera." The woman trembled. "It's me, Ule."

An examination of the creature revealed no clues to whom or what had caused its death. While the desert shifted with a different type of life than what she originally cultivated, it also offered no answers. Rubbing her forehead failed to ease the ache in her mind or stop the relentless memories which had urged her descent into this world.

She had run away. To take a break from her realm for a little while, she told herself. To avoid her Mentor too. Mostly she wanted to return to this paradise, where sunlight had imbued warmth into every blade of grass, tree leaf, and blossom. Memories of being revered by the world's inhabitants and long, lazy days with Elishevera promised a happiness she had once known.

If not for her studies or the building of other worlds, she tried to convince herself, she might have returned to make note of its evolutionary changes. For an eon, it floated on an onyx pillar, silently spinning in such a way it seemed not to be moving at all. The stillness evoked disinterest and ignoring the 24-60-60 model planet with few technological advancements had become second nature.

"A zillion worlds are populated with humanoids that putter around twenty-four hours a day," her Mentor complained. "What a waste of imagination!" He called the world generic.

She called it Elish.

Yet, for some reason, Elish—a culmination of creative efforts during her late childhood—had been assured a place in the Vault.

She thought it strange to watch other Masters, Mentors, and Students scan the world, scratch notes in their fat books, and amble on to observe other nebulas or galaxies with more unique and sophisticated hierarchies of organic systems. No one ever spoke to her about Elish and yet she often caught them, her Master included, watching her as though she might do something terrible again.

Their behavior intrigued her. She mimicked them peaking into the upper stratum of the planet's atmosphere, tried to understand what they found so fascinating. Air whipped through every molecule of her being as she straddled the boundary between her realm and the world's. Two states of existence fought for dominance. The sensation of being simultaneously colossal and infinitesimal always intrigued her.

She should have descended into the world more often, as was their custom. Yet, because she had spent the latter part of her childhood and all of her adolescence interacting with its early evolution, she had been instructed to let it be. She obeyed and moved onto studying more complex architectures, most of which she found tedious and unnecessary. Now, she needed to return. She needed to see her old friend again, to rekindle their connection.

Despite the passing of time, Elishevera would still know how to subdue Ule's moods, no matter how dark; she was certain of it. The flower beast had told the best stories and exuded brilliance that rivaled the sun's. Indeed, groves ripened and flowers blossomed in its presence long ago. The warmth of a single petal often eased Ule into long, deep sleeps, where she dreamed and enjoyed the love which flowed freely between them.

Love.

She wrinkled her nose and silently chastised herself for wondering if her Mentor, Ibe, could ever be receptive to a love from anyone other than himself. Instead of enjoying her impromptu dances, he much preferred to focus on this old world and its odd behavior, and brought it back to the safehold of their Laboratory for observation.

She was surprised when no one—not even their Master—noticed the world's disappearance from the Vault, but she said nothing. She delighted in Ibe toiling over her lackluster work, basked in the attention his solutions provided. She followed his instructions, even obeyed him which went against her independent nature, for she finally had his attention.

Their conferences about the world had felt almost intimate at times. Ibe pointed out flaws in its design; errors, he called them. They weren't worth their Master's attention, he told her, and she didn't mind that their Master knew nothing of their tinkering in the Lab. Ibe was finally attending to her work more than to the work of his other two Students. For the first time during their assignment to one another, since her childhood, she mattered again.

Just as Ibe had ignored her flirtations, she ignored his warnings not to interact with the world without his knowledge. She descended, air flowing through her as she shifted in size, her form pulling into something small and compact yet no different from how she regularly appeared to her kind.

Upon her arrival in the receptacle within Elishevera, she adjusted to the sensations in this new state of existence. For the briefest of moments, her heart stopped. The single, long heartbeat she was accustomed to quickened and changed to a double beat. Nerve endings doubled in number, increasing sensation as her flesh came into contact with other solid forms. And time, momentarily, sped up then slowed down until she acclimatized to the world's spin.

She had remained curled tight lying on her side, anticipating the receptacle walls to ripple with energy and swell with breath. Anger boiled inside and she waited for Elishevera's welcome in her mind—a soft, soothing whisper which would cut through her pain and simmer her mood. Instead, she heard silence, felt an absence of energy, and crawled out of the flower.

She squatted gracelessly, a toe trying to dig into the hard shell of the creature. Tiny and lithe, her long, straight flaxen hair pooled in the lap of a pale yellow dress. Eyes glistening the color of sky, she grazed her fingertips across the cold ancient beast.

"What happened to you?"

In the early dawn, Ule cried.

— 2 —

SHADOWS EXPANDED INTO distorted shapes, elongating as the folk they belonged to woke from their slumber. Yawning and stretching, those who had slept on Elishevera during the night rose to their feet. A gathering crowd below began to climb and crawl over the petals. They reminded Ule of ants until they stopped to blink at the new dawn and utter morning salutations.

Shielding her eyes, she noticed how the sun's cool light obscured the pale skin of her raised arm, a contrast to those around her whose deeply bronzed faces reflected a myriad of hues.

"That's a nutmeg," she muttered to herself. "And he's a peppercorn." Other spices came to mind quickly: paprikas, turmerics, cumins, mustards. There were even folk pale as herself—a sprinkle of salt. If not for the low rumble in her stomach, she wondered if she might have described their complexions another way.

Good morn's rose from the maze of tents and shanties which wound around Elishevera—a spiral of chaotic sprawl which looked unkempt and very wrong. Ule remembered a circle of pillars had once surrounded the flower. Pink marble walls marked the inner sanctum of a temple, where libations were set upon altars, and Priests and Mystics conspired against one another.

Nearby an older man ambled toward her.

"Who are you?" she asked him.

He grinned, nodded, and walked on.

She asked others the same question, adjusting her language to what she heard around her. At first she thought they did not understand but they did. They murmured among themselves instead of answering, and Ule felt the curious sensation of being on display. Some examined her, gaping with wonder, while others shuddered and hastily wandered to the far side of the flower beast.

"I am Ule," she finally declared to a woman bound tightly in white linen.

The woman nodded, said her own name in return but nothing more.

"Do you recognize me?"

The woman shook her head and, after an awkward silence, shouted at two children striking the flower beast with stones.

Ule's stomach lurched at the stippled dents left behind in the shell of her friend. Elishevera deserved better than that, even during death. The sooner Ule made everyone aware of her, the sooner they would stop their desecration.

She told others her name, waited for them to recognize her.

"I'm Ule. Surely you must remember me."

They muttered her name, shook their heads, frowned or patted her on the shoulder. The smoothness of their flesh simultaneously comforted and repulsed her.

Suddenly she recalled a culture lesson from her youth: No being in any world created would remember its creator once enough time had passed. The collective memory of the original inhabitants *would* fade, her Master assured her.

Determined to prove him wrong, to ensure her memory did endure, she had suggested repeatedly that statues be cast in her image and stories sung in her honor. Yet no matter how well she had tried to influence the ancient people, her efforts must have failed. No memory of her had survived to the present. She was a stranger, and she imagined her Master all smug and satisfied by the confirmation of his wisdom.

Searing anger shuddered throughout her body. She needed Elishevera to be alive, to feel the caress of a petal, to entangle their minds in an effortless exchange of ideas, moods, and emotions, and laugh about the humans and the funny rules of conduct they made for themselves.

"I created all of you," Ule seethed.

If anyone heard her, they said nothing.

The swell of her emotions peaked and ebbed, dipping into sadness. Sagging, she called out to the flower beast again. "You were my last friend."

"Be you well child?"

Coldness crept along her flesh as she looked toward an older man, who stood craning a wrinkled neck toward her.

"Elishevera, what's happened to her?" she asked him.

"What do you say?" The man's voice warbled. He shuffled toward her. "Here? Do you mean this statue, child? Why, it be here a very long time." A deep, rattling sigh escaped his lips. "Perhaps it be here much longer than any of us will ever know."

They were pilgrims, Ule learned from the old man. Royalty,

clergy, soldiers, merchants, farmers. All kinds of folk traveled to this place year round for the same purpose—to contemplate the mystery of the flower in the desert.

Sometime long ago, they must have plucked the tiny sunstones from the fine lattice of veins on each petal until they were gone. Now, they climbed the plundered beast, struck it, and listened to hollow tones resonate and diminish somewhere deep beneath the ground. Some people tapped rhythmic codes representing sacred notions and waited for a response. Some carved images and symbols into the stone, hoping to manifest a dream or desire.

Children dug into the ground near petals partially buried by sand. They tunneled as far as their tiny arms could reach, fingers wriggling along thick roots which snaked beneath the earth. Ule wondered why they bothered. Come morning, their dug holes and tracks would be wiped clean by the night wind. They would only have to dig again.

The old man stayed by her side, rambling on. In any season, on any day of the year, hundreds of people milled about the flower, he explained. They told stories. The kind of stories which sought to explain the existence of the object. What it had once been. How it had come into existence.

Ule knew Elishevera's origin. She had created the beast, long, long ago; in the beginning. Part octopod, part lily, and part sunstone, Elishevera loved unconditionally and she loved everyone. Regardless of how enlightening, silly, and untrue the pilgrim's stories sounded, at least they agreed the flower had to be sacred. How else could anything endure the storms of the dry, abrasive desert?

Hard, cold stone began warming beneath Ule's feet as the sun rose. She imagined Elishevera coming back to life and wished the gentle beast as something vengeful, shucking the humans from her petal limbs and flinging them into the wasteland. She saddened at the thought that her fantasy would never happen; Elishevera was too kind. And never again would Ule feel her friend's strong, supple embrace.

This was the nature of death. Creations evolved in ways their creators couldn't control, and sometimes they died. Ule knew this from first hand experience.

As a child, she had designed a world of lava populated with creatures, one race of gypsum and another of granite. Both races fought over who revered her the most, and she admired the rapid development of war strategy among the Granites yet loved the

Gypsums for letting their spines evolve into long, arcing, powerful third legs.

Growing bored by the escalation in battle between the two races, she eventually shoved them into lava pits or knocked them together until they surrendered. At her Master's command, she put aside the world and let it be despite her insistence that the two races needed proper attending.

"Guidance neither manipulates nor usurps," her Master explained.

She tried to understand.

"It nudges," he continued, "toward a course of action—a prodding of free will, an offer of suggestion. Nothing more."

Eventually she allowed the lava world to flourish on its own. Yet, upon her return, the rock races had ground each other into dust. Lava rivers had hardened into thick, black veins; seas had dried into cracked plateaus of clay. Mossy green creatures slithered over a desolate planet pocked with shadowy lakes.

She felt her Master had tricked her into letting the world become some ugly, creepy thing. Had she not felt so betrayed by him, so angry at herself for listening to him, she might not have done what she did—an act worthy of severe punishment.

Spite possessed her. Ule trembled at the memory. She had struck her Master with both fists. Then she wrenched the lava world from its dais in the Vault. Racing through hallways, she dove into the Laboratory, let out a wild shriek, and smashed the planet against a wall of rock samples.

The planet's atmosphere ignited on impact. Whips of energy lacerated everything in the room, including her. Laboratory tables and shelves buckled from the force of the planet's iron core exploding. Nearby, two other worlds, both with emerging new life forms, were knocked from their pedestals. They spun briefly before erupting into flame.

"Destruction is forbidden," her Master had taught her. Of all their laws, this one remained absolute. "It's a delicate matter. There is protocol. Done incorrectly, destruction will diminish the An Energy within our realm and every world we've constructed."

The resulting inquiry had been a lengthy process of being mentally poked and prodded by the Council and her Master. The calm temperament of her Master faltered twice during the process. At the start of the inquiry, he admonished her glib remarks in a burst of fury.

"Wipe that smirk from your face!"

Near the end, an unnerving despair shuddered through him when the Council announced its disciplinary action. She remembered their steely tones and grim appearances as they explained the punishment.

"You will have your memories temporarily blocked. You will be detained in a holding cell in The Void, where invisible walls will confine you in quarantine." Their voices droned on. "There will be no supervision. You will be alone. You will be expected to tap into and remember the joy of creating, without influence."

She understood, but the chorus of contempt continued.

"You will be denied the comfort of belonging until you can prove to respect our ways. You must learn to understand your failing toward us."

Within her prison cell, after her memories had returned, she had felt remorse for destroying the world of lava and granite people. Yet persistent Isolation only urged her to interact with Elish, the new world she had created, making reintegration back into society difficult.

No one had recognized her at first glance. She had left a vivacious, expressive child yet returned a subdued and deeply introverted adult. Though her Master did well to coax what little remained of her personality from a guarded, internal place, his effort failed to bridge their divide. Those who remembered her, kept their distance. Friends from her youth had developed close bonds with one another of which Ule was no longer a part.

She walked in the realm yet did not belong. Her distrust for everyone grew, no matter how hard she tried to fit in. No amount of effort changed their opinion of her. At times she wanted to knock their heads together, pull down the Laboratory and the Vault stone by stone so she could rebuild their realm into a place where she belonged.

"It's the lava world all over again," Ule moaned, peering across the desert. A strong urge to destroy everything pulsed within her mind.

A young man stopped to ask if she was well.

She shook her head. "There used to be rolling fields and gardens." She gestured to the desert, nearly shouting. "Green, green, and more green everywhere. And there!" She pointed to the east of her. "Where's the grove of oranges gone? They had the sweetest nectar. And here!" She indicated the area about the flower. "There was a wondrous temple with Priests and Mystics. They documented rituals, squabbled, and argued. Wow, could they bicker! Where has it all gone?"

According to the young man, there had always been desert.

She stamped her foot with a huff. Another wave of mourning swelled inside. She swiped at tears dampening her cheek and shouted at no one in particular, hoping to gain everyone's attention.

"This is Elishevera and I'm Ule!"

Sharp pain jabbed within her temples.

A woman clucked and shook her head. She squeezed Ule's shoulder and spoke the true name of the place—*Lishev*. She reeked of old sweat and fresh ale, and her fingers felt like bark as she explained the sanctity of the place.

Ule squirmed from the woman's grip. She knew better than anyone what Elishevera meant.

She heard their mutterings: Hid in the flower, did she? Fell asleep there and na remember? Na right in the head, she be.

"I'm Ule!" Her words echoed through the air and into the flower. She felt the gentle vibration through her toes.

Her grief diminished again. "The name Lishev has no meaning," she ranted to everyone nearby. "*Eh-lish* means 'love' and *ever-ah* means 'eternal'. I should know, I made your language. I made this being and all of you." She waved her hand across the crowd.

As a Student, she was limited to using her power within the Laboratory and within any of her created worlds; those were the rules. In the early phase of a world's evolution, using power in the presence of other life forms was often necessary, but once the Root Dimension stabilized and the An Energy diffused, demonstration of magic in front of other life forms was prohibited.

Tired of all the rules, she didn't care if punishment awaited her when she returned home.

"How dare this world forget me! You all loved me once. I will make you love me again."

She arched toward the sun. She envisioned multicolored fireballs streaking toward the horizon. Sharpening her focus and intent, she summoned her will and stretched her arms skyward.

Not even sparks flew from her fingertips. She shook her hands and tried again, extending both arms, wriggling every finger, holding her breath, yet the dawn sky remained a constant blue.

The An Energy resisted.

It hummed in her ear, faint and distant. No matter how much she pushed her will, bright lights failed to shower down from the sky. The An Energy flowed around her instead of through her as it should, denying any access.

She fell into a heap on the flower struggling for air. Searching for any possible reason to explain the An Energy's defiance, she finally let out a long sigh. "It's this awful desert!"

Puzzled and rejected, she found herself surrounded by folk attending to more pressing concerns—discussion of their dreams. Strange tales from the sleep realm pervaded while they nibbled on figs and cheese.

Their attempts to comfort Ule with a pat on the shoulder only added a layer of irritability to her frustration, grief, and anger. Beneath these feelings, fear pervaded in an ever-swelling chill.

She forced a deep breath, marveled at the expansion of her lungs and her heartbeat returning to a solid, even thump-thump in her chest. A soft breeze tickled the fine blond hair along her arms. The sun stung her eyes. Silently she cursed at the degree of sensitivity she felt being in this form.

"Enough of this dreariness," she muttered.

She had come to the world to bathe in the remnants of her youth and remember what she liked best about herself, to commune with a friend, to soothe away her disappointments. Now that Elishevera had died and all that was familiar about the world had vanished, she much preferred to return to her realm.

Ule's gaze turned inward and upward, toward the middle of her forehead. After a slight push of will, she felt the molecules of her body shimmy and prepared to ascend back to her realm, not caring if anyone saw or if she was reprimanded by her Master for being careless.

With eyes closed, she perceived the desert vividly in her mind. Perspective shifted, Elishevera flattened, and the horizon arced a degree or two before she slammed back into human form.

A tremor wracked her body.

Her eyes fluttered open. She glanced at the people squatting nearby but they were preoccupied with drawing symbols on Elishevera with stumps of charred wood. Perhaps the old man who first spoke to her might have seen something, yet when she saw that he sucked at a leather bound flask, studying her from a safe distance, she doubted his rum-skewed perception could offer any help.

Hitching her dress above her knees, she considered another position and sat cross-legged, toes pointing downward, pelvis tilted, head slightly bowed, neck straight. The alignment was challenging, but after she adjusted her hips and legs, she found ease in the posture and attempted ascending again.

Familiar warmth engulfed the length of her spine. She clung to the rising energy and with one last fierce push of will and bated breath, she collapsed, slumping slightly backward and to the side.

Beneath the mid day sun, darkness overcame Ule.

— 3 —

ULE AWOKE TO discover her legs sprawled in the sand, her head and shoulders cradled in the stiff curl of a petal. She imagined herself having slid down the side of the flower during her unconsciousness and thought it strange no one tried to revive her, until she saw others curled up in nearby shadows softly snoring.

Lying there, she felt like a new born being presented to a swelled, radiant father. She winced at the bright sun, at the tightness of her swaddling dress twisted about her thighs and hips, at the sting in her skin after brushing sand from her warm, sticky cheeks. With a sigh, she crawled deeper into the cool shadow within the petal.

Trailing her fingers over eroded ridges of ancient veins and pockmarks where sunstones were once fixed, she admired what remained of her work. Creating a being that was a mix of animal, vegetable, and mineral had been an interesting exercise, one she had only tried once, and she mentally chastised herself for not checking in on the beast. Now, without her notebooks, she would have to guess at the number of generations since she last descended into the world.

"You must have died shortly after my last departure." She clicked the tip of her thumbnail against her teeth, staring at nothing in particular. Worry threatened to cloud her thoughts.

"There aren't any new volcanoes I can see." Self talk had always helped her stay focused and calm. "No indication of a massive flood, that's obvious, even though all of this area, in the very beginning, was a salt lake."

Her foot began to jerk and twitch. "Don't suppose someone might come look for me since I didn't bother to tell anyone I was descending." A wavering breath slipped between down-turned lips. She hoped someone would notice her missing and look for her. She flicked the sand with her toes. "Stupid!"

She scanned her mind for details.

"When was I here last, Elishevera?" And she imagined Elishevera responding.

"Shortly after the First Age, little monkey. Shall I tell you a story now?"

"Tell me the one about the An Energy."

In Ule's mind, Elishevera cooed to mark the start of a tale. "In the beginning, the An Energy was abundant. It concentrated wherever most of your world building happened, making that place very magical."

A pang of grief saddened Ule. "You're magical."

"Yes, once, long ago," Elishevera agreed. "Would you like to hear more?"

Ule nodded at the imaginary voice in her mind.

"During the First Age, every human could speak with me, and you, little monkey, inspired their devotion toward me."

She remembered now. "The An Energy diminished, shortly after I caused that teeny little earthquake to reveal a quarry of pink marble-"

Someone in a nearby shadow sleepily shushed her.

Reluctantly, she lowered her voice to a whisper. "Marble holds such pretty architectural details, I just had to unearth it somehow so someone could find it."

She rolled onto her side, propping her head up on an arm. Setting Elishevera's story aside, she began reviewing old studies.

"Everything seemed fine. The An Energy diminished beyond human perception; normal." She drew an imaginary check mark on the petal next to her. "Your psychic voice grew faint; also normal." Another imaginary check mark. "When devotees couldn't hear you anymore, they began cultivating a belief system centered on your sacrificial libations. An Energy or not, you still needed nourishment." Another check mark.

Narrowing her eyes, she frowned. "That's when it turned strange. Some of the devotees still communicated with you. I didn't think it possible without concentrated An Energy. And they wanted nothing to do with the rituals being developed."

The disparity between two types of worship began to widen. Some insisted the act of ritual was the only way to honor Elishevera while others—the passionate ones—insisted on direct communication. Like the Gypsum and Granite rock races Ule had once created, worshipers fought one another until finally the group split into two separate factions. Those who chose ritual called themselves Priests, and those who desired direct communication with Elishevera were called Mystics.

Hot tears suddenly stung Ule's eyes as she wondered which of the factions had turned on the flower beast, the Priests or the Mystics.

Deep breaths helped ease some of the tension in her neck and the ache at the base of her skull. She kept a constant focus on clenching cool sand between her toes until the ruddy hues of day's end marbled the horizon. Relaxed again, she crawled from the petal onto the cooling sand and lay on her back.

Sprays of fine dots freckled the darkening sky.

"So many of them," she murmured.

The stars were an illusion, of course. The cosmic glitter consisted neither of stars nor suns, she reminded herself. It was a boundary separating this world from her realm. She imagined this planet floating on its pedestal in the Vault, where projects cluttered the vast chamber.

Supported by hundreds of simple white pillars and plinths, the expansive room archived living worlds worthy of study. There they remained, evolving and aging until they winked out of existence and were replaced with newer models.

Some worlds spun on daises, others hung suspended from the ceiling, and the older ones, those which had flourished for generations, were tucked away in niches or alcoves.

For an eon, she had longed to return to studying in the Vault, where the vastness suggested no end to satisfying her curiosity. Yet, all it took to make her want to leave, to descend into Elish, was a brief encounter with Ibe.

She had waited for him, hoping to explain that her dancing wasn't intended for his friend's laughter or the reprimand of their Master. She hoped to soothe Ibe yet when he arrived, he wasn't alone.

Disappointed, she slipped into the shadow of an alcove and watched as he and one of his Students approached a dais. Speaking quietly to one another, a deep, resonating laughter suddenly burst from Ibe. He nudged the young man playfully, who smiled in return.

Yearning to bask in Ibe's laughter, Ule emerged from the shadow, joined them at the dais where a binary system whorled, and broke the silence. "Will you be descending?"

The Student wrinkled his nose at her.

She knew immediately her presence was unwanted. "It looks beautiful," she cooed, hoping to be invited along.

Ibe winced. The expression was slight but noticeable. The

brilliance in his eyes hadn't lessened any, so she knew he couldn't be angry with her. Something she said had annoyed him, however, and she remembered her Master's note about how she made Ibe uncomfortable.

She stared at the binary system, waiting for Ibe to respond. Life was more evident in the world than in him during the moments that followed. Deflected by his blank look, the world drew her into a swirling dance of colors looping in a figure eight around two tiny stars.

Ibe and the Student diminished. The stars began swelling in size and intensity. Unconsciously she had begun to descend, and just as she dipped into the world, a fierce unbridled thrum of energy blasted her.

"Ule," Ibe warned. "Stop!"

She shook her head, felt her body snap back to the Vault. Orange and cinnamon overwhelmed her nostrils, and she knew from the magic scent that the binary system belonged to Ibe, not the Student. Any invitation would need to be granted by her Mentor.

"Sorry. I didn't mean—"

He chuckled and shook his head. "You know the rules, Smashcrow."

The Student smirked at the nickname Ibe had given her, and she shuddered at the reference he made to her past transgression.

"Do you want to be punished again?"

The rules of conduct among her kind were numerous: Students could explore another Student's creation by invitation only. Mentors required invitations from everyone except the Students assigned to them. Yet Masters could descend into any world of their choosing, for any reason, at any time.

The rules were always heeded and the breaking of the rules seldom ignored. Ule knew this from experience.

"Can I join you?" she asked Ibe.

He always appreciated candor in his other students, and she hoped he warmed to her forwardness.

He shook his head. "A world can be more than a single planet, yet that's all you could envision during Isolation."

"I had to relearn everything." The words felt heavy in her mouth.

"The An Energy responds to what's in our minds, doesn't it?"

Ibe's Student nodded.

"And out of your infinite potential, from a clean slate," Ibe pointed to his head, referring to her memory loss, "you create a rudimentary world. How can you appreciate the sophistication of my work or anyone else's for that matter?"

She wanted to run from Ibe's beautiful face. A trembling came over her. Since her release from Isolation, opening herself up to express her feelings—to trust anyone—had been difficult. And she wondered if reaching out to anyone had been worth the effort since she only seemed to be causing more trouble.

Try as she did to resist the feeling, love for Ibe still coursed through her that day in the Vault, for he had taken an interest in her when no one else had. Unusual phenomena occurring in Elish had prompted more advanced instruction. Consequently, they spent more time together in the Laboratory, where he showed her *fixes*, as he liked to call them.

During each conference, conversation flowed easily between them, although she remained aloof. Eventually, she began returning to her room directly after each encounter, where she sat and buried her nose in the folds of the dress she wore. His magic scent clung to the fabric, and she inhaled citrus and cinnamon till her nostrils stung.

Interaction between them became more synchronous. He started touching her—a pat on the hand, a squeeze of the shoulder. Whenever he skirted the table to acquire a book or scan the world, his palm rested in the gentle arch of her lower back. Often he uttered short, humorous comments close to her ear and his breath warmed her neck. And she always leaned into him.

It seemed only natural that the need for entanglement began to blossom. Yet, for all his strength—his preference for being forward and direct—he complained to friends, Students, and eventually their Master, about how Ule's flirting made him uncomfortable.

Fierceness and intensity blazed from every molecule of Ibe as he stood next to his Student, admiring the binary star system—two tiny orbs swirling about one another in a beautiful exchange of pink, white, and red dust tendrils.

"Stay here." His voice became more ethereal in tone as he and the Student dissolved during the start of Descension. "I deny you permission."

Ule reeled from a child-like tantrum thrashing about within.

"It'll be no fun," he said, his voice fading, "if you can't keep up with us."

Laughter diminished into a whisper as they transformed into dust-like creatures, each creating a tendril of color—pale shades of blue and purple. She realized each swirling mass of pink, white, and red was a living creature, rushing about each star in an unending race.

Ibe and his Student re-formed into new colored tendrils many times as they progressed through several generations while interacting with the world, which surprised her. Ibe seldom transformed into something inhuman. He preferred the shape of his thick bowed arms and legs to any form less than humanoid. Although, one time he grew extra legs to see if they might make him stronger but only found them humorous instead.

Most of her kind usually kept to their true form, which is the first shape they embrace within inception. While some chose animals, feline and canine species being popular, others chose hybrid creatures: a lion's head on a reptile's body or a serpent with webbed spider arms. Most, however, preferred the form of their ancestral species—humanoid.

Confident and assured, Ibe's profound masculinity was constant and magnetic. He was older than her by hundreds of generations at least, and for that she expected more maturity from him.

Age mattered little among their kind. Once they became adults, experience defined their stage of maturity. Childhood and adolescence evolved quickly, usually the length of an eon. After that, they could live hundreds of eons if they managed their generations well enough.

The longer they lived, the better their chances of transcending. After the Quietus, their final death, their forms unraveled into black fine threads from which worlds were woven, and their spirits evolved into a species who, instead of manipulating already existing energies and dimensions, created them.

Transcendence seemed unlikely for Ule. The numerous errors uncovered in Elish and her inability to seduce Ibe reflected flawed reasoning and judgment, yet she still tried.

She gazed at Ibe every chance she could. She stood close to him, sometimes accidentally bumping into him. She learned which corridors he walked the most and made sure to walk there too. None of this, however, seemed to pry him away from his Mentor duties or the need to test the limits of his own virility. Her compliments only incurred a snort or a laugh, which was a better reaction than none at all.

That day in the Vault, Ibe's words spun her. She wished she could extract her love and display it on a dais to show everyone its flawed and unfortunate design, to warn everyone. Instead, she had descended into Elish, where she now lifted herself from the sand, stood tall, and patted dust from her dress.

Unexpected indigos and strange warm grays smudged the moonlit sky. Unrecognizable eerie sounds and haunting wails floated through the air. This desert certainly held no beauty the way Elishevera's gardens had.

She imagined the land the way it once was.

Wild flowers speckled fields of moss and heather, marked by patches of quack grass and purple clover. Copses of thin tall trees with angular canopies of brown and gold needles dotted the veld, home to a relentless chorus of chirrups, tweets, and buzzings. Leathery purple vines crept over tree and ground, and occasionally tried to bridge the many streams and rivers meandering in and around the great temple at Elishevera.

A sprawling temple, constructed with faintly colored granite, clay, and egg stone circumscribed the flower beast. Within these walls, an inner sanctum of pink marble glowed beneath the sun. Over the generations, additional rooms created a second floor and then a third. When the foundation could no longer support the weight of a forth level, they dug down into the ground, carving out subterranean caverns which became vast libraries and treasuries.

Ule smiled at the memory of splashing in warm water within the temple's inner courtyard, marveling at how it soothed her body. Elishevera had always offered a fleshy petal as either a diving platform or a slide. Now, that joy and vitality had vanished.

A pang shot through her heart. She missed Elishevera's calmness and grace, the soft murmur of the creature's thoughts. She hadn't thought anything had gone wrong with it while she created the world—her power and sensitivity had still been developing during adolescence. Had there been errors, her Master was certain to have discovered them while scanning her mind upon her release from Isolation. He would have detected her experiences interacting with devotees and realized they maintained a psychic link with Elishevera.

His examination of the world was lengthy and thorough as well. Afterward, he told her to let the Mystics be, that perhaps with a little more time their connection with the flower beast would eventually cease.

Again, her Master proved him self correct. No evidence remained of Priests or Mystics residing at a temple in the desert. Centuries of wind and sand storms had either buried or worn away the ancient place into a fine dust.

Dull sand littered with chiseled gray rocks and boulders offered little inspiration, even less so beneath the shadow of night. Even with its strange, dark green prickly plants, the wasteland depressed her.

"How long has this rudeness endured?" She glared at the horizon and reflected on the shift in her mood. At the beginning of the day, she had gone from yearning to be in this world to wishing she were home again. Any further attempts at ascending proved futile, and she suddenly felt trapped.

Understanding the elusive An Energy seemed the only way to return home, she thought, and then she tried to recall all the adjustments she had made to the world.

She had destroyed a chasm that had torn through the Root Dimension and threatened to breach her realm. She had added additional veins of iron to the world's core to increase the magnetic field and prevent the atmosphere from leaking into their realm. And finally, she infused a barrier into the planet as a safeguard.

She shivered at the thought that she might have misunderstood or misinterpreted Ibe's instructions, which might explain the An Energy's odd behavior.

"It doesn't make any sense," she muttered to herself. "I did ascend... but just a little bit."

Beneath the dark of night, a thought became illuminated. She needed to locate someone to help her figure out what stopped her from ascending, someone who sensed certain energies the way the Mystics had long ago.

— 4 —

A BOUQUET OF unusual smells tickled Ule's nostrils: spiced stews, smoked meats, pungent herbs, and tobacco. Curious, she strolled toward the nearest clump of campfires, ignoring the growling in her belly.

Evening campfire light flickered against wooden makeshift lean-tos, casting shadows and silhouettes on the yellow fabric of pavilions and tents.

Intrigued by whispers emanating from a nearby tent, she leaned in closer to listen and discovered soft moans of pleasure. Her face flushed as she flung herself away from the tents and kept to the makeshift paths lit with lanterns.

She skirted the perimeter of tiny camps clustered together and discovered a boy with dark disheveled hair and a red mark on his right cheek. No more than ten or eleven years old, he sat alone before a small fire turning a long stick over the flames. He gazed intently at the few bits of oddly shaped meat curled around the tip of the stick.

Whatever he roasted smelled spicy and wonderful. She inhaled deeply and moaned.

"Oh, hello," the boy said, glancing at her.

"Where's your mother?"

"Na have one," he replied. "Sometimes I find a soft, pretty *bes* and sleep next to her during the night, if she'll let me."

She wasn't sure what he meant by the word *bes*, but he spoke it kindly. The world was full of odd new words, and she didn't care for how the people spoke.

A long silence ensued between them before the boy spoke again. "Has anyone said you be pretty?"

"Oh yes!" She flopped onto the ground in front of him, letting out a huge sigh. "Back home, not so much. Here, a long time ago, all the time," she continued. "They'd shower me in beautiful flowers from the gardens and cook delicious feasts and bathe my feet and style my hair." Pulling at the ends of her dulled blond hair, her fingers brushed out tiny bits of sand.

"Well, I would na go that far," the boy snorted. "You be pretty, just saying. Na many girls wear their hair so long and loose. And your face be nice and rosy now, na pale like before."

She touched her face and winced. Heat rose from her cheeks and she imagined her skin had burned from lying in the sun unconscious for half the day.

"But you talk funny," he said.

Ignoring him, she stared at the rippling fire. "What do you know of this place?"

"I know plenty stories." He laughed. "But let me tell you the true story."

She blinked as the boy immediately rambled on with 'A very, very long time ago' followed by 'There once be.' She let out a long sigh.

The boy stopped. "What?"

"Which is it?"

"Which be what?"

Ule huffed. "Either it's 'A very, very long time ago' or 'There once was.' It can't be both."

The boy laughed. "You be one of those."

"What do you mean?" Straightening, she scowled.

"You be all about the rules," the boy explained, glancing at the charred meat at the end of the stick. "Making them, following them." He leaned forward a little, eyes growing wide. "Making others follow them."

Breaking them too. She was exceptional at that, Ule thought.

"Do you want to hear the story then?"

"Not really," she mumbled, but the boy hadn't heard her or, if he had, he didn't listen.

"A very, very long time ago," he began again.

She hugged herself, wondering just how long ago this story took place and how long she would have to endure his rambling.

"There once be a merchant. He cherished wealth above all else. When his wife popped out a baby boy, he named him Ertoi—a great name should you ask me, which means *ever lasting*."

"No it doesn't," Ule blurted. "It's not even a real name. Even if I did create that name, it would have to mean something like... snail sludge."

The boy hushed her. After he wedged the roasting stick between two stones, he continued his story.

"Ertoi grew into a strong, handsome man. Had a talent for carving, he did. Could make everything from just about anything: clay, brick, stone, wood. Since Ertoi could make valuable treasure from common junk, this made Ertoi's father very happy, what with his love for money. Na that bad at all, eh?"

A gaggle of children led a woman toward the fire, where they sat beyond the circle of light. The woman and her children were wrapped in black shawls to ward off the cold. Their gaunt olive faces floated in the air as they listened.

"The town's ale maker had a daughter. She be a kind and shy girl, always glanced down at her feet whenever Ertoi walked by, so he never much noticed her until one day when she walked by with her head held high."

The young boy jumped to his feet and sashayed around in a tiny circle, bouncing about with light steps and twirling invisible long hair. "G'day," he said in a high voice, acting the part of the ale maker's daughter. Then he strutted, raking his fingers across his chest. With a sniff, he spoke in a low tone and replied to himself. "G'day."

The children snickered at the boy's impression of Ertoi. Even Ule couldn't help smirking at his antics.

"Their eyes met and Ertoi wondered if she always be so beautiful.

Now the merchant absolutely hated the ale maker and thought him a bit of a drunk. On and on he lamented about the girl's parentage, a family who built their fortune on the fumes of alcohol. What a yeasty bunch!"

The mother laughed this time.

"Is there a point to this story?" Ule tried to interject as more people gathered around the campfire, drawn in by the boy's words and dramatic gestures. Her question went unanswered.

"Ertoi fell in love na the less. When his father denied their union, Ertoi fled home and lived the rest of his life in a forest which now be this desert."

"It was never a forest," Ule complained. "A grassy knoll maybe, with the odd small wood, but never a forest."

The woman in black tutted at her. Affronted, Ule gaped at the woman and again at the boy when he resumed the story.

"It once be an ancient forest with ancient trees, and Ertoi spoke to each tree, asked which of them would be willing to die for love. Of them all, the oldest and the largest bowed with a creak and declared, 'I will die for your love.'"

A pang of envy struck Ule. She kept her discomfort to herself.

"Ertoi lifted his ax." The boy's arms wobbled as he pretended to lift some heavy, invisible ax into the air over his head and brought it down to the ground with a slam. "With every blow of the ax, the tree whispered 'for love', and he carved a man and a woman on a flower. They be entwined about one another in that love embrace I'm na supposed to know about yet. To this day, sometimes if ya strike the flower and listen real close, you'll hear that old tree whisper, 'For love.'"

A murmur of pleasure rippled around Ule, and she wondered how anyone could enjoy such a flawed story.

"So where are the figures of the man and woman?" She pointed past the boy in the direction of Elishevera.

"Centuries of sandstorms wore them away," he replied.

"Why have the figures of the man and woman eroded and not the flower too? And why a flower?" Ule slapped her lap. "Why not a bush or, or, or a squash?"

She was determined to tear open the story, reveal its untruth, but the crowd complimented the boy on his interpretation and began offering their own. In one, Ertoi's object of love had been a goddess in human form; in another, Ertoi died of old age before completing the carving.

She ignored their renditions because she knew the truth.

Stories like the boy's at least touched on the sacredness of the place; for that she was grateful. Otherwise, none of the pilgrims honored Elishevera by climbing her, carving initials into her petals or calling her by a meaningless name such as Lishev.

At last, the boy's stories came to an end, and Ule wrinkled her nose. "Oh vomit!"

The folk fell silent, hushed by her outburst.

He tilted his head. "What bothers you?"

"Who is this Ertoi?" She glared at everyone around her. "What's the name of the woman he loved?"

People from the crowd uttered their theories and speculations. The young boy shrugged. A throbbing had settled into Ule's head, her mind reeling at the distorted fictions failing to remember the flower beast accurately. Wasn't it enough she had just learned of Elishevera's death?

"Ertoi be me," declared the boy.

"Excuse me?" She squinted at him.

"Ertoi, he be every man." He pointed at other young boys and a nearby man. "It be him and him." He pointed at the woman dressed in black. "Ertoi's love, the woman, be her." Then he pointed at Ule. "And she be you."

Ule huffed. Hardly, she thought. The boy's suggestion tugged at the last of her reserve. Remorse, anger, and bitterness tore her open, and she ranted, "It's *not* me! It's *never* me!" She smacked the back of her hand in the palm of the other. "No one wants to love me back, ever."

"You best lay off the rum, eh?" The boy laughed.

Her rage quieted as she glared at him.

After accepting a pat on the head and a few coins from some of the listeners, the boy sat before the fire and resumed turning the roasting stick.

"Hungry?"

Her stomach growled in response. She touched her abdomen. Now that she was in humanoid form, she needed to take care of her body properly, which meant she required sustenance and sleep. Fond memories of her last visit rushed into her mind, of how she had enjoyed delicious sweet drinks and sauce-drenched meats, the soft caress of fine fabric on her skin, and how she had made a game of being in the world.

"Yes," she replied, acknowledging her appetite.

"Here," he said, pulling a piece from the charred twisted lump at the end of the stick.

She took the small bit of roasted animal flesh. It had caramelized into deep browns and black with little prickly bits sticking out. She bit into it, finding the outside chewy with a delicate, flaky, white meat on the inside.

Deciding she like it, she asked, "Ooh, what's this?"

"Spider," the boy replied.

Her stomach heaved. She spit out half chewed roasted spider, imagining crispy hairs stuck to her tongue.

"Hey!" The boy pinched her arm. "There's na else to eat. Go beg at the pavilions for better beast."

She bolted to the nearest shadow of the desert and bent over, the boy's voice trailing after her.

"Good luck to ya, they be snoots like you."

The rest of the spider came up in a forceful heave. Angrily she kicked sand over the mess. If the people had tended to the groves as they had been instructed, the veld would have thrived and spiders wouldn't need to be eaten.

Wrinkling her nose at the acrid odor, which made her want to heave again, she turned back toward the little campfire and stepped on something hard and smooth.

— 5 —

THE ARCH OF Ule's foot ached as she leaned forward and plucked a stone from the sand. Cradling it in the palm of her hand, she noted its pale yellow color and the wavy black streak through its middle, like some nocturnal animal's eye staring at her.

Turning it over, she humphed. She had created many different types of rock matter in this world, and although she recognized the stone was mostly granite and quartz, she failed to understand how they could combine in such a perfect pattern.

She brought it to her nose and sniffed. A hint of fresh earth and mildew lingered. She couldn't tell if it was a natural odor belonging to the desert or the residue of magic scent.

"Be you alright?"

She turned toward the familiar quavering voice of the old man who had spoken with her that morning. Though frail, thin, and hunched, he must have been impressive in his youth for he still towered over her.

"Yes, I'm fine," she said, wiping her mouth.

"I see the sun kissed you today."

Cringing, she gently patted her cheeks. "It feels more like it slapped me a hundred times."

The man snickered.

Ignoring the glassy look in his eye and the smell of rum on his breath, she eyed him from head to toe. He was certainly very old and could possibly be wise enough to tell her what she needed to know.

"Perhaps you can help me," she began. "Where are the Priests?"

The man's face lit up. "Oh there be quite a few in Woedshor, and a couple in the temple just the other side of the desert that a ways, and well, they be just about anywhere if you ask around."

She glanced at the rock in her hand, ran her thumb against its smooth surface. She really needed to find someone with a link to the An Energy, someone who was aware of magic. "What about witches?"

The man blinked. He stared into the air, scrunching his nose. "What is *which-iz*?"

"How about sorcerers or wizards? Shamans? How about diviners or seers?"

"These be strange words." He shook his head. "You do speak strange."

Frowning, she peered at the ground and considered the possibility that there were no living creatures with special sight or knowledge of anything beyond their tangible world. Only some form of magic maker could detect and work with the intangible energies that permeated all matter.

"What of magic?"

The old man smiled. "Yes? What of it?"

Her heart fluttered. "Who are the magic makers?"

"They be the Mystics."

Although she was relieved to hear a culture of magic existed, she thought it odd these ancient devotees had been the ones to develop it.

Darkness overcame the old man's face. "What do you want with them?"

"Where can I find one?"

The man squinted, hesitated, and with a pull at his beard he finally answered. "The closest would be Sondshor."

She frowned. The Mystics had always been fierce and determined, willing to turn away from the Priests but unwilling to abandon their loyalty. She wondered why they had abandoned Elishevera.

"What is Sondshor?"

"You truly na be from around here," the old man mused. "Sondshor be the Magnes realm at the edge of the desert."

"Where exactly in Sondshor would I find a Mystic?"

Grimacing as though it pained him to answer the question, the old man spoke softly. "Na matter which shor, they always be found at the castle."

Panic curled about her heart. "Castle? Whose castle?"

"The Magnes, of course."

She stared at him. An anger like no other rose through her body. She never wanted magic and politics mixed together. She saw what it had done to her Granite and Gypsum peoples—centuries of war, generations never knowing peace, the transformation of their world into something ugly.

In this world, she made sure the Priests wrote down her law that magic always remain sacred, confined to the temples only, beyond the reach of any Magnes or other kind of political leader.

With a deep forceful breath, she hurled the yellow stone.
It struck the sand with a soft thud. She curled her hands into tight fists, stomped a foot on the ground, and shouted. "Holy great suns!"

Trembling, the old man stepped backward.

She stormed away from him, the boy, and the camp. Delving into the dark desert, she began to rant. "You just can't leave anything alone. It just turns into a big mess."

"Child," the old man called after her. "The desert na be the place for wandering at night. There be nomads."

"I just wanted to be with a friend, find some comfort, feel good about myself, trust again," Ule carried on, ignoring him yet again. "Feel belonging, you know, be with someone who accepts me, loves me, oh, and have a little fun, but no! The Priests or, or, or the Mystics abandoned her, killed her. How dare they?!"

The old man hissed, his voice breaking from strain. "They na be kind to strangers." He made no effort to follow her. "Death will come to you fool!"

"Leave it alone, he says!" She placed the bulk of her blame on her Master. "Let it be, watch what the worlds become, and learn about yourself... What good is that if they just destroy themselves in the process?!"

The pleasure of shouting—finally letting her emotions stream out—drowned out the concerns of the old man and compelled her to continue ranting. Somewhere, very far away, an unseen beast howled in response. She ignored it, ranted on, stomped her feet deeply into the ground, marching in no particular direction. Only the light of a half moon dimly lit the footprints she left behind in her tantrum.

Occasionally she stumbled. She swore when her toes struck shadows that were really stones, fueling her ire. Her cheeks burned and her heart pounded. She ranted until her throat grew sore, stomping until her foot came down on the edge of a piece of slate and cut her heel.

In the wake of her fury, she finally paused. Breathing deeply, she mentally pulled herself together. The rage diminished. She came to this world seeking comfort in a friend and instead discovered only more heart ache.

Fatigued, hungry, her face on fire now, she felt her energy slipping away and knew only food, water, and sleep could restore her. Unable to heal herself or outrun anyone or anything, she needed to return to the camp, perhaps even befriend that boy again. He did find her pretty after all. Together they could conspire to find something better to eat than spider. Once recovered to full strength, come morning, she would travel to the castle in Sondshor and find herself a Mystic.

Unsure of which direction she wandered, she turned to scan the desert for any sign of the orange glow of campfires near Elishevera. A low flowing wind swept the top layers of sand and filled in her footprints, obscuring her trail.

At last, she saw something in the dark and marveled at the distance she had come. How long had she been ranting? She rubbed her eyes, just to be certain, for she saw the glow of not just one cluster of campfires but two, each a considerable distance from the other.

A blast of cold wind blew across her back. Her thin dress flapped against her legs. Shivering, she wrapped her arms across her chest and studied one campfire then the other. Each beckoned to her with a dim orange glow, promising food, warmth, and companionship. One had to be the camp near Elishevera, and the other…

What had the old man said, something about nomads?

No matter how hard she tried to find some outline or silhouette of Elishevera, the bone flower blended into the sand becoming a vast stretch of dark gray, indistinguishable from the rest of the desert. Without daylight, determining which of these campfires belonged to the devotees was impossible.

Her stomach growled and, as if in response, a haunting howl floated through the air. The hairs on her arms stood on end. She noted the sensitivity as she rubbed the prickle in her flesh. Somewhere out in the desert, some form of beast wandered about.

She began chewing a thumbnail as she considered which direction to go. If she waited until daylight to determine a destination, weakness might prevent her from standing altogether. Sleep would partially restore her, but she worried she might wake in the belly of a desert predator.

Swaying slightly, she realized she needed to make a choice soon. If she didn't start walking again soon, her trembling knees would relinquish their last bit of strength.

"It felt like... there," she said, pointing to the smudge of orange glow to her left. Her tongue rolled over a fine grit along her teeth, which she was certain was sand.

"But that one," she pointed to a similar smudge of orange to her right, the collective glow of another cluster of campfires, "there's a big shadow near it as well. Perhaps it's Elishevera. Or it could just be a big rock."

To the left, her intuition urged. "To the left it is," she decided grateful to be moving again.

A sharp pain tore through her left heel every time she bore down on it. Her knees throbbed and her lower back ached. The sooner she arrived back at the camp near Elishevera, the sooner she could start begging for food and water, be nourished, then curl up into a ball to sleep and restore her flesh.

To dream.

Recalling the phenomenon was peculiar to this humanoid form, she looked forward to dreaming. The experience often evolved into a sensation of her conscious mind rising above streams of dream bubbles, where she floated in a dark, seemingly empty place, which reminded her of the Void. Often, she had awoken to a mix of visions reflecting Elish, the dreams, and what she saw happening in her realm.

Once, she experienced a dream in which she suffered a fever. During the fever, she began another dream in which she slept and woke to discover her legs had turned into legumes. She found the imagery odd and irrelevant. Yet the dream within a dream, although curious, felt comforting.

Smiling at the memory, she felt her inner energy begin to

weaken. Dread flooded her at the thought of collapsing in the desert only to be gnawed upon by a creature. The feeling propelled her toward the dark silhouette which rose behind the glow of campfires.

Hobbling closer to her destination, she strained to peer into the shadows, searching for a curl of petal or any distinct, identifiable detail belonging to Elishevera. A puff of air blew across her back. She stopped. The hairs on her neck bristled again. Had her reserve of energy been fully restored, she could simply shift her molecules to pass through any medium—air, water, ground—and outrun the desert creature.

Stiffly, she peered over her shoulder into the dark, sensing some *thing* had silently crept by. A coyote or jackal, perhaps. She strained to see into a pocket of nearby shadows, but they remained impenetrable and still.

Hobbling, her pace slowed with every step. She focused on the looming camp, where the dark silhouette against the sky grew taller and taller, appearing nothing at all like Elishevera.

— 6 —

A WIDE TRACT of thick grass poked through thinning sand. Small tents and large marquees draped in bright red fabric pillowed and flapped in a blustery breeze. Crimson flags slashed the sky. Caravan wagons marked the edge of the encampment, where camels slept, some standing still while others lay with legs neatly tucked beneath them.

Through the firelight, the large dark silhouette shimmered and revealed a dense cluster of trees. Bare, bowed trunks supported a thick rippling canopy of dark feathery leaves.

Two figures stood side by side at the edge of the camp, peering into the darkness. Farther along the perimeter, another two figures stood. All wore white cloth tightly wrapped about their legs, torsos, and heads.

Ule suspected they might be guards, and she focused on the two closest to her, trying to remember what the old man had told her about the nomads. What had he said, something about them not being kind to strangers?

She gulped. The movement aggravated the raw burn in her throat. Exhaustion and hunger seemed to offer no choice and urged her toward the camp.

"I always have a choice," she mumbled.

Two options came to mind: return to the desert to sleep a little while and face whatever lurked in the shadows, or trust the nomads to show some kindness. She chose to meet the unkind nomads.

Nearing the camp, she leaned against a wagon to catch her breath. She called out to the two guardsmen. A faint croak stuck in her throat.

Helplessness overcame her. Even worse, she felt naked even though she wore a dress which snapped frantically, twisting and untwisting about her legs. Vulnerability spurred the desire to build a wall around her so thick nothing could penetrate.

She began walking again, the last of her energy slipping away. She reached for the guards, tried calling to them.

They must have heard something, perhaps even seen her, for both stiffened, reached behind their heads, and withdrew swords from sheaths strung across the backs of their shoulders.

"Please!" Ule forced the sound through her dry throat. She stumbled and managed to stay upright, her left heel throbbing and demanding attention.

Riveted to their posts, the guards raised their swords and peered into the darkness. Firelight reflected in the white cloth, creating the illusion of flame flickering auras.

The beginning of rough grass pricked her soles. The guards advanced. One grabbed her by the arm with a tight grip; the other hastened to sheath the sword, leaned into her, and spoke in a low tone.

"You na look well, young bes."

Strong arms pulled Ule along. Her vision faded in and out, yet she saw the glint in the guards' eyes and their soft curves nearly hidden beneath white tunics. They kept her upright, guiding her toward the inner camp and calling out to others.

She eased into the warmth of a nearby fire. She would have slipped into unconsciousness if cold water hadn't trickled over her lips and chin. She reached out for the source and clutched a clay vessel. Tipping the water into her mouth, she gulped it down and let it soothe her cracked lips and parched tongue until it hit her stomach with an icy fist.

Clutching her belly, she groaned to keep the water from coming up. The cramp released slowly. If it weren't for feet padding along the ground nearby or being prodded in the flesh by warm hands, she might have succumbed to sleep.

The pulse of pain in her heel increased sharply then subsided. Something wet and sticky soothed the burn in her cheeks and arms. Why that old man would think the nomads unkind to strangers, she couldn't understand.

Gentle fingers continued prodding her body. She gave into the weariness and her head lolled to one side. For a brief moment, she lifted heavy lids and glimpsed a figure walking among the tents.

A tall, graceful woman strode toward the fire. A small, round face jutted from an elongated head, which swept upward much longer than a skull should. The woman's legs tapered from full thighs down to narrow feet, every muscle firm and chiseled, breasts small, hips narrow. Her glistening black eyes and charred wood complexion nearly blended into the night.

"That's a kokum," Ule mumbled.

She blinked at the strange woman, felt the last of her strength slip away, as questions poured into her mind. Who were these people? What business did they have in the desert? What did the word bes mean? But most importantly, where did the strange woman hide her arms?

Ule woke to a brilliant sun just past zenith. Groggy and thirsty, she batted fine sand dust from her face. Beneath the shade of a tent, she found herself covered with a soft red cotton blanket, and she assumed the nomads had tucked her away for the night.

Sandalwood incense burned in a clay cup near her feet. Beneath her, a wicker mat creaked when she moved. Nearby something spattered, crackled, and stank like fish cooking. A blankness cut through the powerful odor, which meant water was also nearby. Inhaling deeply, moisture in the air soothed her nostrils.

Vaguely remembering she had dreamed, she breathed heavily, waiting for the images to flash in her mind. The dreams remained murky and dark, yet she had the strangest sensation that someone had been looking for her. Now, the thought felt more like a wish.

Rising from the mat, she stretched. The subtle scent of moisture wafted from a half-full barrel of water. This time she drank slowly.

Dozens of nomads milled about the campsite, which had settled onto grassland surrounding a wood of tall trees. Curious, she thought as she walked about the encampment, limping slightly when her left heel touched the ground.

The caravan consisted of only women, both young and old. When she asked where they had come from, they answered with an assortment of names referencing many different places in the world. Some of the names were familiar; others sounded distorted yet reminded her of towns and cities from long ago, when the world was very young.

"Are there any men here?" She directed her question toward a round woman with dark hair and a cherry mark on her cheek, who reminded her of the boy she had met the day before.

The woman swore. Spit shot from her mouth with precision. Ule barely leaped out of the way before it marked the spot where she had been standing. Remembering the old man's warnings about the nomads being unkind, she wondered if he really meant they were unkind to men.

The woman with the cherry-marked cheek lectured her about how they need not answer to men. Eventually she hugged Ule fiercely in a reassuring embrace, told her she had come to the right place to learn about the way of bes. Among them, she would be free from the shackles of men and love again.

Ule cringed. There was that word again—love. She turned away from the woman.

Wandering among the tents, she chatted with the nomads and learned the caravan never stayed in one place too long. They replenished water supplies from the oasis within the wood, visited Sondshor Market to buy food, and obtained monies by stealing coin pouches from desert travelers and from trading odd items discovered buried in the sand, like small caskets and books written in strange old languages.

The day unfolded in a series of conversations, Ule talking to nearly everyone she met. As the sky darkened, night urged the women to speak in whispers. All the women, young and old, gathered in a clearing lit by torches and a small bonfire.

Burning branches snapped and crackled in a stone rimmed fire pit. Nearby, the soft whoosh of tents fluttered in a steady breeze. Around the bonfire, just within the edge of the firelight, women sat in twos and threes. Cross-legged or with legs tucked to one side, they settled onto folded blankets or pillow-seats set before wide wood benches, which stood no more than a foot above the trampled grass.

The benches filled up quickly with bread loaves and bowls of various foods. The women tore into the food, dunking chunks of dark bread into tiny bowls of yellow sauce.

Ule's stomach growled. Eager to eat, she sat on the ground next to two young girls. They shook their heads and pointed toward an empty round pillow-seat several benches away.

"Come, young bes," a silky voice called to her.

Light-headed from hunger, mesmerized by the fire and the prospect of a feast, Ule sank to the ground, sitting on a firm cushion covered in slippery blue and gold fabric.

Wishing to thank the strangers for their hospitality, she finally glanced at the two women seated at the table. Words caught in her throat. Across the mahogany table sat the woman with the black eyes and the charcoal skin. She wore a red dress and her strangely shaped head was also wrapped in red cloth.

"I am Bes," the woman said.

Eyes twinkling, thin charcoal lips spread into a gentle smile and narrowed her fine prominent chin and aquiline nose. She sat back from the table. Elevated a few inches above the ground by a square wooden platform, the elaborate chair extended upward into a back rest carved in swirled leaf patterns. An orange cotton cushion puffed around her thick thighs.

Ule was certain the woman had waved yet there she reclined, armless. Even more surprising, Ule found herself gaping at the armless woman's companion—a corpse encased in a glass box. Gray and withered, eyes and lips sewn shut, the enshrined woman had been mummified and incapable of speech for a very long time.

Ule slapped a hand across her mouth. She was certain the second woman was alive. Her initial surprise faded into fascination. Curiosity stuck out its claws and latched onto the two strange women. Lowering her hand, she blinked at the corpse inside the box then at the armless woman.

"What be your name?" Bes spoke softly, smirking.

"U-Ule." Questions buzzed in her mind. She latched onto the first one. "What is *bes*?"

Bes smiled wider, displaying a row of perfect pearl white teeth. "It be a title," she answered. "But it be an idea first. Here we create a way to honor being bes."

Ule smiled at the mention of creation.

During the First Age, devotion toward Elishevera had been a foundation for all beings in the world, a way to connect, bond and remain civil to one another, especially after the An Energy began to diminish. They had revered Ule also, finding ways to create.

If not for the shrines and temples built in her honor, if not for song and dance or the invention of glyphs with which they told stories, Ule would not have been immortalized, and cultivation of these abilities was paramount to her memory enduring throughout Elish's history.

She could never tell people what to do or think; this was considered interfering, according to her Master. She could never trick them; this was manipulation. Both ways broke their rules so she taught the Elishians to be curious, leading by example. She asked a lot of questions. In time, they too began to ask questions. They asked for guidance, what fabrics she liked best, the name of her favorite food, and other ways to best honor her.

Except now, the ancient world's efforts had proved futile. No one she met recognized her. She had no power to remind them. A Mystic, however, might know how to help.

"What is this idea you're devoted to?" Ule tried not to stare at the sharp edge of Bes's shoulders, or the unblemished smooth indents where arms should be, or the unusual size of her skull.

"To the feminine aspect, to its authority within us," Bes said. "You be a young bes. I be *the* Bes, leader of the Bisi Nomads."

Ule sighed. Something of the original language had remained after all. Although she didn't recognize the word bes and assumed it to be new, she did recognize the pluralization rule and was grateful it had stayed intact—Ule and Bes and the withered corpse counted as three bisi.

— 7 —

A YOUNG WOMAN approached the table carrying a wide rimmed bowl. She sat before the chair with the orange cushion, sudsy water slopping about, and began bathing the Bes's feet. Fascinated, Ule watched the woman pat dry Bes's heavily callused soles and wrap them with the cloth.

"What happened to your arms?"

"I be born this way," Bes replied, a tint of boredom in her voice as though she had answered the question a thousand times. She reclined slightly, her upper back hunching forward as her toes scrunched the cloth.

Ule's eyes widened. She knew humans underwent rare, drastic physical changes in their forms. Sometimes the mutations were revered, but usually they were feared and destroyed.

"Does it hurt?"

Bes gently laughed. "Na, young bes."

Six young attendants carried large silver trays heaped with grapes, apples, oranges, dates, and an assortment of nuts. They set trays down at various tables about the clearing. One of them attended their table.

"I be too warm," Bes said to her.

The girl's response was swift. Tenderly, she began unraveling the red cloth from Bes's head.

Ule held her breath, wondering if the oddly elongated head was yet another error in form, some strange eruption of bone and skin stretching her skull. Yet when the cloth fell away, she saw a sculpture of shiny black hair. It was intricately braided, curled, and pinned. It towered nearly a forearm high and sat on top of a perfectly normal head with a smooth, high forehead.

"You must have very long hair," she blurted.

"Longer than my height, I be told."

Before Ule could ask if someone could style her hair that way, Bes leaned backward. Raising one of her long, limber legs, she shook her foot free from the cloth wrap and extended it toward a bowl. With her toes, she plucked a shiny red grape from the vine and brought it close to her mouth. Her foot lingered as she leaned forward and sucked the fruit into her mouth.

The woman couldn't possibly be more flexible, Ule thought until Bes reached with her foot toward a wooden goblet of red wine and slipped the stem between two toes. She brought the vessel to her lips in a graceful arc, the muscles in her thighs shifting.

Bes's dark eyes locked with Ule's as she sat tall, tipped the glass, and drank deeply until a trickle of wine spilled from the corner of her mouth. She set the goblet down and wiped the wine away with the side of her big toe.

"We consider it a sign of respect," she began, a slight curl to one side of her mouth, "for guests to dine in the same manner as their host."

A little stunned at first, Ule regarded the tarnished silver goblet in front of her and shrugged. Determined to drink wine with her toes, she extended a leg up toward the low-rise bench.

A hush fell over the clearing.

Reaching with her dusty foot toward the half-filled goblet, she shifted slightly to accommodate the flex in her hip. Faint titters floated in between the crackles and spits issuing from the fire pit. She clenched her toes about the goblet stem, which began to tip as she lifted her leg. To prevent the wine from spilling, she shifted her balance and keeled sideways, tumbling from the pillow-seat.

Reverberating laughter erupted from Bes.

Ule scrambled to her sitting place grateful to discover she hadn't spilled wine everywhere. Relieved the goblet remained upright, she finally heard the Bisi's swell of laughter throughout the yard.

A flush of embarrassment warmed her cheeks. She began smoothing her dress, waiting until their mirth settled down.

Bes threw her head back and laughed again. "Good jest, na?"

Realizing Bes had played a prank on her, Ule snorted. "Funny," she said. Half-smiling, she shook her head and laughed.

A thrum filled the clearing as women returned to their dinners and gossip. Although an easiness overcame Ule, her curiosity was still not quite satisfied. She glanced sideways at the glass-encased box, wondering about the strange corpse with its curled hands, leathery skin, and wiry white hair. The stitches in her eyes and lips made death seem so solitary, internal, and indisputable.

An urge to say something finally loosened her tongue. "Does your friend prefer figs or dates?"

Bes threw her head back and laughed again. Though her hair seemed likely to tumble down, it held firm. Regaining herself, she leaned forward.

"She be the first Bes, the way the stories tell it. Every evening she be honored, a reminder of the sanctuary she created."

Ule realized the Bisi Nomads were no different than the people who traveled through the desert to honor Elishevera; they both sought a sacred place. The woman in the box had acted on an idea, brought it into existence through action. She had created. Ule felt an immediate connection with the dead woman.

"I created this world, you know," Ule said.

Bes arched a thin eyebrow.

Ule interpreted the facial expression as one of disbelief and quickly returned her attention to the first Bes. "So why did she create this caravan?"

"Love," Bes replied.

The fig Ule bit into tasted bitter. She rolled the gritty seeds around in her mouth, not wanting to swallow. Before she could protest, Bes began the story.

"Once she loved a man. The more she loved him, the more he struck her," Bes said. "It be the only way he know how to express his love. Their ways be too different from one another to find any happiness, and she knew if she na walk away from him, she would die."

Ule frowned. So far the love story was depressing, just like the one about Ertoi and the ale maker's daughter.

"He knew it be wrong to hurt her but he could na stop himself. He feared losing her and he could na let her go. See, when she ran, he hunted her down, dragged her back home, until one day she ran far enough away."

Ule waited for the rest of the story, hoping for some kind of happy ending, the kind of happy ending she heard happened with some people, people other than herself.

"She needed a place to heal herself, a place where na person could find her, a place that always be changing. She became a nomad, gathering together other women and girls like her, and they now be called the Bisi Nomads."

Ule's stomach churned but not in the usual nauseous way she had become accustomed to at the first mention of love. Now her stomach felt as though it were getting ready to bring up a spider.

The strange woman tilted her long head, peered at Ule with beetle like eyes and asked. "Have you ever been hurt by a man, bes?"

Nearby, Ule watched the women hunch, mirth erupting amongst them and fading away in waves. "Do emotions count?"

For a moment, Bes sat still and finally nodded. "Cuts scab," she said. "Bruises fade. Emotions? Those take the longest to heal."

"And sometimes they don't heal at all."

Bes stared at her briefly, eyes narrowing. "You be smart."

So far Ule had heard two love stories since she had descended into the world, both of them tragic, neither of them hopeful. She didn't need to be told these tales. She already knew no good came from loving someone.

She really needed to return to her world.

"Are there any Mystics among you?" She hoped the change in topic might lead toward a more comfortable conversation.

Bes scowled. "Only certain kinds seek their services." Her eyes locked onto Ule. "What do you want with a Mystic?"

Shifting nervously from the woman's scrutiny, Ule's uncertainty about telling the truth prompted her to lie. "I want to become one."

Her host winced. "You have the vision?"

Ule nodded, lying again, unsure of what to make of the woman's question.

Bes sneered, looking sidelong at the bonfire, where four others gathered carrying musical instruments: two tall, skinny drums; a long, hollow wooden pipe; and a wide diamond shaped board adorned with taut strings on one side.

"Do you not like the Mystics?" Ule asked.

Picking at what remained of the grapes and almonds, she watched the musicians begin to play, the voice of each instrument melding into enchanting music. The slow rhythmic beats made her want to jump up and swing her hips in big ludicrous circles.

"Do you like people who frighten you?"

Ule remained silent, not wishing to tell her host she feared very little in this world, least of all the people.

"Why else do the Magnisi collect them? They be weapons." Bes huffed. "One Magnes uses them to keep another Magnes in check, and all the Magnisi keep the world under their control."

Hearing the word Magnes again, Ule wondered what it meant. Before she could ask for a definition, Bes snapped her fingers and silence fell over the clearing.

"Enough with this nonsense," she declared. "Stay with us and I'll teach you our way."

Bes released her leg, letting it settle back on the ground. She hunched over the table, eyes closed. An earthy tone began to rise and fall within her throat. A slight shimmy overcame her body, and Ule wondered if the woman was about to vomit.

Tilting her head backward, Bes rocked both shoulders back and forth. She folded both legs beneath her and jumped to her feet, letting out a wavering cry.

Around the campfire, the women watched intently, some rising to their feet. Wide-eyed, they waited until Bes raised a knee high up and drove her foot down into the ground. Cries erupted around the fire as though the gesture signaled a beginning.

Legs wide, knees bent, Bes swung her hips in a large figure eight, first side to side then back to front. When she tired of that, she undulated her torso muscles, back and forth, from her pelvis to the top of her ribs. Even though she didn't have arms, Ule could see them swirling through the air.

She sighed at the lyrical beauty encircling the bonfire. Others joined in the dance. The desert hardly seemed rude now. Still, she knew she would need to find a way home eventually. Until then, she might as well enjoy herself. Stuffing the last grape into her mouth, she joined the nomads.

The rhythm of the drums beat faster. The girls stomped vigorously on the tough grass. Ule didn't mind it prickling her feet or the throb in her heel when she stomped. Elation whipped about within her. Despite the limitations of her body, she abandoned herself to the movement in the music.

When she felt the first bubbles of joy rise through her, she twirled on the spot, enjoying the lightness of being pushing through her. She barely felt the prickle of grass on her feet anymore. Only cool night air swirled around her.

Gasps broke through the rhythm of the music. The melody, the tone, the beat—each of the instruments voices faded one by one. The silence and a wave of murmuring interrupted her mindlessness. She opened her eyes to a dark sky spinning with stars and a sliver of moon, and just below her feet, faces turned upward to stare at her.

Ule clapped as she witnessed herself literally dancing on air. Somehow she had accessed the An Energy and floated several feet above the ground, an expression of her power in the world at last. Her satisfaction soon slipped away when she saw upturned faces glare and gape at her.

The stern countenance of Bes unnerved Ule the most, binding her joy into a knot of anxiety. She fell to the ground and scrambled to her feet as the An Energy receded. The hairs on the back of her neck rose. All joy of dance fled, and a strange mood overcame the women gathering close to the fire.

Bes didn't need to point with an arm. Her glance alone indicated something accusatory. She said nothing. She didn't have to. Someone among the group spoke first, and the others uttered the word as though it stung their tongues.

"Demon!"

Ule blinked in disbelief at what she heard.

"Your kind na be welcome here." Bes's voice was firm and rose above the whispers.

Strange comments spilled out of the women about how she looked nothing like a demon and how could they ever know the difference if they all started to look entirely human. None of what the women said made sense.

"You're mistaken," Ule began to explain, "I'm Xiin-"

The first rock struck her on the cheek.

She blinked. Angry, fearful faces cast in shadow by the flickering fire sharpened into focus. She shielded her throbbing cheek, felt her hand tremble. Shock barely registered before a second rock struck her in the stomach. Tears welled in her eyes from the sting of the stone. Anger rushed through every muscle in her body.

Beneath the dark of night, the women shouted, telling her to return to the night where she belonged. Bes's voice rose above them.

"Just because you walk among us, look like us, behave like us, does na mean you be one of us."

The guards who had aided Ule the previous night reached behind and unsheathed their swords. Other women searched for more stones to throw. Ule flinched as young girls poked her thighs with long sticks used to stir the fire, the heat of their tips searing her flesh with tiny red dots. She marveled and lamented at how quickly their adoration turned to hatred and violence.

Glaring at them, Ule wished upon them a searing white hot physical pain. She wished them screaming in agony, writhing and shuddering while they submutated into lizards and snakes. For all her intent and focus, the An Energy ignored her, and the effort threatened to knock her unconscious again.

When a third rock struck her in the chest, her entire body shook. She could have picked up the stones and flung them back, but that would not protect her. She was outnumbered, and her access to the An Energy was erratic and unreliable.

A cascade of small stones thumped against her arms and stomach. Sticks poked her hard, prodding her to move. She swiveled, shielding head with arms, but some young girls would not let her pass.

"Be gone from our sanctuary, little demon!" The words Bes spoke encouraged the Bisi to pummel and poke her with more fervor.

Despite the jabbing, aching pain, Ule sucked in a deep breath and pulled at the energy between her molecules. All at once, they loosened and shifted her into a state which allowed her to pass through materials. She still hurt even though the sticks and stones ceased making contact with her flesh, and was relieved to know she maintained that ability.

The sticks passed through her much easier than the stones, for their dense matter of fiber was more porous than compressed earth.

The Bisi gasped and fell back. Some screamed. Even Bes stepped backward, waving at everyone to seek a safe distance. Ule imagined she looked like what her kind usually do when they shift—a translucent image of her former body shimmering in the air. A ghost.

For a moment, she reveled in their fear, as girls collapsed to the ground shivering and older women waved their stones, riling themselves into a deeper rage.

Ule groaned. The pain in her shifted state tore through her with more intensity. The energy with which she used to modify her molecular structure was fading quickly due to her wounds. She turned and ran. She hoped the image of an eerie gray blur whooshing across the sand into the darkness of the oasis would be enough to keep them from following her.

She ran between the outermost trees, breath tearing through her throat. Once engulfed by the darkness of the woods, she stopped and gulped for air to ease her ragged breath. She shifted back to a solid state and peered back toward the bonfire.

A slow steady beat of drums punched the air.

— 8 —

A TREE TRUNK at her back, Ule slid to a ground cushioned by decaying leaves. Her heart sank, disappointment making her wish pain on the inhabitants of the world. She massaged her forehead as tears streamed down her cheeks.

"This isn't me." Although she wanted to dispel the emotion, she couldn't deny her hatred—a sensation of lava shifting inside. If she stayed in the world much longer, that lava would bubble, erupt, and spew her rage.

What she couldn't understand was how the Bisi Nomads chose to enact the same violence they strove to protect themselves from. Or how they failed to recognize an expression of the very power they honored and revered. Or how they could turn on a bes so quickly.

When in doubt, talk it out; at least that's what her Master had told her. Oddly, the self talk had comforted her many times during Isolation.

"They didn't see me as a woman," she whispered. "I had become…"

Throbbing welts, burns, and bruises melded into an ache she could no longer ignore. It pervaded her body in a way being burned by the sun hadn't. Even her cut heel had been tolerable. Her thoughts began to cloud, and she needed mental clarity to navigate this evolving world.

After three long, slow inhales, she tapped into the remaining reserve of energy within and began pushing around her biological systems, urging the physical wounds to heal faster.

Cuts scabbed over and faded into faint scars. Bruises cycled through blues, purples, greens, and yellows until they rose to the surface of her skin and faded.

Grateful she didn't need the An Energy to rejuvenate her body, she knew that for the amount of energy expended, the demand on her body to restore balance would be fierce. Pain ripped through her flesh, muscles, and bone. Clutching her stomach, she doubled over and gasped for breath.

Food would quickly restore her energy and ease the backlash of healing. Water too. Fatigue, however, forced her muscles to sag. She needed to find a comfortable place to collapse and let sleep partially restore her.

A well-traveled footpath wound between the narrow trees and disappeared into shadow. With effort she stood. Dried twigs snapped underfoot as she inched her way through the darkness, feeling her way until the trees opened into a clearing which smelled of fresh water mingled with earth and decay.

Issuing from the shadows, a distinct babble and soft splash of water suggested a spring spilling over rocks. When she peered into the darkness, she discerned objects by their silhouettes: a sapling tree here, a pipe cactus there.

Eventually her hands encountered a large, warm boulder. She collapsed on the ground next to it, wondered how the stone radiated warmth, and sighed in gratitude for it kept away the chill of night.

"Sleep," she mumbled, but her mind failed to succumb immediately. Her, a demon? The thought was ludicrous.

Demons only existed in the earliest stages of world building. They were cast-offs of dark aspects during a time when the An Energy was heavily concentrated. When enough inhabitants of the world shared a fear, incapable of accepting, tolerating, or reconciling it in any way, that fear took form.

At least it tried to.

Once dispossessed, demons were merely vapors trying to take shape. Like phantoms they wandered the world, waiting to pass over into the Chthonic Dimension, where they could evolve into ethereal beings or fade away altogether. All worlds evolved toward this separation.

The Bisi Nomads having knowledge of demons was an impossibility. Only magic makers would know about such beings, about the An Energy. Even if the Mystics weren't familiar with these phenomena, they should still sense them. For that reason, the Mystics seemed the best choice for helping her find a way home.

She needed to rest first, just long enough to recover enough energy to drink from the spring. The babbling water lulled her into a deep sleep, where she dreamed of dancing in the air.

High above the desert, she spiraled upward. A flame of red swirled around her, laughing. She recognized Ibe. She wasn't sure if his presence was actually him or just a figment in her mind. Regardless, she swatted at the flame and lamented. "I just wanted to love you. Why did you have to be so rude?"

Although the welts and burns had all vanished, by morning her flesh still retained the memory of those wounds. Pain surged, the sting returned, and she winced. Rubbing her eyes, she pulled her sore, stiff body upright to examine the oasis.

At the center of an oval clearing, a large cairn of black rocks glistened in the morning sunlight. Steam clung to thin rivulets cascading into a pond of rippling water. Rough-hewn stone steps encircled the structure, leading to the top where travelers stopped to fill their tankards and wineskins with fresh drinking water. Once sated, they could bathe away the grit of the desert in the pond below, or simply sit and enjoy a reprieve from sand and sun.

Cautiously, she dipped her big toe into the warm pond water. She usually wouldn't give much thought to walking about nude, but she stopped and looked about the clearing to ensure she was alone before slipping out of her dress. Regardless of how the thin fabric was, it still shielded her body from the world.

Wading into the water, she frowned at the growing self-consciousness within her, how the slightest noise threatened to roil her emotions. She hunkered down until only her head remained above the surface and melted into the liquid warmth embracing her.

Once again, she scanned the grassy clearing spotted with stones and boulders. Her paranoia satisfied, she examined the fading scars on her flesh. Rage whipped through her and receded, residual hatred lingering like an afterimage.

This wouldn't do. The feeling crept like an illness through her body. She came here to wallow in the very thing that seemed so elusive to her, love. While water restored her energy, loving and being loved would restore her in other less tangible ways, and Ule didn't want to know what she would become without this feeling.

Submerging beneath the water, she tried to wash away everything: dirt and sweat, mostly pangs of anger and grief. Eyes open, she watched long matted hair swirl about her face as she crawled along the bottom of the pond, examining round stones littered with leaves, seeds, twigs, and...

She broke the water's surface and gasped. Wiping water from her face, she glanced around the clearing. It was practically empty except for a few large boulders and scattered stones. Frowning, she considered an error in her perception, a flaw in her memory, because something was missing from the landscape and she couldn't figure out what.

"I can't lose my mind, not now," she mumbled.

Doubting her memory triggered another surge of rage. Plagued with doubt since being released from Isolation, she hated how certainty evaded her when she needed it most—during world building, when she spoke with Ibe, and now, in this hostile place.

She'd heard the stories about how others like her had given themselves over to their worlds, lost themselves to madness, unable to keep their physical forms intact, spinning out of control or dying prematurely.

The surge of anger eased.

Doubt was her curse. It slowed her down in both thought and action or spurred uncontrollable impulses, like the time she had destroyed three worlds when she discovered her Granite and Gypsum races had ground each other into dust. Destruction of other worlds in the Laboratory had been an error in her judgment. She meant to ruin her world only, which felt righteous and imparted a despicable yet effective message to her Master.

He was too strong, too confident. His control of the An Energy both unnerved her and, on occasion, ensnared her in a state of breathless awe. She envied him these abilities. She wasn't surprised to discover that after her punishment, well on her way to reintegrating with her kind, the contrast between his abilities and her vulnerability and chronic indecision made his presence unbearable.

After release, she questioned everything she thought, felt, and did. She never understood why when someone spoke with her, she searched for words and found her responses insipid and unsatisfactory. Articulating the source of her doubt had been difficult.

Eventually, she began to understand. She had been locked away according to a set of rules she had no part in creating. She was expected to obey them without question. To be without question was contrary to her nature—all of their natures. Worst of all, fulfillment of the punishment didn't seem to satisfy anyone for they continued to judge and avoid her.

Withdrawing socially from their confusing system and behavior came naturally. The distance it created, however, only made her yearn for connection again, the way she had in the Isolation chamber. If it weren't for Ibe, she might not have ever found a desire for connection.

Being near him eased her anxiety, brightened her mood, stirred her to action. She wrote poetry, lingered in the Laboratory longer than she should, and even stole a kiss once.

She hoped he appreciated her affectations and the effort it took. Instead, he reported her to their Master, who questioned her endlessly.

"You can speak with me," her Master encouraged her. "That's one way I can help you, if you let me."

She didn't respond.

"At least look at me." His voice was stern.

She couldn't look him in the eyes or she might feel smaller, disappear altogether beneath his scrutiny.

"What don't you want me to see, Ule? That you hate everyone?"

The truth in his words caused her to shudder. The candidness in the way he spoke only incurred more envy of him. She hated all of them for their doublespeak and their politics.

Shame pulled at her. Tears pushed their way onto her cheeks. She forced herself to look at him. "I don't want to."

In her admission, she found some release from resentment but not from guilt or sadness. She stopped smiling. At times she stopped breathing, forcing herself to rejuvenate her body. Everything and everyone danced just beyond her reach. And when it all became too much, she didn't turn to Ibe or her Master or any of her kind. She turned toward Elish—a world where she played as an adolescent on the verge of maturing into an adult.

It was an unremarkable planet, except she felt happy there and befriended a gentle giant flower beast that now lay still in a desert, frozen by death.

Ule sensed some part of her wanted to die, reminding her of a flame fading in the dark or a smoky tendril evaporating into air. Whatever had once been interwoven with her desires, dreams, and needs began to unravel.

"I can't fall apart." She drove these words deep into her mind while she stared at her wrinkled finger tips.

She crawled from the water and climbed the cairn steps leaving behind a trail of puddle footprints. At the top of the spring, she knelt and drank until the pain in her muscles and flesh diminished to a tolerable ache.

If the desert and its people were any indication of what to expect in the rest of the world, she worried she might fade away like those unfortunate others who had succumbed to their creations.

"Not in this dreadful place."

Returning to the pond's edge, she tried finger-combing the tangles in her hair that had begun thickening into stubborn dreads. Giving up, she struggled to pull on the dress which clung to her damp skin.

Only partially rejuvenated, she knew food would quickly restore the remainder of her body's lost energy. She set out on the well worn path back toward the edge of the woods, where she could spy on the Bisi from a safe distance. From their hostile reactions, she doubted they would willingly give her a few apples and figs, so she began to scheme a way to steal some food.

Safe behind a tree, she took a deep breath and craned her neck around to watch the women. What she saw made her stumble into the sunlight. All the camels, wagons, and tents had vanished. The bonfire, along with a half dozen scattered small fires, still smoldered. Everything, including the Bisi themselves, had gone.

She wandered over the flattened tract of grass, saw impressions of split hoofmarks, footprints, and wagon wheels in the ground. When had the Bisi abandoned the oasis? She rubbed her brow at the sudden aloneness.

Walking about the abandoned site, she plucked a wineskin from the ground, no doubt dropped in haste while the caravan packed their wagons. She also found a small saddle bag packed with dried meat, apples, and thinly woven gray linen, which she gratefully wrapped about her hot shoulders and head to block the sun.

She found other items abandoned in the sand: a stick of figs and a leather pouch filled with seeds and nuts. Except for the wineskin and an apple, she stuffed everything into the saddlebag and secured it about her waist. Returning to the pond, she filled the wineskin with water from the spring and slung it across her shoulder.

Recalling conversations with the nomads about how they visited trading towns at the desert's edge, she decided to follow their tracks. As long as she stayed a safe distance from the hostile women, eventually they would lead her to less desolate land. Free from the dreadful desert, she could then focus on finding a Mystic.

"Sondshor Castle, was it?" She bit into the yellow apple and savored its sweetness.

No one answered.

She kept her eye on the tracks created by the caravan, aware of a pressure building inside her. Another explosion of hatred threatened to escape. She pushed it back, knowing the feeling was born out of fear of not fully understanding the nature of the changes in the world, like the unstable nature of the An Energy. How could she dance in the air yet fail to make fireworks or turn the Bisi into lizards?

Occasionally sand drifts wiped the terrain clear of all tracks. Ule hunted until she found evidence of where the caravan trail resumed, grateful the weather remained temperate. At times the air felt so hot and dry, it burned her lungs to breathe. She persevered, following tracks and observing changes in desert terrain.

Black slabs of slate jutted at angles, interrupting the flow of sand. The variety of cactuses grew. Some were round and others were mutated spiny creatures twisted and curled into odd shapes. She stayed clear of them, not wanting to be pricked by their fine needles.

Basking in solitude, she squeezed the apple core between her fingers, debating whether her stomach was strong enough to digest the seeds and extract their powerful energy. If she threw the core away, she wondered if a tree would struggle to grow in a sea of cactuses, if its bark could endure being pricked by spines. Would it need another of its kind or would it survive on its own?

Ule decided she could get by without intimate connections. She didn't need anyone; not really. She'd spent half an eon entirely on her own. She only needed to appreciate herself and her ability, no matter its stage of development. Without Master or Mentor to curb her behavior, she could become whatever she wanted.

Releasing her fingers, she let the core fall to the sand.

Skirting a large boulder, she passed a tall cactus which stood at least three heads taller than her. Stunned by its remarkable appearance, she stopped to marvel at how all its bulges just happened to coincide with the muscles of a human body.

Round spiny red scions clustered on what could be shoulders. Along the backs of forearms were rows of thin red spines of varying lengths. More red spines spanned large calves. Everywhere smooth flesh was marked with widely spaced ridges running the length of its body.

"Just like a human," Ule mused as she turned on her heel.

"I be better than human," the cactus replied.

— 9 —

ULE FROZE.

The voice had issued from the cactus. Lowering its arms, the cactus lifted a distinctly human head with masculine features: black eyes hooded with a thick brow bone, a wide nose, squared jaw, and dark green lips.

She blinked in quiet fascination at the stealth and agility of the cactus as he stretched. His arms swung back and his chest thrust forward. She did not remember ever making such a plant or animal.

"I didn't mean to scare you," the cactus proclaimed.

She didn't believe him. The tone of his voice was laced with sarcasm and menace. She felt as if no good would come from the creature, no matter how well intentioned his words might be. Everything that had happened to her since her descent into the world may have contributed to her overall uneasiness. Her instincts warned her to be careful.

"You didn't," she assured him. "Thought I was alone. You startled me, that's all."

A silence ensued between them. She had the distinct feeling the creature before her was anticipating or expecting something to be done or said.

Pulling one foot from the ground then the other, he uprooted himself, shaking away clumps of sand which had stuck to his well-defined calves and feet. He was considerably taller than any human she had seen so far, and he leered at her.

"Afraid of me?" he asked, tilting his head. Warmth failed to flicker in his face, even though a slight smirk curled at the edge of his mouth.

Considering how the Bisi had treated her, a nagging worry pervaded Ule. Physical wounds she could heal, and with her energy fully restored, in the ideal environment, she could flee if she needed to. Unable to ascend was worrisome. That the inhabitants of Elish had become as duplicitous as her own kind irked her. But fear. She had felt it a times, creeping about in the lower depths of her mind. She knew nothing good ever came from letting the fear beast free.

"No," Ule answered, keeping her fear caged. "Should I be?"

The cactus snorted.

"You do know who I be, do you na?" He shifted his balance to one leg, thrusting out a hip and rubbing thick, callused green fingers across his ribbed chest.

She stared at him blankly.

"I be Istok."

"Oh," she replied. "I'm Ule."

She had seen the devotees of Elishevera greet each other in many ways, which often involved the arms or hands. They hugged and sometimes grabbed each other's forearms. Some patted and squeezed each other's shoulders. Most shook hands. Upon seeing fine spines jutting from the backs of Istok's arms, she quickly reconsidered extending her hand.

"Everyone who lives in the desert," he continued, "or passes through, knows me." He bowed slightly, nodding toward her. "Usually they tend to cower."

Coldness crawled down Ule's back. Doubt flickered inside her. If she understood the cactus man properly, she wasn't reacting appropriately, and she couldn't help wondering if this beast was a King or a Lord.

In need of clarity, she carefully asked. "Does this cowering include a lot of trembling?"

"Yes. Yes, it does." He stood a little taller. His glare grew intense. "They shudder and shiver before they... *run*."

Ule smiled politely, pushing away doubt. A quiet deep breath settled her nerves. The cactus was not a reigning authority. He was a tormentor. She was certain nothing he could do would be any worse than what the Bisi Nomads had done to her.

Istok stared at her for several moments.

"Do you know where the closest town is?" she asked.

In two long strides, he stood before her, a hint of mildew wafting from his body. Ule knew to keep her ground. Giving into the beast, even just a little, would indicate her submitting to his domination and reveal a fear that hadn't entirely surfaced.

"Very few talk to my kind the way you do?"

"Your kind?"

"You really na know who I be or what I be, do you?"

Ule sighed in the following silence. She really just needed to keep moving through the desert.

"I be a demon," he announced.

"Oh." Ule frowned at the revelation, wondering why he hadn't passed through the nexus into the Chthonic Dimension. Yet another error, she told herself.

Her understanding of the demon realm was limited. What she knew related primarily to world building, during which a Chthonic Dimension spiraled into existence along with the Root Dimension. Connected by an invisible portal which they called a nexus, the dimensions often mirrored one another except in one way—the Chthonic Dimension lacked substance.

"You should be afraid," he demanded.

"Hardly," she lied. Her breath shallowed.

Although unnerved by his presence, if he was indeed a demon, she marveled at the complexity of his shape. "You're truly impressive, considering demons are usually smoky. You've actual solid form, don't you?"

She poked his chest to be certain. Firm, thick flesh resisted her touch. The smooth, supple texture reminded her of Elishevera when she was alive. "People must truly fear the desert in this world," she commented.

She turned on the spot and began walking, his image remaining within her peripheral vision. After her encounter with the Bisi Nomads, she exercised caution and turned her back toward him only partially—just enough, she hoped, to convey to him how little she regarded him as a threat.

"Usually they do." His soft words floated over the dry air, and they sounded as if he whispered in her ear.

Keeping a distance from him, she searched for the tracks of the Bisi Nomads but couldn't find any. She heard the light thump of Istok's feet as he lagged behind. In mere seconds his gait matched hers. The ease with which he had done this chilled her. Walking side by side, his movement created a familiar, breezy sensation. Her heartbeat quickened.

"You were near the Bisi camp the other night, in the desert," she said.

"Yes, and in the oasis." Leaning toward her, he smiled. "You snore."

She shivered.

The cactus. Ule remembered now what had been missing from the clearing come morning.

"I mostly roam the desert." Keeping pace with her, he rubbed his upper arm, toying with the scions on his shoulder—tiny cactus buds which were bulbous and covered in short red spines.

They walked in silence, Ule observing him with a sidelong glance. He looked as though a bad stench filled the air.

"Are you all right?" she finally asked.

Istok scrunched his face with disgust. "I be a demon, and you should be sensible and feel at least a peck of fear."

"Sorry." She frowned. "Knowing demons are manifestations of fear, well it takes away the mystique."

He huffed.

"Besides, you look very human," she continued, detecting his sensitive ego and hoping to lift his mood. "Just like a real man. Very masculine."

He patted his lower abdomen and genitals. "In every way," he said.

"I can see that," she said, returning her gaze forward again, just in time to see a black scorpion scurry over the sand and slip beneath a large rock.

"I'm told I be a very good likeness," he continued.

"I believe you." Ule fussed with her saddlebag, repositioning it across her shoulders, fighting both the urge to laugh and to run.

It was common for her kind to interact with inhabitants of the worlds. As long as the interactions were consensual, they were free to gain experience and learn about themselves through all sorts of activities, even intimate ones.

"I used to be much bigger," Istok said.

She quickened her pace to a brisk walk.

Figuring out how to access the An Energy was far more important than consorting with a demon. While curiosity was inherent in her species, she had no desire for intimacy with him. Instead, she fought the urge to ask how he remained in the Root Dimension and how he attained solid form.

"Height-wise, that is," he explained, effortlessly keeping pace with her. "All the cactuses be giants before the desert came. Rivulets and the veld nourished them well. They stood two men tall some of them, had spines long enough to pierce through a man's body. It na be a wonder why they be used in executions."

Mystics and Priests had told stories of cactuses during Ule's last days in the world before she departed, long ago when Elishevera still lived. They spoke often of bloodshed and gore at the edge of the veld near the forest, but she was young and only wanted to play. War bored her, and she had no desire to involve herself in the politics of her creations again.

"Being stuck like a pig," Istok continued, "left hanging to bleed out. Entrails spilled along with tears. Their fear, that be how I-"

"Came into existence," she finished his sentence.

She heard him huff and sigh. Glancing toward him, she saw he had stopped crinkling his nose and his dark green lips. He pouted instead.

"You are far too human," she lamented, feeling herself relax a little by the thought. "The demons I saw were vaporous. Some slithered around like wisps of serpentine smoke, others puffed a lot, and the odd few would make and hold shapes."

"Hmm, yes, some of them," he said, his voice slow.

"There's only the one kind," she assured him.

"There once be this chasm demon. She appeared like a long dark split in the air," he said. "She swallowed people whole."

"Areel!" Ule remembered what people had called the tear in the world's reality, even though it hadn't been a demon at all. The error, as she now referred to all anomalies in the world, was one of many Ibe had instructed her to fix.

"An earthquake killed her a long time ago," Istok told her. "I na think it possible for our kind to die. I be here forever."

"At least until the end of the world," she muttered to herself.

"That long, eh?"

Glancing toward the horizon, she scolded herself for saying too much.

Istok rubbed his fingers across the back of his neck. "Even though most people na remember why, they continue fearing me. It be a thrill."

She nodded.

He sidled in front of her. Turning around to face her, he began walking backward. "How do you know so much about demons, little human?" He tilted his head. "How do you know of Areel? She died long, long before your time."

Ule's throat tightened. She needed to be more cautious about what she told others, otherwise she might create unwanted attention. The Bisi Nomads and their attempt to stone her was an excellent reminder that the world no longer remembered what or who she was.

Then she felt an odd sensation—a presence urging her mind to open up. She wondered if the demon was responsible for the prodding of her thoughts, even though she didn't think it possible for a demon to have that kind of power.

"The silent treatment," Istok said. "Mulga does that."

"Who's Mulga?" Grateful for the digression in their conversation, she focused on keeping her mind guarded.

"My lover."

"Really?" She ground her back molars together. "Good for you."

Istok smirked at her, rubbing his finger across his upper arm again. This time he caressed a small, dark green globe unlike the other scions on his shoulder.

"It be a flower," he told her. "Blossoming be a rare occasion."

"I love smelling flowers," she told him, remembering how Elishevera uncurled her petals to bask in the sun and how she smelled a little bit like lime and peppermint.

Istok grimaced. "I like pulling off their petals. Mostly, I like to watch them wither and die."

Her stomach knotted. "But you have flowers."

"These be special." He grazed a bud with his finger tip. "More powerful than any flower in the ground or even that ancient beast, Lishev."

She stopped walking and Istok did the same.

In the following silence, his words turned over in her mind, in particular the reference to her dear old friend. She carefully touched the demon's arm. His flesh felt slightly cool and pulsed with currents of energy. She jerked her hand away.

"You knew Elishevera?" Her voice was soft and tentative. For a moment, her heart wept.

"The beasts of the veld were na tasty enough, she tried to eat me," he sniffed. "Rather rude of her." He scrunched up his face, looking out across the desert. Lowering his voice, he asked. "How can you know her ancient name?"

"Books," she quickly lied. "Scrolls and tablets," she added just in case one of the mediums had failed to survive to the present time.

"Liar," he said softly. His laughter slithered over her. He snapped his fingers and pointed at her. "I know what you be!"

She stepped back a pace and ground her heel into the sand, bracing herself to flee. Her heart pounded as she waited to hear the demon's revelation.

"Yes," he said. "You must be a Priest. Or perhaps a Mystic."

"Sure. That's it." Her nerves eased a little at Istok's suggestion. Had the trek through the desert not addled her brain, she might have thought up this lie herself. Of course, the Priests and the Mystics would have maintained knowledge of the ancient world.

"Which be it?" The demon tapped a finger against his lower lip, waiting for an answer.

She considered which of the two choices better explained her knowledge and insights regarding demons.

"Mystic," she finally answered.

"You must be an apprentice," he conjectured.

"Why's that?"

"Arch Mystics reek of protective spells." He leaned forward and inhaled deeply. "You smell of desert and... apple."

Ule began to sweat.

Istok tutted. "A pity for you."

— 10 —

"I'M DREADFULLY BORING, according to my Mentor," Ule announced, hoping to disengage the demon's interest in her. A constant companion now, his presence spawned a self-consciousness which made the trek through hot sand more tedious.

They both began climbing the steep incline of a small dune, and although Istok's stride was longer and should have tipped the peak before hers, he lagged behind. She felt his steady leer whip all over her body.

"Na, na, you be very interesting," Istok assured her. "You be a different kind of chase. More mysterious."

His words created a new kind of tension in her body. The kind where she wanted to move faster. The kind which made the air feel like water, making every step heavy and slow.

Patiently he accompanied her through the desert, occasionally chuckling to himself whenever she stumbled or stubbed her toe on a stone.

She pushed over a dune crest and discovered another one loomed ahead, obscuring the horizon. She longed to see beyond it and simultaneously needed to keep her attention partially focused on her companion.

Starting down the steep slope, her feet slid in the soft sand. At the bottom, her feet hit a solid tract of coarse ground spotted with boulders and cactuses. She fell back against the slope. Frantic, she stood and tried to locate the demon.

Something hot pricked the back of her neck.

She smacked her hand over the place where her flesh stung. She expected to find an insect. Instead she extracted something long, thin, and hard from her neck. A sharp pain seared through her back and arms as she examined the strange object—a red spine, like the kind all along the cactus demon's forearm.

Noticing the spine's tip broken, she felt a lump in the tiny wound and knew it remained lodged beneath the surface of her skin.

Light-headed, she spun toward Istok. The desert wobbled. "What did you do?"

He shrugged. "I be curious. That be all."

"About what?" She tried to yell but her words tumbled out breathless and weak.

"To know what you truly be at heart."

Her mouth dried and everything in the world brightened. The open blue sky pulsed. White sand glowed. Istok appeared like a tall pipe cactus standing on the crest of the jittery sand drift. If it weren't for the smirk on his human face and the gleam in his black eyes, she would have thought him a harmless plant.

Then she remembered the oasis, the many silhouettes at night. She had seen a cactus stretching skyward. Come the morning, only boulders littered the clearing. He had watched her sleep, witnessed her rage and tears.

An emptiness pervaded Ule. Everything she saw, everything she felt and heard, blended into one another. Her body began to thin as though her flesh became air. Instead of arms and legs, her limbs tapered into floating smoky tendrils.

The buoyancy was similar to what she felt in her own realm, except there she controlled her motions. Here, in the desolate desert, she controlled only her thoughts, for her body had begun to change under the influence of some kind of magic.

Neither able to speak nor move, her vaporous body felt like it was being sucked through her belly button—imploding into an impossibly tiny space. The lightness of being shifted back to a heavy, solid sensation only more compact, smaller, colder, harder—simpler in design.

Her new form hung suspended in air for a fraction of a second. Then the horizon tipped, and she fell toward the ground.

She tried to move but rigidity and stillness persisted. She expected the impact to hurt the way a fall might. Instead, she felt herself rolling wildly within some invisible container. The violent upheaval invoked a madness she struggled to control.

Only when calmness settled over her did she recognize the state of rigidity within the new form. She had turned into an object belonging to the mineral class. A gemstone, she concluded, based on the crystal lattices which now made up her body.

Seldom did she enjoy or find submutation comfortable for any length of time. The complex molecular systems within a biological form deeply contrasted with the simpler constructs of a pebble. Movement, which was required to exist as a living humanoid, had been reduced to the tiniest of spaces.

Of all the types of transformative power, she remembered submutation was the most common form used among magic makers in any created world. A witch or sorcerer or, in the case of this world, a Mystic would study a lifetime learning and developing this ability. But demons? They weren't meant to be magic makers. They weren't meant to exist in the Root Dimension at all.

Ule's anxiety blossomed as she considered Istok's power. It was directly connected to his physicality and not his mind like other magic makers. He didn't just make magic, the demon embodied it, and this was beyond her ability to understand.

She began willing herself back into humanoid form. At first she pushed gently, discovering a resistance. She pushed again. The fine threads of energy refused to respond to her suggestion. All around her, energy coursed yet refused to yield.

She began exerting her will wildly. She tried to affect change in any way by mentally thrashing against the energy binding the molecules together. When that failed, she tried ascending again. The An Energy still eluded her. Even descending into molecular spaced failed.

Surrounded by impenetrable walls, she felt trapped. Within, anxiety prickled as the claws of a dark beast crawled forward, reminding her of a similar place from long ago.

Isolation.

She had woken to darkness. Her eyes strained to detect even the faintest hint of light, not certain what she hoped to see. Her muscles tensed as she sat upright and stiffened, afraid any move might be her last. Her breath quickened.

Hard and cold, an invisible floor pressed against the underside of her crossed legs. All around her blackness hung in thick tapestries. The place seemed so empty yet was full of some other *thing*. She sensed it, felt its thrum.

Heavy breaths burst from her gaping mouth. The hard pulse of her heart ached with every thump. She uttered a tentative, slow hello to the darkness. When no one answered, she explored the floor with her toes and flinched with every touch. Finally she lay down and crawled on her stomach, in a desperate search for light.

Her head tapped something hard. Flinging backward, she cried out. Shakily, she reached out again, fingers twitching over the hard, cold surface. Once standing, she pushed. The darkness would not yield.

She pushed again and again, for she was too young to understand that she was too weak to push down a wall. Cautiously, she felt along the surface for any impressions which might indicate where she was, until she realized there was no way for her to gauge how big the place might be, or how small.

Panic seized her lungs. She gasped for breath. She called out weakly at first. Curling a hand, she struck the wall again and again. Anxiety snaked through her arms, and she pummeled the darkness until her bones ached. Heaving, she collapsed to the floor.

Knowing a place where she could imagine anything she wanted, she closed her eyes. Turning inward, she shuddered. Where there should have been memories of experiences and dreams, she discovered darkness—empty and unfamiliar, as though she had never existed.

From deep within her belly, Ule screamed long and hard until her lungs emptied. Tension poured from her body. Sagging from the exertion, she hiccuped and sputtered for air.

Her teary eyes twitched, detecting some dim light, and eventually they adjusted to its frequency. Variant shades of gray undulated about her, each casting a subtle sheen of indigo or crimson. There was a floor after all, and it gently curved away from her, casting no reflection.

She wiped at her cheeks, smearing cool tears. Uneasiness prickled the tiny hairs along her arms and neck. Peering into the space, she discovered millions upon millions of fine black threads, each one vibrating softly.

She pulled at one of them, and it trembled in her fingers. Smooth and soft, it wriggled free. She caught it again, squeezing harder. It struggled fiercely, wrapping tightly about her knuckle, turning it white until she finally let go. She caught it again and this time silently willed it to stay. It obeyed.

Some innate tendency urged her to explore, to reach out into her immediate surroundings. She gathered a handful of these filaments, rearranged them into a strange pattern and willed them into a form. The mass of thread mewed. What came into existence was feline in nature; not quite a cat, but rather a cloud of stealthy, light gray ribbons rubbing against her knee.

Intrigued by the creature keeping her company, she realized the processes of weaving and willing seemed the most natural of instincts, like scratching an itch or brushing the hair from her eyes. The sense of having done this all before flashed in her mind, then faded into a vague thought and disappeared entirely.

She turned her attention toward those strange little threads, each carving out a portion of some distant white backdrop until the least amount of light remained. Again she pulled at them, twisting and folding.

Rapping and clicking emanated from this new arrangement. Although it was mechanical, it was not anything that had ever existed in any world before. She made a third, fourth, and fifth form, each one different from the other, until at last one uttered the structured sound of a language.

She felt ideas connect within and became aware of an innate ability to understand language, in fact, any language—dead, alive, or yet to be. Warmth flowed through her at this little discovery.

Captivated by this new creature, she cradled it in the palm of her hand. A tiny turquoise flame flickered there, and it asked in a hollow voice, "Who are you?"

Although it whispered, its voice resounded within her mind and sparked a recollection, a name. "I'm called Ule."

"*Oo-lay*," the small voice repeated carefully. The flame spoke again, and its voice shook through her. "What are you?"

"I'm not sure. I can't seem to remember." She pondered momentarily. "I think I was punished." She stared at the form inquisitively, looking for guidance.

The flame trembled. "Why were you punished?"

"I don't know," she replied. "Must've done something bad I suppose." She cast her eyes downward. "I'm not sure I like it here."

"Well, if you don't, I don't," the flame flickered.

"I don't know what to do," she said.

"Neither do I."

Ule pouted, staring sadly about her.

"I made you," she said to it.

"Yes, you did." The flame bowed toward her, rippling orange and yellow around its blue core. "I came from within you and now exist outside you."

Ule considered this.

"I like to make things," she declared. "It's fun, don't you think?"

The small flame shrugged. Then it began to shrink, diminishing into a wisp of smoke. Only long limp lines remained in its place, which slipped over her hand and melted into the floor below. Other creations fell out of existence at the slightest mental suggestion, also disappearing into the floor.

She lay down. Fractured images cascaded without flow, snagging her mind here and there. Partially formed ideas paused in her mind. She focused elsewhere, on her breath at first, and the faint single-beat rhythm of her heart. She heeded that rhythm then applied it to her thoughts.

She rolled over and peered into her imagination, reached for a handful of threads and began to play with them. She experimented, creating various configurations until the forms were satisfactory. She quickly learned the rules for creating more complex forms.

She turned a ball into iron ore, fashioned granite and lava, designed stones and trees, air and water, until a tiny new world spun before her. Spiked fish flopped around in primordial seas, and snarly, eleven-tailed, furry creatures roamed through the forests. This was only the beginning.

She played just as well as any child. She gave herself over to imagination and boundless energy, understanding she had lessons to learn. Eventually, the gap in her mind began filling in, as though every time she created a four-eyed serpent or six-winged lion or other form, she was rewarded with the return of an old memory.

She aged. She created. The games she played changed to match her evolving maturity. More and more, she missed her kind and longed for companionship. In her solitude, she peered deeper and deeper into the Void, searching for anyone other than herself. When she found no one, she wondered what it might be like to build a friend, one fashioned from mineral, flower, and flesh...

Ule forced her will against the molecular structure of her new form, imagining elements disintegrating. She would die in the process yet afterward be free to deathmorph into a new form. When the energy still would not yield, she propelled her inner sight to begin searching past the confines of the gemstone for someone who might help. Not her old friends though. Not her Mentor. Instead, she searched for her Master.

Peering through the molecular construction, she pushed through the lattices and interstices until her inner sight breached the surface of the stone.

The patterns faded, and she found it difficult to adjust to the panoramic, fragmented vista. Accustomed to looking through two eyes in one direction, she did her best to focus through one fragment at a time in all directions.

With practice, her vision adjusted to the brightness of peering through multiple facets of stone simultaneously. Each facet captured an image, and the images overlapped one another until the desert appeared whole again.

Desert and sky stretched all around and above, bright and open. Black birds fluttered nearby, smudges of feathers blotting the sun. Beneath her, sand glittered. A giant now, Istok scanned the ground.

Yet again, a presence prodded her mind. Certain the intrusion belonged to the demon, she resisted and pushed her thoughts outward.

Unable to stretch, reach, or curl up, because she had no body with which to move, she realized that without vocal chords, she would be limited to projecting her thoughts.

Still and stagnant, unyielding and heavy, she wondered how long it would take for her new physical state to begin affecting her mind.

In a fit, she hurled her thoughts outward.

"Change me back!"

Although she had no ears, she interpreted the sound of sand crunching beneath large feet. The slow pace grew louder. A green wall blocked out the brilliant blue sky. A sheen of black flickered.

She adjusted her perception and wanted to scream at what she saw. Dark and empty, save for the hint of light reflected by the world beyond, a demon eye blinked at her.

— 11 —

"YOU BE ALIVE?"

Large fingers curled about her, momentarily blocking out all light. She felt herself sway and sunlight flooded her vision again. The demon stood tall, his arm bent to his chest and the palm of his hand beneath her.

"Let's have a look at you," Istok said. Grinning, he examined her. "Sort of crimson, translucent, tiny facets," he muttered.

Irked by the scrutiny, Ule appreciated his verbal observations nonetheless. They confirmed she had submutated into a gemstone.

"My first Mystic," he cooed. "A difficult kind to kill usually, since you all secret yourselves away in towers drenched in the stench of your magic." He wrinkled his nose.

"I said change me back!"

He chuckled. "Ever the na! You be the first to live. Had I known Mystics could survive, I would've hunted your kind down long ago. You be a rare beast. Perhaps one with a power to be tapped. Perhaps a power stronger than any of my kinsmen may possess, like Kaleel. Have you met him?"

She remained silent. She knew nothing of any creature named Kaleel and, as long as she stayed a stone, doubted she would ever meet anyone again.

"He'll hiss with envy at *me* for a change," he mumbled. His strange naked brow crinkled into a frown. A green tongue glided along black scalloped teeth.

She struggled, pulling herself in one direction then pushing herself in another. No matter how foreign or complex a substance, she always found a way to move along or through the energy it contained. Her search for a way to be free from the demon's magic kept her puzzled.

A need overcame her, urging her to descend deep into the stone until the space within an atom felt like another universe, yet nothing of the lattice pattern would yield. The restriction only created tension within her mind. Needing to stretch or breathe or jump, and knowing she couldn't do any of those things made the space within small and unbearable.

Istok brought the stone to eye level, inspected her adoringly. "Pretty how the light makes you glow. You be a powerful creature indeed." His eyes widened. "Another demon, perhaps?" He tapped the stone with a black fingernail and finally muttered, "Perhaps na."

"Why not?" The Bisi Nomads had thought her a demon.

Istok shook his head. "You be too human."

"Release me!"

Her command went ignored.

No amount of begging deterred the demon from holding her up to the sun. Light passed through her, bounced off each facet in different ways, refracted in endless permutations. She appreciated the gemstone's beauty—the ribbons of bronze, the elongated crystal fomrations—yet worried about how she might change if she stayed this way for too long.

"You can't mutate just anything," she tried to reason with him. "There are rules."

"I like breaking rules," the demon admitted.

The absence of menace in his tone cowed Ule into using another approach, one which might convince him to undo the magic.

"Submutation isn't *that* special," she announced.

"Submutation?"

"Changing something complex into a simpler pattern," she explained.

Istok narrowed his eyes. "Be this Mystic talk?"

"Y-yes," she lied. "And submutation's quite common. It's certainly a lot easier to visualize a simpler form."

Caws from black birds nearly interrupted her attempt to appeal to the demon's ego, but he showed no interest in anything except her.

"Go on," he insisted.

"Going the other way, making a simple design into one more complex, that takes real skill."

"What kind of skill?"

"A lot of energy, focus, and *power*." Ule hoped to peak the demon's curiosity and his desire to demonstrate the full extent of his ability. "You look like you can supermutate anything you want."

Silence overcame the demon. He appeared to mull over her words. With any luck, she may have appeased his ego enough for the demon to change her back.

"You have a greatness na seen in any of the stones my spines have created."

She sighed.

"With you in my possession, I could unite the demon folk, make humans more resourceful and productive." He hunched over his hand and quietly explained. "They need much prodding." After a silent pause, he added, "I could rule the world."

Not in this world! Ule cringed at the thought. Magic had no place in politics. How dare the demon suggest it. She knew first hand what policy makers did with power; they created mountains of rules and then conspired to confine you to a powerless state.

Like Isolation.

She hurled a long string of profanities, reciting every curse word she had ever heard, learned, and created, including some she heard Ibe mutter when he thought no one was listening.

Her voice trailed off from exhaustion, ending with a sharp squawk from one of the black birds now pecking about Istok's toes.

"Impressive words. I recognize only a few."

She felt oddly flattered by the compliment.

"What other strange words will you utter once you see what lies beyond this dune?"

She paused before asking, "What do you mean?"

Brushing past the black birds, Istok climbed the side of the dune in long loping strides. His feet sank into the sand at the crest of the hill, where he stopped and raised his hand.

And Ule saw.

Desert faded into grassland. A forested horizon feathered the sky in dark greens. Between the edge of the desert and that far away forest, small farms spotted the land and stopped at a deep ravine which receded into the distance and appeared as a fine line.

Sprawled along the far side of the ravine were clusters of buildings merged into a collage of rectangles. Ule recognized the organic sprawl pattern, which had once been an assortment of markets coalescing over time.

"Can you see?" Just to be sure she could, he held the stone higher.

"It's a town." Her words felt empty, sad, and futile, just like everything she had done and said during her life.,

He nodded. "Yes, a town."

Coming close to finding civilization beyond the desert, where someone might be able to help her return home, struck a nerve. She projected her thoughts with ferocity, hoping they snapped at the demon like a whip.

"What did I ever do to you?!"

He laughed. Turning back toward the desert, he slid down the dune. "You could've feared me, just a little." And he held her to the sky, admiring her again.

She swelled with a font of emotion—frustration, disgust and, dare she think it, revenge.

"Did you know you glow?" he asked.

"It's my rage!"

The demon chuckled.

With the amount of regenerative energy stored inside her, she imagined she looked like a tiny lamp through the translucent gem, and she noticed other creatures drawn to her light.

One of the black birds flew to Istok's shoulder and landed with a wild flapping as its claws clasped a cluster of prickly, fuzzy scions.

Another bird flew to Istok's head, tiny talons pricking his scalp. Yellow-rimmed eyes seemed to catch and reflect the color of the demon's flesh somehow. She didn't like the look of this bird at all and she squirmed beneath its scrutiny.

Istok spoke to them. "A beauty, yes?"

The bird on his shoulder squawked a reply, and she imagined the feathered beast hungrily agreed to some secret conspiracy.

Istok made no effort to remove either of the creatures. The demon's dark eyes twinkled as a third bird plodded about his feet.

She wondered how deeply he was amused by the avian attention, for she found the feathery trio an unwanted nuisance.

Pinching the stone between thumb and forefinger, Istok held the stone up to the sky. The birds remained fascinated by the shiny toy, even when he began slowly moving his hand through the air.

She moaned at the back and forth movement, wishing he would stop.

Istok chuckled at how the birds remained riveted to the object, chirping excitedly. To provoke them further, he tossed the gem into the air and caught it in his palm.

Upon impact she grunted at the force, and just when the waxing and waning within finally eased, the bird on the ground stopped, tilted his head, and bolted toward her.

Pink tongue curled, the bird let out a soft gurgle as its beak securely caught the stone's facets and bolted into the sky.

"Put me down," she urged the bird in flight, wondering if her thoughts would even register in the animal's mind.

As much as she detested the cactus demon, she strongly suspected she was safer with him. At least the chance of her being restored was greater. For that reason, she preferred being in the demon's possession.

In the desert panorama, he grew smaller yet she could still see his deeply furrowed frown track their flight through the sky. He turned his forearm toward the rising bird. A red spine shot out, striking its underbelly.

She felt the vibration of the transformation, watched eruptions of amorphous form and shifting color as the bird collapsed and imploded on itself. Then, in the very same space, a new shape exploded into existence, something gray and jagged.

The momentum of increasing speed swelled into a pervasive nausea. Falling toward the desert, a second stone accompanying her, she dreaded the impact of landing in the soft sand.

The black bird launched into flight from Istok's shoulder. It rose toward her, curled a talon around her, but its grasp was weak. Still the bird lessened the velocity at which she fell, and she tumbled onto the sand with a long roll, finding the swirling movement easier to endure then rocking back and forth.

The demon swore loudly as the bird settled next to the gemstone and tried to grab it with its beak instead.

"No, no, no," she scolded the bird, trying to protect it from the demon's magic.

Istok kicked the bird and it fluttered away squawking. As though in retaliation, the bird perched on his head drove a sharp beak deep into green flesh. Green, thick fluid began to ooze from the gash. Smacked hard by the demon, the black bird settled with a soft thud onto the ground silent and unaffected.

Wincing, Istok kicked at both birds until they half-scrambled, half-hopped away to a safer spot.

Ule fixated on the bird with the green rimmed eyes, watched as they darkened. They seemed unnatural, she thought, as though two sets of eyes peered out into the world instead of one.

Eying them carefully, Istok plucked her from the sand. Despite her new state of being, she was relieved to be in his possession again.

He dabbed at the wound. "Pathetic little pests!"

One of the birds flew directly at him, and she waited again to find herself hurling through the air clasped in the little beak. Instead, the bird steered toward the demon's shoulder, plucked a large green bud, and gobbled it down in a swift gulp.

Istok gingerly touched the spot where the bud had been growing. Fury creased his face.

The black bird landed next to his green eyed companion with an ungraceful thud, for its talons puffed into twisted human feet with black toenails. The body swelled into a squashed version of a human torso. One side of the quivering chest remained covered in black down and the other turned into pink flesh. Feathers still jutted at odd angles from its neck. It made a half caw, half human cry.

"I knew it!" Ule declared satisfactorily at evidence the demon could mutate forms into ones far more complex in design than stones. Her joy quickly faded, however, once the supermutation began to express errors.

Its head swelled and only one eye took on the shape of a pale gray iris. The beak curved down into a long vulgar nose and wide pinched lips. A swollen pink tongue flicked experimentally at emerging thin lips.

The black bird became grotesque. Half bird, half human. Floundering along the ground, it attempted flight. Lithe, graceful wings had swelled into thick, bulbous limbs resembling feathered human arms. It tried again and again, stumbling every time.

The final black bird, the one with the strange eyes, bolted into the sky, abandoning the unnatural thing crawling in the sand.

Istok laughed and spoke to the bird. "Serves you right for eating my blooms."

"Oh, please," Ule begged. "End its misery."

"Ever the na." He turned away from the beast, which dragged itself toward the dune. "It snatched an orange blossom."

"The form has gone wrong. It must be terminated," she explained.

As a child, she had attempted to transform a steam train into a cat. Instead, a hideous deformity shuddered into existence, refusing to die.

"In the event of dysmutation," her Master had instructed, "you may undo the work. This is the only time you are permitted to destroy."

Saddened and relieved, she had unraveled the creature back into fine black threads and now wanted to do the same to the bird thrashing about in the sand.

"An orange blossom!" Istok spat. "The bud about to blossom be orange."

"It's just a flower."

He scowled, leathery green flesh crinkling around his eyes. "Mine be special!" he yelled at her.

Yes, she thought, they certainly are. Without a mouth with which to swallow, she realized, there was no way she could eat one to see if it might return her to human form.

A shadow fell across her. The demon curled his fingers, securing the stone firmly to his palm. The world split into a multitude of similar vistas, each overlapping the other. Some of them filled with the dysmutated bird crawling along the ground, each grasp of talon becoming weaker. The images disconnected, moved around, like tiles being shuffled back and forth.

She lurched and slid in all directions, slamming into the walls of her prison. The to and fro motion indicated the demon's hand swung back and forth to balance out his long strides.

An ache began to grow. Ule groaned.

— 12 —

THE DEMON STROLLED and despite the low ebbing pain his motion created for her, Ule focused on the desert. No two rocks looked the same. No two trees or cactuses twisted in the same way.

Yet she noticed it all.

Left at a large round purple cactus.

Right at a granite boulder spotted with black mica.

Around a worn tree, a bone finger pointing toward the sky.

They came to the edge of a narrow, deep ravine, the one she had seen in the distance near the town. "Have we come back around to where we were?"

Istok slid down the steep slope of the ravine and resumed walking along the bed of what must have once been an ancient river, no doubt the main tributary which had brought water to the orange groves near Elishevera.

"Hush!"

Ule heard the annoyance in his tone, saw him sneer a little. He had to know his attempt to confuse her failed. "Did you really think you could trick me?"

He frowned. Scratching his chest, he grimaced. "You have problems with seeing."

"I see just fine—"

He shook her.

Pain swelled but she refused to give Istok any satisfaction from it. In the receding ache, she remained silent and watchful as the demon follow the riverbed. It brought them to a spot next to a bone white tree.

Beyond them, Ule saw fields of corn and farmland blend into the hayfields of another farm, the ravine snaking around and damming the flow of vegetation from spilling into the town. A group of pipe cactuses clustered in a troop formation on a hill at the edge of the nearest farm, as though they guarded the desert.

"Home at last," Istok said.

Ule saw stones stacked in two pillars. Spanning the supports was a solid slab of granite. The structure was an archway, a precarious one. Through it's opening she saw tufts of quack grass poke out from sand which spread toward a desert horizon, where the sun began to cast the world in a ruddy glow.

"Where's the rest of it?"

Snorting, the demon blinked at the shifting light in the sky and bid the wasteland a fond goodnight. He tapped a pillar, which she was certain shifted slightly, and they passed through a space of darkness.

Most of her time in the world so far had incited anxiety. Now Ule worried most about what kind of darkness the space opened into. Light eventually returned to her vision. A strange, unnatural glow began to illuminate her new surroundings, and she was grateful to see again.

Around her, a cavernous room loomed. Tall, curved stone walls were draped in fabrics and tapestries of red and gold. A blue floor cast an ethereal light, looking as though somewhere below sunlight shimmered through deep, dark moving water.

Embers glowed in the hearth beneath a cast iron pot partially filled with stew. A dirty bowl lay upside down on the floor near an ornate table.

Istok kicked the bowl. It skidded across the floor, smashing against the stone step at the hearth. Fine lines appeared within the floor, creating eddies and ripples wherever the bowl touched. Eventually the turmoil faded into long, wandering waves and found calm again.

"That lazy cow," Istok muttered.

"Who?"

"Never you mind," he told her.

He walked from one windowless room to another, the floor rippling with every step. Suffused in a soft white light emanating mostly from the floor, Ule detected gilded lanterns adorning the wall; they flickered as though someone had not fueled them.

"Oh Mulga," Istok sang.

Ule listened for a reply. None came.

He strained his head around corners, looking for someone—his caretaker? perhaps the companion and lover he had mentioned?—and came to a stop in a roundish chamber.

There, in a vast round bed in the center of the room, a figure lay beneath thick, puffy blankets. Ule tried to imagine who, or what, might be reclined in such comfort. Woman. Man. Beast.

Istok stealthily walked toward the edge of the bed, leaned over the still form and shouted, "Mulga!" His voice sharpened on the last syllable.

The lump in the bed flinched.

"Look what I found today," he said, holding up the gemstone.

Mulga sleepily turned over. Long chestnut hair contrasted deeply with her pale face. Her large, dark brown eyes widened at the sight of the treasure.

"F-for me?"

Istok snorted. Ignoring her question, he strutted around the room. "Imagine Kaleel's envy when I tap the power within this stone, when I show him. Do you think I should visit that stench of a grove he calls home or wait till he makes an appearance in the desert?"

"Kaleel?" Mulga wiped her puffy eyes with thick fingers.

"Your old master," Istok spat. "Kaleel the Rex. The one I saved you from?" He jabbed her in the forehead. "Something in there still na working."

Ule shuddered at the vile condescension in the demon's tone toward the woman. Had she not been a gemstone, she would have certainly defended Mulga since she showed no desire to stand up for herself.

"I guess you do na listen, eh?" Istok smirked and added, "Dumdum."

Ule swore at the rude comment. Neither the demon nor the woman seemed to hear her.

Large eyes cast downward, Mulga whispered, "I know who you mean." She hugged the blankets toward her large bare chest. Her skin was pale with the exception of an oval, brown birthmark, which streaked her collarbone and neck.

Wondering if the woman could hear her at all, Ule braced herself for retaliation from Istok and projected her thoughts forcefully. "Help me!"

Mulga frowned, rolled over in bed, and ducked under the blankets.

"You have to hear me," Ule cried. "Somebody. Anybody. Help, I'm trapped."

A light danced in Istok's eyes again. Her desperation amused him.

Smiling, he approached a narrow horizontal rock which jutted from the side of the wall. The ledge displayed glass boxes, each filled with objects. Ule saw a bracelet of polished human bone decorated with fingernails and a violet human eyeball, which couldn't move yet watched her nonetheless.

He gently set her down inside an empty case and closed the lid.

"Let me go," Ule cried. "Please! You there under the blankets, Mulga, help me."

The lump in the bed stirred.

"She probably can na hear you," Istok whispered to her. "Perhaps only demons can, maybe other Mystics, but you be neither. You be something else, eh? Something more powerful, something worth tapping. Then perhaps the other demons will follow me, even Kaleel." He admired her crimson facets and he smiled a wide, toothy grin.

"Now Mulga." He spoke softly, turning toward the bed. "Remember, na touching. If you do, I'll know. Then you'll be sorry."

She shifted in the bed.

"I be off to find a Mystic," he told her. "Someone to teach me the mechanics of magic." Eyes cast downward, consumed by thought, he made no affectionate gesture toward the woman in bed as he exited. "It may take a while."

The smack of each foot created dark blue ripples in the floor. Bursts of soft blue light snaked along the delineation between crests and valleys as they collided with one another and collapsed back into stillness. In the same way, Ule's anxiety and panic swelled and diminished, a dark tide of fear waiting to pull her under.

She struggled again, pushing toward the spaces deep within the molecular structure of the stone. She was still unable to ascend, descend, or shift. No amount of focus in her mind beckoned the An Energy so she could change herself back into human form, to move the way the floor moved.

She called out to the demon, "Let me go, please!" The floor returned to a calm swaying, and she sensed no one else in the cavern except for the woman in bed.

Mulga shifted beneath the blankets.

"Please," Ule wailed. "Help me!"

Throwing off the blankets, Mulga lazily sat upright and stared at the ledge before pulling herself out of bed. She was naked. A curtain of brunette hair fell to the backs of her knees. Large breasts sagged against a thick torso. Wide hips waddled and plump thighs rubbed one another as she approached the ledge.

"Shh!" she said, nodding toward the gemstone.

"Y-you can hear me?"

"Yes I can," replied Mulga. "You be very loud."

Relief flooded through Ule. "Please tell me you can put me back?"

"Oh yes, I can," Mulga declared. "He thinks I na think, but I know how."

Ule's heart silently soared with hope that this woman was a magic maker who could return Ule to humanoid form so she could walk, jump, and dance again.

Mulga popped open the lid of the glass box, took the gemstone from the case, and held it up to her face. "Tell me where you came from," she said, "so I can bring you back to where you belong."

"That wasn't quite what I meant." Ule's hopes began to crumble. "Do you know anyone who can put, I mean *change* me back?"

"Istok can," Mulga said. "But why would you want to?" She proceeded to place Ule back in the glass case.

"No, no, no!"

Mulga listened. She stopped and held onto the stone, staring at it intently. The woman was no magic maker; that much was discernible. At the least, she offered to be helpful.

"Mulga, that's your name right?" Even though the woman sounded a little dimwitted, Ule needed to try explaining her situation. "I used to be like you, human, and Istok changed me into a stone. Now I'd like to be changed back into a human."

"Why?" Mulga whined. "If Istok changed you, it be only to make you better."

"How is this better?!" Ule snapped, surprised by her outburst of anger.

Mulga sat on the side of the bed, her thighs melding together. She held the gemstone with care. Her eyes grew vacant, as though she had forgotten what she was doing. She remained frozen, fixated on Ule until her eyes regained focus.

"Istok will treat you well," she said.

"Does he treat you well?"

Mulga paused a moment then said, "I be free. I be... *more*."

Ule wondered how terrible this woman's life must have been for her to find living with Istok a better option.

"He na always be my master," Mulga explained.

"Yes," Ule agreed, remembering Istok had mentioned a fellow demon. "Something The Rex."

"You knew my old master?" Mulga gazed wide-eyed.

"Who?"

"Kaleel." After a moment, Mulga seemed to forget she was waiting for an answer and said, "Did you know all cat demons be called Kaleel? My old master, he be Kaleel the Rex." Mulga smiled. "Wrinkly, skinny, eyes like water. Very tall, with the longest of claws. Wears a belt of bone and gold. Have you met him?"

"No, I haven't," Ule replied softly, hoping she would never have to. Who she needed to meet was a Mystic. Before she could ask the simple-minded Mulga to take her to the nearest one, the woman stood again and wandered around the bed.

"Tell me," Mulga demanded, "where did you and Istok meet?"

Time was essential, Ule thought. Istok might return any moment. "In the desert," she answered quickly. "Listen, I need you-"

"Do you want to know how I met Istok?" Mulga asked.

Ule wanted very much to be as far away from the cavern before the demon returned. Instead of yelling instructions, she submitted to answering the question. "Sure."

"It be during night in Kaleel's farmyard. I be sleeping-"

"In a farmyard?"

"Yes." Mulga nodded. "With others, the chickens, and the rooster. The grass be cut in the fields... oh, I love the smell of grass!" Although she paused, it was not long enough for Ule to offer a response.

"And Istok saw me, told me Kaleel valued me most so I be very special. Then he gave me a flower." Mulga smiled. "Istok took me away, brought me here."

Although Ule was having a difficult time understanding the story, she decided the woman had been a slave or servant at one time, because their kind often slept in barns and their masters sometimes had favorites.

"Still, if Kaleel treasured you, why is being with Istok better?"

"Being with him changed me. I slept on straw before he took me away. I simply love him," Mulga replied confidently.

"Even though he will never truly love you in return?"

Mulga gulped. Her smile faded. "He loves me," she said. "One day he'll give me a token of his love, something from his shelf. That would be... nice."

"No, he won't," Ule declared, growing impatient with the woman's ignorance. He'll never give you anything but heartache, Mulga. Never."

"*Na-ver?*" Each sound came out choppy, the way a child learns to pronounce new words. Her squarish face drooped into a frown, large lips curling into a pout. "But why?"

In the brief time she had known Istok, Ule sensed what he cared most about was the effect he had on others, how much fear he could generate to subdue those he met.

"I don't think he can love you in the way you want."

Mulga shuddered. "He loves me, he does!" A strangled scream rose from her throat.

The movement was swift, arcing, and upward. Ule braced herself. Trembling shook through her that wasn't her own. She felt the motion originate from the woman.

With both arms raised above her head, Mulga whipped the gemstone against the floor.

— 13 —

THE BLACK BIRD ambled in circles. Round and round a pillar, it finally slowed to a stop, head tilted toward the stone archway. Moments earlier the cactus creature had passed between the pillars and vanished, leaving in its wake the smell of damp earth and rust, which should only be encountered in a forest or on a farm, not the desert. The smell lingered and persisted—the way magic scent does.

The bird resumed walking clockwise around the column of precariously piled stones. After a few rounds, it skittered across the sand letting out a long warble and a sharp nod with its tiny sleek head.

In a burst, the bird flew to the top of the archway, where it stared down at the space between the columns. It perched there for many hours, silent and attentive, until the green, prickly demon exited from some invisible place. Beyond the gap, where there should have been an entrance, the desert shimmered briefly.

And the bird perched as still as stone and observed.

Istok tapped the column to his right twice. He turned toward the heart of the desert, sand crunching beneath his feet. "Fehran's Mystic be a bastard," he muttered through gritted teeth. "He be too powerful anyway. Too difficult to manage. Need one less educated, more... yielding."

Incoherent vehement ranting issued from the demon yet the bird remained still until the demon climbed a dune and gradually disappeared over the crest. In a flutter, the bird floated down along the right column landing with a soft thud on the ground. Walking counter-clockwise this time, the bird stumbled before completing the first round.

The air shimmered, pushed the bird backward. A magic door. Invisible. Locked.

For a moment, the bird eyed the column Istok had tapped, then pecked one of the stacked smooth stones twice. Pushing forward, the bird shivered as magic pressed around him. The air shimmered, the light of white sand and blue sky rupturing into a darkness which slowly brightened again.

Where there should have been sand, a great expanse of blue

marble-like floor rippled with dark and pale blue lines. Every wing flutter and talon prick set off ever expanding, distorted rings. On the far side of the chamber embers crackled in a stone hearth, emitting a steady orange glow which stank of sulfur.

The bird began exploring the shadows behind chairs and beneath tables. Save for the slick sheen of its feathers, the shadows hid the tiny creature well.

"But why?"

The lament of a soft voice stopped the black bird. It waited, listened, and took to the air, swooping past the warmth of the hearth and along the curve of a short hallway into another smaller chamber then another. Clinging to the shadows, the bird hovered close to the ceiling and landed softly on a narrow wardrobe.

At the center of the chamber, beside a disheveled bed and a shelf fashioned from rock, a naked woman held something above her head. Her thick arms jiggled as though the object were heavy. Anger pinched her round face. She flung her arms down and something hard struck the floor.

The bird flinched at the sharp crack and watched the object skip and spin across the marble floor.

Bright blue swirls exploded at every point of impact on the floor until the bright, crimson gemstone came to a rest.

The woman's puffy hands clawed at her cavernous mouth, eyes fixated on the gemstone. Also riveted to the object, the bird bobbed several times before standing still. Green-rimmed eyes danced over every facet until the woman pounced on the stone, scooped it into her hand, and examined it closely.

"I be sorry," she whispered.

The black bird trembled.

She gently shook the stone. "Hello?"

The silence persisted and a blank expression overcame her. She stared and blinked as though she failed to recognize what lay in her hand. Then her eyes focused again.

"Oh na oh na oh na," she cried. "I broke it."

The bird bobbed up and down, stifling a gurgle in its throat. For all her crying, she couldn't hear the bird's talons clip against the wood of the wardrobe.

"You na look broken," she said, eyes narrowing suspiciously. "Why you na talk to me?"

Silence again.

"You want Istok." She nudged the gemstone. "You want him for yourself."

Concealed by shadow, the black bird's chest swelled. It shook its head and craned forward, eyes again peering at the stone.

"I know you can hear me," she seethed. "You na can have him!"

Anger stirred her. Curling her fist around the stone, she pulled a finely woven red linen dress over her head, fingers lightly touching the subtle edges of gold embroidery. Black linen covered her head. She pinched the fabric together beneath her round chin and rushed from the room.

The bird dove from the wardrobe, silently gliding behind her until the shadow cast by the hearth offered camouflage. Small thin rings expanded across the floor only to be swallowed in the wake of ripples set off by the woman's clumsy footsteps.

She stopped before a portion of wall. Bricks shimmered subtly in the light cast by the hearth's smokeless fire. Tilting her head, she reached out a hand, and it slipped through the illusion.

"Na like him to leave the door unlocked." Her words softly echoed. She held her breath and felt her way through the invisible portal.

Wings pumped and the bird climbed the air, diving through the magic barrier and emerging into the brightness of white sand and sun. From above, the bird followed the woman, watched her stop and return to the archway, lightly knock on the right column twice, and turn toward the grassland where she passed tiny farmlands and occasionally stopped to catch her breath.

The bird absorbed the world below. Arching footbridges tore into a maze of buildings, food stands, shanties, shacks, and pavilions, all nearly piled on top of one another. Rooftops sloped and slanted, hiding narrow alleyways. Dirt paths and cobbled roads converged into a vast market center.

The woman grew increasingly distracted by the wares in the market. She stopped at a small tent soiled with mud. Garments hung around a table made of warped wood which threatened to buckle under bolts of fabric. The woman ran her thick fingers over a black dress with billowy sleeves and sighed.

Resuming her journey, she slowed near a small hut where a skinny old man with deeply wrinkled cocoa skin offered her a handwoven veil of sheer turquoise, insisting the color suited her brown-eyed beauty. She blushed and continued on.

She stopped again outside a small shack with a portico, where the smell of broth hung in the air. Painted in tiny handwritten print,

Sunrise Soup Kitchen sprawled across a wooden slab. Outside, rickety tables were laden with every variation of sweetness—cakes, pastries, fudges, candies—and she sniffed them all.

In a junction between two vendor heavy areas of the market, she stopped before a small house with a double split door. The upper half hung inward against the wall of the house while the bottom half remained shut.

Settling on the edge of the roof, the bird's talons slipped, raking fine gray lines into the slate tiles.

The woman rapped lightly on the bottom door.

"Yes, a moment," a voice called from within the house.

A wiry man poked his head through the opening. Fine lines creased his brow and eyes. He wore a long beard which was confined to the peak of his chin. The remainder of his rough flesh was clean-shaven, and although he looked older than thirty years, his calm, buoyant tone sounded youthful.

"I've na the time for spice tea today, Mulga," he said.

"But I have something for you." Breathing heavily, she held out her hand to show him the stone.

Slipping again, the bird gave up its tenuous hold on the tile and dropped down onto the wooden ledge of the bottom half-door, where it found better balance.

"That bird be a bold one," the man said.

Mulga flapped both hands at the bird to shoo it away.

Each wing fluttered, one at a time, and folded neatly into place. Preferring the new perch, it resumed staring at the stone, which in daylight appeared far more purple and cooler against Mulga's pale flesh.

"He be enraptured by the stone," the man told her. "Birds! They love treasure. The shinier, the better." He reached for the stone then stopped when his forefinger brushed one of its sharp edges.

"Where did you find this?"

"In the desert," Mulga replied.

"Of course, the desert." The man gazed long and hard, then gently curled Mulga's fingers closed. "By rights it be yours then." He glanced at the bird and nodded. "Do you na agree?"

Remaining still and silent, the bird stared at the man's sunken cheeks and brilliant eyes.

"Please take it." Mulga pushed the stone into the man's palm.

Her arm clipped the bird's beak, forcing the bird to scuttle backward.

The man held the stone up to the sun. "Why be you so generous with me?"

"You be kind," she replied. "Do you remember? You helped me home the first time we met." Mulga rocked her shoulders back and forth. "And you always invite me to tea."

The bird stayed focused on the man, who wrapped his fingers around the stone and scooped out several coins from a leather pouch fastened to his belt.

"This be far too valuable to give away," he said softly and handed her the money. "Take this, in exchange for the stone."

Mulga's eyes widened. "Thank you," she gasped. Batting her eyelashes, she asked, "Will you tell me your name now?"

The man chuckled. Leaning forward, he lowered his voice. "Goyas," he told her. "I be the Magnes Fehran's Arch Mystic."

Her face froze. She glanced down at the gold coins in her hand. A struggle unfolded in the following brief moments. Some conflict of desire played out in the twist of her lips and the wrinkle of her brows. Finally, she snapped out of her daze, decision made, a soft smile on her face.

"Good day to you," she said and hastened toward the market.

The bird craned its neck, following her movement which defied gravity as she lightly bounced along the narrow paths winding among the vendors.

"Mulga, Mulga, what have you found?" muttered Goyas.

Together, bird and man examined the gemstone beneath the late day sun. White light reflected off the facets, and a strange glow within warmed the crimson hues.

When Goyas turned away ever so slightly, the bird scrambled, eyes darting over the man's wiry arms and straggly red hair, and peeked into the small house. Inside, an unkempt bed, a littered work table, and rows of shelves anchored to one wall cluttered the one room house.

Goyas began shutting the upper half of the door, patiently waiting for the bird to fly away. The bird shuffled along the ledge, staying within the decreasing gap, and simply wouldn't budge.

Tapping a bare foot on the floor, Goyas smirked. "In or out?"

Accepting the casual invitation, the bird glided through the gap into the house.

— 14 —

INSIDE THE SMALL house, the bird settled on the highest shelf—a narrow slat of aged wood anchored to the wall with iron brackets. Walking toward the corner nearest the worktable, the bird left behind tiny prints in thick brown dust. Below, rows of cluttered wooden shelves descended to the floor. Running alongside them, an equally cluttered table filled a third of the floor space, leaving little room for a narrow bed, a side table, and a stool.

Goyas leisurely stroked his red beard. A slight sneer disrupted his calm face as he gazed up at his new guest. Man and bird watched each other for several moments, their stares battling one another until finally the Arch Mystic backed down.

"You be like Mulga," he said. "Not quite what you seem, eh friend?"

The bird cawed at the cold tone underlying the word *friend*.

"Mulga, now she be less than what she seems. I say these things to you," and he pointed at the bird, "because I know you understand what I say. You must sense in her what I do. She dreams of grass and hands squeezing her breasts."

He lowered his arm and rolled the gemstone over in both hands before setting it down on the table.

"And there be unfilled spaces in her being, as though she barely lived the life of a full grown woman. Her mind be much too big for so little experience. Now you..." He looked up at the bird again. "You be *more* than what you seem. Difficult to read but intelligent. Yes, the glint in your eyes gives you away."

He turned toward the door and slid dead bolts into place across both upper and lower portions and fastened all four windows, one on each wall. Gesturing in small circles with his right hand, he muttered strange words. Though nothing visually changed, a tremor rippled through the air.

The bird twitched from the sensation, after which a strong and peculiar magic scent of onion and sandalwood wafted throughout the house.

"That should make it seem as if no one be home, at least for a little while," he informed the bird.

After rubbing his gaunt face, Goyas stretched his eyes wide in what seemed an attempt to stay awake. He shook his long, beige shirt from his pale body, raked knobby fingers through thick auburn chest hair, and unfastened a leather brown belt. It fell to the floor with a thunk. He made no attempt to clear the clothing and turned his attention toward the gemstone.

Straddling a stool, he sat near the middle of the long table strewn with books, scrolls of parchment, unusual tools, and trinkets. Amid the chaos, he found the gemstone and held it upward. The crimson color glowed slightly, capturing his attention as well as the bird's, which cautiously hopped to a lower shelf on the wall and craned its neck.

Goyas glanced sidelong at the movement. "Come, look closer."

After a moment, the bird hopped down onto the table and waddled along the far edge, stopping beyond arm's reach of the man. It peered into the gemstone, equally enthralled by the fluctuations of light exuding from within, and flinched when Goyas lightly tapped the stone.

"Certainly you must see the light too." He craned his head backward and rubbed his chin. "Only living beings emit light. Color as well as brightness reflects their species and degree of power. Humans are mostly blue, sometimes green. Beasties are mostly red."

He sat in silence, and it was quite plain to see by his furrowed brow that he had begun to think. The bird watched, as that was all it could do.

Eyes narrowing on the bird, he spoke solemnly. "Be that you sneaking about in my mind?" He sat upright, squaring his shoulders in a stance of power.

The bird backed away from the table with a flap of its wings.

"I suspect I be the only human here, eh?"

Inching closer again, the bird ducked its head low to the table and jumped back again the moment Goyas extended his hand.

"Hush, hush, little demon." He squinted, picking up a loupe with three lenses stacked on one another. "If you be a demon, it matters little to me. I've battled bigger ones than you." He sniffed at the air. "Strange, there be na smell to you. Your kind usually reek of magic."

Hunching forward, he dug the base of the loupe into the flesh about his eye. Squinting, he kept the contraption in place and peered through magnifying lenses into the gemstone. The smallest and outer most lens settled against a facet making a faint click upon contact.

"And they try too hard to be human."

Sitting upright, he relaxed the muscles about his eye. The loupe fell onto the table and rolled into a stack of parchments.

"Whoever, whatever this be, it still be alive," he declared. "And very powerful, for the brightness conceals the color." He shook his head. "Perhaps in better light, the color can be seen."

From beneath a scroll, he pulled a small oil lantern missing a glass globe. The tarnished brass base was covered in a fine layer of dust which he blew away in forceful huffs. Setting the lantern before him, he traced a finger over the small brass dial on its side.

The bird shuffled toward the device, catching a talon in the feathery blade of a discarded quill. Shaking himself free, he stumbled into a book then shuffled back to a safe distance again.

"Caution be a trait I respect in all creatures." Goyas chuckled. "Though it occurs rarely in demons."

He turned the small dial and a low hiss grew in volume. Head bowed forward, lids half-closed showing only the whites of upward turned eyes, he began to whisper indiscernible words. He retreated into a meditative state until a tiny bubble of light began to flow from the lantern.

The bird lowered its head again to watch the tiny flame change from yellow to dark orange. It flinched when the light forcefully shot upward emitting a harsh white light.

Pulling out of his trance, Goyas squinted. "Dimmer," he commanded.

"As you wish," the flame whispered, and its luminosity lessened into a pale blue.

Riveted by the flame, the bird side-stepped in one direction then another and finally settled on a position closer to the gemstone.

"This be my meditative flame, Lucens." Patting the base of the lantern, Goyas nodded toward the bird. "Lucens, my new friend."

The flame arced in a brief bow.

Holding the gemstone before the flickering light, Goyas peered through the facets. The bird craned to look too.

From within, a beautiful, unusual glow darted about. Frenzied and fierce, the color shifted erratically along the spectrum from red to blue, flickering from crimson to a cool purple.

"That be unlikely," Goyas muttered.

The black bird cawed, making the man flinch.

"I never thought it possible for colors from opposite ends of the spectrum to come together like this," he explained. For a moment, he sat in silence, his attention devoted to the bird.

"Tell me Lucens," he began. "What do you make of my new friend?"

The flame shrugged. "It watches."

"And what of this?" Goyas turned the gemstone over in his bony fingers.

"Xiinisi," the flame said in a rush.

"What be that again?"

The flame spoke the word slower and fell silent.

"What be those?"

Although faint in volume, Lucens spoke encouragingly. "You know."

Goyas played with the word by repeating and distorting the sounds. He recognized the plural form and began to sound out the singular. "*See-an-os—*"

"Na, na, na," Lucens complained. "That na be how your da called them." The flame straightened. "One *zeen-ehs*, ten *zee-*"

"*Zee-nuh-see.*" Goyas repeated the word again exaggerating the pronunciation. In the flickering light, his eyes widened with recognition. "But they be myth," he snapped. "A bunch of stories told by old, burnt out Arch Mystics. Those toothless gobs of fading power with nothing better to do than scratch their asses and sputter on about the gods of yore while their minds unravel with age."

In the aftermath of his rant, silence ensued.

Daylight had turned ruddy and dim. A cursory glance through the window beside the half split door indicated the sun was about to sink behind the Sunrise Soup Kitchen.

"Brighter," Goyas commanded, finally calming down.

"As you wish," replied Lucens.

The black bird blinked, watching the flame flicker, swell, and then brighten.

"Thank you, friend." After a moment's pause, he asked, "Now tell me, what have I read about Xiinisi?"

The flame shrugged. "A little. But as you know, I cannot cast light into minds where that light has not yet shone."

Nodding, Goyas lightly set the gemstone onto the table near the lantern. "Yes, I know," he muttered bitterly. "What good be you then?

"I help you remember what you forget." Lucens huffed.

"There, there, friend." Goyas began scanning the shelves across the room. "A little help locating books be all I need. There must be something written about them here. I remember my da's tales, but there be others. Ones not tainted by intoxication or slur."

The bird listened as the Arch Mystic listed titles of books, their authors and summarized contents. He even listed the location of each book—the castle, a library in Woedshor, a shelf within the tiny house itself.

"I read a lot," he assured the bird.

"He skims," Lucens corrected him. "And he ignores the notes."

"Na true. I read them sometimes." Softly chuckling, he glared at the flame. "Most notes be mindless scrawl of guess makers and idiots longing for intelligence."

Spinning about on his stool, he stood, skirted the table and began randomly grabbing books from the crooked wooden shelves on the far side of the table. Nearly every wall in the tiny house contained shelves stuffed to the brim with books, stacks of yellowing parchments, rag cloth scrolls, scopes, loupes, and prisms.

"Oh, that one!" Lucens excitement compelled Goyas to retrieve a thin volume bound in green leather. On the cover, finely tooled in filigree lines, was a sun.

Resting the small book in the palm of his hand, he began skimming the first few pages. Determined to read the book as well, the bird flew to the nearest shelf and settled next to a mark of dried ink from a toppled jar.

Many different styles of writing filled the book, some of the print nearly worn away in places. Glyphs were neatly stacked in vertical columns at the center of each page. In the space between the columns and all the wide margins, arrows linked alphabetical writing to elements within the symbols.

Educated guesses at possible meanings for the glyphs were partially faded and marked with brackets, and a single page of the manuscript reflected a history—the evolution of writing systems from the dawn of Elish to the present time. The book was old and what it contained, within the glyphs themselves, unfolded another story.

"Sacred be Elishevera," Goyas began to translate. "The first and the last; worship and adore her; nourish her by libation and orgy; there forth her heart-warmth? Heart-heat, perhaps?"

"Both interpretations be accurate," the flame offered. "So would life, pulse, and passion."

Arching an eyebrow, Goyas ran his finger along the smooth rag paper. "Whatever Elishevera be, it imbues the world." Shaking his head, he asked Lucens. "What does this have to do with Xiinisi?"

When Lucens remained quiet, he turned the book toward the bird. "What do you think?"

The bird pecked at a particular symbol on the page then craned to look at the flame.

"It motions to the symbols *there* and *forth*," Lucens told Goyas, and after a pause, the flame addressed the bird as though it had spoken. "Yes," Lucens agreed, "that word indicates a physical place."

Ignoring them, Goyas trailed his finger up and down the page, and resumed translation. "See here," he said and pointed to a row of glyphs. "The Priests invited everyone into the temple, taught them how to worship Elishevera—a god perhaps, a goddess even. Back then anything or anyone could be a god."

Leaning toward the bird, he shook his head. "This book, it be written by Priests who worshipped some rock in the desert. Priests na be the brightest flames in the fire." Gesturing wildly above the open book, he rambled on. "They never make up their minds. See this." He pointed to another symbol. "Here Elishevera be love."

"Elishevera could be a god, love, a place—all these ideas. Any reason for the Priests to fashion their stupid rules," he muttered, his eyes wandering over the text. Momentarily he paused and blinked at what he read. Hesitant at first, he resumed translation. "There be others who..." Leaning toward the flame, he whispered. "Cast your light on this one, remind me accurately."

"Direct communion, meditation," Lucens responded. "As not to be confused with the less direct, like ritual or statesmen."

Goyas chuckled at the flame's subtle humor and continued translating. "There be others who commune directly with Elishevera and The Sun Child. A god and its sire."

His finger roamed into a side margin where the name Alephos appeared in tiny block print letters.

"Ah, he reads a side note," Lucens chirped. "How refreshing?"

"Shush!" Shutting the book, he scratched his earlobe. "Only a god can sire another god. The Sun Child could very well be a metaphorical description for the brightness of Xiinisi. I need a text from a perspective other than Priests."

He abruptly stood. The stool toppled. Scanning the wall full of shelves once again, he asked, "Where be *Dialogs with Lishev*?"

— 15 —

"THE SHELF ABOVE the bed." Lucens swayed back and forth as he gave more directions. "In the chest."

High above the disheveled bed, a broad, thick shelf hung suspended from iron chains. There, squeezed between thick tattered tomes sat a large wooden chest. Goyas retrieved it, carrying it carefully toward the table, where he set it down and gently released the tarnished latch.

Upon lifting the heavy, warped lid, he pulled out a dozen oversize thin books bound in soft leather. Several were the color of green apple and others pale terra-cotta or cobalt blue. He set the books on the table, spread them out and examined their frayed bindings.

The bird scurried over to the books. Leaning over the nearest, it tilted its head and gazed with one eye for several seconds before moving onto the next. After scrutinizing every book, it returned to a terracotta one inlaid with strange gold symbols and gently pecked the cover.

"How did it know which book it be?" Goyas asked the flame.

"It understands writing," Lucens replied softly.

"How much of the beast's mind can you read?"

"Only what it allows."

"It won't let me in at all," Goyas grumbled. Pulling the stool to the far end of the table, he sat before the book titled *Dialogs with Lishev* and opened the cover. The broken spine yielded easily and he began reading the text.

"Here," he stared pointedly at the bird, "you'll find this bit interesting."

Sidling up to the book, the bird cautiously peered at the glyphs and words again. Sound gabbled in its throat.

Goyas began to translate. "The Mystics na be trusted by the Priests, thought my kind killed Elishevera and pretended we still communicated with her to gain control over the temple."

Pausing, he gnawed at a callus on his forefinger. "When Mystics began mysteriously dying, they discovered the Priests were poisoning them. A war began between them." Goyas addressed the bird. "To this day, we hate each other. Trust me, you be better off in my company."

Turning about, the black bird faced the man. A loud, abrupt caw resounded throughout the house.

"He wants to know about the Xiinisi," Lucens explained.

Goyas smiled. "Impatient." Grinning from ear to ear, he chuckled. "You must be human after all. Cursed perhaps?" He snapped his fingers, growing excited. "The victim of a submutation spell for some crime. What did you do? Witness a murder?" He leaned back on the stool, thin lips curling into a crooked grin. "Rut with someone's wife? Maybe their daughter? Perhaps their son?"

The bird cawed in agitation. Focused on the book, it pinched a corner of the first page within its beak and began to sidestep. The page buckled.

Goyas helped turn the page and flipped others while watching the bird scan the images and text. A page saturated with additional notes in different handwritings incited a fervent warbling. Humoring the bird, he obeyed and began to read the text.

"Elishevera's voice began to fade. In a last effort to keep her alive, Mystics transcribed their meditative conversations with her." Pulling the book closer to himself, his eyes focused on the words. "Yes, yes, this be it!"

"A Mystic asked, 'How be you born?' Elishevera replied, 'Xiinisi created me.' Another Mystic asked, 'What be Xiinisi?' Elishevera replied, 'A race of beings that live between the stars.' 'Why did Xiinisi create you?' 'To learn.' 'What appearance be Xiinisi?' 'Anything you wish, but for those who can see into their…' What is this, Lucens?"

"Essence, inner light," the flame answered immediately.

"Their essence be… of red and blue?"

"Purple." The flame shimmied.

Curious, Goyas held the gemstone up to the flame. With daylight gone, he detected within a frenzy of movement which warped the air the way heat does in the desert. A purple tint shimmered more red than blue. Setting the stone back down on the table, he hastily flipped through the remaining pages of text.

He paused at the back cover and pointed to a citation in regular cursive scrawl. Disappointed, he sat back.

"Oh, I should've remembered a title like that."

"I could've told you," Lucens complained.

"It na matter," he said. Standing, he retrieved his shirt from the floor and pulled it on. "I na have that book."

"The nomad in the market does," Lucens commented.

Buckling his belt, Goyas leaned forward and gestured to his face. "The one with the delicate features?"

The flame bobbed.

"He is a *she*," he whispered. "I'd bet fifty gols she be a Bes." Leaning toward the lantern, he began to turn the dial.

The flame began to diminish. "Will you call again?"

"Soon."

With a whoosh and a burst of bright light, the flame vanished.

Fully dressed, Goyas sifted through cups and bowls until he found a pouch with a long leather strap. He fastened it around his neck and tucked it beneath his shirt.

"Care to join me at Sunrise, *friend?* I've seen that nomad there many an evening. Perhaps plied with enough booze, I can get a good deal on that book out of him."

Extending his arm, he waited for the black bird to respond.

It walked back and forth along the edge of the worktable, as though stuck in thought.

Using his other arm, Goyas moved his hand. The gesture was slight—a spiral movement which sent a tremor through the air again. Onion and sandalwood arose as the seal on the house evaporated.

With a flutter of wings, the bird floated up and settled on the Arch Mystic's shoulder.

The Book of Alephos sat propped open on a small easel. A thick tome with ragged edges, its sullied pages offered the oldest stories written in the most archaic system—ticks, dots, curves, and slashes were presented in widely spaced vertical lines down each page.

Silence pervaded the small house as Goyas and the black bird scanned the book well into the middle of the night. Flickering with solemnity, Lucens cast warm light over the book and waited to assist.

Upon turning a page, the ones behind fell out.

"Hmm, I paid good money for this."

The loose pages were heavily scored with tiny printed notes in every available space.

The bird hunkered over them and scanned the words.

"This Magnes Alephos be vile," Goyas mumbled. "Hangings from forest trees and impalements on cactuses na be the acts of a kind man. However, it be fascinating to learn he ruled an ancient forest where the desert now be."

Lifting the loose pages, he translated: "There be mention of a tome lost to time, written by Alephos, ruler of the ancient tree world? Tree realm?"

"Forest." Lucens sighed.

"In which a child god delivers instructions to devotees to fashion a temple at Lishever, the veld at the edge of the forest."

Clicking and clucking, the bird tossed its head back and walked about the table.

"He sees the name be similar to the others," Lucens interpreted what thoughts the bird revealed.

Nodding, Goyas turned the page. "Diminishment. I see this all the time in ancient writings with place names especially. Elishevera becomes Lishever, then Lishev. Who knows, perhaps one day the place will be known as Ish."

"Let's read on, shall we." He turned over the first of the loose pages and scanned the markings. "What be this? A race of world builders?" His fingers clenched the page tightly. "A race of beings whose light resides on the edge of perception," he continued. "A cool crimson on the verge of becoming purple." He perked up. "This be Xiinisi."

Lucens sighed again.

Tilting its head, the bird craned to see around the edge of the pages Goyas held upright.

"The name of a child god be pronounced *ool* or *uhl*, a reflection of the color of sun and maize. The name be written *Ul* based on remnants of ancient seals. Ul be worshipped during the dawn of the world and be associated with the grove, war, Lishever, and iron ore cuprite."

Goyas sat upright. Eyes wide, he glanced at the gemstone briefly before resuming reading.

"The seal depicts a spiral for a body, perhaps symbolic of a serpent or snake. Like all gods, Ul be replaced in favor of new ones, namely Areel, who be associated with mining, war, and chaos."

Squinting, Goyas set the pages down and tapped his finger on the table. "I always thought Areel be the source of all demons. Curious." He picked up the gemstone. "Be you *ool*? *Uhl*?"

The flame huffed.

"Yes, Lucens."

"I be bored," it lamented.

"Help me then." He flipped open the lid of an ink jar, grabbed a quill and a nearby blank parchment.

The bird fluttered about as the parchment slid from beneath its talons. It finally found stability on a portion of exposed wood, where it shook itself and gabbled in annoyance.

"Now, now," Goyas consoled. "Come Lucens, assist me with first contact."

Flickering with excitement, Lucens replied, "Of course."

Bowing his head, a low, deep sound crawled from somewhere deep within Goyas. When he raised his head, both eyes fluttered upward, the whites of his eyes gleaming with a strange intensity. With his free hand, he touched the gemstone.

"Hello," he said.

His other arm moved slowly as he dabbed the nib of the quill into the ink jar and poised it above the parchment, prepared to record any message which might issue from the ancient god.

The bird eagerly listened too, waiting for a response.

"Hello!"

Jolted by the sound, Goyas caught his breath. The whites of his eyes receded. Scored into the parchment was a dark brown smudge of ink.

The bird cawed.

The voice they both heard belonged to Lucens.

"Are you playing?"

The flame tittered and nodded.

"I be working," Goyas grumbled.

"It matters na." Lucens said. "Something within the stone deflects your thoughts. You sensed it. I know you did. You know it too."

Not one to give up so easily, Goyas spoke to the stone again. He asked it questions, gently rubbing each of the facets, offering respect and promises of libation, but what or whoever resided at its center did not respond. Well into the morning, he persisted until his shoulders slumped.

Turning off Lucens and the other lanterns, he retreated to the unkempt bed, where he pulled the blanket over his face to block out the rising sun. Curled next to his chest, his strongest hand clutched the gemstone.

The bird took to the high shelf again, where it nestled in a tight ball of feathers and listened to Goyas begin a steady low humming. Whispers floated along the walls and the bird shivered. The soft, heavy breathing associated with slumber finally overcame the man, and in the early morning, the bird watched him lash out fitfully.

Something thudded against the floor.

The bird jolted at the sound. It flew down to the straw carpet next to the bed and saw the gemstone. Glancing around the room, it examined each closed window, sniffed at the lingering magic scent from a second sealing of the house, then returned to the stone.

Even without a loupe or lens, the bird detected a fine red sliver lodged deep within a facet and began pecking at the odd feature. Light stabs pushed the stone along the frayed rough weave of carpet and heavier stabs cracked the bird's beak.

Come morning, when Goyas woke, the bird eyed him carefully and unfolded its wings to reveal the gemstone and a split beak caked in blood.

"I still na know what to make of you," he mumbled at the bird and retrieved the stone.

A beige and black spotted mare snorted, shifting about in a stall next to the tiny house with the split door. Goyas opened the gate and the horse marched into the street.

"Eager this morning?" he spoke to the beast and the mare snorted again. "We've a long journey ahead. We be off to Fehran's castle today," he told her, while securing the saddle to the horse, then the bags to the saddle. "I be in possession of a curious item which would be better understood using the resources of my laboratory there."

Earlier, the bird had watched Goyas pack his tools, parchments, and strange instruments—even the talking lamp—into saddle bags. The gemstone, however, he kept in a pouch on a leather strap, fastened around his neck and tucked securely beneath his tunic.

The mare folded her neck toward the man and nipped at his arm.

"Seems everyone be playful these days," he mused. "You, Lucens, even that bird. If only the Xiinisi in the gemstone came out to play, then I be able to ask it questions. Perhaps it could teach me new skills."

With a final glance at the tiny house, he mounted the horse and leaned forward. "Go now," he whispered to the horse. "To Fehran's castle."

He neither dug his heels into the beast nor pulled the reigns, yet somehow the horse craned its head forward and huffed before cantering down the street toward the outskirts of Sondshor Market.

— 16 —

THE BLACK BIRD soared through the sky, cleaving small wispy clouds in half. Below, Goyas and his mare plodded along a dirt road. Dropping out of an air stream, the bird descended and settled onto a saddlebag to rest.

Hoarse breathing accompanied by a low hum issued from the man, in a rhythm which matched the cadence of the mare's plodding gait. Together, for a little while, the trio traveled roads which wound around farms and skirted the forest of Woedshor.

A blast of air ruffled the bird's feathers as it turned about on the saddlebag, talons sinking into the soft leather. Green-rimmed eyes blinked until the wind diminished. The black bird finally stretched its wings and shot into the sky.

Within its inner ear, a twitch signaled a drop in air pressure. Arcing wings rode a current all the way back to the desert, to the stone archway where it sneaked inside. Treading softly, the floor responded, sending out small waves across its magical surface. Eventually the small waves were swallowed by larger ones flowing toward a black hearth.

Concealed by the bulbous and curvy leg of a table, the black bird watched.

The woman, Mulga, sat on a small red sofa placed sideways before the hearth, occasionally tapping her bare feet. She wore the black dress with billowy sleeves she had admired in the market the previous day. In her lap, she unfolded a white cloth and revealed several glazed pastries. Apple, cinnamon, and honey sweetened the air.

On the other side of the hearth, a young man sat in a wooden armchair, eyes bulging. He struggled against invisible restraints, bearing down on his boot heels yet failing to free himself.

Bruises marked his round cheeks and bare arms. His tunic was torn at the collar, his leggings smeared with dirt. He screamed, the force pushing at lips that wouldn't part, forcing his voice to resonate in his chest and throat.

The bird shook its head at the man with his jaw constrained by an invisible gag. Magic scent emanated from him. Mingling with the aroma of pastries, the air reeked of iron and earth.

Shattered glass echoed throughout the room.

Mulga flinched and the man in the chair stiffened. Both froze. The rippling floor calmed to a peaceful lapping of ever changing dark and light waves.

"Where be it?"

Mulga trembled. She gazed into the hearth's fire first, then at the finely decorated bowls and vases which lined the black stone mantel. She spoke softly. "Where be what?" Her faint voice carried throughout the chamber and down the hallway.

Storming into the room, green ribbed muscles taut, fingers curled into fists, Istok glared at her. Blue waves exploded across the entire floor, obliterating the fluid stillness. "The stone, Mulga!"

She stared into her lap, tentatively touching the pink glaze on a chocolate square. "What stone?"

Despite the demon's calm, a rage flickered in his black eyes. Jaws clenched, he seethed. "The gemstone! You know what I mean." He stood behind the armchair and laid his hands firmly on the shoulders of the bound man.

Shivering, the man inhaled sharply.

"If na for the gemstone," Istok began to explain, his eyes darting over her dress and pausing on the pastries in her lap, "I na risk injury finding this fellow." He gave the man's shoulders a friendly squeeze.

The man moaned.

Mulga lifted the chocolate square, nibbled it, and set it back down on the napkin.

"Do you have any idea how difficult it be to capture a Mystic?" he shouted.

She glanced at the bound man. Either the look of terror in his eyes or the smear of blood along his brow forced her to stare at her lap again. She shrugged.

Leaning over the chair, Istok ground the heel of his hand into the gash above the Mystic's brow causing him to struggle, scrunch his eyes, and gurgle. With a tiny laugh, he stopped, sniffed the air and glared at the baked treats in her lap.

Mulga quivered. Careful and coy, she glanced at him then averted her gaze. She brought another glazed pastry to her mouth, hesitated then sunk her teeth into the crunchy, thin layers.

Momentarily distracted by flickering firelight, Istok turned toward the hearth. His head fell back, a small laugh bursting from him. "What did you do with the gemstone?"

Calming himself, he spun around. His expression softened into a childlike display of innocence as he slowly approached the couch and leaned over her. "Really, I won't get angry."

Mulga pouted. "I sold it," she replied. The corner of her mouth slightly down turned, she nibbled and sucked on the sweet dessert.

The bird backed away from the table and pressed against the cold wall of the room, entranced by how rage flowed through the demon's body. His muscles thickened. Tendons and veins popped along his neck and arms.

Istok sneered. Eyes darted back and forth between Mulga and the man, who had slumped forward in the chair and breathed heavily, sweat trickling down his bald head and chubby neck.

Chewing slowly, Mulga's cheeks bulged. She poised another pastry at her lips before even swallowing. A heavy slap struck her hand. The pastry flew into bits and scattered over the floor.

A small piece stopped at the leg of a table, ripples in the floor expanding into large amorphous ringlets. The bird crept from the wall, snatched the crumb with its beak and threw back its head swallowing the sweet morsel.

"Who did you sell it to?" His voice boomed throughout the chamber. He grasped her face in his claw-like fingers.

Eyes wide and vacant, she smacked her lips as she continued savoring the sweet.

"Focus, Mulga," he demanded. His fingers gripped harder, digging into her fleshy cheeks. "Tell me who you sold the gemstone to!"

"If he be a Mystic..." Crumbs spilled from the corner of her pinched lips. She pointed at the bound man, her hand trembling. She tried to turn her head to look at him, but Istok kept her head still. "Then what be an Arch Mystic?"

Reeling backward, Istok curled his fists, bracing them against his temples, as he let out a short, choked cry.

"It be mine!" He seethed. "Do you even know what you cost us?" He leaned over the red sofa again, pumping his fist before the woman.

Mulga froze.

Rearing upright, Istok threw himself against the hearth. He caught hold of the mantel, causing the vases to rattle. He braced himself, heaving for breath.

"No more hiding out in this hovel. Freedom to roam." He turned on the spot. Hunched over, he raised his fist again. "Humans..." Sucking in a breath, he grimaced. "On their knees!"

He tore a spine from the back of his forearm. "Power." He held the red spike before his face. "I could have ruled the world with that stone you stupid cow!"

Gripping her by the hair, he pulled her to her feet. What remained of her pastries tumbled to the floor. Crumbs cascaded over her chin as Istok held the spine close to her face, pretending to draw random lines over her trembling cheeks.

Lowering the spine, he roamed the point over her breasts and collar bone. Shaking his head, he turned and whipped the spine at a nearby tapestry. Finely woven silk burst into a rain of red dust.

Istok reared upright, spewing a barrage of vulgar curses. They resounded throughout the chamber, harsh sounds stirring the floor into shallow eddies. Again he squeezed Mulga's face between his fingers, watched her cheeks cave and yield. Her eyes grew wide, brimming with tears.

Nearly forgotten, the man in the chair whimpered. Istok tilted his head at the sound, peered over his shoulder. His eyes sparkled, enjoying the man struggle with all his might against the magic which bound him there.

A slow calm came over the demon. His face softened. He released his grip and intoned. "Oh, don't cry." Black talons combed through Mulga's dark hair. Leathery green finger pads caressed her cheek. He kissed her on the lips and nodded.

With a sniffle, Mulga collapsed on the couch. Forlorn, she gazed at the pastries spilled over the floor. Next to her she discovered a chocolate stick which had rolled between the seat cushions. Looking toward the hearth, she retrieved it and bit off the end.

"Any Arch Mystic be a challenge in magic play." Istok ran his fingers over the smooth skin of the captive's scalp and face. "Especially Fehran's Arch Mystic. Insightful, powerful, incorruptible. It be a waste of time trying to retrieve the gemstone from him."

Sneering, Istok circled around the man bound to the chair. A flash of delight softened his features. "The cur can have it." Smiling, he patted the man's cheek. "I'll make another."

Mulga stopped chewing on the chocolate stick and shuddered.

The rage returning, Istok huffed. After a few deep breaths, he yanked a spine from his arm and stuck it into the center of the man's forehead, letting out a grunt as he used his thumb to drive all of it into the source of his new gemstone.

Steely white light burst through the air and flooded the room.

The bird peered into the light, inner eyelids blinking repeatedly, determined to witness the change.

The man shimmered and shrunk into a gap of space a foot above the chair. The light folded in on itself and vanished. For a split second, the object hovered then fell onto the seat cushion.

Grinning, the demon descended on the chair to claim his prize. He held up the object to the hearth. The rough surface of dark gray rock glinted in the firelight. All trace of the man's human form had disappeared.

Istok frowned as he examined the rock. "Hello?"

The only sound in the room belonged to Mulga, who licked the last of the chocolate from her lips.

Shaking the stone, he glowered. "Do you dare na speak with me?" Silence persisted as he turned the stone over and over.

Turning toward Mulga, he held it before her nose.

She flinched.

"What does this look like to you?"

Tilting her head, she shrugged. "A rock?"

"Do you think it pretty?"

She shook her head. "N-no."

"It's pronounced *nah*, you simpleton." Holding the rock up to the firelight, he huffed. "Looks like basalt." He ran his finger over the surface again. His eyes twitched.

"There be nothing precious about this. That gemstone, it be more than a Mystic." Clicking his back teeth, he blinked profusely. "Perhaps another demon? One of my kind who has finally become human." He stared at the stone in the palm of his hand, brushing a thumb over the jagged ridges. "That be true power," he mumbled.

With a grunt, he whipped the rock against the hearth. Slivers and shards rained into the fire unsettling the flames. They wavered and hissed making the shadows in the room flicker.

The black bird sneaked back behind the table leg, head swiveled toward the shimmering wall which marked the exit from the hollow.

"That gemstone be mine." Raging, Istok descended on Mulga again. "You thief!" He grabbed her by the hand. Squeezing her fingers together, he bent her wrist backward, forcing her to stand.

Whimpering, Mulga struggled against her captor as her arm folded at an awkward angle.

Through clenched teeth, Istok growled, "I must have it back!"

Having seen enough of the demon, the black bird unfolded its wings and dove from the shadows through the shimmering bricks, out into empty sky.

Turning away from the reddening horizon, it soared high above the market. It followed a cobbled road which turned to dirt past the bridge and side-winded toward Woedshor. Darkness fell. By the light of a crescent moon, the bird found Goyas and the mare plodding onward.

Easing onto one of the saddlebags, the bird listened to the rhythmic hum and breath of the Arch Mystic. Reigns slack and intertwined loosely about his fingers, he sat slumped forward deeply immersed in meditation, ignorant to the rising sun and another new morning.

The horse steadily strolled through sprawling farmland, tracts of coarse grass, wheat filled valleys, and a thick forest with blue-green pines. Yet, what interested the black bird most was the knot of leather strap poking out from beneath Goyas's tunic.

Deftly lifting into the air, the bird settled on the mare's head, ignoring when she whiffled at the contact of talon against her flesh. There, it closely watched Goyas.

Descending into a valley, the land began transitioning. A medley of greens—grass, brush, and tree—flowed into a collage of color marked by a maze of shanties, shacks, tents, and markets. The mare deftly navigated the tiny crooked streets and passed through a gateway in a high wall made of white stone.

Beyond the archway, guards dressed in silver armor watched over cultivated fields. A dirt path wound around a look-out tower and snaked through a field of staggered pumpkins and squash. Uneven ground exaggerated the sway of the mare's gait, causing the pouch to tumble from a fold in the tunic. The bird tilted its head, espying the way the pouch hung there. Wings rearing backward, the bird relaxed its grip.

Only the whites of his eyes showed. His eyelids fluttered. Crisp blue irises rolled forward to focus on the bird. A slight curl on his lip, his fingers alighted on the pouch. They lingered a moment before tucking it deep inside his tunic. As though waking from a sleep, he blinked at the landscape around him.

"Nearly home, I see." His voice was thick and gravelly. He forcefully coughed to clear his throat.

Flinching from the sound, the black bird turned on the spot, talons pricking the warm flesh of the horse.

A tall turret with a broad girth capped the end of a wing of the castle. Decorative bricks marked the peaks of the tall narrow windows, and the tiny ones too, which dotted the seven floored tower.

Purple moss feathered the white stone which made up the base of the tower, nearly concealing an ornately carved wooden door bracketed in iron.

"My laboratory. Na other in the world rivals mine," Goyas told the bird. "Funded by the Magnes himself. Everything I could ever need or want. Apprentices, adepts, equipment, but Fehran holds the reigns tight."

He dismounted from the mare, unbelted the saddlebags, and allowed a young boy to lead the tired beast to a small stable across a field near the edge of a woods. The woods ran alongside the castle and dipped down onto a vast steppe of land which sprawled toward the borders of Woedshor.

The bird fluttered from the mare's head to Goyas's shoulder, wings poised wide. Once secure, the bird relaxed, folding each wing back into place as Goyas entered the large door propped open with an iron brace.

Inside the turret, a musky incense thickened the air, yet beneath the scent a strong odor persisted—a blend of sandalwood and onion which clung to the tall brick walls.

Browned ancient world maps and once folded star charts papered the empty spaces of the one room laboratory in a seamless collage of diagrams, symbols, and numbers.

A row of lanterns hung from beams along the twelve foot ceiling. Through the center of the vast chamber, starting just a few feet away from the main door, a long, wide, dark wood table divided the honey-colored plastered floor in half. Near the main door, past a series of narrow windows and a bookshelf which extended to the ceiling, another door stood.

Goyas began filling the table with items from the saddlebags: the special lantern and *The Book of Alephos*, which told of the god Ul; strange ocular implements, some mounted on long tubes, some on small tripods; and round glass lenses cased in brass which showered specks of reflected light.

"I know you desire what lies in the heart of this stone, bird," Goyas whispered, tapping the pouch tucked within his tunic. "Stay here as long as you wish, but understand this—the stone be mine!"

— 17 —

THE BLACK BIRD crept along the top shelf of a bookcase. Six of them were positioned evenly about the laboratory, each one stopping just beneath the ceiling beams. They were crafted of thick slats of mahogany and anchored to the bricks and stones with bolts.

Between each bookshelf, surrounding the large table, clusters of workbenches wound about the room. The bird often stopped to bob at any Mystic who disengaged from their workbench and leered at the creature. When the bird remained well behaved, they returned to their work silent and sulky.

Upon the bird's arrival, the adepts and apprentices had sensed in it what Goyas had and expressed their concerns: It be more than a bird. Its mind be like rock, impenetrable. It must be a demon!

Goyas assured them the bird was not a demon for it had never displayed any magical ability. His words failed to assure them, for the apprentices residing in the dormitory just above the laboratory complained of a strange presence which woke them at night.

"Might it be you lurking about in the lab?" Goyas winked at the bird.

The bird's sharp, defiant shrill echoed throughout the tower.

"There, there," he assured the bird. "Na offense to you."

Gaining the trust of the adepts and apprentices proved difficult, and one afternoon, Goyas presented a birdcage. Coal colored rectangular walls supported a similar roof with rough, uneven welds at each corner. Tiny holes not much larger than a finger's width spotted the walls, allowing for air to pass through the simple black box.

"This be cast iron," he told the bird, opening a solid black door. "Na the strongest of metals, but solid enough to contain you."

The bird paced back and forth along a shelf, twitching occasionally.

"For night time only."

Silently, the bird fluttered toward the birdcage, landing on the open door. After examining the darkness within, it climbed inside and began a low moaning warble.

"I know, I know," he consoled the bird as he shut the door to the cage. Carrying it, he carefully climbed the stairs to a small landing, where he showed off the imprisoned creature to the apprentices, who sighed or sagged in relief. Goyas continued just past the first floor dormitory, where he stopped and opened an unlocked door.

Locked and secured in the cage for the night, the bird glared through a hole, watching the Mystic sleep on his back in the narrow bed of a long, arcing room which had been built into the outer wall of the turret. Like the laboratory and the house in Sondshor Market, the room stored more books than furniture.

The bird searched for exits. It spied the ornately carved wooden door next to the foot of the bed and, above the table, a double slat window. The tiny panes of glass seemed invisible against the dark of night.

Sounds of tinkling and creaking drifted through cracks in the wooden floor. Goyas clambered to his feet instantly. He peered over his shoulder toward the cage.

The bird fluttered his wings to remind the man of his presence.

Stealthily, Goyas unlocked the cage, letting the black bird climb onto the sleeve of his tunic. Once he opened the chamber door, the bird took flight, swooping along the stairwell past the landing of the first floor and down into the laboratory below.

"Eck!" The cactus demon leaned forward over the long work table. "Keep birds in the lab do you?" Glass flutes toppled over where he rested his elbows on a stack of books. "What might the Magnes think?"

"Quiet! You'll wake my apprentices." Across the laboratory, Goyas stepped into the main floor and faced the demon, squinting in the dim light emanating from lanterns above.

A change overcame the man. His muscles grew taught, tendons popping and stretching his skin. His cheeks, chin, and nose sharpened as though all bones were being pushed to the surface of his flesh. The unruliness of his red hair might have made him seem insane if it weren't for his focused gaze and steady tone.

"What be your purpose here?"

Istok stood and trailed his finger along a parchment, smearing the fresh ink. He glimpsed the bird nestled safely on top of the highest bookshelf. Recognition glinted in the demon's eyes.

"I understand now. Your usurping of this beast be the cause of its intelligence," Istok mused. "Only weak men make beasts their minions."

"Then he must be *your* friend."

"What do you know?!" Istok snapped at the verbal jab. He rubbed his fingers over the recently scabbed gash along his scalp.

"I know you be an idiot." Goyas remained fixated on the demon. "The beast is loyal to whoever possesses the stone you've been tearing my lab apart to find."

"You have it still then?" Istok asked softly. When the Mystic failed to respond, the demon shouted in fury. "I want it back!"

Goyas squared his shoulders. His knees cracked as he stepped forward. His flesh paled, nearly becoming translucent.

Silence persisted between them.

Istok stretched, paused a moment as though time had stopped. He flicked his hand, balling it into a fist, and aimed the back of his forearm toward Goyas.

A red spine shot across the room.

Instead of avoiding the projectile, Goyas stepped toward it, hurrying the impact. The sight of the spine turning to black dust lit his face with maniacal delight.

The bird alighted on Goyas's shoulder despite the man's tenseness.

Istok laughed with disgust.

"I na enjoy our meetings," Goyas said, repeatedly circling his hand in the air. "You ought to know that by now."

Consternation overcame the demon as he watched the movement intensify. The air thickened and distorted with every turn. He flinched when Goyas simultaneously stomped his foot on the floor and hurled something hard, heavy, and invisible across the room.

Istok flew into a workbench, crumpling to the floor. Vials hurled against the wall and smashed, dripping thick amber contents down the stonework. He cradled his stomach. Wincing, he sprang to his feet and bolted for the open door. At the exit he stopped, cast a bitter glance at the man and retched. "Ugh, your magic stinks!"

Goyas nodded vehemently and grinned. "As do you."

In the days after, the bird found itself being regularly fed by the Arch Mystic. Small clay bowls, one of water and one of seed, were constantly being shifted about the long work table.

It was early in the evening when the seed passed the bird's gullet and a moment later its tiny heart, which already beat fast, quickened. Fierce spasms consumed the bird, as it scrambled toward the edge of the workbench and collapsed. The spasms diminished. After a final shudder, the black bird relaxed into stillness, unable to cluck or move yet still able to see.

Goyas nudged the tiny creature in the chest, then examined a handful of seed which began to crumble into tiny dark brown bits under his prodding finger. Tasting a crumb, he licked his lips at the bitter flavor.

"Coffee bean," he announced. "Sorry my friend," he said to the bird. "It na be my intention to poison you. It certainly be someone else's though."

He discreetly scanned the laboratory, glancing at the faces of his staff. Some glanced nervously toward him while others remained fully absorbed in their work.

Fumbling through the implements of a nearby table, Goyas grabbed a glass bowl full of discarded stone and bone fragments and emptied the contents onto the table. He placed the body in the bowl.

For a moment he stared at the bird, as if waiting for something remarkable to occur. He carried the corpse out into the yard. Beneath the dimming sky, he saw large, wide footsteps in the earth.

"Silly demon, still skulking around," he muttered.

Cradling the bird, he shook his head and buried it next to a young sapling.

Darkness descended. Beneath the cover of a night sky, only a sliver of moon witnessed a stirring beneath freshly dug soil. The pale green leaves of a sapling trembled as the black bird folded in on itself, stretching and pulsing.

Finally it settled into a new form—something dark and shiny, which crawled out of the earth and skittered toward the turret.

A cricket leaped onto a stool and jumped to the long worktable, where it boldly straddled a brass loupe next to Goyas.

The man leered in the direction of the lens. "We na be imagining chirps after all," he said aloud. He jabbed the point of his quill at the air. "Always on nights when that blasted demon breaks into the laboratory. Do you know you wake everyone with your racket?" He leaned forward and whispered, "Thank you. You've saved us a lot of grief."

The cricket resumed its focus on the gemstone. Ambling over parchment, it skirted a compass. The needle twitched and slowly wandered from its mark on North, following the weaving movements of the shiny black bug as it roamed about burners and candles.

Goyas squinted at the cricket, eyes deeply furrowed. Voice tentative, he softly asked, "Be that you, friend?"

The cricket answered with a quick chirp and to leave no doubt in the man's mind, it jumped on his shoulder in the exact same spot the black bird had once perched.

He tensed as the creature turned toward him. "That be a pretty nasty curse you have. What will you become next, a worm?"

The cricket stared, rubbing his legs with a soft hum.

"You na be very terrifying. Icky for certain," Goyas rambled. "The Magnes tolerated a bird at my side well enough during counsel, but a cricket?" He scratched his chin through his thin beard and chuckled. "Thankfully he be young and easily amused."

Through many long nights, the cricket crawled over stacks of books, scrolls, magically imbued magnifying lenses, and elegant, precise measuring devices. Whenever the demon returned to ransack the turret, the cricket scrambled beneath the bookshelf, where the hollow between the first shelf and the floor increased the volume of its chirrups and always stirred Goyas from his sleep.

The cricket remained his constant companion, sitting and

watching him fill many scrolls with fine handwritten text—observations and minuscule details about the energy inside the stone. Hue, luminosity, rate of vibration, temperature, and even the nuance of the energy's continually shifting patterns, consumed both of them for days.

Goyas finally spoke after days of introspective silence. "It may be afraid or in pain. What do you think?"

Crawling over a parchment with isolated words written on it, the cricket hovered above the word *yes* and rubbed its legs.

"At least we agree on that assumption." He proceeded to focus his mind and thoughts, and spoke often to the stone in a soft coaxing tone.

Glancing over the rim of tiny lenses balanced on his nose, Goyas hunched over the worktable. The last of the adepts had adjourned to their rooms, and he sat at the end of the table closest to the open main door, enjoying the cool of night and the quiet company of the cricket.

Grasshoppers chirruped in a massive chorus. Goyas heard every nuance of click and buzz, and the soft, even footfalls padding along ground outside, alerting him to the presence of someone approaching the turret.

Goyas maintained a focus on the book he read and slid another along the table until the open cover hid both gemstone and cricket. Ignoring his attempts to protect the insect, the cricket slithered to the edge of the book and regarded the familiar demon, who loomed in the doorway carrying a cat.

Two yellow wide eyes stared helplessly through a collar of long ruddy fur obscuring its maw. Aside from two tufts of white at the tips of its ears, there were no other discernible markings on the feline.

"Would you be responsible for the tunnel discovered at the east rampart?" Goyas asked, not bothering to stop reading.

"It be big, eh?" Istok answered, amused by his work.

The cat hung from the demon's grasp, forelegs made immobile by the demon's hand wrapped around its upper ribcage. Hind legs dangled as he pressed the back of the cat against his belly and pinned her there.

Something in the air prevented him from entering the turret. He pushed forward a second time; something pushed him back.

"Yeah, a big tunnel full of dead burrowers of all kinds." Goyas finally looked up from his work and eyed the squirming cat. "Some animal, some demon, all worked to death. Minions of a weakling na doubt."

Istok huffed at the insult.

The cat, desperate to find some leverage, curled her hind feet. With claws extracted, she began searching for anything in which to stick them. Istok pressed her harder against his stomach, and she went limp again.

"Oh, how it must keep you from tending the lab?" Istok asked innocently, craning his head to see through the doorway and over the worktable

"The tunnel reeked of iron and fresh earth," Goyas stated, setting his book down. "Of course I knew it be you, so I sent my best Mystics to deal with your diversions." He sat back and yawned. "I've better things to do."

Grimacing, the demon stretched his neck and smiled when it cracked. "Like casting silly magic spells?" He poked a finger at the space in the doorway, pushing it in with great effort. The barrier yielded but very slowly as it pressed around the demon's finger. When his finger began to pale, he pulled it back. "Nice trick."

Nearly choking, the cat stuck the claw of its hind leg in the demon's wrist to find leverage.

Istok snarled at the jab of pain.

Pointing at the cat, Goyas smirked. "Why the feline?"

"Something in there be chirping," Istok complained. He hoisted the cat into the air as if momentarily displaying it, and gently tossed it through the door. "She'll make a meal of the tattler."

The cat landed on the floor unaffected by the magic. She froze in the center of the room and stiffly skulked, searching for a place to hide.

Scampering out from the shadow of the book, the cricket jumped through the air and landed on the floor directly in front of her.

Frowning, Goyas leaned forward and watched his little companion become the target of a predator.

The cat locked wide yellow eyes onto the cricket, her predicament forgotten. She hunkered down, shifted her hind legs, and leaped. The cricket twitched once as her paw scooped beneath it and launched it into her cavernous mouth.

"No more cricket racket to keep you all up at night." Istok smirked. "You should thank me."

Fangs sheared both antennae and severed its thorax from the

abdomen; in one swallow, the cricket slid down the cat's throat. Within her stomach, a tiny life ceased. The broken parts of the cricket began to melt, changing into black matter which folded into the stomach of the cat. It seeped into tissue, muscle, and tendons, entwining itself around the essence of the feline, and possessed the creature.

The cricket became the cat. In a graceful arc, she leaped on the corner of the workbench, where she sniffed at Goyas while stepping across the open book that once had shielded the cricket.

The book slid out from under her hind leg and fell to the floor.

"Not even a thanks," Istok mumbled. As he turned from the door, his eyes lowered toward what the fallen book had concealed—the gemstone. He stopped and rose to full height, his hands resting on the door frame. Fixated on the treasure, he sucked in his lower lip, and pinched at the green flesh with his black teeth.

With a deep inhale, he lunged at the doorway, driving himself into the thick air. The cat hissed at him, a long drawn out warning ending with a harsh spit.

The air behaved as though it were water pressing all around him. He kept pushing into it, and it pushed back. When he reached the corner of the table, the pressure around his body began to increase. Bringing his fingers together, he tried to use his hand like a knife and drove it forward. He only moved slower.

The cat swiped at him—an effortless movement. Graceful, swift. Claws extended.

Istok pushed backward. Despite his strength, his movement was slow. Sharp claws raked the green flesh of his arm several times.

Goyas sat back bemused by the cat's deep lamenting belly growls and the demon's determination to reach the gemstone.

Istok pushed with all his strength. Tightness constricted his chest. Eyes bulging, he finally turned back around. The closer he came to the doorway, the less the air threatened to squeeze him to death.

Pulling himself free of the strange thick barrier, he staggered outside and sucked in gulps of air. Recovering, he turned to glare at the cat. Slowly, he backed away and receded into the night.

Goyas cautiously reached for the cat and ran the tips of his fingers along her back. As the cat rose to his touch, she turned and blinked at him. As though burned, he snatched his hand away.

The flat, bright yellow eyes had become beveled by a ring of bright green around the slitted pupil.

— 18 —

FOR SEVERAL DAYS the cat wandered about the turret. She poked about the laboratory, then skulked about the apprentice dormitories above, all five floors. She'd gone as far as the top of the tower where adepts gazed through long, skinny telescopes directed toward the night sky. Along the winding stairwell, she stopped at the short landings in between floors and charmed her way into the private rooms of adept Mystics, who kept their doors locked day and night.

Goyas was nowhere to be found. Even his bed had not been slept in.

During the day, she perched on a beam above the main door of the laboratory, where she peered down and observed the tedious ongoing experimentation. In between tests and final applications, leftover ingredients disappeared into the robe pockets of apprentices. The adepts didn't pay much attention while they nipped at flasks of whiskey and wine. Despite their indiscretions, they all exhibited a passion and devotion for their work.

At night, the cat retired to Goyas's bedroom. The door remained unlocked, allowing her to slip into the room and leap onto the narrow bed. A sheet of ruddy fur began to form on the linen where she slept.

Curled there, she rested with eyes half closed until one evening, a stirring at the door startled her. Her ear twitched as she watched the doorway.

"Oh," Goyas grunted, "still here?"

The cat stood, arching her back and curling her tail.

"I'm na so stupid," he told her. "You think because you be cute, I'll let my guard down."

Sitting on the bed, he yawned loudly and huffed at the sight of her. Picking at the accumulation of fur on the blanket, he said, "Have I been gone that long?"

Ignoring his paranoia, the cat leaned forward, stretching one leg at a time, paws reaching toward his tightfisted hand. After the stretch, she spilled over onto her side and pawed at the same hand.

"You be too clever for your own good." Opening his fingers, Goyas turned his palm upward and revealed a thin, oval shaped piece of glass. "Five days of incantations and meditations with the glass blower. A patient fellow he be, putting up with my chants."

He held the lens up to the light of the window, and the cat rolled forward and sat up to watch distortions flow across the glass.

"Come." He lightly patted the cat on the head. "We've

experiments to conduct. This lens be na good on its own." Then he patted his chest just below the collarbone, indicating the place where he kept the gemstone in the pouch.

In the laboratory, the other Mystics reported to Goyas about the latest news in a rattled cacophony: A new tunnel at the southeast rampart breached the treasury. Na corpses be found. Nothing stolen either. The placed reeked of iron. The breach be sealed against demons.

The ramparts were far away from the castle.

"It must be another attempt to lure us away from the turret," he muttered. "Damn cactus!"

He gave the Mystics instructions on creating a device to detect subterranean movement and settled at his workbench, where he began drawing schematics for a personal project—a tall, narrow cage molded in brass and plated with gold.

Once designed and constructed, he slid the lens into the beveled base and beneath that he set a lit candle. The candlelight changed in quality as it passed through the glass into the main cavity of the cage. The orange glow transformed into a soft, diffuse light which pulsed.

The first objects subjected to the cage were a quill, a scroll, and an apple, all of which floated in the main cavity and turned about unaffected by the pulsing light.

"To witness if the lens truly heals, we need to find injured critters," Goyas whispered to the cat. "I know you do na play but might you go hunting?"

Experimentation quickly resumed on injured animals—a mouse with a clipped tail, a bird with a broken wing, a vole riddled with tooth punctures. Each in turn hovered above the lens, squirming slightly, but otherwise yielding to the force as their wounds slowly mended.

Finally, Goyas retrieved the gemstone from within his tunic and placed it in the device. A new candle in place, he lit the wick and turned the lens toward the gemstone.

The diffused light passed through the stone, at first. Seconds later, disparate beams veered away from the core of the machine. Intense sprigs of light arced, zapping a nearby glass-encased bookshelf. Fine cracks splintered through the glass in strange patterns yet the glass kept its form and shape.

Cries and shouts filled the laboratory as apprentices ran for the main door. Adepts ducked behind bookshelves or beneath the work tables, remaining behind to satisfy their curiosity.

"That be strange," Goyas muttered, retrieving the lens from the device before the light sparked again. "Unexpected." He did his best to calm everyone, as apprentices cautiously returned to the room.

Spooked by the rays of light, the cat's tail bristled twice its normal size. Along its spine, fur stood on end. With dexterity and determination, she began washing the fur flat.

"Disconcerting how the light turned destructive." Brows deeply furrowed, Goyas began pulling on his beard and returned to the worktable, where he sighed and hummed as he considered the lens.

Reluctantly, apprentices resumed their stations. The adepts, however, offered their services but Goyas declined, preferring to solve this matter on his own, promising to evacuate the lab before attempting any future experiments.

Alone, he sat hunched over the main table, where he examined the lens in candle light.

The cat padded over disregarded scrolls and books and struck his forehead against Goyas's. Sitting back, she blinked sleepily and purred. Until then, she had limited affection to the occasional leg rubbing as a way to remind the man of her presence.

"Be that necessary?" He rubbed his forehead, devoting his attention to the lens.

The cat chirruped and stared wide eyed. It ground its forehead into the man's again.

Goyas sat upright. After a moment, he rubbed the space between his eyes. "I rather like my thought lines, thank you," he told her.

Balancing herself on hind legs, she stretched upward and gently tapped the man on the forehead before collapsing back onto all four paws. Afterward, she laid across a parchment with random words written on them and lightly licked the ink, leaving a small wet spot next to the word *Lucens*.

The man shook his head. "That blasted demon stole my special lamp. There's no way I can speak with the flame." Flipping over the lens, he gently touched the middle of his forehead.

The cat stretched out in front of him and patted at the lens.

"Do you mean here, like this?" He placed the lens at the middle of his forehead.

The cat scrambled upright. Legs neatly poised before her, she began to purr.

Goyas strolled toward the stables. Bundles of quack grass pricked his leggings, and once in a while he slapped his arm to kill an insect. He stopped in the middle of the grass field. Behind him, the cat bounded along, stepping precariously over small rocks.

In his hand, he held a skull cap. Lovingly he examined the mulled leather stained to a deep red. Strange symbols painted black adorned the edge and converged at a deep point which covered the center of the forehead. The lens had been stitched into the leather and aligned with the location of the third eye.

"The tanner was most co-operative to sit up with me for the past few nights, tooling each symbol under my guidance." He tapped the lens before slipping the cap onto his head.

Power surged from his forehead. It was immediate and unexpected. Beneath the brightness of the morning sun, the energy that radiated from the lens was a nearly invisible blue ray of light.

Twitching, the cat skulked through the high grass in search of a safe perch. It found a large boulder and climbed onto it.

Goyas practiced controlling the fluctuating nuances of the beam of light as it collided with stones, grass, flowers, and insects. Stones cracked and grass smoldered. Anything living curled up and died.

For many days, he practiced controlling the blue beam, which resulted in a partially burnt field, forcing the horses to be taken elsewhere to graze. Finally, he found confidence in his ability and directed the lens toward the gemstone in a more controlled environment. To make sure no one might be injured, he sent his staff away for the day.

The blue beam surged and he grimaced. Gritting his teeth, he fought to keep the ray of blue light from veering away from the gemstone. After only a few seconds, he yanked the skullcap from his head and fell to his knees out of breath.

"I na be strong enough," he complained. "Perhaps there be another way to work this lens." In his room, he placed the skull cap and the gemstone on his reading table, next to the window and sat up through the night meditating.

In the early dawn, he sat cross legged on his bed. He still muttered meditations while sunlight streamed through the window, passing through the lens, bathing the nearby gemstone in soft rainbow hues.

A squealing whistle pierced the air.

He bolted from bed, scrambling to his feet wearing only leggings. A deafening boom rattled the room. He flinched and knocked a lantern to the floor. Above him, a wooden ceiling beam splintered and creaked.

In the dim light, he lunged toward the table and scooped up the gemstone and lens, which he slipped into the leather pouch secured about his neck. He yanked the bedroom door open and flung himself into the stairwell where dark shadows stirred and flitted. Descending from the first floor dormitory, pale panicked faces accompanied by lanterns bobbed in the dim light along the stairwell.

Hunched, eyes bulging, Goyas pressed the pouch against his chest to prevent it from swaying back and forth.

The cat wound itself about his ankles, fur bristled, pupils enlarged, ears attuned to every sound.

From the laboratory below, concerned voices chattered with one another.

"Who be working this late?" Goyas demanded as apprentices began huddling on his landing. They fumbled for words but from their frazzled comments, he discerned that two of them had stayed up that night to count inventory, and a newly anointed adept was attempting to derive a new formula for the subterranean movement detector.

A second whistling shrilled, closer this time, and a second explosion shook the turret. Goyas braced himself as the beam in the room behind him crashed onto the floor. Bricks and stones popped from their mortar, breaking apart as they hit the floor. An apprentice toppled forward from the landing and spilled down the stairwell, letting out a moan when he came to a graceless stop part way down the stairs.

From below, groans arose from the fading cacophony of brick, stone, and timber colliding and crashing.

Goyas shot down the stairwell, debris cutting his bare feet. The cat whooshed by him, sailing with agility and ease, ears flattened and head forward. They sailed over the stunned apprentice who clung to the wall.

At the base of the stairwell, Goyas emerged through the doorway and examined the laboratory. In the wall opposite him, a gaping hole spilled into piles of stones. Workbenches and shelves had collapsed under the weight of the debris. A ceiling beam lay at a precarious angle, only having partially fallen.

Two terrified apprentices huddled in the corner.

Goyas coughed as mortar dust hit the back of his throat.

"Be you injured?" he asked the apprentices.

They shook their heads and spoke quavering *na's*.

"And him?" He nodded toward the newly anointed Mystic, half buried in rubble.

They shook their heads.

"They only be whistler bombs, the kind demons make," he explained to them. A vein across his left temple thickened. "Unless demons have all declared war, this be the doing of that vile cactus. He probably be hiding out in the woods."

After a pause, he strutted to the main door and shouted into the smoke riddled morning. "Show yourself you coward! At least come a little closer to enjoy the misery you be inflicting." Turning back toward the laboratory he snarled. "I'll happily give you my misery."

He suddenly cocked his head, hushing the whimpering apprentices. In the silence, a low groan grew louder, higher, more shrill. Mentally he began to count: One, two...

"It na be coming from the woods," he muttered. "And these walls will na withstand another blast."

...four, five...

He rushed toward the stairwell door and shouted, "Evacuate now!"

...six...

Apprentices, young and old, hurried past him, flowing out the turret door as the whistling increased in pitch. Goyas remained until the last of the Mystics fled. The cat hunched near his feet, mewled, and ground her head into his calf, urging him to go too.

...seven.

The third explosion tore out the main door to the turret, blowing outward. Escaped Mystics hurled through the air. Some were dashed against the castle wall while others were slammed to the ground.

Propelled backward through the archway of the stairwell door, Goyas struck his head on the bottom stair. When the dust settled, he lay dazed and unfocused, perhaps for the first time in his life. Next to him, the cat lay bleeding and battered.

She curled into a tight ball. A tremor coursed through her body and ceased. All tension in her small muscles released. Uncurling, a long breath rattled through her. The glow of green receded from her eyes, and black smoke spilled from her nostrils, eyes, and ears.

Coalescing into a cloud, it looked like a shadow within a shadow. It hovered just above the floor and began to crawl, gliding over fallen beams and stone debris. It climbed the broken wall, spilled through a gaping rift in the mortar and slithered across the ground into the woods beyond.

At the edge of the woods, the smoke observed soldiers descend on the fallen turret and tend to the injured. Eventually Goyas staggered out of the gap which had once been the entrance.

"Did anyone see the direction that one traveled?" For the first time the Arch Mystic's voice trembled, yet he still managed to shout above the commands of soldiers.

An adept nodded.

Pointing at him, Goyas shouted again. "I counted seven seconds. Where is that ugly gob of a demon?"

The adept dropped to his knees, tore up a spot of grass and began etching calculations in the bare soil. He pointed and muttered a location.

Goyas swiveled around, looked beyond the turret and the nearby woods.

The smoke looked too.

"The Steppes of Woedshor?" He spat on the ground. "He'll be long gone by now."

The smoke retreated deeper into the woods, to ensure it avoided detection, and began exploring new shapes. Finally, it settled on the form of a man.

The man grew taller, then more muscular and broader through the chest. His hair changed length until it stopped at a shaved head with a strip of short hair which ran from his crown to the back of his nape. The hair turned blond then brown, red even, then black and remained that color. Around him, residual smoke fluttered into a brown cotton shirt and leggings which settled over his nudity.

The strange man who had been a cat, a cricket, and a black bird, turned and walked into the heart of the woods. No matter what changed, one feature remained constant—eyes the color of saplings and tree seeds and sun drenched leaves.

— 19 —

THE MAN WALKED through a farmer's field and slept among the haystacks. Come morning he bid farewell to stoic cows chewing their cud, his presence even more unusual for he walked barefoot and without any tools or weapons.

He strolled into a combat training square located between the outer rampart and the castle grounds, nearly opposite the ruins of the Mystic's turret. Armed soldiers stopped sparring and officers ceased talking to watch the odd man as he watched them in return, scanning the marks of their ranks for an officer.

He strode toward a soldier dressed head to toe in steel plated armor. Towering above the officer, the man glowered. "How do I enter your service?"

The Major stepped back. Haughtily, he eyed him up and down. "You look strong enough, but just because you work the farms does na mean you can fight?"

The man nodded, smiling at the jeers and laughs from other soldiers in the yard.

"I want to prove myself?" The man inquired softly. "I want to join your army."

The Major pulled at the sleeve of the man's cotton shirt to examine it. "Without weapons, a sparring match hardly seems fair. Except—"

The Major snapped his fingers and nearby officers descended on the man. Faces distorted in rage, arms flailing, soldiers shouted and cursed at him. They tore off his leggings and shirt while other soldiers around the courtyard roared, raising their swords.

The noise triggered the man's nerves, and the world became a little brighter.

When he hadn't run and the soldiers had retreated, he stood naked before everyone. Arms cocked at an angle, fists clenched, eyes darting all around, he stood his ground and glared at the officer before him.

The Major stepped backward, armor clinking. "We are born into this world naked, destined for struggle, forced to fight with the only weapon that truly matters." He pointed to his head. "Unless you be a farmer."

"You," the Major pointed to a nearby officer with a purple serpent painted on his chest plate. "Be witness. The farmer will fight me if he still wants to join us."

The naked man flinched.

"We must teach the farmers to stay with their cows."

Before anyone signaled the fight to begin, the naked man punched the Major. Both fists struck the soldier's chest plate at once. His knuckles split as the armor buckled beneath the impact.

Rasping for air, the Major unsheathed his sword and swung it. The man ducked, grabbed the hilt of the sword and twisted sharply, snapping the officer's wrist.

The Major howled in pain and unwillingly dropped the weapon, which the naked man claimed as his own and smashed the pommel into the officer's helmet, setting off a loud clang.

Dizzied by the blow, the Major crumpled to his knees.

The naked man dropped the sword, wrenched the helmet free, and spun it around. He stared long and hard at the soldier beneath, who struggled to regain his breath. Quietly, the man donned the helmet.

Outraged the Major flung a limp arm, a weak attempt to defend his honor, but he collapsed on the ground. Plate by plate, the man began unbuckling the steel shields and unhooking the mail beneath until the Major wore leggings and shirt.

Every time the Major attempted to stand, the man drove his knuckles into his face hard enough to make the skin split but not so hard as to knock him out.

Piece by piece, the once naked man fitted himself with the armor. Hands swollen and bruised, he rose to full height and assumed the rank of Major.

Sprawled on the ground, the Major sputtered and tugged at his sweat drenched leggings and shirt. Kneeling next to him, the officer decorated with the purple serpent examined his fallen comrade. After a moment, he looked up and crossed his wrists, one over the other, a signal to the man to cease any further attack.

Lifting the guard to the helmet, the man who once had been naked asked, "I be a soldier now, eh?"

Leaning against the vast circular mahogany table, Goyas squinted at the Marshal, who sat across from him. They shared suspicious glances with one another, which had become a long standing custom during counsel with Magnes Fehran and the other Advisers. The Marshal didn't mind. He had been hearing rumors about himself for years.

He was the soldier who had been granted the rank of Major by beating it out of another. Fehran's Arch Mystic, Goyas, guffawed the ancient practice of stealing rank at every opportunity over the years. His suspicion was stalwart, and one day the Marshal discovered why.

"Those eyes of yours be an interesting shade of green," Goyas had said once. As though rubbing salt into a wound, he added, "My *friend*."

The soldier's mouth had twitched in response, betraying his otherwise calm exterior. The expression was slight and automatic but noticeable. Black bird, cricket, cat or soldier, it made no difference: Goyas knew some *thing* walked among them and had for many years, and he tried to warn the others.

"He na be trusted."

"If you, the most powerful Mystic in all the shors, can na read my thoughts," the Marshal countered, "then I be the best at securing our military stratagems and our Magnes."

Unable to argue his logic, Goyas begrudgingly withdrew his vocal accusations. As the years passed and the chill of oncoming death began to seep into his flesh and bones, he and the Marshal continued their stand off in silence.

The last of the Advisers claimed their seats at the counsel table, around which time had trampled on all of them. Even the best of these reputable men had been ravaged by aging, having all swelled and faded to silver. Goyas, whose red hair and beard had whitened, looked more gaunt in the face. The glint in his eyes, however, revealed a mind sharper than in his youth.

The soldier had aged too. Towering in chain mail and leather, he was scar-dented and weathered, and had gone bald. Stone-faced, except for the flicker of intelligence in his green eyes, he listened attentively, respectfully.

Withered and frail, Goyas sat forward.

"As you all know," he began. "This be my final counsel."

Protests exploded around the table. Goyas raised his hand and the Council quieted. He fetched the pouch from within his tunic and shook it until a red gemstone tumbled into the palm of his other hand.

Riveted by the sight of the gemstone, the Marshal licked his lower lip and bowed his head slightly. The motion went undetected by most, except for Goyas whose quick eye detected every nuance of the man.

"This be found in the desert." He rolled the stone around in his palm then gave it a squeeze.

Magnes Fehran squinted at the object. Age had rounded his features, and he had blossomed into a stout, bald, and austere man. "Pretty. What be its worth?"

Goyas snorted. "For years I thought it quite valuable." He pointed to the stone. "You see there, at the center."

"It glows," said Magnes Fehran.

Nodding, Goyas fondled the stone. "That be a powerful being." He paused, raising a finger to shush an excited Adviser. "Could very well be the one who created this world."

The Marshal stiffened. He glanced around the table at the various men as they began murmuring among themselves. Resuming focus on the gemstone, he adjusted the tunic around his neck to deflect his concern.

Magnes Fehran hushed his Advisers and asked, "How do we tap this powerful source?"

Goyas tutted. "Hmm, it na be possible. Tried for many of many years." He set the gemstone on the table.

"Perhaps the stone be a tomb," the Marshal spoke. "A trapped ghost."

Goyas snorted. "How refreshing. A soldier with tragic sentiments."

Leaning forward, the hilt of the Marshal's sword clicked against the table. He flared his nostrils and furrowed his brow.

Magnes Fehran's patience faded quickly. He raised his hands toward both men. "It na matter what causes the glow." He tapped the stone. "What be this made of?"

"Cuprite. Pure cuprite," replied Goyas. "More rare in occurrence than diamonds," he explained. Hunching forward, he dragged his fingernails across the table. "Too soft to be carved but if we set into another object like a cup or crown, it could still be an invaluable treasure."

Magnes Fehran sat back. He spoke then of ancient gods and their remnants left behind in nature, of how to best honor their fading memory and how the people could come to revere this rock as a beacon of hope and divinity.

"The stone belongs in a scepter," he finally announced.

The Council agreed. To ensure the safe handling of the gemstone, Goyas oversaw the design and smithing of the scepter. The Marshal vowed to personally protect the Arch Mystic and keep the stone safe.

In the days that followed, the scepter was fashioned. Upon its crest, claws of gold alloy clasped the gemstone, set into the center of a fine, filigree flower. Triangular petals were tipped in white gold. Silver and gold laurels and vines intertwined with one another along the length of the staff.

Goyas conducted incantations and instructed strange symbols to be set at intervals along the staff as additional Mystical protection of the gemstone. Upon completion, the Magnes Fehran uttered a blessing upon the jewel, which the Marshal thought sounded more like an apology. Locked away in the treasury, the scepter remained in a glass case guarded day and night by soldiers.

Nearly skeletal, desperate for air, Goyas lay in a bed in the infirmary within the castle. Diminished and withered, a lifetime nearly coming to an end, his mind remained clear and focused.

The Marshal stood nearby, hopeful to learn any last wisdoms he could from the man before he passed. He'd learned so much from Goyas already.

"Bird, cricket, even as a cat, you seemed harmless, but now, you be like one of us." Goyas rasped. "Tell me, what be your curse?"

The Marshal looked out across the rows of beds. Most were empty except for a few. A little girl coughed fitfully, pulling at her sheets. Several men with broken limbs moaned.

He grabbed a wooden stool and set it down gently on the bright blue tiled floor next to the bed.

"I hardly be cursed," the Marshal admitted. His knees cracked as he sat, and he shuddered as Goyas's bony fingers snagged his tunic sleeve.

"Can you na die?"

The Marshal laughed. "I die well enough, it just does na stick."

"Neither does your body." The Mystic sneered at him, coughed sharply and shifted under a wool blanket. "Answer me this," he demanded. "What do you want with the gemstone?"

"Like you, I want to understand." He grimaced at the strength of the old man's fingers digging through the soft leather of his tunic.

Goyas pursed his lips as though having tasted bitterness in his mouth. After a moment of silence, he said, "You be a demon after all," and released his grip.

Leaning forward, the Marshal spoke in a low, intense voice, "Tell me Goyas—"

"Do na intimidate me creature!" He raised a gnarled finger. "I may be dying but I still have skills."

The Marshal smirked. "Have you tried everything to infiltrate the gemstone?"

Lowering his hand, Goyas nodded. "I've done more than ten Mystics could do in their lifetimes. And to leave behind any knowledge of what lay at the heart of that gemstone would—"

He breathed deeply to catch his breath. "I dare na think what wars it might start." He paused, then whispered, "I dare na think what might happen should it fall into *your* hands." He shifted again, lifting his arm to touch the Marshal's chest. "I might not be able to pierce that mind shell of yours," he muttered. "But I can pierce something else."

The Marshal shook his head. Frustrated by the Arch Mystic's paranoia, he lightly smiled until a glint of light caught his eye. Peering down at this chest, he discovered Goyas pressing the lens from the skull cap into his leather tunic.

Grinning, Goyas hurled one last thought like a dagger. He pushed his powerful mind through the lens, which sharpened it a thousand fold, and speared the Marshal's heart.

The Marshal gasped at the twinge he felt in his chest. He didn't quite feel the impact until Goyas withdrew his mind, and a deep burning tore through his chest. Each heartbeat ached in his throat and radiated along both arms.

"Perhaps this time death will stick," Goyas rasped. His body shuddered and lay still.

The Marshal collapsed onto the floor clutching his chest, struggling for air. The room darkened. Sound diminished and beneath it, a thrum surrounded him, low and indistinct. Blood congealed in his veins and warmth slipped from every pore.

The Marshal remained still, as a corpse should, until his body was buried in the catacombs, then he rose from his casket on the stone shelf far below the ground and shifted into a dark shadow.

It seeped through the soil to the surface, slunk into the darkness of the forest, and took on a new form. It became humanoid again, young and unmarked from life, starting again.

Sometimes it chose to be a man and sometimes a woman. It became animals and insects again too. On rare occasions, it possessed another life form the way it had possessed the cat.

Whoever, whatever it became, it lived—aging, succumbing to injury and illness, healing, dying. Magnes succeeded Magnes. Generations of peace passed over into war. No matter how time turned, it always stayed near Sondshor castle, close to the gemstone.

During the days which would become known as the Era of Calm's End, it roamed Sondshor Castle as a spirit and had grown accustomed to visiting newborn Magnisi. After two hundred years, each child appeared the same—pure, innocent, unmarked, waiting for experience to shape them into something more distinct and capable of wielding power.

The newest babe, born to an unbroken line of heritage dating back to the Magnes Fehran, seemed no different from all of his predecessors. He lay swaddled tightly, a cocoon nestled in his exhausted mother's arms, eyes partially open. Unlike other babes, whose look locked onto their mother's eyes, this child stared directly at the shadow of the spirit in the same manner he regarded the wet nurses—as a solid, physical object.

The babe lived when he should have died from the same pox that consumed his mother the night he was born. The child seldom played, for his mind was set on determining how everything in their world worked. When his court doted on him, the child despised them their sentiments, for his attention was focused elsewhere—on the strange presence in the castle.

Fleeing, the spirit sought refuge in the woods by the garden, where it remained hidden while watching the boy grow and develop.

Unusually quiet, the boy liked to wander about the garden, examining rocks and flowers with a focus of incredible intensity. He was often heard mumbling to whatever object he studied. As heir to the throne, no one dared correct his behavior.

One morning, the spirit hid in an oak tree and observed the boy, who was nearly eight years old. He swiped short black hair from a tawny expressionless face. Dark eyes scanned flowers and bushes and stopped at a spot on the far side of the garden. He walked toward it, unafraid and determined.

Brushing his hair back again, he peered up into the branches of an old oak tree and gazed at the trunk. He tilted his head slightly. After a moment, he spoke.

"I see you."

— 20 —

ULE SEIZED AT the staccato of pain. Bashed and barreled inside the tiny space, she braced herself and waited.

The impact against the marble floor with its illusion of fluidity should have cleaved the interleaved latticework of the stone—broken her. Instead disjointed pricks and jabs inflamed and melded into one another. The tremor increased in motion, each turn in movement aligning with the next, growing stronger until it spun and swelled into a pervasive, overwhelming agony.

Stopping the roiling within was impossible. She sank into the chaos and searched for an eye to the storm. Wild energy whipped through her, persisting like a hot desert sun beating down until she felt worn away into sand.

She cursed the desert, the demon, and the Bisi.

Succumbing to the frenzied heat, she melted into the pain, and the world receded.

Structure began to scatter.

Cohesion disintegrated.

No more than one sentence—a simple, complete thought—existed in her mind at any given time.

"I am Ule."

Focus... scattered.

Dragged along by the gale of affliction, she felt something interrupt the pulse of the storm. The tiny disturbance captured her attention, sharpened her focus as she tried to determine what had caused it. A thought within a sound, a mere word raked over her—*Uhl.*

The utterance of her name began. It rippled through the pain and receded before finishing.

Fury obliterated the intrusion. After acclimatizing to the raging pulse, she remembered that a moment ago something had caught her attention. Just as she was about to wonder what that had been, her focus scattered again.

The storm intensified. A whirlwind now, it flung her about, tearing through both body and mind, whipping her round and round. Only pain existed.

Another ripple disturbed the roiling.

Her focus returned.

"Is... someone... there?"

Her projected thoughts bounced back from the whirlwind, which felt thick and solid. The echo created spasms of discomfort and wrenched her mind into silence.

The pain began to recede. She hung suspended in a pause of time, her focus returning. She didn't know what to make of the calm or the writhing mass of energy or how she had been disconnected from it.

Discordant energies like none she had known before collided and bonded, knitting themselves into stronger ropes of energy. Like an immune response in the body, they bound tighter and surrounded her as though she were a wound.

The wall of energy pulsed and throbbed just at the perimeter of her perception. She thought it odd she perceived the energy as biological matter, reminding her of wounded human flesh.

She examined the layers of lattices of her new form and realized she had no nerve endings with which to feel physical sensation. The memory of once being flesh had affected her perception, she realized. Now, on a physical level, she felt an absence.

"Is anyone there?" The projection of her thought echoed and diminished the way echoes should. She tried again. "Anyone?"

The storm of pain still circled her, even though it had retracted its toothy tendrils. It throbbed and pulsed at the border of consciousness. No longer close enough to afflict her, the intensity remained a constant menacing presence.

Words and visions spun around in her mind, drifting into one another and coalescing into more complex thoughts. Relieved to be regaining her mental clarity, she panicked as a piercing brightness struck her. It seared through her mind, obliterating her thoughts with white brilliance. A pattern of energy emerged and she recognized it as a sound. Strong and steady, the thump-thump of a heartbeat resounded within.

She had no heart of her own, being a gemstone. The pulse had to belong to someone else. A connection had been made between two body states.

Focused and fierce, Ule projected her mind.

"Hello?"

Ule failed to understand the stillness around her. It reminded her of the Isolation chamber from her youth. At least during her imprisonment, she was able to create a world.

As an experiment, she imagined herself breathing, and she did. With cells instead of crystals, she breathed deeply. Then she imagined flesh and bone, and sat upright within a female body, long blond hair spilling over her bare shoulders.

Around her the wall of energy continued to exude a visceral quality. Like raw, irritated flesh, the energy glistened. She hated the sight of it. Slowly, bit by bit, she imagined a more serene vista, and around her a horizon of blue began to knit together and block out the prison.

Although she could no longer see the pain that now encapsulated her, she still sensed its presence as she stepped onto a cool black rock. Ripples formed around it, swelled in ever-growing circles away from her, receding, and revealing new earth stirring with emerging life. Soft green tendrils shot into the air. Earthworms and grubs unfurled from the force and burrowed back into the earth.

Even though it didn't feel real, the imaginary vista was more appealing than the raging cocoon.

A tiny rivulet broke through vibrant moss spotted with tiny purple flowers, trickling cool water over Ule's feet. Perpetual gray cast an eerie glow over a valley of groves. Lush trees sagged with branches weighed with ripe oranges. Their thick, pitted skins gleamed with yellow light despite the persistent gray sky.

She gazed upward. Moon and sun sank and rose rapidly on the horizon, day and night melding into a perpetual dusk. She tried to halt the sun at zenith, but it did not abide.

Longing to rest, she wished for a home. Grass and trees bent and twisted into archways, domes, and ceilings. The flora succumbing to her will, reforming into what she desired. A temple.

Then she wished for people to tend to the temple and for beasts to wander the open fields. No matter what living creature strolled passed her, whether it be a doting maid or a slathering lion serpent, she knew they were only figments of herself.

Everything within the lucid dream changed at her command, except for the sun and moons, which she thought strange.

The temple shifted from moss to ceramic tiles. Beige, blue, and soft pink fragments fashioned themselves into geometric shapes along the floors, walls, and ceilings. Red and dark blue threads wriggled through the tile cracks and wove together into luscious crimson carpets.

Sapling trees spiraled upward from the floor, twisting into chairs, tables, and a bed. Smoke crawled along the floor, curling into four legged creatures. One by one, each pulsed into full feline form. A few were black in color, others gray and beige. A ruddy kitten clung to her leg as though she were a magnet, rubbing its thick torso along her calf.

Ule scooped up the purring beast. Looking into its golden eyes, she still saw only figments of herself. If she must reflect, she thought, what better than to gaze upon a room of cats.

Cradling the kitten, she walked the room. For how long, she didn't know. Turning toward the bed she had conjured, she stopped at the sight of a young man sitting cross-legged.

He sat at the foot of the bed surrounded by the disarray of white cotton sheets. He was naked, except for the expression of curiosity etched in his face.

She tilted her head. "I don't remember making *you*."

Straight hair pooled into his lap like ink. He ran his fingers over the soft cotton mattress.

"What is this place?" He unfolded lean muscular legs and stood. His dark eyes locked onto her naked body.

"This is a dream," she said, letting the kitten spill from her hands onto a tree chair, where a pillow finished knitting together. The kitten landed with a soft thud and curled up into a ball.

"You must be dreaming too." She returned to her bed. Rolling onto the mattress, she wound her body into one of the sheets. When she stopped, she pulled the edge up to her chin.

"Who are you?" the man asked, sitting next to her on the bed.

"Ule." She sensed he didn't belong in this place. Nothing about him reflected her mind. Suspicious, she narrowed her eyes. "Who are you?"

"I am Adinav. A pleasure to meet you." He touched her gently on the cheek and she shivered. He definitely was not a figment for nothing about him felt familiar. He felt beyond herself somehow. His presence sparked hope.

"Can you help me escape here?" she asked.

"I don't know how," he answered, eyes wandering over the tables, chairs, and tapestries of the temple. "I do have... abilities." He resumed looking at her. "I don't entirely understand them or how to use them."

"Oh," she said sadly, as though his ignorance was a terminal illness. She touched the back of his hand in a gesture of comfort.

"How did you make the grass change to tile?" he asked.

"Using the An Energy." Sitting upright, she hugged herself. She shrugged. "It's what makes things move. Without movement, none of the other energies can stick or change or come apart. All magic makers try to tap into it but they usually can't find the focus to do much with it."

"I like magic," Adinav said. His fingers touched the edge of the sheet wrapped around her body and gently tugged it down. "It brought me here... I think." His fingers touched her collarbone and trailed down between her breasts. "Are there others like you?"

"Yes."

He suddenly stood, releasing her from his touch. Brows slightly furrowed, he searched through doorways and nearby windows. "Are they here?"

Throwing off the sheet, she stood next to him. "No," she replied. "They live beyond here."

"Somewhere better?" Excitement washed away his expression of curiosity.

"No, just... different," she answered.

For a long moment, Adinav looked at her. His eyes roved over her body and stopped at her breasts.

"I can make them bigger," she offered.

He seemed unsettled by the notion.

"Or smaller," she quickly added.

"They be quite... fine," he told her.

He brushed his fingers across the peak of a breast and her flesh prickled. Taking her by the hand, he led her back toward the bed. "Tell me more about this...," he struggled with the pronunciation. "...*ann* energy?"

"*Ahn*," she corrected him.

"An Energy, yes." He kissed her on the lips.

"Its a fundamental energy," she began, slipping beneath the crumpled sheet of the bed. "There are all kinds of energies."

Adinav crawled into the space beside her. "How many?"

"Depends." She tilted her head, propping herself up on an elbow. "On how many dimensions you're familiar with."

"Dimensions?" He kissed her again, and fell back against the bed, folding his arms behind his head.

She touched his solar plexus. "Your body is one kind of dimension. It creates certain energies."

"And what do you do with these energies?"

Biting her lower lip, Umera thought a moment and replied, "I manipulate them."

— 21 —

BRAIN OOZED FROM a gash on the dead soldier's forehead. Blistered forearms and a bloated stomach indicated the middle-aged man had been dead nearly a week. Putrefying flesh slid over bone as he lunged between toppled benches.

Swiveling sharply, a blacksmith curtailed the point of the corpse's long sword. Weighed down by shield plates and a bulky leather apron, his thick arms and chest glistened. With skill he parried with the corpse and when the space between them had widened enough, he sank his sword into a spot just below the solar plexus.

The corpse slumped forward onto its knees. The blade twisted easily in the buttery entrails. With a soft slurp, the smith withdrew his blade, severing a tendril of energy which controlled the undead man. For a moment, the body hung there. With a groan, the magic released its hold, and the corpse crumpled onto the white marble floor.

Sweat dripped down the smith's scarred face. He wiped his square jaw. Stubble prickled his cheeks and neck except for the end of his chin, where a thin braided beard fell to his chest. He tucked the end of it back inside the apron and adjusted a red leather skull cap over his bald head, grateful for the strange writing and the lens in the brow which showed him what others couldn't see—filaments of light connected to the dead.

A tall lanky creature strode toward him wielding a lowered saber and spoke. "This bodes well, my friend." Bright almond-shaped blue eyes scanned the slop of carnage in the throne room.

The smith caught his breath, reared himself up to a looming height yet still found himself a couple feet shorter than his unexpected ally.

"I'm not your *friend*," he said. With sword slightly raised, he backed off, examined the room for any more possible threats then focused on his new companion.

Feline features slightly distorted a lean, human figure. Pale, slightly wrinkled flesh covered its body. Unlike others of its kind, this demon wore clothes: brown leather trousers, a belt fashioned from small bones, and a sheath slung across his shoulder.

"Adinav's army is nearly finished," announced the demon. He wrinkled his nose in disgust. "Soon there'll be nothing but bone to resurrect." He motioned to the corpses. "Why else might he raise the dead again?"

"To exhaust his enemies," the smith suggested.

"Perhaps." Bemused, the demon turned about to face the throne, flinging the blade of his saber over his shoulder and letting it rest there. "A century of sucking dry nearly every resource in the world, all for what? To channel magic. And all this time I thought Adinav a pig and vain to want to rule the world. To tap demon magic? Some other goal drives him, but what?"

Still cautious, the smith wondered too. Getting close to the Grand Magnes had been difficult. And for the last decade, the ruler had locked himself away in the heart of the castle, surrounded by his closest confidantes and inner court noblemen.

"You're Kaleel right?" The smith lowered his sword. "The one who's been freeing demons from Adinav's control. How is it he hasn't manipulated you?"

The creature flashed a smile that deeply curled the tips of his thin lips and elongated a rounded maw protruding from a human shaped head. "I have a certain charm."

"Most of the demons have fled back to their hovels because of you." The smith spat, wondering why the one before him hadn't returned to the shadows along with his kind.

"Be thankful we're not fighting them." Kaleel's brief laughter deepened the wrinkles on his face.

Short black whiskers twitched with the curl of his pale pink lips. Red blood dripped from cuts across his sinewy, furless chest. The tip of a triangular shaped ear had been torn and crusted with old blood.

"Not to worry," he continued, "you and I, we want the same thing."

Before the smith could object, a guttural grunt echoed over the marble. He raised his sword and froze. Something sharp grated along the floor. A stirring of bodies arose throughout the throne room.

The demon hunched forward. "Tell me Green Eyes, what do you see?"

An uneasiness consumed the smith. The presence of the hulking demon had been disconcerting and now he proved to be perceptive too. "Puppet strings," he answered, wary of how the demon's black claw-tipped fingers re-gripped the hilt of a curved saber. Fist clenched about his own weapon, he waited for an attack. "Can't you see them?"

"No, but you can, eh?" Kaleel turned his back toward the man and raised his blade. "I recognize your gear. It belongs to the Mystic trade."

Reluctant at first, the smith raised his sword and turned his back toward the demon. Backs against one another, they joined forces to defend themselves against the dead rising yet again.

"Adinav's got them by the heart this time," the smith finally answered, watching soldiers rise for the third time. A blue white shimmer of fine tendrils issued from the upper chest of each corpse.

Kaleel hissed. "How else can Adinav tether these poor souls?"

"The throat, the crown of the skull, the groin—"

"Enough!" Kaleel peered down over his shoulder and squinted. "What be in your fireworks?"

The smith pulled from his apron a steel sphere with a tiny button, which fit perfectly in the palm of his hand. "This one's clear fire," he replied. "It'll incinerate anything organic within this room, including us. There's a twenty second delay, enough time to get out of its way."

"You're that weapons smith," Kaleel shouted. His eyes narrowed. "You're the one Adinav can't control." He grinned. "Good for you."

Not entirely believing in the demon's praise, the smith pointed toward a narrow doorway beyond the throne. Shattered wooden panels hung in splinters. Loud grunts and shouts reverberated through the opening.

"Let's go!"

Kaleel scanned the lumbering dead trying to rise to their sludgy feet. Nodding, he followed.

Together they side stepped bloodied soldiers straining to pull themselves to their knees. From the doorway, a young soldier spilled into the room clutching his throat. Blood streamed through his fingers and he collapsed on the floor. Curling into himself, he shuddered. Limbs remained still for a few seconds then began to twitch back to life.

Kaleel walked over the fresh corpse and paused in the doorway, where beyond a din of shouts and clashing swords spilled down the stairwell.

The smith hurried into the stairwell, where he pressed the button on the grenade with a callused thumb. Something inside the device clicked, activating a mechanism, and he hurled the grenade through the doorway into the throne room. It landed on the floor with a clunk and began to spin.

Dozens of dead soldiers found their footing and recovered their swords. The emptiness in their half lidded eyes and slack faces swiveled toward the stairwell. Their mouths gaped and a howling flooded the chamber. Together, the dead rushed toward the two allies.

The smith and the demon pushed their way up the narrow steps, each vying for space until the smith pulled ahead. Below, a drawn out crackle-hiss blasted into a thundering boom.

Blue-white light licked along the walls around the doorway, momentarily illuminating the roughly plastered walls of the stairwell. The aftershock rolled up the worn marble steps, lifted them off their feet, and knocked them to their knees.

When the clear fire vanished, all that remained at the doorway were several piles of plated armor and a scattering of weapons. Before them, the skirmish continued onto the next floor.

The few living soldiers who fought, had been compromised by Adinav. Clouded eyes and blank faces failed to express any pain from cuts and slashes on their bodies. The smith and Kaleel dodged their mechanical thrusts and parries, and pushed their way toward the Inner Sanctum of the castle, a place of counsel where the smith had sat and given advice as a Weapons Smith, and before that as a Mystic, and long before that as a Marshal.

A low hum began to resound over the stone walls. The smith shivered at the static undertone. Searching for the source, he discovered it close at hand.

"Does your saber make that noise often?"

Kaleel regarded the arced weapon before him. "It's only ever made that sound around Areel, the first demon. She disappeared long ago. But I've heard, since Adinav's reign, she's rumored to have returned."

They ascended onto a landing that widened into a hallway. Bodies of soldiers and beasts were piled against the walls. Among the dead warriors, servants and residents of Adinav's Inner Circle had been strewn or cast aside. Bloodied and beaten, their deaths had been brutal.

The smith braced himself, waited for the dead to rise again, but all that shifted was a figure in the shadows near the end of the hall. He nodded toward the movement. "Something guards the way."

Together they moved toward the tall, humanoid creature shifting from leg to leg. Back lit by lantern light and an eerie glow from the open door of the Inner Sanctum, its left arm extended long and straight, ending with a large block.

A clang of swords back toward the stairwell ceased. The only sounds remaining were their heavy breaths, their footfalls, and the low hum of the saber.

The smith heaved for air, the hairs on his arms bristling. From the darkness drifted a long mournful sigh.

He motioned to Kaleel to keep to the left and was surprised when the demon obeyed and said, "I know this one. He's that cactus bastard."

"Istok," the smith grumbled.

"You know him?"

"We've met, unfortunately." The smith slowed his pace to step over crumpled bodies. A woman in a blood stained satin gown and a man in a wrinkled suit were twisted about each other in a limp embrace.

"I'd bet money he'll run once he's released from Adinav's power." Kaleel stopped to gape at the broken body of a young boy adorned in a suit of blue velvet.

Emerging from the shadows, Istok stepped into the orange glow cast by a lantern. Glassy black eyes flitted back and forth mindlessly. In his left arm, bits of steel glistened. The maul he gripped hung low. Studs ran the length of the wooden handle and adorned the double headed, woodblock hammer.

He swung the maul low, bringing it across his waist. Green biceps flexed. The butt of the weapon grazed the plaster, and fine cracks splintered the wall. Effortlessly he swung his arm back.

The smith stumbled, the wide heel of his boot sinking into the chest of a corpse. Jagged steel studs grazed his arm as the woodblock dug into his lower ribs. He let out a loud grunt. Bones fractured as the maul slammed his body into the wall.

Istok withdrew his weapon, preparing to strike again.

The initial shock burst into a flood of pain as the smith struggled for air. Breathing into his wound, he recovered some strength and lifted his sword again, hoping to inflict some damage in return.

The maul rose.

Kaleel lunged forward. The tip of his saber slid into Istok's belly just below the ribs. He withdrew it slowly and delighted in the trickle of green blood which flowed along the blunt edge of the blade.

Raising the maul, Istok's flexed muscles trembled. He moaned through clenched lips, blank eyes roving about. He aimed for the smith again, driving the hammer down.

The smith jumped forward and braced himself for a burst of pain when he landed. Sucking in a sharp breath, he turned. With his full weight, he wedged his sword into the fold of the cactus demon's elbow. The blade slid through green flesh and hollow bone. Both maul and severed arm tumbled to the floor, one settling with a clatter and the other a faint thud.

Istok wailed, clutching his wound. He keeled sideways against the wall. Plaster cracked beneath his weight and crumbled onto the floor, where he gaped at his forearm curled next to the maul. He blinked a few times and shook his head.

"If the pain doesn't break Adinav's hold on him, nothing will." Kaleel inched forward carefully, saber raised again.

Istok fell onto a pile of dead noblemen. His eyes flitted back and forth with focus. He studied his foes while cradling his amputated arm. "What's happened?"

Relieved the magic hold on the demon had been released, the smith staggered toward the Inner Sanctum determined to defeat the Grand Magnes. He faltered at the pain in his chest. It dimmed his sight yet he still detected an air of vengefulness overcome the cactus demon.

Istok clung to the wall, eyes narrowing. The act was quick, the motion automatic. He simply bent his good arm, aiming his forearm, and shot a red spine at the smith.

— 22 —

COLD DREAD SEEPED into the smith. He veered to the side to avoid the projectile and gasped as the muscles around his broken ribs failed to release. Kaleel's reflexes were much quicker, however. He swept the corpse of the young boy in blue velvet from the floor as though he weighed nothing. The spine struck dead flesh, and the boy exploded into a shower of white sand.

Istok pushed himself up, reeled along the wall, and tripped over a soldier. Sprawled on top of the dead, he snatched his amputated arm, scurried through the hallway and fled down the stairwell.

"One less puppet to worry about." Kaleel turned toward the entrance of the Inner Sanctum. "Can you go on?"

Both arms trembled when the smith breathed deeply. He

nodded, determined to push through to the end, and stepped aside to let Kaleel creep into the tower chamber first. Clutching his side, the smith ambled behind, sword held low to reserve his energy for necessary combat only.

A vaulted ceiling peaked the uppermost tower floor. The plastered walls echoed a cacophony of blast, pops, and fizzes. The hum of Kaleel's sword, which he held sideways guarding his chest, began to emit a sound and joined with the strange chorus of dissonance.

The smith scanned the familiar room. Most of it remained the same as he remembered it. On the opposite wall, a tall stained glass window glowed blue, red, and yellow, reflecting a reverse image of a tree on the round counsel table. The same colors speckled the plastered walls and white marble floor. Tall tidy bookshelves stood erect like guards on each side of the square room.

Magic scent hung thick in the air, a mingling of sweet, bitter, and rancid, which reminded him of wine, radishes, and rotten meat.

What had been added were laboratory workbenches, one on either side of the stained glass window. They were skewed across the corners of the room to accommodate for their length. Flutes and flasks neatly lined in rows made the atmosphere seem untouched by the chaos of war just beyond the door.

High above the counsel table, a strange blue light emanated from a fissure in the air. The tear shimmered brightly about the edges. At its center a strange distortion reflected a flow of beige, black and blue shapes, none of which made any discernible form.

The blue light snaked around the fissure and leapt through the air toward a man, who stood back from the laboratory workbench. Long black hair clung to his turquoise robe. The translucency of his skin failed to reflect any of the fissure's blue light or the man's age. For having lived a hundred and twenty two years, Adinav still maintained the unnatural youthful appearance of an eighteen year old.

Kaleel glanced over his shoulder at the smith and shouted, "Areel *has* returned." He bowed slightly toward the tear. When she did not respond, he hissed. "She must be under his influence."

With great calm, Adinav acknowledged their presence with a graceful nod. Fine blue veins popped on the back of his hand as he gripped the Scepter of Sondshor and slowly inscribed the air.

"I hate that he's not afraid," growled Kaleel.

"Why should he be?" The smith began to feel an appreciation

toward his demon companion. "The man can reanimate the dead."

Kaleel hissed again as the Grand Magnes Adinav resumed his fascination with the strange dance of light between scepter and tear, fine arcs of bright blue flitting back and forth.

"That," the smith nodded toward the fissure, "is not a demon." His voice strained to speak above the din. A fatigue began settling into his body. He pushed to stay alert by fixating on what became of the fissure.

Something in the rift shimmered. All at once, colors and shapes merged into a wavering, fluid image of a large dark iris looking down at them. Suspended in the air, blue arcs of light climbed around the tear.

A fear like none other disrupted the smith's exhaustion, snapping him awake.

Kaleel raised his weapon. The humming of the saber had become a low, guttural drone. "If not Areel, then what is this beast?"

Grimacing, the smith examined the ever shifting edge of light as he watched himself being examined by what resided beyond the rift. Dread coiled around his heart.

"The world tearing apart," he shouted. Or perhaps a doorway opening, he thought, as more arcs of blue light skittered over the scepter and converged around the gemstone in its flower crest.

Inching closer still, Kaleel's saber had a similar effect on the fissure and continued to drone.

Suddenly interested in the weapon, the smith urged his ally to stop. "Where'd you find that?"

"Forged it myself." Blue light shimmered along the steel except for where green blood had dried. "Long ago, using metals from Areel's chasm. They sang to one another."

Cringing with pain, the smith raised a finger and pointed at the eye in the fissure, which began to swirl and dissolve into the image of long crooked fingers. "Did Areel look exactly like that?"

Kaleel nodded. "My kind revered her." He sniffed. "According to stories, Lishev gave birth to humankind and Areel to demon kind." His maw elongated, long lips arcing downward. "She's not a demon, eh?"

At the reference to the familiar name, the smith shook his head. "Do you mean Elishevera?"

Kaleel blinked. Narrowing his eyes, he sucked in his lower lip. "You know her ancient name." The tips of his upper fangs glistened. "You look too human to be a demon."

The smith snorted. Pain flooded through his side. After regaining himself, he straightened. "Your sword sings louder the closer it comes to the fissure."

The demon shrugged. "If it wants to sing, let it. I'd much rather focus on controlling the turn and aim of its blade."

The word *focus* struck the smith as being meaningful. He observed the nature of the Grand Magnes, comfortable, pleased, and deeply entranced as he inscribed a semi circle in the air with the scepter.

The crimson gemstone set in the scepter's crest glowed brighter as it came closer to the fissure. The lightning spears shortened, arcing more severely. The snaps and fizzles multiplied. And the tear stretched.

"What other fireworks are in your apron?" Kaleel tugged at the smith's apron pocket.

"Explosions will only worsen the tear," the smith explained.

Riveted to the floor, he observed the subtle movements of Adinav's lips as he continued inscribing patterns in the air. The gemstone seemed to respond with sprigs of blue light which fed the growing fissure.

"We need to split his focus."

Agreeing to the idea, Kaleel grunted. He hunched closer and spoke loud enough for the smith to hear. "I'll attack Adinav from this side of the table. You, go to the other side. What do you say we meet in the middle?"

After a moment of thought, the smith nodded. "Let's see which of us can strike him first."

At the sound of his name, Adinav glanced at them. "You've nothing to fear." His voice was calm and soothing, as though he spoke to frightened children. "In a few minutes I'll take you with me. Beyond this world, there's another."

The smith leaned into the cat demon and shouted, "Go!"

They both began skirting the large girth of the counsel table. Kaleel made great strides. Clearing the fissure first, he sprung onto the table. The movement was sudden, and the smith was stunned by how unaffected the Grand Magnes behaved.

Adinav frowned. Irked by the sudden proximity of the demon, he sighed heavily and raised the Scepter of Sondshor. Leaning toward the gemstone, his lips moved again as though he spoke to it.

The smith saw opportunity to drive his sword into the small of Adinav's back. He lunged forward. His blade veered away from the man as though it had struck an invisible wall of stone and dove into the marble floor. He cringed as his ribs clenched from the impact.

Swiveling slightly, Adinav circled the air with the scepter. A long, jagged filament of light burst from the gemstone and zapped the smith square in the chest. The force knocked him to the ground. The left side of his body seized with pain. Tiny dots floated in his vision as he pulled himself up again.

"My turn," hissed Kaleel. The thrum of his sword became deafening as he leaped toward Adinav. Saber poised overhead, tip pointed downward, he aimed for the man's chest.

Saber and scepter collided in a storm of blue electricity. Cracks of thunder exploded throughout the room. Whatever force was unleashed within the collision hurled Kaleel backward and dashed him high against a bookshelf.

Books tumbled to the floor along with the demon, who scrambled to take up his sword. Flames licked along the edge of the blade where blood from the cactus demon had dried.

The collision propelled Adinav backward toward the stained-glass window, where he barreled into the corner of a workbench. Flutes and flasks tumbled to the marble floor and smashed. Yellow, red, and blue elixirs mixed together into muddied puddles.

Adinav rose to his feet still clutching the scepter. His look was an odd mix of delight and curiosity. "Give me your weapon now, Kaleel, and I'll spare you."

"Spare me what?"

A blade of white light erupted from the flower crest. Impressed by its sudden appearance, Adinav held the scepter high above his head, directing it at Kaleel.

"The wrath of my goddess."

Desperate to find any weakness in the man, the smith lunged again. This time the invisible barrier had vanished and the blade slipped into his middle back, piercing a kidney and tearing a lung. Pulling himself free, the smith shivered as Adinav regarded what should have been a fatal wound with a passing glance. The cut ceased bleeding and sealed itself in mere seconds.

The blade of light arced in a different direction, and the gemstone sheared in two, still caged by the gilded prongs of the crest.

A glimpse of humanity returned to the Grand Magnes. His arm trembled. Anguish contorted his face. He wailed as the sprigs of blue light flared and began to fade away. High above the table, the arcs which danced around the edge of the fissure began to fizzle out one by one. The tear in the sky began to shrink until it disappeared altogether.

Relieved by the sealed tear, the smith knew the man's seat of power did not reside in the Scepter of Sondshor. To prove this true, Adinav began inscribing the air with simple gestures of the hand similar to those of the Arch Mystics.

Advancing again, this time the smith lowered his sword and raised his forefinger.

"You're only a weapons smith." Adinav's laugh was honest and almost sweet. It was a gentle laugh which echoed slightly in the silent room.

Eyes narrowing, the smith lowered his head until the peak of his skull cap lined up with his target. "I'm many things," he growled.

Adinav straightened, rigid fingers dug at the air as though he carved into somewhere unseen. From that secret lair, he pulled out a spider of energy. Fine white tendrils snaked about his palm.

The smith loathed to be close to the man. He reeked of lavender and mint. Their faces close to one another, the smith smelled the rot in Adinav's breath and reluctantly glanced at the tendrils of energy snapping beside him.

Straddling Adinav's hand was a large, sinewy black spider covered in an exoskeleton of fine white light. A front leg reached toward his shoulder.

"I'll tell you a secret, so you don't waste your energy in these final moments." Adinav tilted his head, leaned in closer until their eyes met again. "My heart beats once a month," he whispered.

"You've no need to lie Magnes." Lowering his head, the smith gazed upward toward the lens of his skullcap and smiled. "Everyone knows you don't have one." He jabbed the air sharply, driving not just one image but two, each like a pin boring through tissue and flesh, deep into the back of Adinav's head till they lodged in each occipital lobe.

Adinav froze at first, all tension draining from him.

The spider launched itself from his hand into the air and landed on the counsel table, where it scurried hastily and dropped to the floor. The sound of its crackling energy faded as it disappeared through the chamber door, out into the hallway.

A gasp escaped Adinav as he clutched his face. When he stumbled backward, his arms snapped outward feeling for something or someone. The smith backed away as Kaleel descended on him.

"What have you done?" Blindly, Adinav whipped the scepter

before him like a baton, hoping to strike something. "What is this... image?"

Slumping against the counsel table, the smith caught his breath. "Darkness."

Kaleel caught Adinav's flailing arm with the scepter and held it firm. Stiffening, Adinav felt with his free hand, reaching along the cat demon's arm, fingers dragging through dried blood and the gore of slain soldiers congealed to the demon's chest.

"You live in a grove no bigger than this room," Adinav gurgled. His fingers tapped across Kaleel's maw and stopped to linger on the points of his fangs. He inscribed a movement in the air but nothing happened. "It's a cage. I could have set you free from this troubled world. All of us... *free*."

"The world's not the problem," Kaleel spat, shoving Adinav backward. "You are." Grabbing his saber in both hands, he slashed Adinav across the chest then stabbed the tip of the curved blade into Adinav's upper chest until ribs finally parted, giving way for the full length of the blade.

Adinav sputtered, eyes searching in a darkness that didn't exist. Weakly, he lashed out with the scepter but Kaleel dodged the broken crest.

In want of his sword back, Kaleel wedged his knee on Adinav's stomach and pulled it free.

Keeling backward, Adinav clutched the Scepter of Sondshor with both hands as though it would help him regain his balance. Beneath his weight, stained glass parted from lead cames. The image of the tree shattered. Tripping, Adinav screamed as he fell, shards of glass tearing through his flesh.

The smith rushed toward the broken window and stared down into the courtyard, four stories below. Adinav lay broken and bloodied, eyes wide, the scepter still clamped in his fist.

"How did you stop his power?" Hesitant, Kaleel approached the window.

"I cast a thought in the form of an image. Something I learned from a Mystic." Catching his breath, he clutched his side. Remembering Goyas, he knew the seat of a Mystic's power resided in their perception, which was both formed and informed within the mind.

"Good for us." Kaleel slapped the smith's shoulder.

The smith groaned beneath the pressure.

"We need to make sure that beast of a Grand Magnes is dead."

Kaleel turned away from the window. "And announce it so the world can take a long rest till the next peacock comes along who wants to occupy the throne who wants to destroy us all."

Silently, the smith accompanied the demon back into the hallway. The spider had long disappeared, and in the distance, the clang of swords and cries were faint as though skirmishes were diminishing.

"I like the world," Kaleel said, recovering the maul from their encounter with Istok. He slung it over his shoulder. "There's no place for me in it, but I still like it. How about you?"

"It's different."

"Yes," Kaleel nodded. "It's good, eh?"

Struck by the demon's attitude, the smith smiled even though he remained unconvinced.

— 23 —

BROKEN COLORED GLASS littered the flat stone of the courtyard beneath the Inner Sanctum. Amid the ruin, the body of Adinav lay crumpled and motionless. The smith nudged his boot toe into the preternatural young man, watching for the slightest hint of life. A limp arm rolled from the corpse's sunken chest.

The smith tried to breath deeply. He coughed at the pain. "Satisfied?"

Kaleel nodded. "No one'll believe him dead, not without a good and proper exhibit."

He raised his saber, which had gone silent once the fissure had sealed, and swung it downward. A single blow severed Adinav's head. Very little blood spilled from the neck wound. Kaleel knelt and braided the dead man's long black hair into a rope which he fastened to his bone belt. When he stood, the head with half-lidded eyes rolled back and forth over his thigh.

The smith raised his hand. "Listen."

Around the courtyard, through a half dozen archways leading into other yards within the inner castle, the clank of metal on metal and battle cries eased. The din of a few remaining skirmishes began to diminish.

Kaleel tilted his head to listen too. "Word'll travel fast now the war's over, what with soldiers regaining control of themselves. Everyone'll know sooner if we prop the head up in Sondshor market."

He patted Adinav's forehead.

The severed head swayed as Kaleel rose to his full height and towered over the smith. He flexed his arms in a long stretch, as though waking from a deep sleep. "Coming?"

"Start without me." The smith toed the scepter. It rolled out of the headless corpse's grip. "I'm going to loot the laboratory for healing tinctures." He touched his swollen ribs.

"You must meet me at Sunset," Kaleel said, "so we can drink to peace before the humans shoo me and my kind back into the shadows now the war's coming to an end." He turned on his paw-heels and strode from the courtyard.

The smith scanned the ground and saw scattered fragments of cuprite among the broken glass. After a few moments, they began to vibrate and slowly shimmied across the flat stone toward each other. Retreating from the area, the smith rested in the shadows of a doorway and watched their strange dance.

Twitching, they pulled together and arranged themselves into a pattern marking key points along an invisible human outline. When they settled on a position, they began to glow, intensifying into blinding whiteness, forcing the smith to shield his eyes. After the light faded, he discovered the body of a young woman lying on the ground and the fragments of the gemstone had vanished.

Across the yard, a shadow moved. The smith leaned forward as the cactus demon lurched beneath a pointed archway, carrying his forearm. Wide black eyes locked onto the sight of the young woman sprawled on the ground.

The woman's eyes fluttered, then slowly opened. Next to her lay a saddle bag. When she felt for it, the form collapsed and turned to dust except for its metal handle.

Istok stepped closer. The smith emerged from the shadows, his movement reflecting the demon's. Their eyes met briefly. Glowering, Istok flung himself back through the archway into the yard beyond and fled.

Groaning, the woman lifted a trembling hand, rubbed her eyes and tugged strands of matted blond hair from her face. Rolling to one side, she pushed herself to her feet.

Stealthily, the smith receded into the darkness of the doorway, where he waited and watched.

※

Ule blinked at the wide blue sky, at the sudden clang of metal and shouts momentarily rising then diminishing from somewhere close by, at the white stones arranged as walls, arches, and supports.

"Castle," she muttered.

On the ground near her, she saw a headless body robed in turquoise, fingers curled around emptiness. Next to it, a broken scepter glittered in the sun. By instinct, she backed away.

Squeezing her eyes, she shut out the corpse. She fisted her hands and trembled, frightened by how nothing she saw looked familiar. Her heart quickened to a furious beat. Confusion reeled through her mind.

Carefully she opened her eyes again. Shakily she began to walk across the yard and through the closest archway. Cool stone propelled her forward, from one yard to another, through an endless maze where she saw dazed men abandon their fights with others and amble toward a vast archway, where steel gates had once hung and now lay twisted, broken, and cast aside. She watched the soldiers regard one another, shake their heads, and she wondered if they had all been affected by the same spell.

The flat stone of the yard ceased at the gate. Soldiers spilled through the opening, each one veering in a different direction across a vast field. Following them, Ule ran over coarse grass. It prickled her toes as she steered toward an open field.

She tripped over the corpse of a strange beast with eight eyes and fell sprawling over another of a man. His armor, slick with blood, dug into her chest. His arm was folded beneath him, his ashen face squished into the mud, helmet askew, his mouth slightly parted. She scrambled to her feet, tears streaming down her face. The man's emptiness consumed her making everything else around her bright and harsh. A chill settled deep inside her bones.

Staring helplessly, not understanding, she carefully stepped over more human remains. As for the corpses of other strange creatures, she understood their parts—muscles, teeth, claws, tails, maws—but not the combination of those parts, for there were beasts made of a dozen snake tails and others with several heads on thick necks or with fine, feathery thin limbs.

She slipped and fell again, losing her breath. A sharp pain tore through her right shoulder. Across the field, the carnage spread endlessly. The dazed soldiers she had followed stumbled over piles of slaughter. Pushing herself up, she grabbed her shoulder and winced in pain. She stumbled onward, mindful there were others alive like herself, wandering among the dead.

On her left, a tall, narrow man with black hair squatted next to a beheaded beast with ten eyes clustered above a gaping, cavernous mouth. He pulled at the beast's hair—dreads which erupted from a skin made of flesh-colored scales. On her right, a woman rose and walked toward another corpse.

Stealthily, Ule approached the nearest of them, the woman, who leaned over the body of a man flung on his back. Her hair was short with a bluish tint. Thick through the middle with solid round arms, she fumbled through the pockets of the corpse's muddied, torn tunic. She stood to examine the contents of a pouch she unfastened from his belt. Tall and dark with a deep olive complexion, she hummed as she peered into the pouch. Fastening it shut again, she glanced upward and slipped it into the pocket of her long skirt.

Ule gasped as their eyes met. When the woman spied her, dark aggression churned in her blue eyes. Tilting her head, she grimaced as a fine steel shiv slipped from the sleeve of her shirt into her wide hand.

The glint of steel, though slight, hurt Ule's eyes. She squinted. Shivering, she cradled her shoulder.

"Oh!" The woman's voice softened. She sagged slightly. Compassion relaxed her hardened features, revealing a heart-shaped face. "Been hurt, have you?"

Ule nodded brusquely.

"That's fine fabric," the woman cooed and stepped a little closer to examine the dress. "Reminds me of the sun."

Ule stepped backward, wincing at the glint of the weapon.

Noticing her discomfort, the woman carefully shoved the pick back up her sleeve and continued toward her. Within reach, the woman gently touched the short sleeve of the fine, yellow dress then dabbed a finger at a blood stain.

"Never seen such work. Must be a new design." She pouted, still admiring the dress. "Only nobility wears such fine cloth."

Ule shrugged. She knew nothing of clothes and design or nobility. She only wanted to understand what had happened and what was happening.

"I don't know," she rasped, trying to figure out how to avoid any further scrutiny.

The woman curled her nose. She was tall and muscular, with thick lips and small breasts. "If anyone knows you're from Adinav's Court, they'll hang you, that's for definite certain."

Ule trembled. Touching her throat, she began to trudge across the field away from the woman, away from death.

"I didn't mean I would." The woman caught up with her. "Your secret's safe with me. I won't tell." She clasped Ule's hand firmly and walked beside her. "You should leave this place."

The touch of the woman's callused fingers slightly anchored Ule. She found the descending sun burned her eyes, and when she looked down to avoid the brightness, death stared back. No matter where she looked, she found no reprieve from her confusion.

The woman's long thick skirt snagged on edges of armor or outstretched limbs, which only prompted her to stop and search pockets and boots for coins, bills, and other treasures.

Ule frowned and turned her back, not quite understanding her disgust at the sight.

"Never mind them," the woman said. "They're dead. They can't bring any of this with them. Not their money, not their things." She stood again. "The jewelry I melt down so no one'll recognize it. Dead is dead. And if it weren't me, it would be somebody else." She motioned to others in the field—men, women, children—crouching over the dead, searching for treasures of their own.

Unsettled by the sight, Ule winced.

"There, there," the woman consoled with heavy handed pats.

The gesture offered little comfort and Ule shrugged it away. Insisting, the woman took her hand again and led them toward a thicket of small trees.

"I'm Yensilva."

Ule remained silent, squinting to force tears back.

"You must have a pretty name being nobility," Yensilva rambled. "Exotic no? You must tell me your name!"

"I don't know," Ule mumbled.

"I promise," Yensilva said softly. "I won't tell anyone. I'll make sure no one'll hurt—"

"I don't know!" Ule's heart raced. "I can't—" She blinked back tears. "I can't remember anything."

Yensilva grunted. "That's weird!"

Silver saplings hid a small wooden wagon weathered gray by rain and mud. Nearby, tethered to a tree in the thicket, a tall brown steed with large beige spots shifted from leg to leg before settling down again. Twigs and brambles clung to his matted beige mane.

Ule appreciated the horse's wild dark eyes. They seemed to be filled with everything, a welcoming contrast to the vacant expressions of the dead. For a moment, she forgot her shoulder hurt. She even forgot her inability to recall anything about herself.

"Here," Yensilva nearly shouted, pulling an unfolded wool blanket from the wagon. "Wrap this around yourself. That way no one'll glimpse that pretty dress and suspect." Then, as an afterthought, her tough exterior softened again. "It'll keep you warm too. C'mon now, climb in. Mind your shoulder. It's probably bruised. It'll heal in no time. You'll see."

Ule obeyed as the woman hoisted her up onto the wagon's back end. Scrambling to the other end near the seat, she pulled the blanket tightly around her body. She sat against a bulky canvas sack filled with carrots and barely noticed how little it yielded beneath her weight, for an impenetrable curtain in her mind hid the answers she sought. No amount of brow furrowing or teeth clenching seemed to pull that thick fabric aside and reveal the slightest of memories.

She sat in thought, raked through her mind, and tried to uncover a seedling recollection which might lead to a clue about her identity. She cried again. Of all the things to cry about, a name. It was hers, and it had been wiped from her memory along with her past.

She rested from trying to remember—her name, where she came from, the name of a friend, a relative even—and watched Yensilva pack away her recently found treasures into a small wooden casket then tend to the steed.

The horse snorted profusely, and Ule thought the beast seemed annoyed at being hitched to the wagon. Finally, he settled down and bowed his head to nibble at a tall cluster of quack grass. Yensilva climbed into the wagon and shook the reigns several times before the horse abandoned its meal.

They traveled mostly in silence along narrow roads which led them through abandoned shanty towns, valleys filled with more dead soldiers and beasts, and a forest which smelled of pine.

"Stinks, doesn't it?" Yensilva said, scrunching her face. "It's not nearly as bad as the dead. It'll be better at the farm." With a heavy sigh, she mumbled, "So much better." Perking up, she snapped the reigns.

Ule remained silent, failing to understand the woman's rambling. Pine scent overwhelmed her, prickling her nostrils and tickling her lungs. She squinted when the forest receded and the road snaked through rippling fields ablaze in pale yellows and golds. Slowly acclimatizing to the brightness and the soft whoosh of wind through the fine wheat stalks, she sank into a deep sleep.

She dreamed of a long, red needle. It pricked her skin. When she checked to see if the wound bled, she saw the needle sewing stitches of black thread into her skin. Threads descended from the night sky and into her hands, her body. She was created entirely of shimmering black flowing filament, and she found it comforting.

Upon waking, she discovered dusk had descended, and Yensilva had stopped to camp for the night. Only fragments of the dream remained in her memory. By the time she ate a chunk of stale bread with broth, the dream had faded entirely.

Ule soaked in sun-heated water, legs bent to fit in the large tub made from beaten steel. She refused to emerge, content to sit in the dirty water, simply because the sensation of fluid wrapping around her body eased her nerves. Though she didn't care much for disrobing in front of the strange woman, being naked outside in the middle of an open yard, splashing about in the water, felt natural.

Relaxing, she began absorbing details of the farm. A small, blue painted, single story house. A large unpainted barn. Several small makeshift shacks stood in odd places around the property. A large basin on stilts towered left of the house, from which Yensilva siphoned rainwater to fill the tub. Beneath the basin, a makeshift wooden shack with a half door revealed a shower.

On the other side of the bathtub, the yard opened up onto a wide, partially tilled field which receded into grassland. Rows of upturned brown earth began near the edge of the yard and ended abruptly half way across. In the other half, a litter of dried, old cornstalks still needed to be turned under.

Small vegetable gardens dotted the perimeter of the oddly shaped yard. A potato patch piled high with soil had been tilled close to the house. Along the barn wall, unruly giant rhubarb bushes fought each other for dominion.

Sighing, Ule sadly watched Yensilva fawn over the soiled yellow dress, cutting away stains which hadn't washed away during a boiling in the pot on her hearth.

"The scraps'll make pretty handkerchiefs," Yensilva told her. "No worries now. I have more practical clothes for you." She pointed to worn, faded pants with a shirt neatly folded and stacked on the front stoop, topped by a pair of thick soled leather sandals.

Ule tried finger combing her damp hair but the long dense knots persisted. Once her flesh began to wrinkle, she reluctantly emerged from the tub, dried herself with a stiff towel, and dressed.

The pants were large and made of light blue cotton. The short sleeves of the beige shirt stopped at her elbow, the hem of the tail at mid thigh.

Still pulling at her hair, she finally spoke. "Do you have a mirror?"

Yensilva frowned at her, then glanced sideways at nothing in particular. "Inside," she mumbled.

"What's the matter?"

The woman shook her head and said nothing.

Ule climbed the stoop and entered the house. In a moment, she returned back outside. "My hair is gorgeous!"

Yensilva snorted. "It's awful. It's got all kinds of tangles."

"It just needs a brush." Desperate, she resumed pulling at the knots.

"It's awful! Believe me," Yensilva insisted, forcing Ule to sit on a stool in the yard. She plucked at the matted hair. "I'll make this better," she promised, and retrieved a brush of thick hog's bristle and shears from the house. After a few moments of tugging at Ule's hair, she asked, "Still don't know your name, then?"

The shears snipped close to Ule's ear. Profoundly confused, she replied, "Nope."

"People call me Yensi. You can call me that if you'd like."

Hunching forward, Ule grunted every time the brush snagged a knot. In this quiet moment, she squeezed her mind for even the tiniest significant detail about her identity. Not even the tiniest drop of information fell into her awareness.

"Oh, this is too much of a nest," Yensilva complained. "It needs a proper cutting."

"No!" Clasping her hair with both hands, Ule shook her head.

"You might be nobility," Yensilva scolded her, "but you can't let people know. A different style could hide you."

"But if someone recognizes me," Ule argued, "they can tell me my name, tell me who I am."

"Later," Yensilva insisted. "When the war is good and over, you can grow it out. For now, be smart and stay safe."

Clenching her jaw, Ule conceded.

"I'm not as good as the girls in town who can cut and style hair so pretty," Yensilva rambled. "Anything I do will still be better than this."

Ule flicked her hand in the air, ungracefully gesturing for the cutting to proceed and listened to the shears begin snipping in random places about her head.

"*Oo*-something," she blurted.

Light cheeriness reflected in Yensilva's voice. "What's that?"

"My name, it's *oo*-something." Slumping on the stool, Ule plucked long strands of hair from her lap.

"*Oo, oo, oo*," Yensilva said softly to herself. She stopped snipping for a moment. "P'haps it's Umera. That one's a popular name these days."

"It seems a bit long." The name didn't sound right. Her name, if she could only hear it, she was certain the familiarity would make all of her memories come rushing back.

"Your hair sure is," Yensilva grumbled.

Ule counted the syllables using her fingers: *oo-mer-a*. "I meant my name."

"Nonsense! Umera's a lovely name." Yensilva paused in mid-snip, tsked, then resumed in a flurry.

When the scissors fell silent, Ule's nostrils twitched. A sweet aroma surrounded her. Yensilva pulled at the ends of her hair, and Ule winced every time. "What's that?"

"Honey," Yensilva replied. "A little in the hair'll give it some shape."

In the mirror inside the house, a stranger stared back at Ule from the silver surface. Short blond tufts stuck out at odd angles and stopped at the base of her neck, reminding her of some small furry rodent. She hated how she looked. It felt and looked wrong. She searched her eyes for recognition. The only memories she had went back to the courtyard of the castle and a headless body.

"*Oo-mer-a*," she said slowly to herself.

"It's better than not having any name," Yensilva said. "At least it's something until you remember."

Ule would remember, she promised herself. Until then she mentally held onto the image of her long hair and yellow dress. Perhaps one day she could resume her appearance and search for anyone who might recognize her.

"Call me Umera then."

— 24 —

HARSH STREAMS OF sunlight tore apart Umera's dreams. Rising through the darkness, she moaned.

"Wake up will ya?" Yensilva poked her in the shoulder. "You're bringing down the walls with your snoring."

Shuddering, Umera rolled over in the narrow bed. She stretched, breathed deeply, and nearly tumbled onto the floor.

"Come on!" Yensilva shook her. "You've lots to learn today," she shouted, rambling on about how the room belonged to her brother who had died in the war, how she had wanted to rent it out, and how lucky Umera was to stay there. "What better place to hide than on a farm."

Rubbing her eyes, Umera scanned the tiny room and noted the paint chipped wardrobe and the scuffed leather chest next to the bed, where her clothes were neatly folded next to an oil lantern.

She abandoned the warmth of the wool blanket, dressed, and stumbled from the room. In the main room, she skirted a thick post that ran to the top of a rustic vaulted ceiling.

"Eat, eat!" Yensilva sat at a round table made of wide, thick planks of oak, where she bit into a large chunk of bread. "Quick now," she urged, her mouth full of food. "We have lots to do."

Breakfast consisted of dense bread and greasy fried meat. Umera chewed leisurely at the bread which tasted of nuts and spice. Reluctantly, she nibbled on the peppered beef. Heavily laced with fat and gristle, she found it difficult to swallow and preferred the bread.

"Eat it all." Yensilva jabbed the table with her fingertip. "You can't work on bread alone." She rose from the table, abandoning her plate. "Meet me near the barn when you're done, and don't take all morning."

"I grew up here," Yensilva explained. An ax slung across her shoulder, she stood by a heavily scarred tree round in the yard near the unpainted barn.

Groaning, Umera rubbed the lump of food in her belly.

"This was my da's land. It was supposed to go to my brother, but they both died in the war, and my ma, she passed when I was young." Yensilva continued. "Now the farm's mine. Been in the family..." She pursed her plump lips and squinted. "...more than thirty two generations now."

Before Umera could protest, Yensilva demonstrated the proper way to hold an ax and split a log. Partially paying attention, she peered across the field, glancing over the eruptions of soil and plant debris and saw something peculiar in the distant grassland. Tall, bristled, green pipes disrupted the flow of tall grass. The sight of them stirred an anger within. "Are those cactuses?"

Yensilva pulled the ax from the tree round and let the steel head thump on the ground. A shudder shook her body and her voice quavered. "Stay away from there."

"Why?"

"Sometimes some *thing* lurks about there." Her face blanched. "But nothing lives there," she added quickly. "We checked."

Umera wondered about the churning deep within her. Pushing, pulling, and climbing through her body was an inexplicable pain followed by rage. The force took her breath away.

"There, there," Yensilva said. "Nothing to fear. You're strong. You'll be even stronger once you start chopping every day."

Accepting the ax, Umera's arms sagged beneath its weight.

"Don't you worry." Yensilva laughed. "You'll have muscles in no time."

Umera didn't want muscles and decided to keep that thought to herself. She swung the ax, missed the log, and wedged the blade deep into the tree round. Yanking failed to pull it free, so she rocked the blade back and forth until it finally loosened.

Yensilva clapped. "You're a quick learner."

Umera plucked a green apple from a bucket beneath the kitchen window next to a rickety cupboard. She was about to bite into it, preferring it for lunch instead of thick oily stew, when Yensilva gasped.

"They're for the horse!" She snatched the fruit and shook it in front of Umera's face. "I don't know how you ate in the castle, but here apples are for horses and pies. Pies are for people though, not horses. Understood?"

"Alright," Umera mumbled.

Easing into a seat at the dining table, she felt an unrelenting ache throughout her arms, shoulders, lower back, and thighs. After having split a small pile of logs, her hands burned with tiny blisters and her stiff tendons could barely clasp the spoon. The ache in her body reflected the ache in her mind, while she endured Yensilva's relentless barrage of instructions.

"Besides feeding the horse every day, you should groom him too. Or every other day. It depends on how busy we get. There's a comb and brush hanging by his stall. Just keep your eyes open. You'll find all the tools you need there."

Still full from lunch, Umera rolled over a fatty bit of meat in the stew and asked, "What's his name?"

"What's whose name?" Yensilva smiled, dunking a large chunk of bread into her stew.

"The horse."

Yensilva's hand fell against the table, making the dishes rattle. "He's a horse. He doesn't have a name."

"He must be called something."

"I call him horse. You and names," she complained.

Umera stared at her sullenly.

"I didn't mean..." Yensilva's face paled and softened. "You'll find your name one day, you will. The war's over but people are scared. When they're not so scared and angry, when it's safe again, you'll find someone who knows you."

Tending to afternoon chores, Umera silently thanked the silence while hobbling stiffly to the well pump. She filled a bucket with water and wondered if the horse would mind her soaking her raw hands in his cold drinking water until she remembered another of Yensilva's rules: "Well water's for drinking, rainwater's for bathing."

Inside the barn, she filled the horse's trough with water from the bucket. She winced when she released the handle and again when she took a brush from its hook on the wall. Starting with the horse's muzzle and the sides of his neck, she made long strokes the way Yensilva had shown her. Oddly, she found the action calming and hoped the horse felt the same way.

"How's that feel? Is that better?"

Occasionally the horse whinnied or snorted, and she imagined him saying, "Just fine, thank you very much."

"I think it's strange you don't have a name," she confided in him.

He blinked at her.

She eased into the stall and brushed his back and sides. There, she discovered his knotted beige mane and began brushing it.

The horse raised its head, whinnied, and kicked both hind legs at once. A crack reverberated throughout the barn as his hooves struck the slatted wall at the back of the stall. Splinters flew into the air and disappeared into the straw covered ground.

Umera flattened herself against the adjacent wall and slowly slid away from the beast. At a safe distance, she slammed the brush on a shelf, turned and yelled. "Are you insane?!"

The horse nudged the air and snorted.

"You're such a crank!"

Later, sitting at the hearth trying to recover from a third heavy meal, Umera clutched her aching belly. She tried to ignore Yensilva, whose mirth and laughter had persisted during the entire afternoon and throughout dinner. Annoyed, she finally snapped. "What?!"

Tittering, Yensilva covered her mouth. "The horse..." She smiled deeply.

"What about Crank?"

"You let me know when he starts talking back, won't you?"

Umera loathed the mornings. As the days passed, she awoke to stiff joints and sore muscles. Her heels thickened and her hands developed calluses. Her slender arms and legs hardened into muscles, and her narrow hips and waist widened.

She welcomed evenings the most, when collapsing before the hearth allowed her mind to drift from the growing discomfort within her body. For several evenings now, her attention was drawn toward a tiny movement in the darkness. Between the stone at the base of the hearth and the ash-covered wooden floor, a large black spider continued spinning a ghostly web.

Beside her, Yensilva embroidered an edge on a square of fabric from Umera's old dress, and the soft whisper of thread sliding through fabric resounded in the silent movement of the little beast.

"The market's all a flutter," Yensilva began. "Rumors are the war's absolutely over, except for some idiots who don't know any better. There's been a couple of skirmishes near the castle. Could be they're fighting for governance. Woedshor's already appointed a new Magnes. It's about time we got a new one."

Umera settled back and listened, wondering if anything in the world might start to make sense to her.

"What's important is the Grand Magnes is dead. His head's locked in a cage hanging in the Wares District. We're best to avoid the market till the celebrating's over."

Firelight reflected warm shapes in the glassy black body of the spider. Long, delicate legs spun and wove fine soft threads, and Umera thought they ought to be black but wasn't sure why.

Tired, she rested her head against the back of her chair and asked, "What's a Grand Magnes?"

She was intrigued by the simultaneous fascination and repulsion she felt toward the spider. Never had she seen a creature that reminded her less of a human yet was creepy and beautiful and familiar...

Whack! Yensilva smacked the spider with an old shoe.

Umera flinched. She hadn't even heard the woman rise from her chair or walk toward the hearth.

"Disgusting, ugly things." Yensilva walloped the shoe against the spider a second time.

Clenched into a tiny ball, the spider uncurled slightly and lay still. The torn web clung to a stone. In that moment, Umera wanted very much to smack Yensilva with the shoe.

"Never you mind about what a Grand Magnes is." Yensilva wiggled her foot back into the shoe and collapsed in her chair with a grunt. "It's been a thousand generations since one tried to rule the world. It didn't work then either." She cut a thread and leaned forward to examine her work. "All that matters is soon every shor will have a Magnes of its own again, the way it used to be. Not that I would know what that's like, I've only ever known what it's like to live during warfare—"

"Is a Magnes like a lord? Or maybe a king?" Before she heard any answer, Umera's mind raced. "That would make Adinav an emperor."

"I don't know," Yensilva whined. "What's a *keeng* or *emp-rer*? You sure do speak strangely."

Umera hacked at dried soil with a hand trowel, carving out a new garden bed between the newly seeded field and the well. Sweat dripped down her forehead, ran along the bridge of her nose, and slid down to her mouth where the taste of honey stuck to her lips.

I hate my hair.

She stabbed the ground.

I hate these clothes.

She stabbed the ground again, harder.

I could be meeting people who recognize me, who can help me remember. I hate this farm, I hate this garden, I hate my name, oh how I hate, my stupid name.

Stabbing over and over again—harder, deeper, faster—Umera gritted her teeth until her jaw ached. The ground opened like a dark, moist wound, and she kept stabbing.

"You all right?"

She stopped, the trowel blade buried to the handle in the earth. She peered upward and wiped her sweaty cheeks, leaving behind a smudge of dirt.

Yensilva blotted out the sun. Her wide face drooped. "I've been working you too hard, haven't I?" Twisting her lips, she stared off across the field in deep thought. "Come on," she said, holding out her hand.

Back at the house, Umera stripped and bathed in soothing tepid rainwater until the walls of the shack shook.

"That's enough," Yensilva shouted. "Shut off the shower!"

Frowning, Umera hastily turned the valve and flung a stiff cotton cloth around her body. By the time she reached the kitchen, the cloth had dampened and clung to her. She stopped and stared at herself in the mirror, admiring how her wet hair lay about her face.

Yensilva flew into the kitchen, her arms laden with clothes. "What are you gawking at?"

"I like the way my hair curls—"

"It looks silly. Everyone wears their hair like this." And she pointed to her own short, spiky brown hair with faded blue tips. Determined to make her point, she demonstrated by strategically sweeping honey through Umera's hair again, sculpting it into tiny spikes.

Umera winced at the sight of her stiff golden locks which reminded her of how cornstalks bowed in a strong breeze. Grittiness itched her scalp once the honey began to dry.

"All that needs fixing is the color." Yensilva continued playing with Umera's hair. "Blue and red are in these days, but we can't afford the tints until we've sold a couple of vegetable harvests, or when the corn's ready to be picked."

"What a shame," Umera mumbled, wrapping her towel tighter.

"Here, put this on." Yensilva held out a dress made of red linen and Umera obeyed.

The full length skirt flared at the bottom, draping over her body and pooling at her feet. Square-shaped straps fell down over her shoulders. Even though she wasn't as small as she used to be, the beaded corset buckled and gaped.

Needle and thread danced in Yensilva's hands. Humming and

hawing, she snipped away the corset and reworked the skirt, cutting a new silhouette, darting the back and front, hemming edges, refastening the shoulder straps until the old dress had become another kind of dress—one that fit snugly and stopped at Umera's knees.

Yensilva tapped her lips with her forefinger as she contemplated her work.

Umera stared off at the wall, listening to her stomach grumble. "Isn't it time for dinner? Shouldn't we start chopping carrots for stew?"

"Not tonight." Yensilva turned to a large chest by the hearth, rummaged through the neatly folded contents, and pulled out a black belt. It wrapped about Umera's waist twice until she measured and cut the worn leather and refastened the tarnished steel buckle.

The belt fit snugly yet failed to cinch Umera's hunger pangs.

"What are we doing tonight?" She slipped into a pair of large black sandals which laced about her ankles and shins.

"You'll see," Yensilva replied.

Abandoning needle and thread, she bathed and changed into clothes of her own—a cobalt blue dress with white trim. Thin leather laces criss-crossed in a narrow strip running from the top of the wide collar to the hem of the full skirt. She styled her hair and smoothed a bright red ointment on her lips.

"What's that?"

"Oh girl, where's your mind? It's lip tint."

In the mirror, Umera applied a little of the tint and saw her pale lips blaze into a brilliant red. With the combination of painted lips, pointy blond hair, and bronze skin, she thought she looked a little too much like Yensilva.

Together they set out from the farm, walking through a field which spanned the distance between the farm and the edge of town. Soft clouds spotted the pale blue sky. The orange of encroaching dusk spread along the horizon as they crossed a small wooden footbridge which gently arced over a deep ravine.

Excitement quickened Umera's breath as she admired the unfamiliar new setting. Her stomach growled loudly. "Are we going for dinner somewhere in the Market?"

"Yes, we'll be eating soon enough." Yensilva nodded as further reassurance.

"I want to ask around about survivors from the castle," Umera announced, already plotting questions to ask anyone she might meet.

Yensilva stopped and huffed.

"I know some people might want to hurt me," Umera said softly. "But don't you think it's worth the risk?" She patted the irate woman on the shoulder hoping to calm her. "There could be other innocents who survived."

A sneer curled Yensilva's lip and she snorted. "No one who ever lived in that castle with Adinav was innocent."

Sadness seeped into Umera. "But I used to live there—"

"Shush!" Yensilva resumed walking. "You've no memory of any of it, and that's why I don't hold you at fault. Others won't be nearly as considerate."

They followed a narrow street which ran along the backside of buildings. Barrels half-filled with sludge and rainwater smelled of mildew and swarmed with buzzing mosquitoes.

Umera strained to see through the gaps between the buildings and glimpsed men and women dressed in colorful clothing. Some walked arm in arm while others clustered about each other chatting, smiling, and laughing.

Through a narrow walkway, she glimpsed an oval cage hanging from a small iron chain on a wooden pole. Wide spaces between the cage rungs revealed an odd shape. At this angle, she saw a knotted rope of black hair and the shape of an empty eye socket. Unable to pry her eyes away from the bone and flesh of the rotting human head, she whispered, "Is that Adinav?"

Yensilva pulled her by the arm. "Forget about it."

"Don't you think seeing him might make me remember?"

Redness seared Yensilva's cheeks. "Stop asking so many questions!"

Unwillingly, Umera obeyed. Oddly, her hunger pangs faded.

— 25 —

UMERA LAY HALF awake recounting a memory from the night before. Warmed by many drinks, music beat into her mind and body, nearly deafening her. Wandering among the dancers and clusters of drunk townies, she explored the tavern until the handsome fellow with tussled indigo hair pulled her into the shadows near a stairwell. He crushed her in his arms and pressed her against the wall.

"Looking for a little fun?" he asked and kissed her before she could respond.

She liked the way his lips and tongue melded into hers. Her heart quickened and her flesh warmed.

Musk, smoke, and stale ale tickled her nostrils. Her eyes roamed, gazing upward at the rails of the stairway and the bevels and beams of the roof. Above them on a second floor, people were tucked away in shadowy corners, hands underneath shirts and skirts, kissing and groping.

Kisses on her neck caused her arms to prickle. Despite relaxing into her arousal, she felt a disconnection, as though the drink had created a boundary of thick gossamer between her and the man.

"You gotta go upstairs to get downstairs," he whispered in her ear.

"There's a downstairs too!" she slurred. "This place is huge."

He laughed at her, said it again, emphasizing each syllable—down, stairs. Then she felt his hand slip between her legs and understood.

"Umera!"

Images from the previous night abruptly stopped. "Coming," she replied groggily.

Yawning, she rubbed at the grit caught in her eyelashes. Her tongue felt dry and fuzzy. Stretching, she rolled onto her back and felt the dress tighten about her thighs. For a moment, the sensation felt familiar.

Yensilva called to her again, accompanied by thumping cupboard doors and clanging dishes, causing Umera's head to throb.

The aroma of baked bread and fried meat filled her lungs, tickling the back of her throat. Her stomach lurched. She jumped to her feet, teetered slightly, and bolted through the kitchen and the front door. Near the earth she tilled the previous day, she retched.

Yensilva's voice burst from the open windows of the house. "You better not be near the potatoes!"

Umera nudged the patch of soil with her bare toe, kicking earth over the spoiled ground. Wiping her mouth, she paused and wondered why this seemed familiar too.

A man's voice spoke. "Must've been the mead."

Spinning around, Umera gawked at the man standing between her and the house. He stood with arms neatly folded across his chest, which creased the black vest and white shirt he wore. Maroon pants and tall black boots indicated he wasn't any of the neighboring farmers. Dark brown hair softly curled about a lean, hardened face.

A gentle huff from his mare interrupted the silence. She stood at the edge of the yard, just at the mouth of a dirt road which connected with others leading to town. She blinked at the ground and occasionally stared at the barn, sensing another horse nearby.

A vague memory of speaking with the man the previous night pushed through the fog in her mind.

He scrutinized the plot of soil.

Hoping to block his view, she stepped in front of her buried mess. "Not even sure I like mead," she told him.

He scanned her from head to toe, and she felt as if every one of her freckles were being documented. Like the spider at the hearth, she felt drawn toward his weathered handsomeness yet repulsed by the scorn in his expression.

Grunting, he turned toward the stoop and spoke in an even cool tone. "If it's going to come up the morning after, be sure to enjoy it going down the night before." Then he raised his voice, calling out. "Yensi!"

A yelp arose from the nearest open window, followed by the thump of heavy footfalls on the stoop.

"Uncle Ellie!" Yensilva flew down the steps and threw her arms around him, engulfing his slight frame in a brawny embrace.

He stiffened, endured her affection, but she refused to let go until he lightly patted her back. The warmth emanating from her in that moment rivaled the morning sun and emphasized the unyielding coldness in the man standing next to her.

"You remember Elusis?" she asked Umera.

And Umera began to recall the night before.

She and Yensilva had walked along the outside of a large building. Dusty plank walls vibrated from music and laughter. The dark walkway opened into the market square where lantern light washed wood, brick, and stone in golden hues. Beyond clusters of people—some dressed in fine clothing and others still in sullied work wear—night hung like a thick black curtain.

She blindly followed Yensilva around a brick jetty attached to a motley building that had experienced years of repairs, rebuilds, and add-ons. Umera held her breath when Yensilva dragged her through the entrance.

Bodies breathed, moved, and swelled with laughter throughout a vast hall. Tiny cast iron tables and stools outlined the outer walls while pitted oak benches ran in lines across the floor except for a space at the far end, where a small raised platform supported a group of men and women playing stringed and percussion instruments.

The musicians pounded out a powerful, energetic song. People danced in lines, stepping, turning, and stomping in unison. Wincing at the harsh, rigid movement, Umera wondered if they danced other ways.

To her left, couples trickled up and down a wide staircase leading to a mezzanine, where faces flickered in the soft candlelight and shadows rubbed against each other. Beneath this, lanterns hung from iron chains. An ornately carved wooden counter ran the length of the stairwell wall, where doorways led into back rooms and, by the smell of apple, pork and cardamom, the kitchen as well.

Umera gently patted her growling belly.

"This is Sunset House." Yensilva carved a path through a small crowd of young farmhands. "The best public house in the market. There's even gambling in the back. According to stories, long ago, the place used to be a couple of tables serving soup. Can't be true, if you ask me. Just can't see the place as a couple of tables, can you?"

Umera shrugged and graciously accepted a tiny glass filled with golden liqueur, hoping food would soon follow.

And she remembered.

She had downed the thick substance in one gulp, wincing at the sweet taste and at the burn which flushed her cheeks. Although it wasn't stew or bread, the drink eased her stomach slightly.

"Asking for punishment, are you?" Yensilva smiled weakly while sipping hers.

Embarrassment deepened the flush in Umera's cheeks as she grew aware of how those standing closest to her eyed her warily, except for one young man with tussled indigo hair and a mischievous smirk.

"Have another while you're waiting," he insisted, calling to a barmaid behind the counter.

Umera considered accepting the drink, but when she saw how slowly Yensilva and the others sipped their mead, she reconsidered. Smiling, she declined.

"Nooo!" he whined, clutching his chest as though he'd been struck by an arrow. He accepted the shot of mead from the barmaid and set it down on the counter between them. "You're going to deny me the pleasure?"

Umera smiled at the memory of his broad face and thick shoulders.

Changing her mind again, she had sipped at the mead. When he rolled his eyes at her, she downed it in one gulp. The alcohol blasted her belly and walloped her head. All at once the public house grew louder and brighter.

People milled about her, chatting with Yensilva and the man with the indigo hair. Then an older man with a slight yet commandeering stature approached. He reeked of whiskey and his eyes were bloodshot.

"Is this her, Yensi? The stray you found at Sondshor castle?"

He had worn different clothes yet his demeanor was the same—austere and shrewd. He shuffled slightly to the side, maintaining a pristine posture. Elusis examined her cautiously.

"A partisan of Adinav sleeping in our homestead," he seethed.

"Hush!" Yensilva looked wildly about them. "Someone might hear you."

"What does it matter to me?"

"Don't be like that uncle," she whined. "You promised you wouldn't say anything to anyone. She can't remember what she was."

Elusis rolled his eyes.

"Besides you haven't lived at the homestead since you were eight." She straightened his tie. "And you barely visit anymore. If she's taken away, how will I find time to have a little fun, find a husband, and visit with you? I've been alone on that farm going on six years."

Umera's head swam.

Pulling away from the man, Yensilva said to her, "Ignore him! He always gets a little mean when he's been drinking."

The grim stare Elusis cast Umera was honest and intense despite his liquored state. Her mood plummeted until the man with indigo hair pulled her toward the dance floor.

She tried dancing like the others, stiffly stomping and stepping in patterns. Eventually she gave into her inner rhythm and moved fluidly, her lyrical twirls incurring laughter from onlookers, including her new friend.

"What were you doing?" he asked, following Umera back toward the counter.

"Dancing," she snapped.

"Ah no, don't be angry."

A third honey mead soothed her ego, melted away all body aches, and eased her anxieties. Inside, she either opened up or some unknown barrier disappeared. She didn't care what Elusis or the other dancers thought of her. She pursued her curiosity. Who was the man Yensilva spoke with? Would her new friend with the indigo hair try to kiss her again? And why, when she returned to the counter, had Yensilva's smile turned into a pout?

Umera reveled in the feeling of recalling a memory, even if it was a recent one. The stink of earth and vomit at her feet forced her to regain her senses, and she noticed Yensilva's wide eyes urging her to respond.

"Oh, yes," she said softly to Elusis. "I remember you."

Elusis listened politely to Yensilva chatter about the new vegetable gardens. He ran a thumb over the beveled arm of the orange tea cup before him. His scrutiny was unnerving as he continued to watch Umera. She felt as though he were searching for the end of the thread that would unravel her entire being and couldn't wait to give that thread a tug. Based on his scowl, she knew not to expect affection or tenderness from him.

Again she found herself drawn to the sensuality of his gestures and mannerisms. There was a confidence in the way he sat, in the smoothness of his movement when he reached into a back pocket, withdrew a flask, uncapped it, and poured a bit of the amber contents into his tea.

She enjoyed the blended scents of burnt toast, caramel, and oak and cringed at the underlying alcoholic fumes.

Yensilva leaned forward, proffering a plate piled with rectangular shaped pastries. "Honey biscuit anyone?"

Umera's stomach tightened. Urgently, she shook her head.

"What do you remember about the castle?" Elusis asked casually.

Yensilva gasped.

He dunked a honey biscuit in his tea, bit off the corner, and nodded in approval at the flavor.

"Uncle!"

He cast Yensilva a stern look at her outburst.

Sitting back in her chair, Yensilva smiled weakly and fell silent.

"Nothing," Umera responded, preferring the taste and smell of the greasy breakfast that cooled on the stove. Drink had helped her forget to ask around about other survivors from the castle, but she wasn't going to let the hangover do the same.

"Do you know of anyone else who might be from the castle?"

"Umera!" Yensilva scolded her. "What have I told you?"

"Now, now, Yensi." Elusis raised his hand. "Who are we to stop her from looking for her own kind." He stretched, running his hands along his chest, smoothing out the already pressed fabric of his vest. "This family's seen enough death. We're all that's left. The further she's away from this farm, the safer you'll be."

Yensilva's faced pinched tightly, lips puckered shut trying to hold back harsh words until she couldn't. "Don't be like that!"

Still upset, she leaned over and patted Umera on the hand and spoke softly. "You can stay here as long as you want."

"To answer your question," Elusis said, "there's the new smith."

"Oh him, I've seen him." Anger rushed away, returning Yensilva to a perkier mood. "He's handsome," she gushed.

"It's good there's more than one in town," Elusis continued. "Hazias is pricey and he's getting old. Sure he's teaching his twin daughters so they can carry on the business once he's gone, but it'll be years before they achieve his degree of skill." He paused a moment and frowned. "The new one, Avn, he has secrets. You can see it in his eyes."

"See what?" Umera asked, dabbing her finger in spilled cream.

"He's a liar," Elusis announced, eyes locking onto hers.

The venom with which he spoke the word *liar* felt intended more for her than the new blacksmith.

"Says he's from the border of Woedshor but one of the clothier's apprentices recognizes him from the castle." Raising the tea cup, he sipped only enough to wet his lips. "No one can hide. Someone always knows something about someone else." He replaced the cup in his saucer. "It's just a matter of time before word gets around."

Yensilva blinked, her grin slowly faded. "Which apprentice?"

"Milos."

Determined to gather as much information on anyone with knowledge of the castle, Umera asked, "Have I met him?"

Yensilva snorted loudly. "You nearly spawned children with him last night."

"Oh," Umera said softly. "Him."

Her raging headache prevented her from feeling ashamed, though it was clear by Yensilva's upturned nose she should. Even the dull thump at the base of her skull hadn't stopped Umera from thinking about this new possible connection to her past.

"Do you think I should talk to the smith?"

"No! You're not who you were, you're Umera now. All these silly questions, I don't see the point." Yensilva shook her head and buried her gaze in the honey biscuit she began to tear into smaller bits. "And a warning to you, Milos is bad news."

Umera appreciated the worry and concern for her well being, but she felt lost and without purpose. Knowing something about her past might help ease the discomfort which crawled around inside her, she insisted with more questions.

"What do you know about the smith?"

Elusis sniffed. "I heard he was severely injured fighting at the castle, then he shows up here with barely a scratch, about a day after you returned with Yensi." With a heavy breath, as though it belabored him to answer, he continued. "He took possession of that run down house in the junction, turned it into a smithy. He doesn't live there alone. He's been seen with that fellow who carts around the strange artifacts. Hoped to have seen the last of him too."

"Sabien?" Yensilva asked.

Elusis nodded. "Yes, him."

Excitement lit up Yensilva's face as she leaned across the table. "Bethereel says he might have a new show—"

"Listen, Yensi," Elusis interrupted. "I'm not here about gossip. I've some news."

The seriousness in his tone made the hairs on Umera's neck prickle. She inhaled deeply and waited.

"Another woman's gone missing," he announced solemnly.

Picking at another biscuit, Yensilva gasped. "Now that Adinav's dead, it doesn't seem likely he's the reason for all the disappearances like we thought."

Elusis nodded in agreement. "I discovered an unusual detail listening to rumors about the women who've gone missing." He leisurely sipped from his tea cup again. "They've all had light colored hair."

Umera squirmed in her seat growing more self-conscious with the way Elusis watched her, until she realized he was examining her blond hair.

"Yet another reason why your presence here makes me uncomfortable." Elusis wiped his hands on a napkin and straightened his vest.

"We were safe last night," Yensilva assured him. "We walked with four others."

"We did?" Umera couldn't remember anything of how they returned to the farm.

Yensilva rolled her eyes. "We walked. You tottered."

"Good," Elusis said. He stood, the legs of the chair scraping against the floor.

Umera cringed at the sound.

"Wait, before you go." Yensilva excitedly hurled herself at the chest by the hearth and fumbled with the latch. "I have something for you." Clutching several small folded cloths, she returned to her uncle.

Umera instantly recognized the pale yellow fabric of her original dress being handed to the man.

He rubbed his fingers over the smooth silky fabric and embroidery. "You've finely honed your sewing skills this year. Very nice."

"Oh, you should see the dress she made me," Umera stood and spun around slowly, showing off the dress she still wore from the previous night. "It's made from another dress." The swirl forced her to lean against the post near the hearth before she lost her balance. "Very clever, if you ask me."

Yensilva stepped in front of her to shield the dress. "It's nothing uncle," she said. "Really, it's not very good. Thrown together quickly."

He gently nudged her aside and looked over the dress as though someone other than Umera wore it. He laid a finger across his pursed lips, deep in thought.

"The next time you're in the market," he told Yensilva, heading toward the door, "stop by the shop. I'll put aside fabric scraps for you to practice with." He nodded goodbye and exited.

A squeal erupted from Yensilva. She clapped her hands too.

Umera groaned and rubbed her head.

— 26 —

UMERA SWUNG HER feet back and forth, dangling her legs from the back end of the wagon. Sacks and buckets filled with a harvest of vegetables and fruits weighed down the vehicle causing the wheels to creak, and no amount of Yensilva flicking the reigns or scolding Crank, could inspire him to move faster.

She settled back against a sack of radishes to watch the landscape slowly drift by. Large puffy white clouds obscured the sun, casting fields in dark shadows. A bouquet of lilac thickened the air, making her sleepy. They passed near a field of ripening corn. She stared awestruck at the wall of towering stalks.

When last she stood in their freshly tilled field, the corn seedlings had finally erupted after several days and now stood as high as her knees.

"How long before our corn's that tall?" Her voice lacked energy.

Yensilva looked over her shoulder and scrunched her face. "Oh, maybe two months. A little longer, perhaps," she replied. "The heat from the desert slows the growth cycle down but it lets us plant crops all year round."

The roundabout roadways encircled farmland and finally straightened toward the deep narrow ravine, which bordered the south side of the Market where they passed over a wide stone bridge.

The thump of Crank's hooves became echoing clops. The wagon rattled and bounced, tossing Umera around. She bolted upright and clutched the railing, still content and satisfied to be away from the farm.

Her smile deepened as she imagined all she might see in the market during the daytime, and scrambled to the front of the wagon determined to memorize every building.

Large worn stones of the bridge gave way to smaller flat stone. The wagon settled into worn grooves in the road and rattled less. She recognized the row of houses and one-level buildings with the sand strewn alleyway leading to the backside of Sunset House.

Taller buildings began to press together. The streets narrowed. Wagons squeezed passed one another, and somehow the market goers still found ways to slip between them.

Some of the people hugged one another joyously. Others huddled closely, talking intensely, and Umera wished she could hear what was being said. In front of a bakery, two elderly men stood face to face, wiry beards nearly touching, and argued about who yielded the best yeast.

Burnt sugar, caramel, and chocolate hung in the air, and Umera leaned over the side of the wagon to breathe in the sweets until the stench of fish struck her nose.

"Since you want to be like a dog," Yensilva said, smacking her on the arm, "fetch a flier from that young fellow when we pass by."

Umera stretched her arm toward a young boy with a turquoise turban wound about his head. He handed out sheaves of small paper not much larger than her hand. Her fingers grazed his white cotton shirt; he understood and stuffed a bill into her upturned hand.

Sitting back, she admired his clothes. "I love his turban."

Yensilva laughed. "But nobody'll see your wonderful hair cut if you wear one of those."

And there'll be no need to put honey in my hair, Umera thought.

"You don't have to worry about being blond, you know. Elusis was just trying to scare us... because he cares. "

Umera began reading the handbill. In the silence that ensued, she read it three times and started a fourth reading when Yensilva spoke.

"Turbans are really easy to make." Her high pitched voice sounded as though she were asking a question. "If you'd like, I can show you later, once we're back home."

Pursing her lips, Umera tore her attention from the handbill. She sighed and smiled. "I'd like that. Thank you."

With a nod, Yensilva snapped the reigns and Crank snorted. Before them, a crowd parted to make way for the horse and wagon, and she called over her shoulder. "What does it say?"

"There's an exhibition opening in town soon."

Yensilva whistled joyfully. "Is it Sabien? His shows are the strangest, and he tells the best stories."

"Sabien the Storyteller Presents the Extravaganza Desert Exhibition," she read. After she folded the paper, she slipped it into her pocket and marveled at a yard lined with rows of different carts and wagons parked close to one another. Stalls and shanties indicated permanent sellers who dwelled in the food district. The rest were temporary booths—farmers like Yensilva selling from their wagons.

Crank pushed toward an empty space in the middle of the chaos. A squat man with a scrunched face failed to claim the same space due to his decrepit nag. Bitter for losing, he obscenely gestured at Yensilva. She merely smiled in return.

"First come, first served," she told Umera, bringing Crank to a stop. "Unhitch the horse and take him to the barn," she commanded.

"Which barn?" Umera scanned the district intrigued by how the stone ground looked as if it had opened up and gushed tubers and grains.

"The love barn," Yensilva sang.

Of what she knew about the market, Umera hadn't ever heard of such a place. "What's that?"

"Oh you know where I mean," Yensilva snapped. "Do you think you're the only one to get too drunk and lusty to bother with a bedroom?"

The venom in Yensilva's voice made Umera shiver as she silently stripped Crank of the tug straps. She guided him through the Food District overcome with an acute sense of shame and guilt. For what, she couldn't figure out.

At the junction, she noticed Sunset House. Briefly, she saw the building in her mind as nothing more than a shanty. Even what remained of Adinav's fleshless skull and flittering matted black hair stirred images of a beautiful, young man. The phantom images drifted from her mind before she could fully understand what they meant.

Rushing past, she spotted what she thought might be the barn Yensilva mentioned. Everything looked different in daylight. Approaching, she passed an old house with a door split into two halves. Beside the house, near the door, a narrow yard was strewn with debris and buckets filled with scrap metal. An image flashed in her mind of something else being there instead of the yard. In her mind, the image was of a wooden stall fastened to the side of the house, which sheltered a beige mare with black spots.

Familiarity washed over her. Stopping to touch the cool tip of a broken rod jutting from a barrel, she didn't doubt the narrow yard to be real, but she couldn't ignore the mental image of the house with a stall; it felt real too.

Crank snorted brusquely.

"Okay, okay," she mumbled, wiping some of the horse's spittle from her ear.

She led Crank to the barn, where all the stalls were full and the rails crowded. The barn keeper refused her money. When she turned to leave, they both discovered Crank had pushed himself between a buckskin mare and a silver dappled colt hitched at the nearest rail. He carefully nosed about in a trough and selectively sampled the oats.

The barn keeper huffed, conceding to harbor one more horse.

"See you later fusswart," she told Crank as she exited, but he ignored her. "Love you too," she mumbled, returning to the swelling crowd in the market.

She let herself be pulled along in a current of well dressed townies, until they veered toward the Wares District. Frantically, she dove against the chaotic mass of people and pushed her way toward the Food District.

"What took you so long?" Yensilva began lowering a large sack of potatoes from the wagon.

Umera grabbed the sack and eased it to the ground. Before she could explain about the full barn, Yensilva handed her another sack and began barking instructions.

"Never take notes. People think any piece of paper with scrawl on it is worth something, but the Moneykeep won't honor anything from away."

Umera settled a sack of radishes against the wheel of the wagon, nodding repeatedly as Yensilva rattled off a list of prices for their produce.

"A kep for a basket of berries—"

"A copper!" Umera wiped perspiration from her forehead and stretched.

Yensilva scrunched her face. "A what?"

Umera pulled out a few coins from her pocket and raised the darkest of them. "It's called a copper." Whatever certainty she felt faded at the way Yensilva froze in mid-lift.

Her face blanched as though she were stunned. Eventually she recovered herself. Brows furrowed, she lowered the sack to the ground. Her eyes darted around warily and finally settled on Umera. In a low voice, she asked, "It's called a what?"

"Copper." Umera held up the coin. "Because it's made of copper."

"It's called a kep." Yensilva set down a bucket of rhubarb spears at the end of the wagon. "The silver ones are sils and the orange ones gols. They've never been called anything else."

"How is it I know it's a coin yet remember it as something else?"

Impatiently, Yensilva sat at the end of the wagon and slid to the ground, grabbing the skirt of her dress as it rode up her thighs. "I don't know," she huffed. "How is it you can remember a horse is a horse, but you forget and talk to it like a human?"

She snatched the kep. "Just remember to check the gols for scratches and gouges. Some like to collect shavings and melt them down to make their own money." She held up the coin and examined it with one eye closed. "The Moneykeep doesn't honor the heavily marked ones."

She slapped Umera across the shoulder and slipped a handful of coins into the pocket of her shirt. "That should be enough to make change. If you're not sure about anything, ask me."

A twinge behind Umera's left eye forced her to blink several times. She felt an ache course through her head. The new words she had heard stitched themselves to old words, and she blinked from the forceful associations connecting within her mind.

A thin, rugged man with curled white whiskers began squeezing the tomatoes. Waving her hands and shaking her head, Yensilva stood between him and the weathered barrel.

"No touching," she demanded and the man stood upright, shoulders thrown back. "Whatever you'd like, I'd be glad to get it for you."

Umera marveled at the mustard color of his flesh and how it darkened slightly around his eyes. He spoke in short staccato sounds, holding up his fingers indicating the number five. When Yensilva filled his sack with five tomatoes, the man shook his head and spoke again.

Yensilva spoke louder. "I don't know what you're saying."

"He wants five keps worth of tomatoes," Umera explained. "For jumble sauce." She waited for the hint of fear in Yensilva's expression to pass. Hoping to change the topic, she asked, "What's jumble sauce?"

"Stew!" Yensilva's temper flared. She filled the man's satchel with tomatoes and his face lit up approvingly when she counted accurately this time.

Umera's mind cinched again—meanings and the sounds representing them expanded, tweaking her thoughts.

Wary, Yensilva bundled rhubarb for a stout townie dressed in a bright pink dress. "You understood him?"

"I did," Umera said softly, realizing she understood almost everything everyone in the market said. Some used different sounds to convey similar ideas yet there were some words she didn't recognize at all. "I must know languages." Excitement blossomed inside at the discovery of a tangible skill. "Do you know what this means?"

Yensilva huffed as she bundled carrots and counted potatoes for another customer.

"I might not be nobility at all." Staring skyward, she let out a long breath. "I may have been a scholar or an official translator, hired by the court. Maybe I taught languages." She gasped. "I must have traveled a lot."

"Shush," Yensilva scolded her. "Don't let anyone hear you talk like that." In a whisper, she added, "If you ask me, you were nobility with nothing better to do with your time but read books."

She pushed Umera toward a slender townie dressed in pale blue. "Stop daydreaming and tend to Bethereel."

Umera smiled warmly at the woman. She admired the softness of her crimped blouse and wide straight pants which cascaded over narrow hips straight to the ground.

Bethereel leaned forward and pointed at the assorted berries. Her dark brown hair had been carefully pinned beneath a pale blue hat, the odd curl strategically folded over the brim.

"Have you heard?" she addressed both of them. "Another

woman's gone missing. This time a widow. Mother of three, all orphans now. I wonder what'll become of them."

Umera found herself unable to contain her smile. Despite the bad news, something about the woman compelled her to smile. Accepting Bethereel's small basket, she began filling it with raspberries and strawberries.

Frowning, Yensilva sighed. "You'd think everyone would settle down now the war's over, but until we've a new Magnes, people will think they can do whatever they want."

Bethereel pointed to the pears, and Umera eagerly slipped a half dozen into the basket as well.

"A scribe returned from the castle yesterday," Bethereel said. "I overheard him describe the appointment of our new Magnes."

Yensilva gasped, her mouth parting slightly. "What's his name?"

"It's Lyanovmal, but he insists his subjects call him Lyan," Bethereel answered and retrieved her basket from Umera. "A nickname. How progressive is that?" She plucked a raspberry from the assortment and popped it into her mouth.

Umera suddenly wanted to lick the woman's lower lip.

"That's such a handsome name," Yensilva cooed. "I wonder if he's handsome."

Smirking, Bethereel shrugged. Turning her attention toward Umera, she rolled her eyes. "As long as he's not a demon sympathizer, who cares how he looks."

Remembering the skull still on display in the junction, Umera didn't think to curb her curiosity and blurted, "Was Adinav handsome?"

Yensilva wrung her hands fitfully. "Please ignore her."

Bethereel smirked. "He was kind of beautiful, in an eerie way."

Gagging, Yensilva stuck out her tongue. "He was creepy and gross. Too young for too long. He looked strange."

Fishing around in a waistband pocket, Bethereel removed a sil and handed it to Umera.

"No, no." Yensilva waved her hands at the coin. "That's too much Bethi."

Bethereel pushed the sil into Umera's hand. "Bake me a couple of those nut loaves, Yensi, and we'll be even." And before Yensilva could object, Bethereel retreated into the crowd and floated gracefully toward the junction.

Umera realized she had uttered only a few words in the presence of the woman, none of them an introduction, and she called after the woman's diminishing figure.

"My name's Umera." Her words were swallowed by the din of the market. "She has a beautiful name," she said, scooping radishes into a customer's basket.

Yensilva snorted loudly. "Poor thing if you ask me," she said, emptying the last few potatoes from a sack into an empty bucket.

"Why?" Umera stood abruptly, handing over the basket to a young man in exchange for a few keps.

"It's too old a name," Yensilva explained. "At least she's a far better choice of fancy than that Milos, if you ask me."

People descended on their stall in waves. At first Umera, stammered and stumbled trying to fill so many requests at once, but she found a rhythm. The ease with which she understood everyone, no matter what language they spoke—she even learned a few new words—filled her with a pleasant confidence and lightened her mood.

When Yensilva wasn't looking, she snatched an apple, enjoyed its sour-sweet flesh, and sucked at the skin when it stuck to the roof of her mouth. Though growing tired and sore, a deeply felt satisfaction kept her going as she continued absorbing the sights, smells, and sounds around her.

People of all shapes, sizes, and colors toured the district. Some were dressed from head to toe, some covered their faces, and some were nearly naked, wearing only leggings or loin cloths. Most were happy and co-operative, while others scowled and glared suspiciously at everyone.

The shadows in the yard began to stretch, and people grew less amiable. Their irritability was contagious, for Yensilva's negotiations became more dramatic and hostile. The change in mood could have been from a long day of haggling or the incessant clangs from two smithies, one at the junction and the other drifting over from the Wares District.

By late afternoon, only a squashed tomato and a couple dozen apples remained, some of which were badly bruised. Yensilva sat in the wagon, urging Umera to deal with one of the barmaids from Sunset House.

"Not all the apples are good," the tiny young woman complained. She brushed a fringe of wispy bleached white hair from her forehead. "Can't you drop the price?" The woman held out a kep and waved it about. "They're for my horse."

"Two keps then." Umera's left eye twitched. Her voice was raw and her cheery mood depleted from an increase in bartering as the afternoon progressed.

The woman stomped the ground, rubbing her freckled face. She seemed as if she were about to cry.

"They could be for your horse or for Sunset's pies," Umera argued.

"Ooh," Yensilva called from behind her. "Good point. Everyone uses bruised apples in pies."

"You're the only ones with any left," the woman grumbled. She pulled out a second kep and gave both to Umera.

Although they bartered for two dozen, Umera filled the barmaid's basket with the remaining apples.

The barmaid flashed a tentative smile and thanked her, leaving quickly.

Umera rested against the wagon and rubbed her temples. Her mind spun with sounds and phrases, words from different languages parading about. Not only could she hear the sounds, she could see how those sounds were written. Playfully, she arranged words to make sentences.

During her time on the farm, she had learned very little about herself. In Sondshor market, during the course of one afternoon, she discovered she harbored a powerful skill. Given more time interacting with the people of the market, she wondered what more she could learn about herself and the world.

She stood and tapped Yensilva on the shoulder. "When can we come back during the day?"

"Next week." Yensilva yawned, as she leaned back against the wagon, staring off in the direction of the junction. "We'll come for the opening of Sabien's show. If it's the big one I've been hearing about, we won't want to miss it."

— 27 —

"GATHER AROUND PEOPLE!" A man's raspy voice broke through the market chatter. He was long and lean, with narrow cheeks, and an aquiline nose. He towered before a large white tent sprawled in the center of the bustling wares district.

"Come, see the latest finds from the desert!"

Pulled along by the crowd, Umera neared the crate where the man stood and admired how his short curled black hair floated like a dark cloud above the crowd.

"Oh, that's him. That's Sabien." Yensilva nudged Umera and began fishing coins from her belt purse. "Isn't this exciting?"

Umera nodded, documenting every detail. Sabien wore trousers and vest in a dark brown with yellow pinstripes. A short sleeved green shirt was unbuttoned wide at the collar, revealing a cobalt blue undershirt beneath. On the tent flap behind him, a freshly painted illustration revealed a beast that was part bird and part man.

They passed the podium, inching along with the crowd toward the tent entrance. Her mind reeled at the impossibility of The Bird Man, as it was called according to the elaborate blue script painted across the bottom of the image. She wanted to make the torso more human, to extract feather from flesh, do anything to separate human from bird. She knew with certainty these forms couldn't combine. The idea felt like one of Yensilva's rules.

"Inside, you'll hear the story of The Bird Man." Sabien waved at a small gathering, urging interested patrons to move toward the tent entrance. "Discover what the Bisi Nomads truly look like and more."

Pulled toward the small tent door, Umera stopped herself from tripping over a rope anchored to a peg in the ground. Nearly dropping the sil offered to her by Yensilva, she found herself behind a group of young women dressed in long tailored dresses. She recognized some of their faces.

Yensilva crinkled her nose. "Bethereel's hair is awful."

Most of the women in the market wore short spiky hair sometimes wisped over the brims of tiny pork pie hats, each showing off their colored streaks. Umera hadn't yet seen any woman with a long style other than Bethereel's natural dark brown hair, which hung shiny and straight until the very ends, where they curled into a single, gentle wave. It reminded Umera of a waterfall and of how long her own hair used to be.

By instinct, Umera touched the faded tangerine orange scarf wrapped around her head. The simple turban was light and fit snugly, offering her a reprieve from Yensilva's shears and honey.

"That's an accident waiting to happen," Yensilva mumbled, pointing to Bethereel's hair.

"Does she work on a farm?"

"She's the niece of one of my uncle's tailor friends." Rolling her eyes, Yensilva added, "She models."

"Hair styles?"

"Not with that death mop!" Yensilva snorted. "She models clothes. She's an odd one. You're much better off if you stay clear of her."

Umera found the woman intriguing, quietly envying Bethereel's courage to speak her mind and wear her hair as she pleased.

Her thoughts of admiration were interrupted by a soft pinch on the back of her arm. Peeking over her shoulder, she discovered Milos. He winked at her. As she was about to smile in return, Sabien pushed between them.

Wiry fingers pressed into Umera's shoulders, as he gently guided her aside. She yielded to his touch, captivated by his intensity and the irregular shaped red birthmark on his temple. Stale pipe smoke and the scent of cherry tobacco clung to his pale green shirt.

He carved a path between her and her friends toward the tent entrance, where he collected sils and pulled aside the entrance flap to let customers enter in twos and threes. Bethereel and her friends disappeared through the doorway, then Yensilva, herself, and Milos.

Inside, daylight cast a diffuse white glow through the tent fabric. Greeting everyone who entered was a human-like creature with flesh the texture and color of black beetles. Two large triangular shaped ears lay flat against a heavily wrinkled and whiskered face. Black glassy eyes stared from beneath half-open lids. Remnants of leather leggings clung to bony legs. Instead of feet, she saw fleshy paws and claws where nails should be.

Milos stopped and compared heights. "Tall one," he said, when the creature proved taller than him.

Umera fixated on the display, intrigued by the proportions of the form.

"Cat demons," Milos snorted. "Every wood's got one. I've seen better at the salons in Woedshor."

She lingered over each display before moving on to the next. Two headed cows, a horse with a second set of legs erupting from its stomach, all mummified and posed.

"Gather everyone!" Sabien climbed onto a crate near a concealed display. His olive skin appeared to float next to the dark red curtains behind him.

She flowed along with the people as they crowded around him. Milos sidled close to her. He extended his hand and she reached for him, until Yensilva squeezed between them.

"Yes come," Sabien encouraged the crowd to press closer together. "Come hear the sad tale of the Bird Man." Pulling at a chord, the small curtains behind him slowly parted.

Yensilva gaped, covering her mouth briefly before letting out a soft giggle. "Oh, that's a good one!"

Gasps resounded throughout the tent.

Umera's eyes danced all over the subject on display. Propped upright, the artifact stood the height of a short man, with almost human arms and legs. One of its eyes bulged grotesquely as though it ogled the crowd in return, the iris a pale gray, the pupil tiny and dark. Except for arms covered with feathers, the remaining flesh was black and mummified. Talons for fingers and toes. A swelled tongue in a mouth too small to hold it. A long arched fleshy nose in the shape of a bird's beak.

Breathless by the impossibility of the form, she searched for a seam, some piece of thread or binding, anything that might prove the creature had been fabricated.

"This poor beast," Sabien told the crowd. "A product of a mother's fear, a woman so terrified by ravens she imbued her unborn child with her worst imaginings."

Umera knew the Bird Man could not have survived to adulthood with its current physiology. Its lower torso was too narrow to accommodate the necessary digestive system. Its neck was too long to support the weight of its head. She shook her head at the odd musings of her mind.

"No mother's love could have saved this child," Sabien continued. "Abandoned. Forgotten. Starved for affection. If it weren't for black birds to nurse and care for him as their own, he might never have known love."

People pushed one another for a closer look. Umera remained still, marveling at how she could know about physiological formations and why she doubted Sabien's story. She kept her distance, unable to avert her glance from the beast. A wave of familiarity washed over her—an image of the Bird Man writhing in the dessert and someone begging for mercy. Disbelief blossomed inside her.

"There, there. Not everyone can handle these sights." Yensilva patted Umera's shoulder. "You're too delicate for your own good."

"You look like you're going to vomit." Milos laughed. "Later, we'll get you full of food and drink. He waggled his eyebrows, as he added, "And me."

Irked, Umera shrugged away Yensilva's hand and called out to Sabien. "How long ago did this happen?"

A hush fell over the crowd.

"Based on accounts, at least a thousand years ago, sometime

during the reign of Kugilla," he replied.

The crowd muttered among themselves.

"The desert mummifies them," he continued, fueled by passionate conviction. "Then returns to us what has been lost so we can tell their stories."

"How can you truly know what happened?" Umera pushed forward, arms folded across her stomach. She brushed against Bethereel, sniffed her lavender perfume.

"From the libraries," he said softly, a palm outstretched toward her. "From other storytellers and scribes, even Mystics. Over time, they pass down and share their knowledge." Narrowing his eyes, he raised an arm, sweeping it across his chest and over the crowd. "Now I share their stories with you. Stories like the Bisi Nomads."

Biting his lip, Sabien pointed his outstretched arm toward another display. When the crowd averted their gaze, he frowned deeply at Umera, and she squirmed beneath his burning glare.

She squeezed between people until she stood before a glass box. Inside, she saw the remains of a woman whose flesh was like black leather. Her eyes and mouth had been sewn shut with black thread. Legs folded up into her torso, strips of gray wrapped the body tightly in a way which reminded Umera of a spider spun into its own web to rest. Near her breasts, the strips of cloth had been unwound to reveal her shoulders, which were smooth, well formed, and missing arms.

A shocking hot white anger whipped through Umera's body. She shuddered at the sensation, not understanding why she suddenly felt the way she did, but the dulcet tone of Bethereel's voice soothed her.

"You alright, Umera?"

After a deep breath, she nodded.

"Much has been written about the Bisi Nomads." Sabien's voice roiled into a commanding tone. "We know," he began, locking eyes with Umera, "*for certain* this is how they honor their leaders because our ancient Magnisi were also buried in glass cases. Before you is one of three Bisi Nomads to ever be recovered from the heart of the desert."

Sabien leaned over the exhibition. "She must have been very special to be made leader of the Bisi." He lowered his voice. "Everyone's heard of their dark magic, how they charm men to love them."

With a long stick, he pointed to the limbless shoulders, then the head which began with a small angular face and receded into a large skull tapering nearly to a point. The flesh across the face was tight and curled away from withered lips to reveal bright white teeth.

"With such deformity," Sabien said, "only charm could lure any lovers?"

"It's just hair," Umera blurted, realizing she didn't know how she knew the woman's head was misshapen by hair and not skull bone.

Sabien bowed forward, raising a hand to his ear. "I'm sorry, what did you say?"

"It's just hair!"

Leaning forward, the blaze of fury in his eyes betrayed his soft, gentle countenance. "Have you ever met a Bisi?" he gently inquired of her.

"No," Umera replied swiftly. "Have you?"

He pinched his lips, reeled upright, and huffed. His olive complexion flushing slightly across his prominent cheekbones. A flurry of whispers and murmurs filled the tent: She's just looking for attention. She needs a wallop that one, so she knows her place. She's crazy to be wearing *that* on her head!

Through the din, Umera latched onto the delicate snicker and lyrical voice of Bethereel. "I absolutely adore a lone wolf," she told her friends who stared blankly and shifted uncomfortably.

Yensilva whispered harshly in Umera's ear. "I'm not taking you anywhere ever again!"

Milos leaned over the display, his usually unkempt hair neatly combed into a tidy wave, making him look more handsome. Watching him caused Umera's heart to flutter.

"Don't let her start again," he pleaded with Sabien.

"What's wrong with questions?" Her warm affection toward him began to cool.

"Everyone knows the Bisi are man haters," Milos explained.

"Amnesia," Yensilva explained to those standing nearby. "She can't even remember the names of coins. I had to remind her."

Being the focus of attention, encouraged Milos to stand a little taller. He raised his voice and began to educate Umera. "If any man approach the Bisi, they're beat, maimed, killed even. They're known to abandon their babies if they're boys."

"But how can they abandon any baby," Umera quickly countered, "if they don't allow men to get close enough for them to go downstairs, as *you* would say it?"

Titters and chuckles flooded the tent.

At the urging of a frantic Sabien, the crowd dispersed to look at the remaining displays. Once the crowd settled into quiet fascination, he retreated to a corner of the tent and stood guard of the exhibits, withdrawn and sullen.

Milos sniffed. "You're lucky to have met me. I don't think anyone else could tolerate you as well as I do."

Yensilva stifled a giggle at the comment.

"I like your questions," Bethereel said. She smiled warmly before wandering off to examine the cat demon.

Leaning over, Milos whispered in her ear. "How about dinner at Sunset after this?"

Struck by the dark, sour looks Sabien cast her way, Umera nodded, vaguely aware of a body pushing its way between her and Milos.

"How about what?!" Yensilva glanced back and forth.

Covering her ear, Umera winced. "Stop shouting!"

"You're so sensitive." Yensilva patted her on the back again.

Absorbing the strange sights helped ease Umera's annoyance with just about everyone except Bethereel. Around the tent she discovered rare insects and birds; a series of severed heads, one with two faces and another with strange growths running down its cheek; and two dogs joined together at the torso, unable to stand on their own.

These accidental creatures opened her mind; each became a window to places beyond the familiar fabric of the world. The exhibit only incited more questions, a hunger to know more.

She remained quiet when Sabien, having restored his calm, resumed telling more stories. While the crowd stood riveted, she chose not to focus on his words but on his genuine warm intonations. She imagined his voice like a hammock, and all she need do was lay back and be rocked by its rhythm into a lazy day stupor. He was undeniably a great storyteller.

The odd, malformed objects of the exhibition consumed Umera. Her curiosity demanded to know more, longed to scrutinize every twisted limb or elongated skull. She would have remained in Sabien's tent if Yensilva hadn't ushered her outside, where they leisurely walked through the market.

Yensilva stopped at the mouth of the junction. Behind her, a calm steady stream of townies hovered over tables and crowded the stoops of merchant shops. In front of her, the Food District bustled in a frenzy of haggling. "Wait here," she barked. Playing with stray strands of spiked hair, she tidied her appearance in the reflection of a shop window. "I want to visit Uncle Ellie. I won't be long."

Grateful to not have to endure the man's comments in his stale fabric shop, Umera sat on a narrow bench in front of a distillery. The scents of pine and cedar tickled her nostrils while she scanned the market. She spotted Sabien standing at the exit of his tent, nodding at patrons leaving the show.

Agitation animated him as he pulled a skinny pipe from his shirt pocket. He stuffed the bowl with what she assumed was tobacco, lit the bowl with a match, then began pulling long deep breaths on the stem. Umera watched him watch the people milling about the tent. When he glimpsed her, he rolled his eyes and looked elsewhere.

Toward the junction, she recognized the house with the missing horse stall again. From this side, she glimpsed the new smith. Avn stood taller than most men. Thick bulky arms worked a long blade as he beat the heated steel with a large hammer. He was older. Deep lines marked his face. His bare head glistened with sweat, and his dark flesh was riddled with pale pink scars. He still kept his knotted beard tucked beneath a leather apron and wondered why he bothered with it.

In mid-strike, he lost his focus and intensity. Resting the hammer, he straightened and looked out across the junction, directly at her.

Umera's breath hitched at the sudden connection. She felt trapped in his gaze, not sure what to think or feel or do. But when the smith resumed hammering, she felt an absence within her. She shivered and found herself wanting to go to him, to ask him to restore what he took from her during that moment.

Leaning back against the railing of the distillery, something pawed at her turban. Looking up, she watched a skinny cat with long black hair stretch down from its perch upon the banister. It felt out for her shoulder and upon contact, slid from the railing. Pausing at her shoulder, it rubbed its head against her turban then crawled down into her lap, where it began to treadle her thighs. When she patted the beast, it stopped and arched its body toward her touch.

By the time Yensilva returned, the cat had curled in her lap, loudly purring.

"Ugh!" Yensilva sneered with disgust at the beast. "Dogs make much better pets."

Setting the cat aside on the bench, Umera gave it one last final stroke before joining Yensilva. They wandered the road toward the Food District and passed the smithy.

"Are you going to get together with Milos again?" Yensilva's question held a tremulous tone, as though she were a young child inquiring about the world.

Despite Milos's attitude during the show, Umera felt a warmth pass through her as she remembered his kisses and caresses, the way he made her feel desired.

"Maybe," she answered.

Yensilva huffed and quickened her pace.

— 28 —

SINCE THAT DAY in Sondshor Market, when Umera assisted selling her first harvest, she fell asleep every night recounting all the languages she had heard and understood. The only fact about herself she could hold onto with undeniable certainty was that she knew languages. Otherwise, for the past month, her nights were filled with dreams: tapestries of black threads breathing and murmuring, a tendril of red smoke spinning—

A half-strangled cry disrupted the quiet of night.

Jolting awake, Umera held onto the dream image of a gargantuan flower not quite understanding how it could be an animal too, but the shriek which followed chased away the dream all together.

Her stomach lurched as she unwound herself from the wool blanket. Still in evening clothes from a late night at Sunset, she bolted upright. Pushing the turban out of her eyes, she scrambled from bed, nearly tripping over the discarded nightgown she couldn't be bothered to change into, and flung the bedroom door open.

From behind the post she scanned the darkness of the kitchen. In the cool light of oncoming dawn, she discerned a bulky shadow crouched before the main door.

The shadow shuffled and mewled.

Umera blinked crazily, forcing her eyes to adjust faster. Dark edges delineated cupboards and the table. The shadow elongated, as though standing on hind legs.

She felt the rough brick wall next to the hearth until her fingers wrapped around the cold, pitted steel of a poker. Stealthily, she lifted it from the hook as the end of the scarf wrapped about her head fell across her eyes.

The shadow returned to its crouched position.

Umera raised the poker in front of her, feeling every hair on her neck and arm stand on end.

"What are you doing?!" The harsh whisper issued from the shadow.

Arms trembling, Umera lowered the poker. Squinting, she inched toward the door, tucking the lightweight fabric into the fold of her headdress. "Is that you Yen—"

"Be quiet!" Yensilva lunged forward, grabbed Umera by the wrist, and pulled her down to the floor.

Umera's heart raced at the sound of heavy footfalls padding toward the door. They stopped. A low, indiscernible mumbling was followed by a forceful, nasty curse. She held her breath until the footfalls withdrew from outside the front door.

Her fingers began to ache, so she loosened her grip on the poker and laid it softly on the floor. Leaning against the door, she hugged her legs, hoping to still the trembling in her body. She squirmed at how mindless fear burst from a cocoon and crawled throughout her, making her feel weak and vulnerable. She hated feeling helpless and angered quickly because of it.

Yensilva let out a long, slow breath. "There's a demon out there," she whispered.

"A demon?" Umera wasn't quite sure what a demon looked like and the familiar tug of curiosity began to push her anger and fear aside.

"Trust me, I saw enough of them during the war," Yensilva said. "You don't want to meet one."

"What do they look like?"

The question prompted Yensilva to stop rubbing her eyes. "If you saw one, you'd know." She shivered again. "Most of them look like beasts, but the older ones who've walked the world since the beginning, they look almost human, and some of them have powers."

"Like Adinav?"

"No, not like that." Frowning, Yensilva slid down the door and sat on the floor too. "Demons can turn invisible or run fast, but Adinav... he could..." She let out a brusque exhale. "He could get inside some people, make them do things they wouldn't want to do, like turn against their family and friends. Make them torture others, or kill them too."

"Is that what happened to your brother?" Umera asked cautiously.

"Yes." Tentative at first, Yensilva's voice quavered when she began to tell her story. "One day he was my brother and the next it was like he was empty. Like everything inside him had packed up and gone somewhere else. My da and I thought him angry with us at first, but there were these days where he just stood there looking at nothing in particular. It was creepy and sad, 'cause my brother was always the kind to laugh at everything."

Yensilva stared into her lap and began picking at her fingernails. "Then one morning he was gone. We'd heard stories about men walking off during the night to go fight in the war, so my da decided to look for him. I begged him not to go and leave me all alone, but he did. I still hate him for that." With a sigh, she sagged. "I miss them terribly."

Umera squeezed Yensilva's hand and held onto it.

"We worried lots because of the war." Yensilva sounded frail and tiny. "It's all any of us have known for as long as we've lived." She shook her head. "When we learned Adinav was controlling people, it chilled me to the bone marrow. People feared they might wake up puppets. Some even killed themselves." Looking up, Yensilva lowered her voice even more. "What's worse, Adinav started doing the same to some of the demons."

The whispering was contagious. Umera spoke in a faint voice. "Some?"

"His power didn't work on everybody," Yensilva explained, "but it worked on enough people and demons to build an army."

Lifting herself, Yensilva hunched and craned to see through the nearest window. A loud clang made her jump in the air and fall back behind the door clutching her chest. "Oh, he's a tall one."

Curiosity sought domination over Umera's fear. She dug her fingers into her thighs to steady her nerves. She wanted to see what a demon looked like. Perhaps her jitters would subside if she knew something of their appearance.

"I need to see it!" Before Yensilva could object, Umera crawled toward the window next to the cupboard. Pressed against the wall, she slid up until she stood and peered through the glass. The stray end of her turban fell across her eyes again. This time, she shoved it deeply underneath, where sweaty hair rolled over her fingers.

A long silhouette cleaved the yard in half until it shifted, and she saw the demon. It reminded her of the cactuses clustered on the hill beyond the cornfield and of a man. Two legs. Two arms. A bald head which slowly swiveled toward the house. She held her breath until the creature returned to skulking about the tools strewn at the edge of an empty garden bed.

He came to a stop, reared to full height, and stretched with arms bent above his head, chest thrust forward. The deep grimace on his face diminished. As the cornstalks beyond him bent in the breeze, he stooped, plucked a shovel from the ground and spun it around, wielding it like a sword. Blurting a venomous curse, he hurled the tool weapon into a nearby rain barrel. The blade speared the surface of the water and sank into the wood.

From the darkness, Yensilva let out a tiny squeal as water slopped over the barrel brim and splashed the barn wall. A shrill, irritable whinny rose from the barn.

The demon froze.

A whoosh arose from the cornfield as the stalks resumed their upright stature. They were slightly taller than the demon and still growing. The demon, Umera realized, stood considerably taller than her, by several feet.

She expected him to descend upon the house. Instead, he swiveled toward the barn. With head bowed, he plucked a tiny flower from his chest. She failed to understand why he stared briefly at the orange blossom before boldly walking toward the barn doors. Her instincts, however, knew Crank was in danger.

"No, no, no," she cried. Dashing for the door, she swooped to reclaim the abandoned poker. Lifting it high, she unbolted the lock.

Yensilva shot upright, spreading herself against the door. "What are you doing?"

"Move!"

"It's just a horse!"

Fierce determination finally stilled Umera's nerves. She shoved Yensilva aside, surprised at how easily she yielded, flung the door open, and ran toward the barn.

Half-way across the yard, she stopped when she heard cooing noises similar to those she would make when trying to coax Crank from his stall. Short derisive snorts indicated the horse's unruly and uncooperative temperament from being awoken before dawn. She also heard the front door of the house shut and the bolt click into place.

"Yensi!" Her throat stung from the attempt to holler softly over her shoulder.

She heard the creak of a window lattice being swung open. Yensilva whispered, "You chose this."

"Knowing the door would stay open!"

A long squeal erupted from the barn, followed by the familiar crack of Crank striking the back of the stall with his hind hooves. His irritability had mounted to annoyance.

Behind her, Umera heard the window slam shut. In front of her, obscenities spilled out from the barn doors.

Digging her feet into the ground, she raised the poker.

Lightning streaked the horizon. Despite the onset of a sunny morning, it began turning a soft luminous gray. The blacksmith persevered as dark clouds roiled on the horizon. His hunt for deer the previous evening, near the border of Woedshor, had been interrupted by the sighting of a familiar green beast strolling along the desert horizon.

Stealthily, Avn pursued Istok's tracks toward the farmlands, where they circled in and out of fields. During the night, he stayed a safe distance from the demon, who wandered from farm to farm, tipping rain barrels and scattering tools, startling cows and opening sheep pens.

Avn's legs ached from keeping up with the demon's lengthy strides, and he relaxed slightly when the tracks returned toward the desert just before dawn. His hopes were dashed when Istok stopped at the farm settled between the outskirts of Sondshor Market and the vast fields which faded into sand. There, the demon paused to admire thriving cornstalks, their tips on the verge of silking.

Skirting the side of the farm opposite the cornfield, Avn scanned the field where the demon had disappeared and fell against the wall of a shack beneath a rain basin tower. He pushed back the hood of his tanned leather jacket. His focus was split between the racket in the barn and her, the woman from the castle who had once been a gemstone, who now wielded an iron poker as her only defense.

Istok stumbled from the barn clutching his chest. Green fluid oozed between fingers shielding a wedge-shaped gouge. Throwing his head back, he let out a strangled cry.

"Ungrateful beast!"

During the throes of his tantrum, he squeezed his wound and the strange flesh stuck together creating a thick scar similar to the one that encircled his left arm just below the elbow.

A low grumble crawled across the sky, drowning out the click of arrows in the quiver strapped to Avn's waist.

"You're real tough," the woman nearly shouted. "Picking on a horse caged in a stall."

The hairs on Avn's neck bristled at her fearful tone, but by the look of the demon, the horse had defended itself effectively, and she need not worry about the beast—only herself.

"Your kind, always misunderstanding." Istok shook his head and spat on the ground. "I only meant to show the beast a new way of being. I've done it before, you know."

Repositioning her grip on the poker, the woman licked her lips. "Done what?"

"Made men out of beasts. Or rather women."

He raised his scarred arm toward her. She stepped backward, waggling the poker before her.

Sucking in his breath, Avn steadied his bow, aimed an arrow, and pulled the drawstring tighter. Large drops of water began to splatter against the weapon's wooden limb and grip.

Pressed between Istok's thumb and middle finger was the flower he plucked from his chest. Crumpled and torn, orange fluid seeped from the petals, ran along his fingers, and sank into his flesh. Blackened, the petals crumbled and scattered into the air.

Avn flexed his arm and maintained his position, peering through the light rain.

"Is that why you're here then?"

"I'm searching for someone." The demon sniffed.

"Me too, but I don't go around scaring everyone!" The woman shouted.

The demon considered her words. Gesturing toward her, he asked. "Who are you looking for?"

The rain began to soak through the woman's white blouse, turquoise skirt, and orange turban, darkening the fabrics. The profile of her face glistened in the eerie green light of oncoming storm clouds.

"Someone who might remember me," she answered uneasily. "Who are you looking for?" She raised the poker higher.

The demon examined his chest wound again and said, "Hmm, met her a long time ago."

A long steady, slow breath soothed Avn's nerves. He shifted his knuckle, rolling the arrow to adjust the curve of the shaft.

"She glowed, like a tiny sun." Istok brought his hands together and cracked his knuckles. "Rough about the edges, but rare and soft, and no matter how hard you dropped her, she never broke." Briefly he closed his eyes. "She lives. Reddish purple, like the madder flowers near the castle." He paused, a smirk curling his lips. After a moment, his voiced drifted through the rain. "Like a bruise."

Though intently focused on the demon, the woman blinked profusely. Her bare feet shifted, dirt caking to her heels. "What do you know of the castle?"

"It would be better ruled by me. I'd make this world a better place for everyone, not destroy it." Anger surged through him. He curled the fingers of his scarred arm, and it took a moment before they responded and tightened into a fist.

"I used to live at the castle." The woman shifted her muddy feet, widening her stance slightly. "Do I look familiar to you?"

The demon blinked profusely, examining her closely. "Not at all. You're thick all the way through, and your complexion's the color of drab. You look like common granite stock." Jutting his jaw, he snarled. "A good thing for you or I'd kill you otherwise."

The woman felt along the slippery ground with her heel and stepped back slightly, straining to maintain her grip on the poker.

"I only ask because I have amnesia," the woman explained.

Avn stretched his neck and felt a vertebra crack. The rain was cold; he struggled to stay focused as steam vapors rose from the ground, the barn, and the house.

"People forget all sorts of things," Istok muttered, regaining his composure.

"Like what?"

He grimaced at first, as though either the question or the attempt to smile pained him. "There was a time when cactuses were three times the size they are now, and poisonous, and criminals and heretics were impaled on their long, thick spines, left to bleed out, to suffocate and bloat."

The woman shuddered.

"I was born from their fear." Grinning came much easier to him. "Fear of pain, of death, by the pricks of the desert." He huffed harshly. "I'm not alone. Others like me wander the world, some older than Areel, older than me, but nobody remembers why they still fear us, which is a good thing."

"How's it a good thing?" Her voice cracked. Trembling snaked from her wrists into her arms making the poker wobble. A flash of anger creased her brow.

"Ignorance keeps people weak."

Avn frowned. He strengthened his grip on the bow, keeping the arrow aimed.

Leaning toward her, Istok tapped his chest. "This keeps me

strong." He laughed. "At every opportunity, they give away their power... to my kind."

Rain splashed Avn's forehead. He blinked as the cold water trickled into his eye. Despite the blurring, he saw the demon lightly scratch his neck, turning his forearm of red spines toward the woman.

Whoosh.

Well aimed, the smith had released the arrow. It cleared the woman's shoulder and sunk into the demon, piercing the bicep of his good arm.

The woman flinched from the movement. Slipping, she fell back onto the ground, the poker tumbling from her grip. Avn hadn't meant to startle her. Focusing on the demon, he ignored her as she clung to the ground and crawled through the mud clutching at her unraveling turban.

Istok grappled at his new wound, his scarred arm fumbling with the arrow. His fingers lacked the strength to grasp the feathered tail, and he swore in frustration.

Avn emerged from the shadows of the shack, preparing the bow with another missile.

Large veins popped along Istok's neck and forehead. "You again!"

A second arrow responded swiftly to the demon's outrage. He lunged aside. The arrow grazed his ear and he nearly toppled over. He righted himself, and as a third arrow whizzed by his head, he turned toward the cornfield. Loping in large strides, he parted the cornstalks and vanished into their rigid embrace.

The man Umera had come to know as the new blacksmith peered down the shaft of an arrow neatly strung in a large hunting bow. He pointed with it toward the house.

"Inside," he commanded.

Unnerved yet relieved by his sudden appearance, she scrambled to her feet, wiping mud from her backside. Irritability triggered a frown as she banged on the door. The end of the scarf about her head was wet and stuck to her face. She couldn't tell which bothered her more: the blacksmith for being bossy or Yensilva for ignoring her knocks.

She banged on the door again and called out, mindful of how the blacksmith nearly clung to her back while shielding her.

"Yensi," she called. "Come on, it's safe. The demon's long gone."

Yensilva still did not response.

"The new blacksmith scared it off—"

The latch clicked and the door swung fully open. Umera scrambled into the kitchen, where she let out a long breath. Reluctantly she slid the turban from her head and scratched at the mess of her sweaty hair. Hoping to thank the blacksmith, she returned to the doorway.

Collapsing against the jam, Yensilva thrust her hip forward, blocking the way. She gazed admiringly at the blacksmith and let out a sigh.

"You're so brave." She smiled sweetly and raised her arm, pretending to tuck an imaginary piece of long hair behind her ear. "Your name's Avn, isn't it?"

The man nodded. Briefly, he scanned the yard, lingering on the cornfield a moment before regarding her.

Umera tried to understand what Yensilva found so attractive about a man who tucked the tip of his long braided beard inside his jacket. Perhaps his only interesting feature was his eyes, which shimmered like eerie green suns breaking through storm clouds.

"Really," Yensilva insisted. "You're very brave for rescuing this fool." She gestured behind her.

Umera ducked to avoid being smacked. Stepping backward, she folded her arms across her chest as suspicion stirred within. Where had he come from so suddenly?

Mud peeled from her short sleeves and splattered onto the floor. She cleared her throat and asked, "How is it you happened to be here at this very moment?"

"Don't be rude!" The blast briefly altered Yensilva's face and quickly faded back into a soft, open expression of admiration toward the man.

Avn released the bowstring with firm control and returned the arrow to its quiver. "While hunting deer," he began to explain. He wiped his damp forehead and focused on Umera. "I spotted the demon and tracked him here. I had to make sure he didn't hurt anyone."

"You must be starving." Excitement stirred Yensilva. She stood upright in the doorway. "Would you like to stay for honey biscuits and tea?"

"I've a blade to finish today," he replied candidly. "I can't spare the time." He bowed slightly toward Yensilva then Umera. "Stay safe." He slung the bow across his shoulders, and with a final glance at the cornfield, walked toward the field between the farmyard and the outskirts of Sondshor market.

Yensilva stepped forward onto the stoop, her gaze lingering on the blacksmith until the steadily increasing rain forced her inside.

"Oh he's a handsome one, isn't he?"

Umera blinked at Yensilva, as though seeing her for the first time. Merely minutes ago, she was a frightened woman cowering behind the door, and now she was a young girl infatuated by a man.

"Handsome, in a rugged way," Yensilva said dreamily. "We must thank him proper."

— 29 —

MILOS PULLED UMERA into his arms. "Where are you running to?"

"The blacksmith," Umera replied, nearly shouting above the din at Sunset House. "Tonight's the night I get answers from him."

"Hazias?"

"No, the other one."

"Oh, him. How long have you been trying to talk with him?"

Since that early morning when Avn had struck the demon with his arrow, she had been trying. Weeks had dragged on. The corn stalks grew taller as she grew impatient. "Nearly a month now."

"And every time you try," Milos sang, "He walks out before you get near him."

She and Milos were surrounded by a band of farmhands, still in their soiled trousers and shirts, who ordered drinks at the bar where they stood. Bracing her hands on Milos's broad shoulders, she rolled onto the tips of her toes for a better look. Idly, she scratched the hairline behind her ear, just beneath the rim of her turban.

She peered over the farmhands and glimpsed Yensilva flirting with Avn. He nodded repeatedly looking partially amused by whatever she told him. Like previous evenings though, he was soon joined by the familiar, lanky figure of Sabien who leaned into the blacksmith with intimate familiarity—a squeeze of the shoulder, of the bicep. Both men nodded profusely at Yensilva then pushed their way toward the exit.

Disappointed by Avn's departure, all thoughts dissipated at the touch of Milos. His hands roved the curves of her hips and backside. The sensation of warm imprints on her flesh distracted her.

Tilting her head, she let Milos kiss her again.

"I don't like the way he looks at you," he said, his eyes wandering along the length of the bar, scanning faces and lingering on the female ones.

"Who?"

"Him." He gestured in the direction of Yensilva, where the blacksmith had stood.

Avn had unnerved her too. Their encounters were few. Each time, the intensity with which he looked at her felt invasive. The attention also seemed to arouse a jealous streak in Yensilva.

"C'mon," Milos nodded upward. "Forget about him for tonight?"

Reluctant at first, she let Milos lead her up the stairs to the mezzanine, where they huddled at a tiny table. A clear glass bowl filled with oil and a floating wick emitted a dim glow, casting them in shadow.

They kissed deeply, his fingers kneading the soft part of her thigh. They dug in and sprang back, lying still in her lap.

"Why did you stop?"

Milos stared down at her exposed thighs. They were thick and fleshy. He shrugged. "Nothing."

Their resumed kissing created a tingling in her abdomen. His caresses were less attentive than usual. She kissed him harder, spurring him on, and the arousal warmed her flesh.

Moans and soft sighs from nearby lovers drifted along the mezzanine, and she felt herself becoming more aroused.

"Let's go somewhere else," she urged.

Milos led her toward the stairs. Upon their descent, a young man with bronzed skin and sun kissed red hair rose toward them. She was impressed by the strength, confidence, and fierceness he exuded, and not at all surprised to find a woman clinging to each arm, smiling and laughing.

"Oh, hello Umera."

Bethereel's long hair spilled over one shoulder. The dark crimson fabric of the narrow dress she wore was equally as vibrant as the man next to her.

As to who specifically prompted pangs of jealousy, she wasn't sure. Was it the beautiful Bethereel or the strange man who reminded her of fire?

Bethereel laid a gentle hand on her shoulder. "Have you found anything about your past?"

Umera shrugged and shook her head. "Can't talk to the one

person who might know something."

She glanced away for fear someone might detect the fantasy forming in her mind. She watched the bartender below tap a new keg of ale as images of Bethereel, the man, and herself discarded their clothes and wrapped their arms about one another in sensual, exploratory embraces.

"You'll discover something soon," Bethereel assured her. Her fingers grazed the side of Umera's turban. "You're such a deviant. Everyone's complaining about your new look."

"Deviant?"

Bethereel straightened, admiring the head piece. "Only men from the North wear these."

"And what do the women wear?"

Bethereel shrugged. "Nothing." A sparkle lit her eyes and she grinned, and Umera wondered if she referred to all clothes instead of just head wear.

Locked in the man's embrace, Bethereel climbed the stairs toward the mezzanine. As the trio passed, Umera blushed when the man with red hair winked at her. Nervously, she scratched the spot where Bethereel's fingers had touched. An image of him pressing his mouth against hers drifted into her mind.

"Do you know him?"

Snapping out of her fantasy, she gaped at Milos.

"Red, do you know him?" he asked again. Frowning he urged her down the remaining steps and through the doors of Sunset House.

"Is that his name? Red?" She inhaled the cool night air.

"It's a nickname, I suppose." He pulled her through the market toward the junction. "It's what my friends call him. He's new in town."

Umera's mood faltered as Milos pulled her toward the barn. The slow, sensuality with which he used to woo her was absent.

"I can't remember his real name," he said. "It was something weird."

Around the back of the barn, they climbed a set of rickety stairs to the warm loft above, where they fumbled with each other's clothes. During their earliest encounters, Milos had always taken his time, made a game of undressing her and admiring her nudity. Lately, he barely kept his eyes open.

Naked, they scrambled onto the straw strewn floor. Musk and the pungent smell of rotten wood overpowered the sweet scent of freshly cut hay as they intertwined.

Warmth flowed through her body, the numbing of honey mead mingling with her own arousal, a tingling energy which coursed through her torso and gathered in her abdomen. She tried hard to focus on the chaos created by Milos's hasty fingers trying to tease her. If it weren't for the honey mead, she thought the sensations might feel more immediate, more intense.

She had hoped by now that he understood her body better, but he was urgent and impatient with his affection. She helped ease him inside her and gave over to his rhythm, hoping to find some synchronicity between them. Their energies collided. His stirred hers into a unified force which swelled. She felt herself melting into him and into the loft floor. They clutched and thrashed, their flesh kneading together until they felt inseparable.

Gasping at the sudden rush of release, the fear of never regaining herself struck her. The places where they touched disconnected. She felt twice her size until the world rushed back to her, intensifying the feeling of separateness.

Their breaths slowed, returning to an even pace, and she marveled at the wonderful throbbing that continued to course throughout her body. Like all their other reunions, she felt relieved to experience some joy—even just a little—in a world which seemed to offer none, even in the stories people told one in another as entertainment.

The absence of tension and stress within her body had created an openness which her body wanted to fill. As her wits returned and she settled back into herself, she watched Milos quickly dress. She probably would have felt insulted by his sudden exit had she not been preoccupied by a spark of recognition at the diminishing sensation of expansion within every portion of her body, and she wondered why that feeling seemed so familiar.

A fine drizzle dampened the yard. Light dirt caked to Umera's sandals as she trundled toward the barn. Inside, she wiped the spray of rain from her face and scooped oats into Crank's feeding bag. The usual lethargy and grogginess she woke up with every morning had recently started lingering well into the afternoon.

Her mind wandered over the previous weeks. Evening jaunts to Sunset House became more frequent as her worry grew. More and more, Milos required prodding to sneak off to the barn, where they could explore their arousal and revel in release. Months of mead and heavy food seemed to be diminishing her energy. At times, it took all her strength to convince him.

Yensilva's solution to eat more only worsened the restrictions Umera started feeling in her body. Bending and twisting became difficult, but what bothered her most was hearing herself huff for breath after the simplest of tasks.

"There's a good horse," she cooed.

He gummed the oats and reluctantly ate them.

"Want an apple instead?"

She leaned over to grab a yellow apple from the bucket. The usual pressure of her belly squeezed against her snug pants until something gave with a snap. From the corner of her eye, she spied the button of her pants pop free, bounce against the barn wall, and topple behind a bale of hay.

"Don't you laugh," she said sadly.

Crank whinnied at her anyway as she examined the pants which at one time were too big for her. Finding a thin chord, she tied it off about her waist. It was uncomfortable but stopped her pants from sliding over her hips.

Hoping to dispel the onset of a bleak mood, she let her mind drift. Retrieving the brush, Crank sniffed her hand before she began grooming him.

At first, he always shifted uncomfortably, yanking his head back when she approached. Now, she introduced herself, as she liked to call it, and their encounters became more amicable.

Crank snuffled her hand, remaining steady as she began gliding the brush over his coat.

She saw herself in the horse, a creature desperate to move and act upon urges yet caged and trained to fulfill the needs of another, allowed only enough space to survive but not to thrive.

She paused to run a hand through her recently sheared hair. It was short again. Too short.

The crack and rattle of the barn wall startled her. She backed away from Crank as he settled down from kicking his hind legs. After all this time, she couldn't figure out what he meant by the outburst. Her soft chatter eased him slightly.

In the following days, he grew quieter than usual. The wild energy in his eyes, which she had grown to love, had diminished. And when she patted his nose and stroked his brow, for the first time, Crank nuzzled the side of her head.

"I know, I know," she said.

Gossip. It was the biggest commodity at Sunset House. Rumors spilled more than ale, and at times Umera found herself enduring the horrible flavor of honey mead so she wouldn't be forced to contribute to conversation. As much as she had grown to despise the drink, she did enjoy the warm, numbing sensation it offered.

She listened though, and she asked around about the war. Retired soldiers refused to resurrect the horrors of battle. Those with few memories, kept to themselves, drowning their own amnesia in spirits. If anyone had willingly worked for Adinav, they denied it, except for Avn, the blacksmith, who became the subject of more gossip.

"If having been a part of Adinav's court is such a crime," Umera asked bitterly, "why hasn't anyone lynched the new blacksmith?"

"Lots of people don't speak with him," Milos said, setting down a mug of dark ale.

"Sabien speaks with him all the time. They're lovers," Bethereel said. She winced as she downed the last of her mead. "I doubt there's much talking between them."

"I've seen Elusis visit him on several occasions. Even you talk with him," Umera said, nudging Milos.

He shrugged. "He hasn't done anything to me. I haven't any reason to hate him."

"It's because he'sss, he's valuable," Yensilva said. She licked her lips and hiccuped. "A man with ssskills—a smith, a farrier, and a hunter. Besides, he protected usss. I wouldn't turn him into the authorities even if they tortured me." Yensilva's thick fingers cradled her tiny glass of mead as she scanned the tavern for the blacksmith, but he hadn't shown up at Sunset House.

"I have skills," Umera complained, wiping perspiration from her brow just beneath her turban. "I know languages."

"You're a polyglot." Bethereel's interjection caused a hush at their table. She flicked the rim of her empty sniffer. "Don't know too many people who know as many languages as you," she said. "Doesn't rarity make something valuable?"

"Pleeaaase!" Yensilva hunkered over the table, cradling her mead, and snarled. "I can only think of wh-one wh-oman sssilly enough to wear a turban and that jusss makes her wh-eird."

Laughter erupted at the table.

Umera envied Bethereel's refined composure for she spoke her mind eloquently and sometimes forcefully, always speaking appreciatively of everyone yet was now being subjected to ridicule for it.

Bethereel shrugged as the conversation turned.

Avn, Umera discovered, was yesterday's news. The townies were now waggling their tongues about the new guy in town, the one everyone called Red.

According to Milos, he came from the north with a caravan of very wealthy merchants. The townies placed bets on which and how many women Red would woo upstairs or into bed.

According to Elusis, as told by Yensilva doing a rather good impression of her uncle, Red exuded airs, the kind associated with courtesans or royalty. He no doubt kept secrets, the kind that might shame his family.

According to Yensilva, he was the most arrogant, cocky, and sexy man in all of Sondshor, and she wouldn't say no to a jaunt upstairs with him.

According to Bethereel, the only person any of them knew who had directly interacted with him, Red's true name was Ibe, and that's all she would tell.

Umera felt as though her efforts to find information were similar to walking in mud up to her waist. The trudging pace frustrated her, as she exhausted herself with little distance covered despite the great effort made. Her head spun, and the mead helped quiet the crazies, as Milos often called those kinds of thoughts. She hated the taste but loved the effect, and she drank until her mind numbed.

— 30 —

CLUNK. THUD. SLAM.

She groaned, turned over in bed and imagined Yensilva throwing herself about the kitchen—dropping the cutting board on the counter, tossing meat on the board and shearing it through with a cleaver. The loud, obtrusive sounds caused Umera's head to throb. She pulled herself upright. At the edge of the bed, she waited for the usual dull ache from a night at Sunset House to subside. This morning, she felt sore all over. She stood and the room wobbled.

"Stop whirling," she complained to the bedroom.

I am never drinking again, she thought.

She dressed in dirty work clothes and ran a brush through her shoulder length hair. Pausing to take a breath, she twirled the hair up, wrapping the faded orange scarf about, keeping it all hidden. She stumbled into the kitchen and collapsed in a chair at the table.

"Remind me to bring kerchiefs tonight." Despite being clear across the room, Yensilva sounded as if she stood directly next to Umera.

"Bring them where?"

"Sunset House."

Umera's stomach lurched.

"You do remember its Bethereel's birthday?"

"Sure," she croaked. "I thought you didn't like her."

Yensilva slammed an empty water skin on the table before her. "Of course I like the girl," she said. "What makes you think I don't?"

"The things you say about her when she's not around." Umera rubbed her face, hoping to dispel her ache and confusion. "How you want me to stay clear of her."

"That's because all you do is ask about Adinav. She knows important people and word can travel fast. Do you want to be arrested?"

She willingly followed Yensilva to the well pump. Having eaten very little, Umera was grateful to be far from the stench of the kitchen. Taking turns they filled their water skins and began morning chores. The water promised to soothe Umera, yet as morning unfolded, a trembling coursed through her body. Daily tasks completed, she mopped her brow and tended to the cornfield.

Umera slipped the strap of the water skin over her shoulder. She turned and stumbled at the edge of the field. The world wobbled. Sweat made her clothes stick to her body. The turban sagged heavily and her skull ached. She blinked at the brightness of everything as she regained her balanced.

"I think I'm still a little drunk," she mumbled. She stooped to twist another corn cob from a nearby stalk.

Slightly muddled by the cornstalks, she heard Yensilva say, "Not surprised after last night. What got into you?"

Nothing, Umera thought to herself, or rather no one. She met with Milos. They drank and danced, his attention always drifting. Come the end of the night, however, Milos made no effort to escort her toward the barn loft.

Cornstalks rustled and parted. Flushed in the face, Yensilva frowned.

"Good gracious girl!" She threw a corn cob into her sack. "Look at you!"

Umera froze. "What?"

"Take that blasted scarf off your head so you can cool down properly?"

Reluctantly, Umera began unwinding it. Her lower back throbbed while her arms were raised. She shook out her damp hair and for a few seconds, she felt cool.

Pointing to her damp hair, Yensilva gasped. Throwing herself across the short distance between them, she tugged at Umera's hair. "Is that a rash?" She tutted, pulling one of Umera's ears forward.

"It's fine," Umera moaned.

"It's getting cut!"

As the heat of the sun bored through Umera, threatening to disintegrate flesh, muscle, and bone, she longed to spray herself with cold water from the pump.

I am never drinking again, never, she thought. Ever.

Umera crinkled her nose at the smell of fried meat. Disgust consumed her. Rubbing her distended stomach, she wondered how she could still feel full after a night's rest.

Yensilva set down a plate heaped with potatoes, eggs, and little bits of meat with a chunk of bread teetering on the rim. "What's wrong with you?"

"I can't." Umera's throat constricted. "I'd much prefer something like an apple."

"Ew! What, you a horse now?" Yensilva dove into her breakfast, chewing with fervor. "How do you expect to keep going," she said as she chewed her food, "through the morning on an apple?"

Poking at a fat drenched potato, Umera struggled with a bout of nausea. "I think there's still roast beef in my stomach from three days ago."

Seldom understanding her humor, Yensilva slammed the table with her knife. "So you want to waste all the good food I just made!" She gulped down her food in frustration. Scowling, she stabbed a carrot on her plate. "You're lucky to have food at all, you know." She pointed the carrot at Umera. "There are folk who can't eat the way we do. Like skeletons, the lot of them. So eat!"

"It's my body," Umera mumbled, longing to feel light and flexible again.

Setting down her knife and fork, Yensilva settled into a tight-mouthed silence and remained that way throughout their morning chores.

By mid afternoon, Umera felt a niggling hunger pang which she sated with a green apple. It satisfied her well into the early evening, when she and Yensilva set out toward Sunset House. Cloud shadows spotted the windblown fields. The tension between them had finally eased as they strolled away from the farm.

Squinting, Yensilva carefully asked, "Should I call you Crank then?" A pout puckered her lips.

Determined to lighten Yensilva's mood, Umera made a neighing sound, shook her head, and galloped a few steps.

Yensilva smirked at her strange antics and snorted. "Horse!"

Settling down, Umera fell in to step next to Yensilva and strolled through the waist high grass. After a few moments of silence, she felt compelled to ask, "Do you like working the farm, Yensi?"

Letting out a long, dramatic sigh, Yensilva answered. "I like that I own it. It's mine, you know."

"You could easily own a shop in town."

Yensilva's face lit up. "Oh, what an interesting suggestion!" Her mood lifted. "A shop in town? Really? Can you imagine waking every morning to the smell of chocolate cake instead of manure?" Her smile faded slightly. "But I couldn't, not really. What about the farm?"

Before Umera could answer, Yensilva did.

"I could sell it." She shook her head. "But it's been in my family for so long?" She perked up again. "Oh! I could it rent it out and become a landlord."

Listening attentively, Umera smiled to herself as Yensilva rambled on about how wonderful life would be to live among people instead of vegetables.

Umera found Milos tucked away in the darkest shadows at the bar. She leaned toward him intent on kissing his lips, until he sidestepped her advance. Smiling, he scratched his head and looked down at his feet.

Next to him, a slender woman with tufted orange hair shifted uncomfortably. Dressed in teal chiffon, eyes heavily rimmed with kohl, she peered upward and away with an air of superiority, purposely ignoring Umera.

"What do you want?" Milos finally asked.

Umera smiled warmly, sliding her hand across his slightly

barreled stomach. "What do you think?"

He swiped her hand free. Nodding toward the woman with the unfortunate hair, he said, "This is *Umerra*, spelled with two r's."

The introduction was interrupted by a burst of laughter from patrons nearby. Confused, Umera found herself momentarily distracted as she regarded a group of women pressed around the man whom the townies had nicknamed Red.

Everything about him glowed—olive skin, his ruddy hair, his smile, his eyes. His exuberant demeanor was impossible to ignore. She wished she waded in his humor instead of drowning in Milos's growing disinterest.

"Excuse us," Milos said, pushing past Umera. He curtly nodded at her, retreating to his group of friends with the orange-haired woman in tow. They laughed among themselves then proceeded to push through the crowd toward Sunset's main exit.

Umera squeezed into the wake they created. Determined to alleviate her confusion, she followed them. A hand clasped about her wrist, and she discovered it belonged to Bethereel.

Dressed in pink, eyes glassy, Bethereel asked, "Care to dance?"

Riled, Umera shook her head. Pulling herself free, she resumed her pursuit of Milos. Outside, she stepped in front of him.

"What did I do?"

Milos shook his head, as though he didn't understand what she meant. His friends snickered and the orange-haired woman acted bored. As he was about to answer, their gathering was overtaken by Red and an entourage of women, who spilled through the doorway. Milos tipped forward from the collision and fell against Umera.

While she delighted in the smell of his cologne and the contact of his warm flesh, she noticed he recoiled when their bodies met, as though he had touched some icky thing.

Red laughed. Jutting his chin toward Milos, he shouted, "Sorry friend, didn't mean to knock you about."

A flash of anger erupted from Milos and he ignored the apology.

Red's women tittered in unison, their faces rosy and eyes glassy from far too much drink. They parted from one another as Bethereel squeezed between them. The women complained as she positioned herself in front of them, craning her head.

Umera found it difficult to breathe, self-consciousness intensifying as the crowd grew.

"Listen," Milos said to her, straightening his white shirt. "I think it's time to take a break."

She trembled. Her cheeks flushed. Even the cool night could not ease her sudden hurt.

"It's just that..." He searched for words, even looked to his friends for some guidance. He finally shrugged and said, "You're not attractive anymore, what with you being fat now."

Most of Milos's friends coughed or shifted uncomfortably. One of them snickered. A few titters arose from Red's women, who tried to conceal their smiles and kept failing.

"Daftpot," Bethereel muttered, shaking her head sadly.

"Ouch!" Red winced as though the comment struck his heart as deeply as Umera's. The mirth in his eyes, however, revealed a jovial sentiment she recognized as mockery.

Her mind went blank. Yearning for Milos had turned into repulsion. Heat engulfed her as though she wielded a forge inside. At its very core, a raw wound pulsed, demanding to be pummeled and shaped into a fierce weapon.

My body is mine, she declared to herself. I'll choose what it eats and who will take pleasure in it. And the crowd would witness this vow.

With muscles honed and sculpted by chopping wood, tilling earth, and carrying harvest, she swung her arm backward and aimed. The punch was swift, direct, and forceful, catching Milos in the middle of his face. A soft crunch shuddered beneath her fingers. She snapped her fist back, cringing at the sting across her knuckles, and shook her hand to dispel the pain.

Milos's head jerked backward at first. He clutched his nose and when the agony failed to ease, he fell to his knees. None of his friends made any effort to catch him.

The women, except for the orange-haired one, snickered. Bethereel, who had covered her mouth in shock, recovered quickly, clapped her hands, and shouted, "Bravo!" The praise made Umera blush.

Yet the one who laughed hardest and loudest was Red. "Nice contact." He nodded toward Milos's friends. "Her feet didn't even leave the ground."

For a moment, his praise washed away her hurt.

Milos scrambled to his feet, blood trickling over his mouth and chin.

From the crowd, Umera heard Bethereel speak above the murmuring. "Any woman who can make a man fall to his knees is a force to be reckoned with!"

Red's entourage of women nodded in agreement.

"Whad's wrong wid you?" Milos shouted at Umera. Pulling his hands away, blood smeared his down turned face and dripped onto his white shirt. "You can always ged skinny again, bud there's no cure for crazy!"

"You know what I wish," Umera shouted at him. She pointed a finger at his face and delighted at how he flinched.

"Led me guess," he said finding his courage again. "Thad you never med me. Real original, Umera."

All around them, she could feel people squeezing for a better look at the damage done to Milos's face. She struggled for something else to say. She saw anticipation in their eyes.

"I wish," she began. "I wish you... flexibility!"

Silence came over the crowd. Confused faces squinted in wonder at her words. Bethereel smirked.

"See, she's crazy," Milos said, deciding whether or not to wipe his bloody hands on his trousers or shirt.

And she found the words to match her thoughts and spoke each one slowly and clearly.

"So you can bend over backwards and kiss your own ass!"

Milos pouted as a deep belly laugh erupted from Red. His entourage of women giggled again. The crowd broke out into laughter.

The orange-haired woman, a smirk on her face, haughtily offered Milos a white handkerchief. When he reached for it, she snatched it away and joined in the laughter.

Head bowed, Milos stomped off across the yard toward the junction. His friends reluctantly followed, begging him to have a sense of humor; he had been rude first.

Bethereel rushed forward, resting her hand on Umera's shoulder. A light perfume of lavender cascaded over Umera as she stared down at the welts forming across her first two knuckles.

"Are you alright?" Bethereel asked.

"Of course she is," Red said. "That was righteous." He took her injured hand in his.

Still fuming, Umera was surprised to find his touch warmer than hers. He looked at the welts, grazed his thumb across them. He was surprisingly gentle. Milos's touch had been gentle too, in the beginning.

She pulled her hand free.

"I could show you how to punch without hurting yourself," he said. He smiled—with his thin lips, his eyes, the muscles in his entire face and body. "If you'd like."

My body is mine, Umera reminded herself.

— 31 —

UMERA SLOUCHED AGAINST the bar, the seat of the stool digging into her backside. She stared at the melting ice in her glass of apple juice, mindful of a hushed chattering throughout Sunset House, as though everyone had secrets to tell all at once.

The band still hadn't taken their place on the worn wooden platform to tune their instruments, and the twitchy barkeeps were solemn, tense, and quieter than usual.

She turned over large chunks of beef in what remained of a bowl of stew, aware of a deeply nagging bout of curiosity regarding the change in atmosphere.

Peering along the bar toward the main doors, she sought out Yensilva and found her leaning against the wall next to the stairwell. Her body shook with laughter as she continued flirting with Avn, touching his wide bare bicep once, twice, three times.

Frowning, Umera jabbed the spoon into a hunk of meat and squished it. Yet again, she had tried to talk with the blacksmith, to ask him about the war and how much he knew about Adinav and Sondshor castle. Yet again, Yensilva shooed her away, chastising her for raising memories any soldier would want to forget.

Umera watched Avn nod politely, his attention seldom wandering. He exchanged a few indeterminate words. Yensilva stiffened. They exchanged a few more words until Sabien slipped through a cluster of patrons, whispered into Avn's ear, and whisked him away.

Elbows out, Yensilva barreled through the crowd clustered along the bar and collided with Umera, nearly pushing her off the stool. "Have you heard?"

"No, you always interrupt me when I talk to him—"

"Shush girl!" Yensilva arced an eyebrow. "Or I won't use the blue tint I bought on your hair."

Delighted by the threat, Umera thought of other complaints to deter any more experimentation with her hair.

Yensilva's eyes widened and her face paled. Leaning forward, she lowered her voice. "You know the barmaid, the one who always buys up the last of our apples?"

"I know who you mean."

"She's missing."

The words sunk into her mind. Dread filled her stomach and she nudged the stew bowl to the other side of the bar. "What do you mean missing?"

"Vanished." Yensilva waved at a barkeep and ordered dinner. "No one's seen her since yesterday afternoon."

Umera knew the girl in a limited way. She bought their apples, always complained about the cost, and smiled appreciatively when Umera slipped her a few more than what they agreed upon. In the evenings, as a courtesy, the barmaid offered her an occasional free drink.

"Is anyone searching for her?" Umera asked. The barkeep scooped up the bowl noticing the leftover meat and muttered, *What a waste!* In its place, he set down a plate of beef and potatoes.

"I don't know," Yensilva mumbled, as she shooed Umera out of the seat and began shoveling roasted potatoes into her mouth. "I'm sure her family is."

Three-beat percussion drummed away all whispers about the missing barmaid. Dancers lined the tiny floor, stomping in unison. Umera found their mirth and the glint in their eyes distressing as she wondered when and where to begin looking for the missing barmaid.

Knowing she could not begin a search until the morning, she sighed heavily and squeezed between two overcrowded tables, where she tumbled forward into the aisle leading to the exit. Patrons pressed against the bar in clusters. There was very little room to move. She began pushing through and nearly elbowed Milos in the back. Relieved their bodies didn't connect, she tried to inch past him.

He stood partially turned toward her, his attention focused on companions standing against the bar. His hair was combed into a dark wave, his square face cleanly shaved, and although she recognized his regular entourage of friends, Milos talked exclusively to the new guy, Red.

Mug in hand, Milos gestured abruptly toward a small woman in a green jumper sitting farther down the bar. Ale and foam slopped over the brim and dripped onto his hand, which he ignored.

"She's a lot of fun to be with." He spoke loud enough for everyone to hear.

His friends craned their heads to stare at the girl. Red sipped at his drink, boredom dulling the edges of his boyish face as he glanced at Umera. His smiled widened, but she looked away, hoping to move past them without being seen.

"Went all the way upstairs with that one!" Milos sniffed as he pulled at the collar of his shirt with one hand and pointed with his mug of ale again, this time at a brunette. "But she wouldn't let me get to the first step on the way down. A waste of time, if you ask me."

Her stomach lurched at how easily Milos discussed his intimations with others, as though all of these women had no significance, including herself. His bragging disgusted her yet she paused when she noticed how he failed to impress Red, who let out a deep sigh.

"What about Miss Orange Head?" Red gestured at his head, pulling at invisible tufted hair.

Blinking profusely, Milos bent his ear forward. "Who?"

With one hand, Red danced an invisible handkerchief between them and snapped it away suddenly; with his other, he pretended to laugh.

Some of Milos's friends chuckled. Sullen, Milos rolled his eyes. "A sword would wilt if trapped between her legs."

Red laughed. It was loud and harsh—a comment directed at Milos for his inability. Then he winked at Umera. "What about the other blond?"

Leaning forward, Milos smirked. "You'll have to be more specific. I've had lots of blonds."

"Yeah," Red snorted. "Did they all punch you in the sniffer too?"

Milos straightened. "Oh, her..."

Red's eyes locked onto her again. He smiled, waggling his eyebrows.

Milos turned sharply, slopping more ale on himself, as he noticed her. His nose crinkled briefly despite the last of the swelling and redness from the wound she had given him. The expression was slight and brief but Umera saw it before he began laughing.

"I'm so clumsy!"

Snaking an arm around her waist, Milos whispered in her ear, brushing his lips against her cheek. "I'm an idiot, eh?" he mumbled, pulling her to his side.

Umera's heart fluttered at the familiarity of his touch and wondered if this was his way of apologizing for his past behavior. She felt her reserve weaken and she was about to accept his apology when his charm was suddenly eclipsed by the presence of Red, who took her hand in his and examined her knuckles.

"Nicely healed."

The glow of lanterns, the thumpa-twang of the band, and even Milos's touch diminished. All that existed was Red exuding fire and warmth, as though a sun lived somewhere inside his chest.

His eyes darted all over her face, her chest, the entire length of her, as he brought her knuckles to his lips. All thoughts of Milos and the missing barmaid slipped from her mind as she found herself caught in the spin and swirl of passion growing ever urgent inside her. He cocked his head to one side and stooped toward her.

"Do you really want to be with a guy who can't take a punch?"

Laughter burst from others standing nearby. Returning to her senses, she shook Milos free wanting to be as far away from him as possible.

"Here!" Red offered a place next to him near the bar, where he waved at the barkeep for more ale.

Without thinking, she squeezed into the spot next to him but declined his offer of ale. She felt a warm hand pressed into the small of her back. The intimate touch reminded her of Milos, for he had done the same when they first met.

"Hands off." She swiped Red's arm away.

Smirking, he bowed forward and asked, "What's your game then?"

Her stomach lurched again. Her feelings didn't exist for the sole purpose of being bandied about. "What do you mean by that?"

Turning to face the dance floor, she discovered Milos and his friends had retreated to a small table. Hunkered over a nearly empty mug of ale, Milos sneered at her.

"You know. Your game?" Red nudged her. "What makes you feel good?"

Memories of late night unions with Milos reminded her that she felt best exploring sensuality—lips and fingertips on flesh, giving herself over to the rising and expanding which seemed familiar and frightening at the same time. To kiss, to be kissed, to embrace and chase that rhythm of union—that was her game.

Turning toward Red, she steered his lips toward hers. When she kissed him, she half expected he would pull away. His lips were warmer than Milos's, more pliable and yielding, and while he didn't kiss her back, he didn't stop her either.

Slowly pulling away, she saw him nod.

"Not bad," he said.

Before she could ask what he meant, his arms circled around her middle pulling her close. She tried not to feel self-conscious about her girth even though she had to squeeze herself into the red dress Yensilva had made her. He lifted and swung her around to his other side.

Crack!

Despite her shock, Umera felt something warm and sticky splash her arm. She flinched as shattered glass spun across the floor, foam spraying in all directions. In the place where she had been standing, the bar dripped with ale.

She looked in the direction from which the glass had been hurled. Burly men with thick arms and thighs grabbed Milos. He resisted and a wrestling match ensued, but he soon found himself being hauled toward the exit. Blood trickled from his nose. His face red from exertion, Milos glowered at her again as he was forcibly escorted from the bar.

Still pinned against Red, she relaxed into his strength, dragged her fingers across his forearm.

A low chuckle rumbled in Red's chest. "Ah, so that's your game."

Red walked close, his arm brushing Umera's every other stride. She shivered when the warm contact broke and cool night air slipped between them. They strolled through the junction, passing the smithy and the love barn, which Umera was determined to stay away from for a while. They ducked down a dark, narrow alleyway. Emerging from the hive of small houses and shacks, they followed a dimly lit back street toward the main road into the market and crossed the main bridge.

"Is your friend always such a worry puss?" Red scratched his neck. Somewhere nearby, an owl hooted. "She doesn't expect you to be escorted home every night, does she?"

She laughed, hugging herself to recover some heat. "Yensi can't help herself, especially since another woman's gone missing."

"The barmaid, right?"

Umera nodded. Theories and rumors about the barmaid had consumed the patrons of Sunset House, for a little while at least. All woes of life had slowly been forgotten as the ale pumps continued flowing late into the evening. What fears and thoughts about the barmaid the ale didn't numb, the music beat into oblivion.

"I wonder if anyone's looking for her." Hard, cold stones beneath the soles of her sandals sent a chill through her bones.

Considerably taller than herself, she glimpsed Red scratch his head. Face slack, he glanced at her. "We shouldn't do this now that we're alone."

Stunned by the odd comment, she tried to determine his meaning and supposed he wanted to know something about her instead of the missing woman. She certainly wanted to know more about him. "Are you from the North like I've heard?"

"Ah!" He nudged her gently, a blast of heat from his arm warming her shoulder. "We're still playing then?"

"Huh?"

He stared at her for a moment. The click of his boot heel diminished as stone gave way to dirt road. "Us," he said.

Her mind sought to understand his meaning. "You mean, like we're playing a game. Us?"

Red nodded.

"No, no, no." She touched his arm, wishing she could wrap him around her like a shawl and keep warm. "I'm not playing with you." Her thoughts reviewed the recent events at the bar. "Do you mean Milos? No, I wasn't trying to make him jealous if that's what you think."

"I liked that part, Ule."

The owl hooted again, a long, drawn out unfulfilled sound. A shiver ran up Umera's spine as she held onto the last word Red had uttered.

"What's *oo-lay*?"

He grimaced. "Umera, right?"

"Yes?" She found their conversation odd and tried her best to ignore it. "I know everyone calls you Red," she continued, gently pushing him toward the middle of the road, away from a wall of unruly grapevines. "But what's your real name?"

"Ibe."

She rolled it over in her mouth: *ih-bay*. "That's a strange name."

"Not among my kind," he mumbled.

"And where are they? Your kind that is. Are they from the North like I've heard?"

When Ibe hesitated before answering, a chill coursed through her again. Annoyance pinched his attractive face, and she felt a pang of guilt. No matter what she said, he always seemed annoyed by it.

As the road arced and split in two directions, she pointed to the left. There, they followed the winding road around empty freshly tilled farm fields until grass penned them in on both sides.

His eyes darted all over her face again as though he were searching for something. He wrapped an arm around her shoulders. His heat bled into her body, keeping her warm until the road they followed brought them to the farm, where she reluctantly pulled herself free.

No matter how late she returned or how drunk, she always said goodnight to Crank. A snort from the barn indicated the horse was still awake. She excused herself and scampered across the yard, eased the barn door open, and slipped inside, where she watched Crank twitch and shift about in his stall. After bidding him a goodnight, she turned and collided with Ibe. Briefly, her heart pounded at his sudden appearance, for she hadn't heard his footfalls.

He folded her into his arms. Staring at him, she found herself simultaneously mesmerized by his intensity yet repulsed by his cryptic manner of speech and shifting moods.

Shivering slightly, she asked, "How have your people fared under Adinav's rule?"

Red winced, shook his head. Umera wasn't sure what to make of his response.

"Apparently the new blacksmith made weapons for his war, but no one's arrested him yet."

"Blacksmith?" Red tilted his head as he examined her face and playfully tugged at her short hair.

"Avn."

Suddenly smiling, he peered into her eyes. "Did you say Avn? Oh, I'm trying to stay clear of him." His fingers brushed the back of her neck, and he muttered under his breath, "Interesting game."

Umera's heart leaped into a frantic pace at his answer. "D-do you know him from the castle?"

"Fine, I'll play. What castle?"

Disappointed by his response, she sighed. Thoughts began to spin in her mind until he kissed her.

Tension slipped away, their clothes too. Swept into a suffocating heat, she clumsily intertwined her body with his. The world vanished. Their bodies grappled for control and finally found a mutual rhythm.

She felt a familiar expansion. Her body swelled. Her mind ballooned. The boundaries between their flesh vanished. She was as much a part of him as he was of her. She became wood and earth and air. Just beyond the elements, everything that made the world what it was, she sensed a vast emptiness and panicked. She struggled to regain the feeling of Ibe's body against hers, but the euphoria of her arousal eased her distress. The world melted, cascading into eternity.

When release burst inside her, the world rushed back into her—the small, tidy barn; Crank staring at her from the stall; the prickle of hay from the bale she had been flung across. She fought for breath as Ibe released his grip and stood.

"I don't know anything about you," she gasped. "You could be a demon, for all I know."

He laughed. "I'm not some fear cast-off." He stood tall and proud and naked in the barn. "Come on girl, you know me and I know you. This is what you've been wanting for so long, right? My sex? The game's been played now. Let it be."

"Game?" She shivered as his warmth receded.

His eyes narrowed on her. His jaw squared. "There's no one else around," he thundered. "We don't have to hide who we are."

She glanced at their nudity. Hoping to bring back the lightness of being which began to quickly fade between them, she mumbled, "Neither of us is hiding much of anything, are we Crank?"

Crank flicked his tail and looked out across the barn, disinterested and bored.

Regaining her senses, his words resonated in her mind. Excitement chilled her. Her stomach fluttered. She sat up on the bale and whispered, "You know me?"

"Of course I do!" He shook his head and kicked at loose straw on the ground. "You went missing. I thought maybe the reason why was something I had said. You don't always do what I say," he complained. "You're very difficult that way."

None of what he said made sense except that he knew her.

"I thought our Master coming here very odd." Ibe glanced over her from head to toe. "Can't say I understand why he keeps his distance. He must have a reason though." Snapping his head back, he strode around the barn floor. "It's been tough avoiding him. If he knew I was here—"

"I don't understand." Shivering, she reached for her dress crumpled on the ground. The strange man stepped toward her, and she froze. Desperate for some shield between them, she clumsily folded her arms across her breasts.

"If I knew you once, I'm sorry," she said, hoping to calm his temper. "I have amnesia."

Silence ensued. He stared at her, blinking profusely. "You're serious?"

She nodded abruptly.

"I've heard stories about this." He began examining her like she was a curiosity in Sabien's Exhibition. "Why hasn't he helped you?"

Since coming to the farm, all she wanted to do was find someone who had known her. Now she wondered if Yensilva, Elusis, and Milos had been correct to deter her from finding out about her past.

"If you mean Adinav, he's dead," she finally spoke. "You don't have to be afraid of him."

Ibe's lips curled into a sneer. "Who's Adinav?" His annoyance faded quickly.

She stiffened as he pulled her to her feet and embraced her.

"I know your past crimes were impetuous and somewhat despicable, but that's no reason for you to stay here in this condition," he said gently into her ear. "I'll take you home if he won't."

Writhing against his grip, she was about to tell him again about Adinav's death, until she felt herself begin to expand. This time there were no tingling sensations in her abdomen and loins, no soft caresses, just his muscles crushing her. Her breath no longer funneled through her nostrils and mouth but through her eyes and ears, through her toes and fingers, every pore within her flesh.

A strangled cry erupted from her as she felt the boundary between herself and Ibe dissolve. The cold air vanished. The barn floor beneath her feet faded. Her body began to crumble apart, determined to fill the vast emptiness beyond. Just when she thought she would disappear all together, she heard Ibe.

A long, drawn out wail curdled in his throat.

Her body returned and the world rushed back, bright and harsh and cold. She collapsed on the ground and glimpsed Ibe stumble. Shoulders sagging, he steadied himself against a post and pinched the bridge of his nose.

"Why can't I ascend?" He shook his head.

Umera scrambled to her feet and grabbed her dress from the ground. "What are you!?" Shielding her nakedness with the crumpled fabric, she ran from the barn. "Stay away from me demon!"

At the house, she fumbled and struggled her way inside. Once hidden beneath the blankets of her bed, the windows and doors of the house locked and secured, she trembled. Determined to remain awake until Yensilva returned, she wondered about the man Ibe and knew, deep down, he couldn't be a demon.

"He's too much like a human," she whispered to herself.

The man from the North knew her and, despite her fear, she realized he seemed very familiar too.

— 32 —

"DECIDED TO SHOW yourself?" Avn glowered at the form Ibe had taken in the world, a male human in his late twenties with unkempt rust red hair and little clothing. The morning sun had not yet risen, and Avn appreciated the shadows for cooling his rising temper.

"How could you know? I've avoided you until now." Ibe rubbed at the sparse hair of his bare, upper chest, as he leaned against the thigh high wood railing which fenced in part of the smithy yard. "Navigating Sunset House while you're there's even trickier."

Avn's lip twitched. "I sensed your presence."

"Can all Masters do that?" With a wandering gaze, Ibe muttered a charming hello at a young woman who strolled by the smithy, momentarily losing his focus.

"No," Avn grumbled. He returned his focus to a flat oval piece of glowing metal and felled a series of blows with a straight peen hammer. Sparks sprayed along the tapering edge of blackening metal.

"You'll need to wear a shirt if you're going to be around the anvil," he shouted over the din.

"If I catch a burn, I'll regenerate." Ibe's swift answer was followed by a short laugh. "That looks like an actual shovel blade. You'd think you were a real blacksmith."

A final hard strike clanged sharply. The hammer bounced in the air and settled against the anvil with a series of fading taps. Laying the tool aside, Avn dunked the glowing metal into a barrel of water. Curls of steam moistened his face and arms.

"Get inside!"

The bubbling, hissing water quieted as he withdrew the tong-clamped metalwork and set it on the anvil.

"Why so upset?" Ibe sneered. He remained where he stood, arms folded across his chest. "I'm not breaking any rules. I am allowed to be here. It's not my first choice of worlds to play in, but it is Ule's. I am her Mentor."

On a soiled leather rag, Avn wiped sweat and soot from his aching fingers. He bit his lower lip. "Now!"

Ibe laughed again, raising his hands in defeat. He pushed off the railing and scratched at his brown leather leggings. He turned toward the house, ducked through the open doorway, and began examining the inside—cluttered shelves, a narrow bed, and a long table littered with delicate tools and instruments.

"Did you know Ule has amnesia?" Ibe shook his head. "Of course you do."

Avn grunted. "Yes, for some time now." He glanced into the yard before pulling the door shut.

"You're punishing her again, aren't you?" Ibe rolled his eyes. "What did Smashcrow destroy this time?"

"I've asked you not to call her that." Avn leaned against a narrow counter and shut the doors to a tiny window overlooking the side street and explained, "She's not being punished."

"She should be for creating this world," Ibe declared, straddling a stool next to the table. "For something so basic as a 24-60-60 model, it's deeply flawed." He sat and spun around on the stool. Facing the table, he began sifting through a stack of handwritten parchments.

"I have been helping her with the fixes," he continued. "And I know she was kept in Isolation for a long time, but you'd think she would know how to contain her atmospheres by now. That's fundamental An mechanics."

"Enough!" The remark was strong and forceful, and Avn was grateful for his Student's silence.

Spinning back around on the stool, Ibe stared at him, both stunned and annoyed by the outburst.

"I always encourage your challenges and rebuttals in the Lyceum," Avn said. He fisted his hand. "But we're not in my hall and this, what we're doing, is neither a discussion nor a lecture."

Ibe stiffened.

A deep breath helped ease Avn's tension. Rubbing his jaw, he paced the floor. "Am I to understand that you've interacted with her?"

Still annoyed, Ibe nodded.

"Did you at any time call her by her name?"

"I don't see why that's—"

"It's important!"

Ibe huffed and sank against the edge of the table. His head rolled to one side. Quiet and sullen, he played with the concave glass of a small lens.

"We just talked." He remained fixated on the lens.

Avn leaned against the door, folding his thick arms across his chest. Soot from his leather apron smudged the pink burn scars along his dark forearms. His unfaltering stare finally urged the truth from his Student.

"I may have called her by her name," Ibe admitted, "but she called herself something else."

"Umera?"

Ibe nodded. "I thought she was playing so I played along."

"Neither of us can coerce her into remembering," Avn began to explain. "I need her to be as strong as *she* can possibly be. She needs to remember on her own, because it's the only way she'll regain and develop her skill and power. Any manipulation from the outside will interrupt that process and weaken her."

Loathe to saying anymore, Avn rubbed his jaw. His Student needed to understand the gravity of their situation. Reluctantly he added, "And she needs to remember before her body dies. The most we can do is protect her until her memory returns."

Disbelief contorted Ibe's face. "If she dies, she can deathmorph."

Avn's words were swift and terse like a series of jabs and punches. "If she has no memory of being Xiinisi, how will she know that she can."

Jaw clenched, muscles twitching, Ibe fidgeted. "Sound logic. I suppose that's why you're a Master." He forced a smile.

Avn sensed Ibe's lack of conviction and maintained a grim composure as he stopped pacing and leaned against the door to the smithy yard.

Ibe stood and bowed slightly, raking fingers through the hair on his head. "You know best how to handle Ule." He sighed and chuckled, eyes darting all over the house. "I would ascend to tend to other worlds, except when we, I... When I tried to ascend, the An Energy wouldn't respond—yet another flaw in her design!"

The frayed nerves and uneasy tone peaked Avn's curiosity. He pondered a moment before uncovering the truth behind Ibe's nervous behavior. "You tried to Ascend with her, didn't you?"

"I-I was just trying to help—"

Avn's fury raged. "Do you not remember any of your training?!"

Ibe tried to keep his calm, but his voice rose. "It seemed like you weren't helping her, so I tried." He scratched his bare chest, leaving behind marks in the flesh. "Thankfully all design, good or bad, responds to the mighty Masters, so if you wouldn't mind pushing me back, I'll be out of your way."

Avn winced, a scowl firmly fixed across his brows. His anger deflated as he dwelt on his own limitations.

"I can't." He unfolded his arms and stood upright. From a high shelf, he retrieved a tall, green bottle. He twisted the cork free from the neck, drank a long haul of the dark whiskey, and then offered the bottle to Ibe.

Accepting the gift, Ibe wrinkled his nose at the potent fumes. His neck tensed. "Why not?" He examined the bottle and quickly returned it without tasting the contents.

"There's a poorly conceived barrier scattering the An Energy," Avn explained. He gulped another swig of whiskey, nodded, and smacked his lips.

"A-are we trapped?" Ibe shivered.

"Absolutely, so unless you want to age or die prematurely, you best reserve regeneration for healing fatal wounds or deathmorphing. Let your body age naturally. Remember, time moves quicker here than in our realm."

Ibe began a series of calculations using his fingertips.

"At last count, I've turned twenty-two generations here," Avn told him. He ran his fingers over the knots in the base of his beard. "It'd be a lot less if I hadn't deathmorphed so many times."

Rubbing the back of his neck, Ibe retreated into his thoughts. "Why—why so many generations?"

"There's been a war here. A long war."

A frailty overcame Ibe, and Avn was at least grateful that something of what he told his Student was finally sinking in.

"But you've only been gone—" Ibe stopped himself, snatched the whiskey bottle from Avn and swigged the contents. Disgust distorted his face. In a raspy voice, he asked, "How long must we wait?"

"Ule created the barrier," Avn explained. "She has to be the one to dismantle it. That can't happen until she regains her memory. In the meantime, perhaps our combined strengths can find a way through it."

Umera peeled the thick green leaf away from the corn husk, trying very hard not to scratch the sticky blue paste in her hair, wondering if it was supposed to burn her scalp the way it did. Fine strands of pale yellow silk spilled over her fingers, reminding her of how her hair once looked.

She envisioned long blond hair falling over her shoulders, hoping the image might push her mind to remember everything: her past, her home, any family who might be strange like Ibe—not demons but Mystics perhaps, which seemed the only explanation for the odd event that occurred in the barn.

Once she had come to this realization and entertained the possibility that her kind might be Mystics, her fear toward Ibe eased. Polyglot. Mystic. Another element to who she once was—who she is—stirred the thrill of being on the verge of true self-discovery. Ibe had the answers she was looking for and she had searched for him when she visited the market to buy mutton earlier that morning. He knew her and he could help her. Yet, when she asked around, no one had seen him.

"Do you want to go to Sunset again?" Yensilva peeled each leaf till they hung from the end of the corn husk. "That Red, he's not fit to be a husband, if that's who you're thinking about." Twisting her wrist, she snapped the stalk, and the leaves came off all at once.

Umera shifted into sitting cross-legged on the ground. The position did little to ease the ache in her lower back or the cramps in her calves. Beads of sweat rolled down her face and arms, despite sitting in the shade next to the barn.

"No," she answered. "I'd rather just shower and sit by the fire tonight. Can't wait to wash out this blue paste from my hair before its dries and crusts."

"Ooh," Yensilva cooed. "I want to see how well the blue takes."

Umera slowly peeled another leaf, considering what Yensilva meant by what she said. "The blue paste washes out, right?" Her muscles tensed. "That's what you said."

"Yup."

She tried to relax, but she knew there was something she didn't quite understand.

"Once the paste dries," Yensilva began explaining, "it washes out and leaves a beautiful blue in your hair. Now you won't be prey to who's snatching blond women."

A searing blade of anger sliced through Umera's belly. Her throat constricted at its sheer intensity. No matter how desperately she tried to stifle the roiling energy, it found release through her actions.

She grabbed a corn husk from the sack next to her, wrenched each leaf with a sharp jolt until they tore free, and slammed them into the basket between her and Yensilva. Other leaves within the basket spilled out and scattered over the ground.

"Watch what you're doing," Yensilva scolded. "Bethereel's paying for *clean* full leaves." Her mood suddenly shifted and she smiled. "Oh, wait till you see her basket purses. They're divine—"

"I've had it with you and my hair!"

"Excuse me?" Yensilva sat stiffly, blinking. "It's the fashion."

"I don't care what the fashion is!" Umera scrambled to her feet, wringing an unshorn corn in both hands.

"But everyone follows the fashion."

"Bethereel doesn't!"

Nodding, Yensilva grimaced. "She's a little strange. I warned you about her. My uncle says she could really go far if she cut her hair."

"There will be no more dying," Umera began to rant, pointing the corn husk at Yensilva. "No more cutting, no more of that stupid honey."

Yensilva frowned, her voice trembling. "I thought you liked honey."

"You like honey! I think it's disgusting."

Yensilva shrugged. "You sure do drink enough of it," she mumbled.

"I stopped drinking it a week ago!" Already Umera was feeling the effects. Her mind was growing clearer, her body more energetic, and her pants less constrictive.

"That explains your mood," Yensilva commented.

A strangled cry erupted from Umera. She hurled the corn husk toward the field beyond the barn, but it caught the fence and toppled to the ground.

"You used to be a lot of fun," Yensilva said. She stacked the loose leaves which had spilled onto the ground and replaced them in the basket. "We'll discuss this tomorrow, when you're feeling better."

"No!" Umera stomped the ground with her right foot. "There will be no discussion. My hair, my way."

Yensilva frowned, yanking leaves from the last of the corn. "You can't wear a turban again, you'll sweat to death. And if it grows long again, you'll tie it back. I won't rescue you when it gets caught in the tools. And you won't be safe from whatever's snatching blonds." She slammed the last of the leaves back into the basket and some flew out again and fluttered back onto the ground. "What if someone recognizes you from the castle?"

Umera jumped up and down. "That's what I want!"

"They might lynch you."

"Nobody cares!" She began leaping in agitation around the yard. "If they did, Avn's head would be rotting next to Adinav's in the market for all the weapons he forged for the war." Breathless and relieved of tension, she collapsed on the ground. "Yensi, can't you see? Mostly people are grateful the war's over."

Yensilva picked at the kernels from the cob she cradled. She looked up, began to speak, and stopped. Squinting, she stared at her fingers. Again, she perked up and spoke. "But..." She shook her head. "Never mind." With a heavy sigh, she dropped the corn and proceeded to shuck the next one. Quiet and withdrawn, she slowly peeled back the thick green leaves.

Loud cracks shook the barn. Umera wearily watched Crank hind kick the back wall of the stall for the fifth time since she began cleaning and oiling the tools.

Crank's just a horse, she reminded herself yet somehow his sidelong glance and gentle huff felt like a frustration, possibly from working and being cooped up in the barn and having little companionship. Or possibly he needed to say what was on his mind.

"I hear you." She grunted as she pushed a wheelbarrow toward the space next to the stall and began stacking split wood.

The disappearance of the barmaid had sent Yensilva into a tailspin. She dyed her own hair completely blue and confined Umera to the farm until she agreed to let her hair be dyed again.

Umera refused.

With her only companion being the horse, she spent many quiet hours on the farm tending to vegetables and beginning the arduous task of turning over the soil in the completely harvested corn field. She too felt frustrated from working and being cooped up on the farm.

Crank kicked the back of the barn wall again.

She wasn't sure if the beast was trying to express himself, but she recognized the desire in herself for communication. To be heard. To be understood. For someone to listen and help her remember something about her former life.

She had talked with other merchants who had conducted frequent business at the castle, but none of them seemed to recognize her. For all her attempts, she was no further along in speaking with the only other person she knew who had worked for Adinav.

Days passed, each one the same as the last, and Umera felt herself fading into routine, becoming increasingly more anxious and unsettled. She wanted to kick a wall too.

The horse kicked the stall again, jolting her from her thoughts. She dropped a piece of wood and nudged it with her foot until it butted snugly against the others.

"Crank," she whined. "I don't understand."

Hand extended, she approached the horse. After he snorted at her palm a few times, she slipped into the stall and stared at him, not sure what to do. As he shuffled, an idea occurred to her. Reaching down, she patted the shin of his hind leg and was surprised at how willingly he bent his knee.

Grasping the upturned hoof with both hands, she examined the shoe. Tarnished and worn thin, it was encompassed with packed dirt. She nudged the edge of the shoe and a flake of corroded metal crumbled into her palm.

Bracing herself against the wall, she released the hoof and examined the other and found the shoe there even more worn. Touching the black triangle of tissue inside of the shoe, she curled her nose at the foul odor it suddenly emitted.

"Something's wrong with your hooves, that much I do understand," she said. She stroked his side and patted his neck.

Crank snorted.

"Can't let you roam the field or work till they're looked at."

She offered Crank an apple and ate one herself, enjoying its warm, sweet pulp. It filled her without feeling like a lump in her gut. Patting her belly, she paused to appreciate that her figure had started shrinking a little every day, for her clothes were beginning to loosen. The desire to climb out of her body and into another with less girth was also diminishing.

Tired, she brushed her pants and shirt free of dirt and bid Crank farewell. Outside, she sagged beneath the harsh sun and strode toward the stoop, remembering the lightness in her body the first time she entered the house, long ago when Yensilva brought her to the farm. Being slender, she realized, wasn't nearly as important as the buoyancy in movement it offered, and she wanted to feel that again.

Slumped over the counter, Yensilva furiously chopped a carrot into wide circles.

Umera reached for a full carrot. About to bite off the small end, Yensilva slapped it from her hand, and it tumbled onto the counter with a loud thunk.

"That's for the stew!" Yensilva huffed, resuming chopping the carrot to make more circles.

Umera stole a slice instead, shoving it into her mouth. She tried to stifle the crunch of her chewing by keeping her lips firmly closed.

"What are you today," Yensilva began to ask, "a rabbit or maybe a horse again?"

Swallowing quickly, Umera wiped her lips. "What's wrong with eating a carrot?"

"It's raw. Carrots are meant to be cooked!"

"Says who?"

Dour and frustrated, Yensilva stabbed the point of the knife into the cutting board.

"Okay," Umera conceded. "I'll eat your cooked carrots." She knew she could sneak any vegetable from the garden, if she wanted. The crunchy sweet flavor of green beans was her favorite. She just hoped the declaration of this sentiment, even if it was a lie, might calm Yensilva's agitated mood.

Thumps and cracks resonated in the yard and drifted through the open door and window. Lasting only a few seconds, the racket settled and the world resumed a soft chorus of drones, buzzes, clicks, and trills.

"What's that blasted horse trying to do, knock down my barn?" Balling her fists, Yensilva locked them to her hips.

Umera quickly snatched another piece of carrot and rolled it through her fingers. "His shoes are nearly worn through and his hooves smell like something's been rotting for a year."

"Are the frogs black?"

Turning around, Umera leaned against the counter. Struck by the unusual question, she remarked in a glib tone, "Frogs are usually green."

Color drained from Yensilva's face. "On the hoof!" Her voice cracked, her mouth puckered, and she began to tremble. "The mound on the bottom of the horse's hoof, is it black?"

"Yes!" Cringing, Umera inched away from the counter toward the door. Beyond arm's reach, she stopped and poised herself to run.

Yensilva lifted the cutting board and slammed it down on the counter. The knife tumbled to the floor and the clatter it made cued a flurry of curse words. Voice strained, energy diminished, she sagged against the counter and moaned. "Hazias is so expensive."

"What about Avn?" Umera offered nervously. The thought of an opportunity to interact with the man rekindled some hope in learning about her past—if only she were permitted to accompany

Yensilva to the market.

Inhaling deeply, Yensilva slumped over the counter and grumbled, "What about him?"

Turning over the disk of carrot, Umera softly replied, "You mentioned he was a farrier too."

Driving the knife into the cutting board, Yensilva left it there. It wobbled on its tip as she mumbled. "Yes." Turning about, she nodded. A smile slowly sweetened her sour face. "Yes, he is. Good on you for thinking finally."

Yes, she agreed mentally, ignoring Yensilva's slight. She was thinking. Her familiarity with Crank far surpassed Yensilva's. Who would be better to speak to Avn about his needs than her? While she spoke to the blacksmith about Crank, a few nonchalantly asked questions about Sondshor Castle might finally give her some answers about her past.

Briefly, Umera closed her eyes at the arousal of appreciation within. She loathed to think Crank's misfortune might provide her an opportunity to learn more about herself. She just needed to convince Yensilva to allow her to visit Avn.

Yes indeed, she was thinking, as she began formulating arguments to persuade Yensilva.

— 33 —

ORANGE LANTERN GLOW lit the alleyway. Dark shadows fell across the scrap yard. Avn scanned the barrels stuffed with pipes and metal bits and nodded briefly as a couple strolled by dressed in their evening best. Ducking back inside the house, he secured the double split door. Both half-doors held firm, so did the lock on the door to the smithy yard.

"And cover that too." He pointed to a window of tiny glass panes above the narrow bed, which was propped open by a tall stack of books.

"Aye," Ibe mumbled. He stuck his head through the opening and blinked at the cramped walkway along the side of the house, leading from the scrap yard to the smithy yard behind the forge. The wall of the barn next door was a little over an arm's length away, and there was very little space for more than one person to walk through at a time. "Whose going to see us from here?"

"You'd be surprised by how many people sneak in there to have a little fun."

"The sex." Ibe snorted. "Tell me about it." He closed the window and fastened the latch. "I forgot how having twice the nerve endings makes you want to fuck or drive your fist through anything that moves."

Avn grunted, agreeing with the sentiment, and tossed Ibe a scrap of black fabric.

Along the window frame, Ibe dragged the fabric across bits of splintered wood and tucked it into gaps between the frame and the wall.

"All the windows are covered now. No one'll see in." He jumped down from the bed and rubbed his hands together. "Let's get on with this."

In what little space existed, bordered by the bed, the worktable, and the counter and cupboards, Avn and Ibe faced one another.

Avn nodded. "Are you ready?"

"Yes, absolutely, whole heartedly," replied Ibe. "Anything to get us home."

He straightened. Immediately his arms and legs began to melt into his torso. Flesh and clothes darkened into a moving mass of liquid that hovered in the air. The liquid began dissipating into tendrils of smoke, writhing and turning into a tiny, slow moving tornado. Dust stirred in the corners of the room. On the table, loose parchments rustled and fluttered to the floor.

Smoke swirled out of the tornado, zigging toward Avn, and pushed into him, through his eyes, nostrils, and mouth. The swirling pulsed and wrapped around his body, which stood still, allowing the smoke to seep into his flesh too.

Inside Avn's form, two entities collided. The young, weaker one submitted to the older, more powerful one. Together they focused on expansion, with Avn directing their focus and intent. Space between the molecules within his body pushed further apart. Their perception of the smithy distorted, stretching and elongating, becoming smaller. The An Energy was nearly within their minds.

Like a curious fish that suddenly sensed danger, the An Energy stopped and whipped away in a flurry. The molecules in Avn's body snapped back to solid form. The force slammed him backward against a cupboard and knocked the door off its hinges. Black smoke gushed from his body into the house and began coalescing into something fleshy and human again.

Ibe rubbed his face then shook his head, blinking a few times.

"You killed the cupboard." His tone was grim, the words forced through clenched teeth.

Avn coughed. Rubbing his neck, he recovered his footing and brushed himself off. "Tell me, what did you feel while we were merged?"

"It started like it should." Frowning, Ibe shrugged. His shoulders twitched. "It disappeared like a mirage. What did you see?"

"Something is altering the behavior of the An Energy. Probably that barrier."

Hugging the edge of the work table, Ibe's fingers walked over the paraphernalia and settled on the peak of the long side of a large reflective prism. "Is it accessible at all?"

"It is." Retrieving the broken cupboard door, Avn set it down on the narrow counter. "I've met two people who have proved that, a Mystic and Adinav."

"There's that name again." Turning on the spot, Ibe stumbled, momentarily losing his balance. He clutched the prism to his chest as he carefully sat on the stool.

"He was a powerful man," Avn said, detecting the odd behavior of his Student. "So was the Mystic."

A shudder wracked Ibe. He rolled the prism over in the palm of his hand, watching lantern light reflect within the glass and from the surface of its facets.

"You must breathe, Ibe," Avn cautioned, but his words went unheard. Mentally he began evaluating the ticks and twitches, the mounting tension. A light sweat dampened Ibe's face and pale lips.

"H-how... How did this Mystic channel the An Energy?"

Curling his nose, Avn huffed. "Through small machines he created. They controlled lasers or magnified his perception until it transformed thought into other forms of energy."

A sour look overcame Ibe. "And Adinav, how did he do it?"

"Using Ule." Avn bit his lip. "This is disconcerting. I have to wonder how aware she was of her actions."

A silence settled over Ibe. His eyes darkened as he glared at the floor. "We can't just sit here!" Blinking, he shook his head.

"We must and we will," Avn commanded softly. His words were intended to be calming. Instead, Ibe began to fidget. "Once her memory's restored, she'll need to figure out how to access the An energy. The energy within the world is imbued with her signature and will only respond to her manipulation."

"I know that!" Ibe ground his jaws together. "Why aren't we

doing something?" His voice rose in volume with every word. He abruptly stood and whipped the prism across the room. The glass struck the upper half of the split-door and shattered.

"You need to calm yourself," Avn said gently.

Ibe spun around, his fists curled. "We might not be in the Lyceum, but under the circumstances, I'd like to have permission to vent."

"You're not venting." Avn braced himself as Ibe's eyes began to dart around the room frantically. He recognized the symptoms. The quick rise to anger, the shortness of breath, the dizziness.

"You're panicking," he said, "because you feel trapped."

Scrunching up his face, Ibe snarled. "I'm angry. I want to go home and I'd like to do something about it." He lunged forward and shoved.

Avn cringed at the blow to both shoulders. He fell back against the broken cupboard, the narrow shelves digging into his shoulder blades. In an instant, he recovered his stance.

The aggression. The need to escape by any means necessary.

"You've never been trapped before, have you?" Avn's throat burned as he kept his own frustration under control. He stepped into Ibe's space, stared into his fury. "It's called Cleithrophobia. It happens to all of us, because normally very little can confine us. It'll subside if you just focus on your breath—"

A long cry of anguish erupted from Ibe. He spun around and flung himself at the work table. Doubled over, his ragged breath quickened. He staggered back and with all of his might, lifted the stool and hurled it against the far wall.

Panes of glass in the window beside the half-split door splintered. The black fabric curtaining the window tumbled to the floor along with the broken stool. One of its legs remained lodged in the broken window.

Avn felt his temper rise. Before he could say anything to convince his Student to settle down, he felt sharp knuckles dig into the side of his jaw. He hurtled backward, crashing into the door to the smithy. A slat of wood splintered beneath his weight.

Wildness consumed Ibe. Avn knew there was no reasoning with him now. He tried anyway. "Calm down!" He braced his hands on Ibe's chest and shoved hard.

Ibe scrambled backward. "No!" Catching his breath, he lunged forward and threatened, "Let me out or I'll shift and make sure everyone sees!"

"You can't shift, not while you're in this mental state," Avn countered. "You're unfocused."

Anguish squeezed Ibe's face. Through clenched teeth, he demanded, "Let—me—out!"

"Not until I know you won't go looking for Ule." Avn dodged a second punch. Ibe fell through the force of his movement and into the shelves lining one wall. Candles toppled and books spilled onto the floor with clunks and thumps.

Ibe barreled head first into Avn, wrapping his arms around his broad chest. They wrestled, spun around, and locked ankles. Still grappling, Avn tripped first, falling across the work table.

Hard, sharp edges of loupes, lenses, and prisms cut into the flesh of his back. Sprawled on top of him, Ibe pinned his arms in place. Both struggled for breath as a long, loud creak reverberated through the house. Beneath them, the workbench collapsed.

Parchment scattered. Refractive lenses cracked and concave ones rolled across the floor. Ink wells tipped. Black smears marked books and parchment, as they rolled over the mess searching for domination over one another.

Avn locked his arm about Ibe's neck, hoping to secure him until he settled down. Ibe strained against his bicep and squeezed through. The sensation of losing grip on his Student caused Avn to shudder, for he dreaded what kind of damage Ibe might inflict in this state of mind.

Ibe jumped to his feet. Wiping perspiration from his face, he left behind a black smear on his cheek. He sniffed harshly and jutted his chin. "Going to tell me to calm down again?"

Slowly, Avn rose to his feet. "No." He curled his fists. The wetness of ink and blood along the backs of his arms and bare back made the hairs stand on end. "Let's do this the hard way then."

The fisted jab struck upward, catching Ibe beneath the chin. He slammed hard against the broken cupboard, rattling the shelves. A bag of lentils spilled onto the floor in a slow, steady stream. A bag of flour hit the ground and burst open. Clouds of white dust shot into the air.

Ibe shook his head and lunged forward. When he found nothing on Avn's dusty bald head to grab, he reached for his powdered beard and wrapped it about his hand several times. With a grunt, he swung Avn toward the smithy door and let go.

The wood splintered beneath Avn's weight but still held. The hinges and lock gave way. The door crashed to the ground near the anvil. Dirt jetted into the cool evening air, causing him to cough. Ibe knelt down to grab either side of the bib of Avn's leather apron and began hoisting him up.

Grinning, Avn relaxed his body and watched Ibe struggle with his dead weight. With the reflexes of a cat, he clasped his hands over Ibe's, drove his knee upward and felt him pitch forward.

Ibe rolled a hard somersault, his steel heeled boots striking the anvil with a sharp clang and releasing a thin cloud of dust into the air.

Both of them scrambled to their feet.

Avn was mindful of a small crowd forming just beyond the railing of the yard. He heard gasps as he grabbed Ibe by the mess of his red hair. Flour congealed where it mixed with perspiration, making his grip more secure, and he dragged Ibe toward the water barrel.

Ibe pried at his fingers. He found his voice. It was a tremulous, plaintiff cry. "No, no, no—"

Gurgles bubbled as Avn planted Ibe face down into the barrel. Water splashed over the rim as he fully submerged Ibe's head then let go.

Ibe snapped back, keeling backward toward the railing. He gasped for air. Wiping water from his face, he stopped and caught his breath.

"You know," he heaved, "that quite helped. Thank you. Thank you very much." Water sprayed from his nostrils as he shook out his hair, dousing a few nearby people in the gathering crowd. "I'm all better now." Ibe held up his hands in defeat. "Really."

Some glint of sanity had returned to Ibe's eyes, for which Avn was grateful. If it weren't for his own frustration, he might have willingly backed down.

"Be sure now." Avn sneered. "I'd be more than happy to go at this all night... if it helps make me—" He coughed. "*You* feel better."

Ibe shook his head, beads of water spraying in all directions. "All night?"

Nodding, Avn cracked his knuckles in both hands.

"That's a long time." Ibe jumped a few times, shaking out his arms. Curling his fists he raised them and hunkered down, eyes narrowed. "I could go another round or two, if you're game."

It wouldn't be the first time any of their kind made sport of fighting one another in the worlds they created, adopting the form and customs of the inhabitants to learn about power, leverage, strategy, and the many ways sentient beings limit one another with a system of rules.

"What about regeneration?"

Avn seethed at his Student's indiscretion. His muscles ached for release.

Ibe suddenly stood straight, his mood lightening. "Or we could just fuck!"

Tittering arose from the gathering crowd.

"Your pain," Avn replied, gritting his teeth, "is my pleasure." He squeezed his fingers tight. "Can't you see," he said, motioning to his fist, "how hard I'm getting."

The crowd erupted into laughter.

Stunned at first, Ibe huffed. "That would be a no, I see."

Avn dove forward, delighted at the surprise and worry which overcame his Student. He plowed Ibe into the railing, their combined weight snapping the wood railings from their posts.

A woman shrieked. The crowd parted as they tumbled into the street. In the flurry of their wrestling, Avn heard Ibe's request, his voice strained and muffled.

"Watch the face."

— 34 —

WITHIN THE SMITHY house, a gentle breeze from an open side window dispelled the stale air. Early morning dew and oncoming rain merged into an earthy scent, which Avn greedily inhaled as he removed what remained of the screws on the hinges of the broken cupboard door.

His knuckles twitched from fresh scabbing and despite the bruising along his arms and back, his muscles were relaxed. A deep satisfaction consumed him, and even more soothing, Sabien's agitated yet still lyrical voice floated across the room.

"Sunset'll be open soon."

Freed hinge in hand, Avn turned about. Sprawled across the narrow bed, Sabien lay propped on one shoulder, lips pinched, eyes narrowed. The orange shirt he wore glowed against his dark skin. He picked repeatedly at the end of a thumbnail, his agitation directed toward Ibe.

He tottered on the broken stool, which had been haphazardly repaired with nails and twine. A scrape ran the length of a forearm and dark purple bruises covered his collarbone and cheek. His lower lip was split and a wet scab glistened.

"Sorry, did you say something?" Ibe blinked profusely, feigning ignorance.

"Sunset," Sabien snapped. "It'll be open soon. Thought you might like to know, in case you wanted to be elsewhere." He stared at the broken glass, twisted metal bits, books, and parchments still littering the floor around the collapsed work table. Then his gaze fell briefly on Avn. "Go break things there," he mumbled.

"Eh?"

Sabien coughed and spoke louder, glaring at Ibe. "A good place for your kind."

Ibe smirked. "And what kind might that be?"

"The kind only drunks can stand."

The slight incurred a hearty laugh from Ibe as he stood. "Avn, what's so attractive about him?" He pointed toward Sabien and laughed again. Struck by an idea, Ibe stopped and snorted. "What's even more curious," he said to Sabien, "is why you're attracted to him?"

Sabien shrugged, ignoring Ibe's attempts at insult.

"He's different."

Avn frowned slightly at Sabien's comment.

"Still haven't figured out how yet," Sabien mused. "He's a lug of mystery. P'haps that's why he's attractive."

In the middle of the room, Ibe kicked aside a broken table leg and began to stretch, flexing his bare chest and arms.

At the sight, Sabien rolled his head to the side, leering at him warily. "You're such a cock-a-doodle-doo if you think the sight of *that*," he motioned to the bruises, "is attractive."

Belittled by the comment, Ibe clenched his jaw as he wandered over to Avn near the broken cupboard. Leaning over the counter, he said softly, "As soon as I'm alone, I'm regenerating."

"No," Avn projected his thoughts, inflecting an urgent tone. "You won't. It'll make people suspicious of you."

Scrunching his face, Ibe peered through the window. After a moment, he relaxed and announced, "Ule's here with her friend."

"Do you mean Umera?" Avn sternly corrected him. He glanced at Sabien and shook his head. "He can't get anyone's name right."

Sabien chuckled. "Is anyone even called that?!"

Through the slightly warped glass, Avn spied the two women just beyond the broken railing. Yensilva jabbed her finger toward Umera and barked orders, while Umera stood quietly, her lips parting occasionally to respond.

"I'll do the talking." Loud and clear, Yensilva's voice permeated the window glass. "You just listen. Not a word about the castle. No! You'll ask nothing of him, do you hear?"

The bed creaked as Sabien pushed himself off the crumpled blanket. He stood on the other side of Avn and ducked to peek through the window. "Oh, it's her."

"You've met Umera?"

Sabien shrugged. "I get around, but not like *him*." He motioned toward Ibe.

Setting the hinge down on the counter, Avn asked, "What do you know about her?"

"Besides being annoying?" Sabien shrugged.

"On that we agree," Ibe chimed. He turned away from the window.

Avn scratched his beard and said nothing.

"Elusis, from the textile shop," Sabien continued, "doesn't trust her at all, but then he doesn't trust you none either."

"Because of the war?"

Sabien nodded. "In secret Elusis spreads ideas about making those who worked with Adinav suffer."

"Is that how you feel?"

Scratching the birth mark on the side of his face, Sabien shook his head. "You might've forged weapons for Adinav, but I've heard the stories."

"What stories?" Ibe tried to participate in their conversation.

"About a smith slaying the risen dead," Sabien remained focused on Avn, "possessing bombs that could disintegrate the forests of Woedshor in an instant, how you defeated Adinav."

"I wasn't alone," Avn admitted but decided against mentioning Kaleel, the cat demon, who fought at his side.

"Consider the source," Sabien said. "Elusis thinks little of everyone, peering at everything through his whiskey eyes. And he was like that *before* he lost most of his family in the war." He pointed toward Yensilva, his finger lightly tapping the window. "She's his last relative."

In the yard, Yensilva primped her hair and smoothed her clothes while Umera sulked, staring off toward the distillery at the mouth to the Wares District.

Ibe let out a loud huff. "I'm bored."

Sabien turned about. Annoyance dissolved into anger, pinching and elongating Sabien's narrow features. Avn frowned, wanting to know what was souring his lover's mood. He turned and saw Ibe sprawled across the bed and propped up on an arm.

"Perhaps I'd be better off at Sunset for a while," Ibe said nervously, sitting upright.

Silence pervaded Sabien. Tight lipped, he subtly sneered.

"Perhaps," Avn agreed.

Rolling from the bed, Ibe inched around the table and unlatched the bottom half of the split door. He ducked beneath the lower half and shut it.

Relieved by his departure, Avn let out a long sigh.

"Miss him already? Was the fighting foreplay?" Sabien pointed at the bed. "Did you two... Did you want to be alone?"

Avn smirked. "No." He squeezed Sabien's shoulder and the gesture settled him a little. "Wait here a moment while I see what the girls want."

Sabien nodded quickly, slunk back to the bed where he sat with his back against the wall. He stretched out along the mattress and began picking at his thumbnail again.

"G'day, Yensilva," Avn said, entering the yard. He left the door open and braced himself next to the simmering forge. "And you Umera."

Umera was about to speak, until Yensilva jabbed her sharply in the ribs. "Never mind her," she told Avn. "She's being weird again today."

He cocked an eyebrow at the unusual description. "Weird?"

"Oh, she's just pretending to be a horse again," Yensilva explained. "Aren't you?" She jabbed Umera again.

Reluctantly smiling, Umera glanced sideways. Her cheeks flushed. In a dejected tone, she uttered, "Neigh."

Avn smiled. "Imagination's a powerful skill. You should try it yourself sometime, Yensilva."

Slightly blushing, Yensilva rocked back and forth briefly. The hem of her skirt swished around her calves. "Speaking of horses," she said. "What do you charge for your farrier services?"

"Worn shoes," Umera blurted angrily before Yensilva could stop her.

"Hers or Crank's?" Avn asked.

Yensilva tittered. "Handsome and funny too!"

The tension in Umera's face softened into a wince as she described the state of Crank's shoes and hooves. Her knowledge of the horse was detailed, the desperation in her eyes intense, and Avn wondered what she truly wanted to tell him.

"Bring Crank here tomorrow afternoon," he instructed Yensilva, assuring her his rate would be far more reasonable than what Hazias offered.

"Can I ask you something?" Umera's attempt to extend the conversation was met with a forceful pinch from Yensilva. Umera yelped and was about to speak again.

Avn's breath nearly stopped as he understood the source of her desperation. She had questions. She was curious. She was searching. He had sensed that she wanted to speak with him for a couple of months but hadn't seemed ready. He could tell by the way she drank and ate at Sunset—she either wasn't ready to look inward for the answers she sought or hadn't figured out how yet.

"No, no, no," Yensilva hushed her. She grabbed her by the arm firmly. Embarrassed, she addressed Avn. "We won't keep you from your business." She hauled Umera from the yard and prodded her toward the Wares District.

Uncertain of what had nearly transpired, he watched both women until they were engulfed by market goers. He returned inside the house and shut the door. Easing himself onto the bed, he gazed at the broken table.

Still somewhat irked, Sabien sighed. "What was that about?"

"The annoying one wanted to ask me something."

Sabien waggled a finger and nodded. "She's been asking around if anyone recognizes her from the castle." He rested his head against Avn's shoulder. "Do you?"

Quiet at first, Avn finally spoke. "I do. She was there when Adinav fell."

Bolting upright, Sabien's eyes widened. "She was close to him?"

Avn leaned back against the wall and waited for Sabien to begin spinning this thoughts.

Sabien gasped. "She must have been his lover," he surmised. "Perhaps even forced. I mean, who would willingly go downstairs with Adinav, eh? Poor thing. No wonder she has amnesia."

Imagination was Sabien's strength and skill, and he had an uncanny talent for accurately reading people and situations.

Avn lowered his voice and spoke close to Sabien's ear. "She was close to him in some way, that much I know. Not a word to anyone."

"I won't." Sabien shook his head. He secured his promise by kissing Avn with firm conviction. "I can say that, because no one believes my stories anyway."

⁂

Hoof clops echoed through the junction, a ghostly beat accompanying the peel of metal grinding against stone. Avn didn't bother to look up. He remained fixated on his work. Sparks flitted into the air and faded into dark ash, as the wheel of the whetstone spun against the blade of a long cleaver.

Snuffling and whinnying broke his concentration. Releasing his foot in mid-pedal brought the grindstone to a slow stop.

"Move him! You're too close to the forge," he bellowed.

Without hesitation, Umera tugged on Crank's reigns muttering an apology. Crank ceased his vocal complaints and shifted slightly until he settled into a comfortable stance farther away from the searing heat.

Umera stood in silent, patient waiting. She had changed over the past few months. She had been thick and heavy and now she appeared smaller. If not for the weight of weariness that sagged in the young woman's face, he thought she looked healthier.

"I asked *Yensilva* to bring him by this afternoon," he reminded her. "When the sun casts shade."

"I needed to bring him now." Umera smiled weakly. "While I had the chance to slip away without her stopping me. She's always up so early, but this morning she's the one sleeping off a hangover for a change."

"You want to ask me about Adinav, like you did the other merchants and soldiers?"

Biting her lip, she nodded briskly.

He set the cleaver aside. Lowering his voice, he spoke evenly. "Take him 'round back to the scrap yard. He'll stay calmer there."

She stood still a moment longer. "I think it used to be the front," she said, leading Crank along the road beside the house.

Seeking out clinchers, pullers, and a small rectangular blade, Avn waited until the woman had rounded the side of the house before he shook his head. "And yet you don't remember me."

In the scrap yard, Avn offered his palm to Crank, who welcomed him with a cautious lick. Setting a stool alongside the horse, Avn sat facing the hind end and instructed Umera to keep the beast as still as possible. On the other side of the horse, he heard her softly whisper, and Crank responded with soft hisses and gentle snorts.

Easing a hind leg to bend, Avn wedged an upturned hoof in his lap and began scraping away the dirt packed around the shoe with a knife.

"Do you remember me from the castle?" Her voice sounded frail and uncertain.

"He'll need new shoes," Avn announced, ignoring her question. "He's got a bit of thrush as well."

Scraping away at the black infection revealed healthy translucent, beige tissue just beneath the surface. With his fingers, he pressed the triangular mound on the underside of the hoof. Crank's hide twitched uncontrollably.

"It's not serious yet, but his frogs are sensitive."

Forlorn, Umera patted Crank. "I always tell him not to keep those kinds of pets. He never listens."

Avn snorted at her humor. "Yes," he said. "I remember you." He jabbed the packed dirt with the tip of the knife and began digging around the shoe.

"Do—" She coughed. "Do you know my name?"

"Is it that important?"

Though he couldn't see her, her tremulous tone hardened. "I like to think so. It's who I am."

Struggling to keep Crank's hoof still, he slipped the knife into an apron pocket and pulled out a small ball of thick string. Unraveling a length of it revealed evenly spaced black marks, which he used to measure the span of Crank's hoof.

"Who you are isn't predetermined by a label," he told her.

"Then what's a name for?" Her growing anger constricted her tone, sharpening her words.

He tucked the string away and released Crank's hoof. "A name's an introduction. A hint at what lies beneath the surface."

Confusion softened her face.

"Like the first two notes of a song," he continued. "A name, it identifies you but it doesn't define you. It won't tell you any more about yourself than what you already know."

"That's just it," she whined. "I don't know anything."

Standing, he pushed the stool away and began examining Crank's legs, running his hand over the muscles. "What's your favorite food?"

"Green apples," she replied reluctantly. "What does—"

"Do you like the rain? Which jokes do you laugh at? Do you run from danger or toward it? Who do you find attractive? What do you dream about?"

"I don't dream," she blurted. "I mean, I don't remember most of them. They fade as soon I wake. Will you please tell me my name?"

The sadness in her voice caused Avn to stop. He stared at her. Almost uttering her true name, he fought the urge.

Embracing her curiosity made her mind open and pliable. Anything he told her or planted there wouldn't be nearly as powerful as what she discovered on her own. And he needed her to be powerful.

"Crank'll have to stay here the night," he said instead. "When I've done with him, he'll need to be ridden and let loose to roam a little. He can't just stand in a stall all day or work."

Nodding, Umera's body sagged. Downcast, she withdrew from the conversation.

Avn grazed her shoulder with his scarred fingertips. "All you need to do is listen to yourself—your body, your thoughts and feelings, your instincts. They'll reveal everything you need to know about yourself."

She fell silent, as she stroked the horse's flank. After a few moments, she patted him, whispered something in his ear and backed out of the scrap yard alone.

"When should I return?"

"Tomorrow, in the afternoon."

Hope glimmered in her eyes, imbuing her with vitality as she turned down the side road which led to the foot bridges near the edge of town.

Soon, Avn thought, she would return soon. He wiped his hands clean, knowing he would wait however long it took for her to return to herself.

— 35 —

"HE REMEMBERS ME."

Umera flinched at the crack of porcelain against wood. Her elation plummeted as she eased carefully into the kitchen and saw Yensilva slam a second plate down on the table then return to the counter.

"I asked you not to bother him?" Her face twisted by anguish, her eyes puffy, she shuddered. "Why don't you listen?"

"I listen," Umera said softly.

Yensilva carved potatoes into large chunks and dropped them into a stew pot on the cookstove. Steam rose from the boiling water and reddened her cheeks. She stopped and looked up.

"Well?!"

The word stung like a punch. Umera shivered at the woman's widening, hardening gaze. "Well what?"

"Do you know your name now?"

"N-no," she sputtered. "He wouldn't tell me." She glanced downward, preferring the dark grained floor boards to the swelling veins across Yensilva's temples. "He told me I can learn who I am by listening to myself."

Yensilva laughed, the steel blade shearing through another potato and striking the cutting board. "If you listen to yourself the way you listen to me, that'll take forever." She scooped up the potato chunks and dropped them into the pot. "I don't know why I keep you around," she muttered.

Umera folded her arms across her chest trying to squeeze the rising anger back down inside. "I don't know why either. You're never happy with anything I do. I work the farm with you, do the chores you demand, tend to Crank—"

"With silly talk. Do you think the beast understands?" Yensilva grabbed handfuls of chopped carrot and flung them into the pot. Water sloshed over the sides, trickled down, and sizzled on the hot burner of the cookstove.

"Enough about the horse, Yensi," Umera groaned. "If I want to talk to a tree or a rock, I will."

"That's stupid!"

"It's my choice to make!" The anger climbed closer and closer to its peak. "So is wanting to grow my hair long or, or... run naked through the cornfield—"

"Nonsense! That would just... hurt." Yensilva paused and shook her head. "Why do you have to talk like that?" She reached for the knife. It slipped through her fingers and clattered onto the floor. Hastily, she bent, recovered the blade and wiped it on her skirt.

"What I wear," Umera tried to recover her train of thought, "what I eat and drink—"

Yensilva tsked.

Before she could interrupt further, Umera gushed in a fury. "When it comes to the farm, I do as you say. When it comes to how I style my hair, the clothes I wear, the food I eat, how I talk, who I talk to, what makes me feel good, that's for me to decide!"

"You're so selfish."

The absence of mirth in Yensilva's laugh caused a trembling through Umera. She had no way of knowing whether or not the comment was true or if being selfish was as terrible as what Yensilva seemed to suggest.

"I don't tell you what to wear or eat or who to be friends with—"

"Oh ho, I'd like to see you try." Yensilva laughed again, and what mirth she mustered this time felt like a dare.

"I forgot!" Umera tapped her forehead. "What makes you feel good is controlling me."

Yensilva drove the tip of the knife into the counter, overcome with disgust. "You're so ungrateful," she complained. The knife stood upright for a moment then began tipping slowly beneath the weight of the handle. "I take you into my home—"

"Why do you do that?" Curling her fists, Umera clenched them to her sides, hoping to hide them in the folds of her work shirt.

"Do what?"

"Change the subject. Try to make me seem... stupid? Is that it?" Umera huffed. "As long as I don't know any better, I'm easier to push around. Do you think that'll control me anymore?"

"You don't know what you're talking about?"

The fury surfaced. The rage seethed. Heat flushed Umera's cheeks. "Just because I don't know my name doesn't mean I'm stupid and it doesn't give you full reign over my existence."

A sullenness overcame Yensilva. Her dark, hardened eyes glared across the kitchen. The thick of her neck sunk between tense shoulders.

"Only I can know what my needs are," Umera continued ranting. "And how to make sure they're fulfilled, and a lot of them don't have anything to do with you!"

A strangled, cry erupted from Yensilva. Storming through the kitchen, she flung herself through the open door.

In the ensuing quiet, Umera heard the pulse of her heart rapidly thump in her chest, throat, and head. This time, the anger hadn't made her feel ill. Instead, she felt like she had run through the cornfield naked. It was exhilarating, just as she imagined, and a little painful.

"Why the fuss over this world?"

Silent and focused, Avn sat on a stool next to Crank, the beast's hind hoof carefully folded back and wedged between his thighs. He dragged a long rasp over the sole, smoothing out the uneven growth. He wished Ibe remained quiet.

Ignoring the light drizzle of an overcast morning, Avn admired the glistening flat stones and the layers of echoes drifting along the roads and converging at the corner near the house.

Breathing heavily, he stopped for a moment and was about to speak when a tall figure emerged from beneath the overhang of buildings just beyond the barn next door. Bethereel glided along the lane, strolling by the scrap yard.

Dressed in a long red dress today, her hair wound in long curls, she seemed unaffected by the fine mist which clung to her. Arms laden with corn husk basket purses, she smiled warmly at both men.

"Bethi." Ibe nodded, acknowledging her as Crank's tail flicked across his face. Remaining unaffected, he blinked profusely and plucked a tail hair from his lower lip.

She laughed softly, bid them both a good morning, and turned right along the road leading toward the smithy yard and beyond that, the Wares District.

"If I remember correctly," Ibe called after her, "it's quicker to your place through the Food District." He pointed to the third road.

Bethereel stopped. "It's less of a stench this way."

"But you're getting all wet?"

She shrugged and smiled, resuming her stroll.

Once she had passed the yard, Ibe scratched his nose. "I like her," he mused. "I'm not inclined to get attached to our creations, but she's different. Can't quite put my finger on why."

Avn swapped the rasp for a knife and began carefully scraping away the rest of the black infection from the hoof, mindful of how often Crank twitched or flicked his tail.

"Other than her, this world's pretty bland. Seriously," Ibe resumed his previous thought. "The way you and the other Masters have droned on about this place—"

"Keep your voice down."

A twitch ran through Crank's hide along his spine.

Retrieving the rasp from his apron, Avn grunted as he filed the hoof into a level, smooth plane. "I'm surprised you haven't noticed."

"Noticed what?"

"What makes this place special." Avn paused. Glancing upward through the drizzle, a grimness came over him. "Demons walk the Root Dimension."

All expression drained from Ibe. He stared blankly for several moments. He wiped his face of moisture. "Demons?"

Avn shifted the hoof between his thighs. "Haven't you seen any?"

"The locals have been keeping me busy." He whistled long and hard. "What do they look like?"

"Like the object people fear and some of them have pushed their bodies into humanoid form." He ran his fingers over the hoof, checking for any snags in the tissue.

"They're corporeal?"

"Several thousand generations from now, they could be indistinguishable from humans. What's worse, some have powers, and I've met humans whose focus of perception resembles our own." Avn resumed filing the edges around the hoof smooth.

"Remember the Magnes I mentioned earlier, Adinav?" Avn's breath grew heavy again from the exertion of keeping the hoof still and sliding the rasp back and forth. "Since he was a boy, he could see the An Energy the way we do."

"So you say," Ibe challenged him. "There might be another interpretation for what you observed."

Halting in mid stroke, Avn caught his breath. "I witnessed his ability first hand, watched him tear a hole in the fabric of this world."

Surprised, Ibe shuffled his feet and muttered, "I thought those were errors in Ule's construction."

"You've seen tears before?" Avn slowly glided the rasp over the hoof. His mind began exploring the possible meaning of such a phenomenon.

Nodding profusely, Ibe agreed. "Nothing more than expressions of weak architecture. Lattices of An Energy running parallel to one another tend to sheer away, so I showed Ule how to interlace them instead."

"And you didn't think to mention these errors to me?"

"Of course not," Ibe said. "Why would I bother you with her poor skills in fundamental manipulations when I could teach her just as easily as you."

Wiping a sweaty hand on his apron, Avn furrowed his brow. "And who inducted you as Master?"

Sputtering for words, Ibe shook his head.

"You're a guide, not a teacher," Avn reminded him.

"It's rudimentary knowledge," Ibe nearly shouted. "My other Students could teach her!"

Dreading the need to debate with his Student over the finer points of Xiinisi social hierarchy, Avn set aside his concerns about Ibe's ability to Mentor. Instead, he focused on more pressing concerns.

"So teach me, Master," Avn began. "Tell me about the first phenomenon to occur near the end of any world's First Age."

"The Chthonic Dimension evolves out of the Root Dimension, and they separate from one another."

Avn detected Ibe's impatience with the subject matter, but they both needed to understand the nature of the world if they were to ever figure out a way back to their realm.

"And the demons pass over to the Chthonic Dimension, right?"

"Yes, yes." Ibe waved his hand in annoyance. "Because the An Energy begins to recede beyond regular perception. This is natural evolution, a by-product of manipulating the An Energy when we cease creating the core world. Everything... separates."

Steering clear of Crank's flicking tail, Ibe skirted the horse and pleaded his case. "Doesn't this prove Ule's incompetence?"

"Incompetence?!" Avn released the hoof from his lap.

Crank shifted to redistribute his balance on all four legs again.

"If it was my world," Ibe insisted, "I would have fixed it."

"It isn't your world," Avn said calmly. He stood and stretched his shoulders. "Somehow," he continued, "Ule's affected an important developmental stage that's not supposed to be within our power to influence."

"If it were my wor—"

"It's not your world," Avn growled. "It's not mine. It's Ule's!" He leaned toward Ibe, curling his fingers and releasing them before he made fists.

"W-why so angry?" Ibe tried to laugh but stopped when he saw that Avn did not share his mirth.

"I've been here far too long," he seethed. "I'm tired. Wasn't that clear enough for you in our brawl the other night?"

"Okay, okay."

Avn rubbed his face, weariness making his bones ache. "I know you coerce your students, Ibe, to convince them to do what you want."

"That's what teaching is."

"You misunderstand. Teaching is theory, fact, and debate. You—" He poked Ibe in the chest. "You're supposed to guide them in their application of the knowledge within *their* vision, not within yours. What will they ever learn about themselves if they create worlds informed by your mind, emotions, and bias."

"All I'm say—"

"That's the entire purpose for our being—to learn about

ourselves. We share similarities, we're connected, but we aren't interchangeable. We all have something unique to offer each other. Collectively, we will see more and understand more of everything if everyone looks through more than one kind of lens." Avn gritted his teeth. "If you continue like this, dominating your students, you'll never make Master."

"So what am I supposed to do?" Tension coursed through Ibe. He tapped his foot nervously, digging his fingertips into his arm. He sneered at no one in particular.

Crank sidled away from him, tail flicking side to side.

"Figuring out where you end and others begin would be a good start," Avn suggested. "And stop underestimating Ule. We need to focus on what we observe," he explained, "instead of calling a new phenomenon an error when it doesn't conform to our expectations of what we already know. This world isn't about us; it's about her and what was going on in her mind while she created it during Isolation."

Around them, the market darkened. Elderly men shuffled along the lanes, carrying tiny lighter lamps in hand. Silently, they began lighting the street lanterns, stopping occasionally to chat with one another.

Shoulders sagging, Avn pinched the bridge of his nose. "What do we know?"

Ibe shrugged. "The Chthonic Dimension didn't form."

"I disagree."

"Of course you disagree." Ibe flung his arms in the air.

Avn snapped his attention toward a group of townies, who stopped and lingered in the lane. He shoved the split door open and yanked Ibe into the house.

"We know demons are corporeal." Avn kept his voice low until he shut the windows. "My thought is the Root and Chthonic dimensions haven't separated. They're occupying the same time and space."

Ibe sunk onto the stool next to the work table. It wobbled slightly under his weight, so did the work table. Between a ten tiered loupe system and a fire lens, he discovered a quill. Playing with it, he splayed the fine nib by pressing it hard into the table.

"Normally the An Energy recedes from sensory perception," Avn continued, leaning against the cupboard. "There is always a small handful of magic makers who spend lifetimes sorting out how to make a pebble float, but here, some of the people are keenly perceptive and powerful."

He peered over his shoulder through the tiny glass panes of the closed window overlooking the smithy yard. Orbs of orange light lit the market and he watched the familiar gait of his lover stride along the road before the distillery.

Cleanly shaved, dressed in pressed cobalt slacks and collared shirt, Sabien dodged a group of sullied farmhands stumbling toward the Food District. Nearing the smithy, he spied Avn through the window. He nodded but Avn purposely looked away. When their eyes met again, he signaled to Sabien to wait.

Sabien stopped in mid-stride. Smile fading, he retreated to the porch of the distillery and occasionally glanced back toward the smithy as he examined jugs of rum set out on a table.

"Let's examine the magic system here. Who are the magic makers here? Witches? Wizards? Sorcerers?" Ibe snapped his fingers. "Shamans! Am I right?"

"None of those," Avn replied. He turned back toward Ibe and squinted. "The only magic makers are the Mystics, and they harness their power through meditation and scientific methodology—some elaborate fusion of transcendental magic, alchemy, and what they've figured out about the physics of light and energy."

"Really, all that?" Ibe muttered and slumped on the stool.

"Then there are the demons," Avn continued. "They don't make magic, they possess it or it possesses them somehow." He folded his arms across his chest. "And how about you? What have you observed since you've been here?"

Ibe swiveled about on the stool. "Sex."

Not at all surprised by the answer, Avn laughed. "What about it?"

Shrugging, Ibe's answer sounded more like a question. "It's always good."

"No, what have you learned about the world by exploring it?"

"I'm not sure how that's going to help." Ibe stood and began pacing around the room. "Let's see. This species has gender differentiation, which is by far the most common genetic dispersion pattern, but not the only pattern, to exist in nature to ensure procreation and the continuation of species."

After a deep breath, Ibe continued. "Socially gender differentiation tends to evolve primarily toward a heterosexual culture." He paused. Tilting his head, he thought a moment before speaking. "There is a very prominent culture of pleasure present here. Usually, when it comes to sex based on attraction and arousal, all orientations manifest—hetero, homo, omni—and along with these differences, their own subcultures. *Usually.*"

"And it's different here in some way?"

Ibe smiled cheekily, "At Sunset, I've seen a man go home with two girls one night and a man the next. Everyone has nearly done it with everyone else. They have curious libidos, show neither shame nor celebration regarding their encounters. It's as though they have one culture of sex, and it is the inclusion of all orientations."

"Or they've no orientation at all," Avn mumbled.

Ibe laughed, sneering at the suggestion. "That would make them like us."

Avn stared at the floor. He considered other ways in which the world's inhabitants reminded him of his kind—keen perception, the blending of magic and science, fluid sexual orientation. He saw the correlations, and coldness crawled over his flesh. His heart stilled.

Or, he thought, they're evolving to become us.

Cocooned in a thin cotton blanket, Umera sat in her usual lumpy chair, eyelids heavy. The sound of her own snore jolted her awake.

"Yensi?" She called out and heard only intermittent snaps and pops from the mound of growing ash inside the hearth.

Moonless night had settled over the world, hugging forest and farm. Inside, embers flickered dimly, their simmering heat failing to keep the room warm.

Next to her, Yensilva's chair remained empty, the door to her bedroom ajar.

Anger still pulsed within Umera's chest, refusing to diminish. Willful and strong, the feeling created an overwhelming sense of security and assuredness. She likened the sensation to the ramparts protecting the castle of Sondshor, and mentally reciting remnants from their argument over and over only reinforced those protective walls.

She wanted to alter their exchange until she realized that if she expressed herself in any other way, it would have been a lie. That dishonesty, even if it meant making Yensilva happy for a moment, would have weighed Umera down with a lingering, lasting sadness.

She hadn't the strength or energy to lie anymore.

She considered apologizing to Yensilva, but anger persisted, urging Umera to remain strong and steadfast.

Still, she worried.

Yensilva had not returned.

"She's at her uncle's," she mumbled. "Staying the night to cool off."

The flickering embers eased Umera into a trance, her mind becoming blank—a dark, never ending space where inky black strands shimmered and thrummed beyond her reach. Her eyelids closed, and she sank into sleep.

She moved through a dreamworld which segued and twisted swiftly, making it difficult to hold onto any particular image. It had been so long since she dreamed that it felt like a new experience.

Then she floated beyond them, watched each dream contract into a tiny sphere of moving images, one followed by another. Like pearls on a necklace, dreams streamed passed by her in a vast, dark place.

A voice called to her.

Beyond the stream of dreams, a blue flame flickered.

The strangeness of the place unnerved her. "Who are you?"

The flame bowed briefly. "A man once called me Lucens. It's a good name, isn't it?"

"Can I call you Lucens?"

"If you want."

Umera paused, uncertain why she needed to speak to the fire. "I am U—" She choked and tried again. "I'm U—"

"*Oo* are who *oo* are." The flame snickered.

Umera wanted to reach across the stream and swat the flame, but she fell into a dream instead. She stood in a vast veld where tiny foot paths made of stone wound across the land. When she moved toward them, the paths recoiled, refusing to be trod upon no matter how much she tried.

"Fine, I won't bother then," Umera complained.

As she began to make sense of the imagery, she woke and remembered for the first time, she had dreamed.

— 36 —

ROOSTER CROWS ECHOED throughout the early morning, prying the world from deep sleep. Umera moaned, shifted to her left side, and slept well past regular breakfast.

Rising slowly, she stretched her limbs and nearly slid out of the chair. Her stomach growled, and she stopped to appreciate the empty sensation. She hadn't felt hunger in a very long time.

"Yensi?" Her voice hitched from dryness. Licking her lips, she peered through the open doorway into Yensilva's bedroom, hoping to glimpse her friend tucked deeply beneath blankets sleeping off a night of drinking at Sunset.

The bedclothes were neat and tidy.

Pushing herself upward, Umera wondered why she hadn't been awakened. Potatoes and carrots needed to be pulled. Fleshy red tomatoes threatened to snap their vines, and she wanted to lay down fresh hay in Crank's stall before she retrieved him from the smithy.

"Yensi?" She called louder this time.

Outside, she scanned the bare cornstalks which had begun turning golden brown. Insects fluttered over the vegetable patches. None of the land had been touched yet this morning.

She ducked her head inside the shower stall, walked the perimeter of the house and the farm. Breathless, she returned to the main yard where she glimpsed the door of the house ajar. She ran, her feet skipping over the front step.

"Yensi!"

Again no answer.

She searched the rooms again, even her own, but Yensilva was nowhere to be found.

The fashion district welcomed Umera with its calm, reserved atmosphere. She squeezed through narrow alleyways, grateful to be avoiding the throng of the food district. She had visited Elusis's shop and home once, where she had waited patiently outside and wandered a little, while Yensilva delivered several loaves of her nut bread and an apple pie.

In this part of Sondshor Market, weathered wood and chipped brickwork revealed this district to be the oldest. Buildings had been built onto over time, like Sunset House, and blotted out parts of the sky. Though attempts to paint and whitewash the storefronts helped give the core of the district a pristine appearance, the soot stained brick alleyways smelled of ash, indicating a great fire had consumed the market long ago.

Store fronts displayed fabrics and clothing draped in austere artistic ways, except for the hat shop, which displayed an assortment of tiny ladies pork pie hats arranged in a blazing rainbow across its main window. If not for the original appearance of the hat shop, she would not have remembered the location of Elusis's shop.

Passing an alleyway, she stopped before the first porch and

climbed the steps. The door creaked as it swung inward, setting off a cluster of tiny bells fixed to the ceiling inside. Her heart clenched at the sound. She had hoped to be discreet.

Inside, she gaped at the narrow aisles which carved tiny paths through towering piles of fabric bolts. She was struck by the division of color. On her left, a collection of cool colors were kept separate from warm colors on her right.

Carefully, she craned her head and saw a couple of old women clawing through a box of zippers. Searching for Elusis, Umera ambled toward the back of the shop. Finely tailored suits and dresses hung from hooks on the walls. They filled each wall from floor to ceiling, and she half expected one of the suits near the counter at the back of the shop to suddenly move and reveal itself as Elusis.

"Elusis?"

Umera paused at the counter. She noticed a partially opened door behind the counter and from beyond, he replied.

"Coming, coming."

Dressed in pinstripe trousers and vest, a white shirt crisply pressed, Elusis emerged from the doorway carrying a small roll of wide black lace. Despite his cleanly shaved face and combed hair, Umera noticed his red rimmed eyes and the smell of sweet whiskey mingling with cologne.

He set the lace down on the counter and began unraveling it, using the distance between his wrist and elbow to measure the length. "What do you want?"

Umera dreaded what she would say. She knew she preferred people's honesty above all else. Finding her voice, she told him the truth. "It's Yensilva. We had a fight."

He sniffed haughtily. "We discussed the matter last night. She told me what you'd done."

A wick inside Umera ignited at his accusatory tone. Like Yensilva, he had no interest in inquiry or considering a viewpoint other than his own. She wanted nothing more than to be gone from the man's presence before her anger detonated.

Elusis cut the lace and carefully folded the measured piece. He waved it toward one of the women and placed it on the end of the counter.

"I never meant to hurt her," Umera said.

He winced then rubbed his eyes. "What matters is she has friends. Real friends who treat her well."

Umera bit her tongue.

He shook his head and huffed. Jaws clenched, he glared at her. "I questioned her about inviting you into her home. She wanted to help you." He smacked his dry lips as he looked about the shop.

Umera doubted the sentiment. If anything, she realized, Yensilva wanted help with the farm so she could have a social life. Yensilva wanted—no, she needed—companionship, someone to share memories with and not just mead.

"And I'm grateful."

"Are you?" Elusis sneered again. "What would your kind know about that?"

Confused, Umera shifted. The hardwood beneath her feet creaked.

"You know what I mean." He pointed a finger at her. "Adinav's folk. You. The blacksmith. There's a certain charm about him I can't explain. You've got it too." With a labored breath, his eyes scanned the shop again. "Everyone likes him but they don't see him the way I do. They forget what Adinav did."

Elusis straightened as the old women approached the counter. Zippers and thread in hand, they placed them next to the lace on the counter and waited until he tallied the cost. Pleasant and amicable, they paid their bill and bid him farewell. And when they turned to leave the shop, they cast Umera dour looks.

"Magic," Elusis continued, ignoring the chime of bells above the store door as the women departed. He stepped back, pulled out his flask from his back pocket, and unscrewed the cap.

Whiskey fumes tickled her nose.

Downing the thick liquid, he winced and let out a slow breath. "He knows the magic, uses it on people. He must. And you!"

She stiffened. "I don't know how to do magic—"

"You're no different from him, bewitching my Yensi." He swallowed a second mouthful with a sharp toss of the head. "You and that smith aren't to be trusted."

"I-" Unaccustomed to such hatred, she caught her breath, struggling to keep her rage in check. The wick had nearly completed burning. Wringing her hands, she stood abruptly. "I just want to speak with Yensi."

"Then go speak with her!" He waved her way. "Stop wasting my time."

Unfamiliar with both his shop and home, Umera glanced around the store and saw an open door behind him. She pointed toward it. "Is she awake then?"

"You'd know better than I." Elusis downed a third swallow of whiskey and screwed the cap back on the flask. His cheeks flushed and his eyes glazed over.

Dread doused her anger. Her pulse quickened. "Isn't she here?"

"She left last evening while it was still light outside." He rapped his knuckles lightly on the counter. "Probably went to Sunset to let off a little steam."

"She didn't come home last night."

He laughed. "Good for her."

"It's not like her to not want to sleep in her own bed," she told him. Panic began to rise inside her. "No matter how drunk, she always prefers her own bed."

Elusis seemed not to understand her, as he emerged from behind the counter and made his way toward the store front. He eased the door open and stood outside.

She threw herself down the aisles, nearly knocking over a few bolts of fabric. Outside, she nearly shouted. "Don't you care?"

He sneered. "I don't know why you're trying to scare me. Is this is a prank?" He reached into his vest pocket, pulled out a watch, and examined it.

She gasped. "Scare you?"

Glaring, he jabbed a finger into her shoulder. "Yes, you alarmist. Yensi's probably passed out at Sunset. Why she likes that place—"

"But she's missing—"

"Stop it!"

Umera shook her head. "No, you're right." She conceded, silently seething. "She could be at a friend's place. Do you know where Bethereel lives?"

Half snorting, half coughing, he shook his head. "What business would Yensi have with Bethereel? She hates her."

Umera rubbed her forehead. Her brain ached. "I'll look for her." She touched the stiff cuff of his shirt. "I'll tell you as soon as I've found her."

He shook her hand free and shambled down the alleyway between his shop and the hat store, heading toward the Food District.

When he had turned and vanished out of sight, Umera ran in the same direction, mindful of how hard her feet slapped against the stone. The alleyway narrowed slightly at the back of the building belonging to Elusis. As she rounded the back end of the building, she nearly screamed when a tall figure in blue stepped out of the shadows and shut a door.

"Bethereel!"

The woman laughed. It was gentle and sweet. "What's your hurry, Umera?"

She frantically caught her breath, inhaling Bethereel's soapy perfume. "Have, have you seen Yensi?"

The woman shook her head.

"When did you see her last?"

Eyes turned upward, Bethereel thought a moment. "Last night, shortly after dinner, lingering on her uncle's porch. Is everything all right?"

"I don't know." Umera's thoughts began entertaining horrible situations. She knew in her heart Yensilva would not stay the night in Sunset House when the place had no proper beds. "She didn't come home last night."

Bethereel tilted her head, suddenly concerned. "Do you think something's happened to her?" She paled and her soft lips parted in a gasp. "Do you think she's disappeared, like the others?"

"I don't know. Would you ask around if anyone's seen her?"

"Absolutely."

Umera slipped past her and emerged into the food district. Fish guts and cabbage assaulted her nostrils. Pushing through the crowds, she arrived at Sunset House where, table by table, she asked the patrons if anyone had seen Yensilva.

A few commented on seeing her lingering around the fashion district but no one had seen her since.

The panic returned, a slow steady churning of anxiety building in her chest. Randomly she began asking people in the market if they had seen Yensilva. After her desperation subsided a little, Umera realized most of the market goers had traveled from far away places and had never heard of anyone named Yensilva.

"G'day Umera. Come for Crank?"

Swiveling around, Umera stilled her riling thoughts and focused on her whereabouts. After inquiring at Sunset House, she had continued toward the outskirts of Sondshor near the junction. She stood near the smithy and saw Avn tossing pipes into a barrel filled with other bits of metal.

His bronze flesh was slick with sweat, his apron layered in fresh soot, and he motioned to Crank. The horse tossed his head back at the sight of Umera and shifted about the yard.

Remembering how Yensilva flirted with the man, she rushed toward the open half-split door and peered into the house, hoping to find her friend stuffed into his narrow cot, content and peaceful. Instead, she discovered the storyteller, Sabien, stretched out beneath a disheveled quilt while flipping through the yellowed pages of an old book.

She slumped against the house. "Have you seen Yensi?"

"Yesterday." Avn nodded toward her. "With you. I expected her today. Since you're here, take Crank and I'll settle the account with Yensilva another day."

He whistled at Crank, who ceremoniously sniffed him and nodded. The horse was antsy, unable to contain himself, as Avn unfastened the reigns and handed them to Umera.

She regarded the leather straps dangling from her hand. Gaping at everything around her, she searched for any glimpse of her friend. Something stirred in the doorway to the house. When she looked, Sabien leaned there, dressed only in leggings, and bit into an apple.

She felt the warmth of Avn's hand press into the back of her shoulder, and she heard him ask, "What's wrong?"

His intense stare intimidated her. "Yen-Yensilva might be missing."

The soft slurps of Sabien's chews ceased. "No!"

Avn searched her eyes, perhaps to assure himself of her being truthful. "Are you sure?"

Shaking her head, she glanced briefly up at his rigid posture. "We had a fight. She ran off and didn't come home last night."

"Perhaps she's at her uncle's."

"I just visited Elusis." She smiled weakly. "She was there last evening but left while it was still light outside. And..." She bowed her head again. "He doesn't believe me, thinks I'm playing games with him."

"The man's an ugly drunk," Sabien said.

Avn nodded. "The only thing he believes in is liquor." He curled Umera's fingers about the reigns. "Take Crank, search the fields between here and the farm. Sabien and I'll ask around the market. Somebody must have seen her."

Avn braced his hands and offered to hoist her onto the horse. With a deep sigh, she slipped her sandaled foot into his grasp and marveled at how easily he lifted her.

She steered Crank away from the food district and down the lane leading toward the outskirts of the market. Clops slowed to a halt at the peak of a footbridge, and she peered down into the ravine below.

Fine cracks forked across the ancient riverbed, and rattlesnake weed climbed the steep walls. Near the main road, a decrepit wagon lay abandoned. Except for a few broken crates, Umera saw no one lying injured or dead.

She retraced the path Yensilva always took, scanning the tall grass and calling her name. All she found was an old rusty hoe and a dead rabbit.

Back at the farm, Umera sent Crank to the field mindful that he required time to roam, and she searched the house, the barn, and the decaying cornfield for the second time.

At first the kitchen seemed silent until tiny sounds merged together. Hunkered over the kitchen table, Umera focused on the constant noise. It grew louder and louder, beginning with the faint squeal as her fingernail dragged along the plate set out for yesterday's midday meal. Behind her, flies buzzed around heaps of glistening carrots in the abandoned stew. Outside, starlings squabbled over grubs in the yard next to the rainwater basin.

Umera longed for a door slam or the smack of the knife against the counter to interrupt the din. Even one of Yensilva's testy huffs would have lifted her mood.

"This won't do." She shook her head at the disarray. "Yensi'll come back when I least expect it, and she'll screech at me for leaving a mess."

She gathered up the clean plates, returned them to the cupboard and wiped the counter clean of stray carrots, beheaded celery greens, and curled potato skins, which she tossed into the stew pot. Grabbing the pot by its handles, she lugged it from the counter, mindful not to slosh the spoiled broth all over herself.

Lumbering toward the doorway, she set out a plan in her mind to wash down the counters and table and sweep the floor when she returned, yet all thoughts of housework tumbled from her mind as her right foot rolled midway down the stoop.

Clutching the stew pot, she braced herself using the side of her right foot, compensated for the shift in her posture, and skated down the remaining steps. At the bottom of the stoop, she regained her balance and paused, slightly dazed that she remained upright and hadn't spilled a drop of stew.

A sharp pain shot through her foot. She set the pot down on the ground and rubbed her ankle vigorously, wincing as she scanned the plank steps where she discovered a round, smooth stone.

Plucking it from the stoop, she examined the dark gray granite dappled with spots of peach-colored quartz.

"Collect rocks?"

Umera gasped. Shadow obscured her vision of the stone, but she recognized the soft, sultry voice of Bethereel and all other sounds around her receded in a flash.

"Only the ones that nearly kill me." She slipped the stone into the pocket of her pants.

"Are you okay?" Still dressed in blue, a large corn husk woven basket purse hung from one arm, Bethereel smiled. "I figured you to be sitting around fretful and worried." She patted the purse. "I brought you a sandwich and an apple. I know you like the green ones best."

Despite the throb in her ankle and the limp in her walk, Umera abandoned the stew pot in the yard and invited Bethereel into the house. "Have you found out anything?"

"Everyone says the same," Bethereel answered. "They saw her at Elusis's shop."

At the kitchen table, Bethereel unpacked the purse, unfolded paper from a sandwich. The bread was dark and thin, the sandwich heaped with vegetables. Umera didn't have to taste it to know she'd like it.

"If I had my memories," she said as she was about to bite into the sandwich, "none of this would've happened, and I wouldn't have had to stand up to Yensilva." Tears rimmed her eyes as she plucked a piece of crust from the bread and nibbled at it instead. "Elusis is right. I'm not a real friend to her. How can I be a friend to anyone if I don't know who I am?"

"Never become other people's doubts," Bethereel said. "Especially when they belong to Elusis. Don't believe him. He's a broken man. You know yourself better than you think."

Wiping her eyes, Umera perked up. "Really?"

Bethereel nodded. "Listening to your heart's a lonely affair, and I've never met anyone so willing to stand alone when it mattered." Taking Umera's hand in her own, she squeezed it. "You're quick to make enemies because of it, and that's why I really like you."

Umera appreciated the kind words. "Do you mean like the time I punched Milos?"

Bethereel nodded. "*That* was amazing." She unwrapped more wax paper, revealing green apple slices which she offered to Umera. "And when you questioned Sabien's stories during his show. Don't misunderstand. I love Sabien, but it is nice to see him squirm once in a while. And wearing a man's turban, that was inspirational."

Silence fell between them. Umera reluctantly moved her hand to accept an apple slice. "Yensilva's just angry," she mumbled. She nibbled at the pale fruit flesh and rolled a small morsel throughout her mouth savoring its tartness. "She's just stewing somewhere right?"

"No matter where she is, we'll find her." Bethereel reached out across the table and wiped hair from Umera's cheek. "Yensi and I have never been friends, but I'm still scared for her. If she's not back today, we'll look for her, okay?"

Umera nodded, relieved to know someone willing to take action. It lessened the weight in her heart, soothed her anger, and revived hope in Yensilva's safe return.

— 37 —

"MAYBE SHE'S FAKING it?" Ibe leaned against the door to the smithy, head bowed as he chewed on a jagged thumbnail.

Avn spread glowing embers inside the cavern base of a small stone and mortar smokestack. The forge fire swirled in a frenzy with every sweep.

"Why would she pretend about Yensilva's disappearance?"

"No, not that." Ibe huffed. "Her memory loss."

"You think she's playing then?" Wiping the sweat from his forehead, Avn abandoned the poker at the mouth of the forge. "What would she gain from that?"

"Attention."

Avn scrutinized the man before him, finding the notion superficial, immature, and strange coming from a Mentor. When they returned, Avn knew he needed to discuss terminating Ibe's position with the Council.

Ibe stood abruptly. "Don't look at me like that!"

Avn laughed.

"Ule is always dancing around me, nattering on about nonsense, wanting to descend into worlds with me."

"Because she's in love with you." Avn regarded his Student with concern. Under his breath, he muttered, "Idiot."

An assortment of expressions contorted Ibe's face, alternating between shock and disbelief mostly. Finally, he settled on disgust.

A heaviness hung in Avn's tone when he declared, "Not everything's a game."

"Trust me, I've worked with her more than you have." Ibe stomped his foot on the ground for extra emphasis. "She's playing."

"Then why is she still searching for Yensilva by herself? The official search party quit days ago."

Blinking profusely, Ibe shook his head. Bewildered, he threw his arms up in defeat. "Who knows with her?"

Silent, Avn mulled over a couple of short blades still requiring a bit more tempering. With a set of tongs, he clasped the end of one of the blades and nestled it into the embers of the forge.

"Her searches have been taking her closer to the border of Woedshor," he said.

"That far?"

Avn sensed the sarcasm in Ibe's voice, how he pretended to understand. "Have you been out that way?"

"Out by that strange little grove that reeks of cat piss and burnt sugar?"

Nodding, Avn retrieved the second blade and set it next to the first in the forge. "The place has a reputation." He stirred the embers, watching the blades blacken, waiting for them to glow with a tinge of red. "People in deep despair have gone there to die or kill themselves."

Ibe shuddered.

"Why does that bother you?" Avn frowned, wondering if perhaps being trapped in the world had stripped Ibe of his sensibilities. "Every world we've ever built has at least one death locus."

"That place, it's something else. I know magic scent when I smell it." Ibe sat on the bench next to the forge and inched away from the heat until he was comfortable. "I steered clear of that place as soon as I smelled it. I don't descend into worlds to tangle with their magic makers."

Avn flipped the glowing blades over in the fire one by one. "Let's hope Ule does the same."

"What about there?" Umera pointed toward a patch of trees in the desert. Soft greens and golds dappled the broad-leaved canopy of the grove while white sand splashed around its edges—an island in the desert.

Crank ground his teeth against the reign bit and bobbed his head.

"Yensi has to be somewhere." Turning over the loose reigns to one hand, she found the end of her orange turban with the other. She unraveled it partially and draped the end of the scarf across her face to shield herself from the sun.

She hadn't thought to come this far until she spotted the grove on her return from the border of Woedshor. Had she known her search might lead her to the desert, she would have worn longer sleeves to protect herself from the sun.

She thought of all the places Yensilva had once mentioned, even the places she hated, like the forest. "What better place to hide than somewhere no one would think to look for you."

Crank ignored her.

Mesmerized by the grove, she watched how it shimmered beneath the late afternoon sun. She steered Crank down a narrow dirt path which ran along the edge of a thicket and faded into a narrow plateau of grassland.

Woedshor forest receded into the horizon, a wall of trunks and indeterminate foliage abruptly halted by the empty plateau. The trees curved slightly, as though they strained to avoid the heat of the desert. Grassland dipped over a small hill and disappeared into the sand.

She couldn't decide what compelled her toward that grove more, the search for Yensilva or a fundamental insatiable curiosity. What she did know for certain was that she would be traveling there alone, for Crank whinnied as his hooves sank into the hot sand.

Umera dismounted, tied the reigns to the remnants of a twisted tree, and patted him lightly on the shoulder. Slightly dazed, she squinted and softly spoke. "Stay here."

One of Crank's ears folded backward.

Umera walked into the desert, the grove beckoning to her.

Claaang. Claaang.

"Why do you keep doing that? Of all the things to do," Ibe mumbled.

Slumped forward where he leaned against the mended railing, he scratched his shoulder then his arm. Wide eyed, he stared at the ground neither flinching nor blinking whenever Avn struck hammer against metal.

"There are other ways to live here," Avn insisted.

Ibe scratched his nose then shivered. Hands on head, his left leg began to jitter.

Avn stopped hammering and shaping a small blade. Both concerned and annoyed by his Student's twitches, he asked, "What's wrong with you?"

Huffing, Ibe slapped his hands against his sides. He stood and began pacing. "How can you tolerate it?"

"Tolerate what?" Avn rested the head of the hammer on the anvil, appreciating the weight of the tool, keeping his hand occupied. He waited for an explanation.

"Being like this." Ibe gestured to his body. "In descended form for so long?"

"You're not going to freak out again, are you?" Avn lifted the hammer and struck the metal blade. He ground his teeth, lifted his arm. Tendons twisted. Muscle flexed. The hammer swung down again.

Claaang. The jolt fired through Avn's arm and into his body, numbing his nerves. The sound reverberated in every molecule, easing his tension. The weight of the hammer, anchored both mind and body. "Find something to focus on."

Rolling his head around, Ibe stretched his neck. "What do you focus on?"

In response, Avn motioned to the anvil. "And figuring out the pattern in the behavior of the An Energy is another way," he answered. "Understanding what I saw of the lattice work in the barrier when we tried to ascend." Between strikes, he mused. "Can't help wondering why she built one in the first place."

"Because I told her to," Ibe said.

Avn stopped the hammer in mid-swing. His tendons screamed. His brain fired question after question, yet all he could muster at that moment was a strained, "Why would you do that?"

"The world was tearing apart."

Stunned by the response, a wearisome fury silenced Avn.

"Could you imagine the damage an unstable core might cause to the other worlds in the Vault? I had to do something." Ibe sighed. "Barriers are built all the time. The basic ones are simple."

Avn released his grip on the tongs. The glowing blade clattered to the ground. Dirt stuck to the cooling metal. Clenching the hammer, his knuckles cracked as it swung to his side and rested against his thigh.

Ibe approached the anvil and hugged himself. "She's more trouble than she's worth." He paused a moment, brows furrowed. "When we get back to our realm, I'd like her reassigned to someone else."

"Creating a barrier is not a simple task." Avn gritted his teeth. His fingers repositioned on the smooth wooden handle of the hammer, grateful for the warm steel head grazing his flesh now and again, helping to keep his rage tethered. "How come you didn't tell me this?"

"Tell you what?"

"That you ordered her to build a barrier!"

Pacing again, Ibe's shoulders twitched. He sucked in his breath. "I don't know, because the barrier we saw wasn't the one I instructed her to make. At first, I thought it was something you put there."

Ibe halted in the middle of the yard. Frowning, he strode toward Avn, finger jabbing at the air. "Do you think I had something to do with this? Oh no!" He shook his head. "No matter what I tell her, she always does something else."

"Keep your voice down," Avn growled. "Tell me, what type of barrier it's supposed to be then?"

"I-I... It's just a basic barrier!"

Avn strode toward Ibe, grabbed him by the base of his neck. Their noses barely touched. The weight of the hammer stopped him from strangling his Student. "What did I tell you about showing some discretion in this world?"

Straining against his grip, Ibe sneered.

Avn gripped him tighter, raised the hammer until the head rested against Ibe's chest. "Were you in the Lab when she built it?"

"I..."

"Tell me, or we'll be going another round," Avn challenged him. "This time with weapons."

"No!" Ibe flung himself away. Scowling, he rubbed his neck. "No, I wasn't in the Lab. I gave her instructions. It's just like her. She can't even follow simple instructions."

Avn bit his lip, squeezed his eyes shut, and vented. "You arrogant bonehead."

"Excuse me?"

"You heard me." Every muscle in Avn's face tightened. His cheeks ached from the pressure. "You're a half-wit dolt if you don't think instructions can't be interpreted in more than one way."

"The instruct—"

"Did I say you could talk?!"

Holding his hands up in defeat, Ibe quietened.

Avn turned away, his fist choking the hammer handle. With a fury, he raised it high and slammed it down on the anvil. A sharp, reverberating clank lifted into the air. His arm muscles spasmed from the blow. He let the hammer go, and it tipped onto its side with a rattle.

Regarding his student again, he noticed Ibe had paled and a tinge of fear darkened his eyes.

A false sense of calm thickened Avn's voice. "Did you bother to check her work?"

Ibe gulped. "No," he whispered.

Avn grimaced. "Get out of my sight. I need time to cool down."

"Okay," Ibe eagerly agreed. Twitching again, he strode across the yard and jumped through the gap in the broken railing.

"And do whatever it takes to keep the Cleithrophobia in check," Avn commanded.

About to say something, Ibe stopped and simply nodded.

Averting his darkening gaze, Avn regarded the anvil. He recovered the tongs and the partially tempered metal blade. Still dimly glowing, he tossed it into the water barrel.

"Find something to focus on," he suggested.

— 38 —

COOL WIND EASED the warmth in Umera's cheeks. The soles of her feet stuck to her sandals and pebbles slipped between her toes, burning the tender flesh there. She waded through a drift and marched toward the grove, grateful for what little protection her footwear provided against the searing sand.

Peering between the trees into the dark underbrush, she searched for a way into the thicket and saw darkness. Around the grove she wandered until she discovered a gap between two skinny, bowed saplings. She ducked beneath them and climbed over the wide girth of a fallen fir tree.

"Such a big tree for such a little..."

High above her, much higher than she would have expected, a thick canopy of pine needles and leaves glowed with sunlight and cast shadows over the ground.

"...forest?"

Turning back the way she came, she stopped. The bowed trees were farther away then she had remembered traveling. Through the gap, she glimpsed the white desert.

Both curious and cautious, she turned around again.

"Yensilva?"

She expected her voice to disturb the birds, insects, and small beasts, to interrupt the twitters and caws within the canopy above, the clicks and hums and buzzes too. Instead, silence persisted, until she stepped forward and made the leaves softly rustle underfoot.

She gasped when her feet began sliding down a slope of dried leaves into a narrow ravine. Wobbling side to side, she kept her balance until she came to a slow stop near the bottom and fell backward against a dry riverbed.

The riverbed stretched on and on, carving into the ground well beyond the perimeter of the grove. On her walkabout, she had traveled over level ground, and the desert showed no indentation for any kind of ancient river.

"This is weird," she muttered.

She climbed the other side of the ravine, wiping leaves and needles from her clothes. Peering between thick gnarled trunks, she examined the underbrush. Counting her footsteps, she stopped at two hundred. Her heart beat a little faster.

By her estimation, she should have cleared the grove by now. Crank should be within reach, waiting for her to pick up the reigns and ride him back to the farm. Instead, a forest still loomed before her.

She continued walking, her feet sinking beneath the leaves. Twigs scratched her ankles and pricked her exposed toes, and she wished she owned a pair of boots.

Entering a clearing, she stopped and shivered at the lone pipe cactus standing in the midst of withered branches and tree stumps. A thick breeze flowed over the ground, stirring dead leaves, and brittle twigs. Around the clearing, trees which hadn't been cut towered with strength and majesty, unaffected by the absence of their kind among them.

The cactus shifted and turned. Upward stretched arms lowered. His bowed head rose. At first, he peered over his shoulder. Then he turned some more. His glassy black eyes snapped toward Umera like magnets and stuck to her as she backed away in the direction she had come.

She sucked in her breath. She whimpered, all the while backing up until she slammed into the rough bark of a pine tree.

"It's you again," Istok bemoaned.

Umera glanced all around the clearing, searching the circle of trees for a gap to escape through. The woods seemed a safer place to be.

A thoughtful look overcame the demon. "Do you live here now?"

Along the right side of the circle, she detected movement behind a tree. A pale face floated in the shadows like a ghostly orb. A finger pressed against its lips. Long dark hair spilled over one shoulder and the contours of tiny, bare breasts. Umera envied the woman for being hidden and just behind the demon enough to be well out of his visual range.

"J-just exploring." Umera struggled to wet her lips. Her throat constricted. "Do you live here?"

"The place is too crowded for my liking."

She glanced around at the seemingly endless forest that barely stirred with life, at the demon, at the woman motioning wildly to her. Counting two people and a demon, Ule agreed. There was one too many of them present and hoped the demon might grow bored and leave.

Inching sideways toward the woman, rough bark scratched Umera's back.

"You're a friend of Kaleel's then?" The demon's voice drifted through the air, echoing slightly, which seemed odd for trees tended to absorb sound.

She froze. "Who?"

Istok smirked. He ran his thumb over the scar below his one elbow, then grazed his fingers across the tips of spines jutting from the forearm.

"A useless cat demon," he replied. "He's always taking what doesn't belong to him. What did he take of yours?"

Shaking her head, Umera thought immediately of Yensilva. "Possibly a friend."

"Possibly?" The demon's laugh echoed throughout the woods. Rage simmered beneath his ribbed skin, the glint in his eyes, and every word he spoke. "He takes everything. Cages them here. Gemstones and cows. Everything. Everyone."

She squinted, not quite sure what his words meant. "What are you looking for?"

"What he stole from me." He plucked a spine from his forearm and twirled it between thumb and forefinger. "He won't even admit what he took. Do you know what he told me?"

"Who?"

"Kaleel!" Istok slapped his hands together. "Pay attention!"

She flinched from the sharp noise and the pop of the red spine as it snapped in half and fluttered into dust.

Shifting his weight onto one leg, he ran his hands over his head, rubbing gently at thin scars.

"He told me he saw it in the castle, in a scepter passed down from Magnes to Magnes, worn in front of everyone to see, once wielded by Adinav. Adinav!"

Clutching the tree, she struggled for air, waiting for the demon's next outburst.

"All this time, right before my eyes."

"A-are you saying h-he stole a gem?"

"The rarest." Istok sighed. "He told me he smashed it, but I'll find her again. She was slender and blond, all sun-like—"

Softly huffing, Umera blinked in confusion again. "Are we still talking about the gem?"

"Your hair." Tilting his head, Istok admired her as though he were seeing her for the first time. He touched his neck. "It's grown quite long."

Chills crawled over her ribs. In her mind, rumors of the missing women being blond collided with a forgotten image, a reflection of herself from when she arrived on the farm—long blond hair, a yellow dress.

The demon's eyes glazed over. "I might've remembered her wrong. We met in the desert. It *is* sunny there. She could look much different now, could be anywhere, be any one. She should've died, but she stayed alive. She can't be human. I'll find her, even if I have to change every single one of you."

Carefully, Umera crept closer toward the tree's edge, where the strange woman now crouched in the underbrush.

Istok suddenly turned away, nose sniffing the air. "Come out, come out my little moo," he sang. "I can smell you."

The woman lifted herself slightly, as though preparing to run. Eyes riveted on the demon, she waved again and began rocking back and forth.

"M-maybe Kaleel can help you find her... it?" Umera suggested still unsure of his meaning.

"He's no better than the Bisi," Istok seethed. "Hiding in his little grove 'cause he can't control what's out there. Clucking about one disappointment and the other, nesting until he's laid an egg of misery to break over the heads of his people."

Her head began to ache. She found herself trapped somewhere between his anger and his verbal digressions. Nothing he said made much sense, and she wanted to flee from his presence.

"He can't control any of you when you're still out there," the demon rambled, pointing to somewhere beyond her left shoulder. "Can't stop you from eating and drinking, holding yourself hostage by your lusts 'cause you can't tolerate the world as it is or what you've all made it into."

She couldn't deny the truth in what he said. The contradiction became painfully clear when she started working the fields—plants grew better in the waste of decaying food. Life grew out of death and death out of life.

Her heart fluttered weakly. He continued ranting as though she had not spoken at all. "You noticed that too?"

He spit on the ground. "He'd have you waste your lives here, in a place that barely resembles the real world. Do you think this a better place?" Istok shouted, raising an arm toward her. "This place makes me gasp for air, yearn for sunlight. It's predictable." He smiled. "The world beyond holds beauty and marvel, mystery and pain. I like the world. This—" He stomped the ground. "This isn't real. Shame on you Kaleel."

She flinched and dug her fingers into the tree bark.

His full lips pulled into a horrible grimace. His voice fell. "He's no better than Adinav. He wanted nothing to do with the world either. All that wretch ever wanted was to leave it behind and take that gemstone with him."

Withdrawing into himself, the demon thumbed the spines on his forearm again and plucked another one free.

Her heart began beating rapidly at the sight of the spine. Unsure of what he might do with it, she remembered how Avn prevented the spine from striking her. She began inching again, surprised at the girth of the tree. She poked her toes about in the thick pile of leaves.

"If I ruled the world," Istok mumbled, "you'd all have real purpose."

Umera's legs twitched. An urge pulled her toward the woman, hidden in the shadows.

"Your kind never took responsibility for us." He touched his chest softly. "You created us in the image of your fears, cast us out, rejected us, forced us into the shadows. This world's just as much ours as it is yours." Lost in his thoughts, he smiled. "I could make it better for all of us. I have a plan."

Umera had a plan too. Eyes riveted on a narrow gap between the trees, she pushed forward and ran.

Determined to stay ahead of the demon, Umera fought the tension in her body which threatened to immobilize her. Hard bursts of breath struck the still air as she raced toward the gap in the trees.

Within her peripheral vision, relief relaxed her muscles when she saw Istok hadn't moved. Eyes narrowed, he raised the red spine to his mouth.

Movement distracted her. The woman behind the tree suddenly swung her arm, hurling something dark and jagged through the air.

Umera froze. Clenching arms to body, she cowered as the rock arced through the air. Uncertain why her flesh throbbed and stung as though she had been struck herself, she exhaled slowly when she saw the weapon was not intended for her.

The rock struck Istok in the chest, jolting him as he blew the spine from his fingers.

Snapping out of her daze, she ran again, skirting tree stumps and leaping over fallen branches. The spine whistled through the air, veered above her head, and struck a giant tree near the gap in the clearing. The sap-riddled bark crackled and turned to pitted, yellow-white bone, spreading outward from the point of impact.

"Is that you little moo?" The demon made sharp kissing sounds as though calling out to cattle.

Umera held her breath at the sight of the blight slithering throughout the tree.

The gap in the clearing neared and soon she would have trees to protect her. Snaps and cracks echoed above her. Heavy branches fell from the canopy, hitting others on the way down, showering pine cones, needles, and sharp splinters of bone all around her.

Shielding her head, jagged splinters raked across her arms and dust blew into her eyes. She slipped through the gap in the trees still running. Echoes of twigs snapped next to her, and when she looked, she saw the woman running beside her.

Long tangled hair bounced against the woman's back, and her small breasts flopped all around. Breathless, she tugged at Umera's sweat drenched shirt. "Follow me," she gasped, steering them in a different direction.

The forest grew denser, darker. The sun seemed more distant then ever and Umera suddenly missed the heat of the desert as the air cooled and dampened.

"Come on, coooome ooon! Little moos, come on." The crunch of twigs and rustle of leaves became ghostly voices echoing the demon's taunts as he pursued them.

A soft whistle passed close to Umera's ear. She glimpsed the red spine briefly and knew where it struck when an old rotting tree suddenly erupted into sprays of fine ash. A second whoosh and a young sapling to her right ossified. It resembled the twisted arm of a strange dead creature struggling to be free of an earthly grave or, perhaps, pulling itself back under.

The woman steered Umera again, around a boulder and a cluster of bushes, across a narrow brook running with clear water, toward a strange green glow pulsing in the darkness of the forest.

Pushing herself, Umera ignored the growing ache in her lungs and sucked in deeper breaths.

Istok still pursued them, mewling and calling out as if trying to lure an animal.

The woman tore through the green glow and Umera followed. Although she would have continued running for however long it took to be safe from the demon, she was grateful to see the woman slow down and stop.

Umera keeled over, gasping for air. "Should... shouldn't we... keep going?"

The woman shook her head. Pulling her hair back over her shoulders, her naked torso rose with every deep breath. Tied around her waist, sleeves of a shirt hung limp around tattered leggings. She was thin, the hollow of her ribcage pronounced, large brown smears marked the flesh across her neck and shoulder.

Umera clutched her chest as she endured the prolonged burning in her lungs and noticed a light dusting of ash all over her own clothes. Loud kissing sounds startled her. She shuddered at the sight of Istok's face pressed up to the green smoke.

"We're safe here," the woman said and ran her fingers through the air above her head. "This magic, it hurts him."

"Come be milked little moo," he sang as he explored the green smoke. Grimacing, he prodded it with a finger and yanked it away, flicking his hand a few times.

Reveling in her safety, Umera dared not step any closer to the smoke. She was grateful to be well beyond arm's length of the green light. With false bravado she yelled, "How dare you call me a cow, you, you sandbox prickwart!"

Smirking, the young woman absentmindedly scratched at her breast. "He meant me," she said softly, stepping up to the smoke. She peered up at the demon, chin stuck out, eyes narrowed.

"I'll milk you again and again." Istok stooped a little, peering at her through the smoke. "Make you beg for it. You used to like that once. Probably still do." He leered. "There are some personality quirks that just don't change, no matter how much you change the rest of yourself."

The woman's face blanked a little. Her eyes remained fixed on the demon. Slowly, she tilted her head.

"Or I could prick you," Istok spat. "Again and again, you scrawny twit."

The woman tilted her face some more, remaining silent. Slowly, she stuck out her tongue and waggled it about.

Struck with fury, Istok curled a fist and drove it into the smoke, toward her face. She sucked back in her tongue and shrugged when his fist bounced back without touching her. He let out a wail of anguish, then spewed a torrent of profanity, which only made the woman smile more.

"He's insulting," Umera fumed. "Say something to him! You don't have to tolerate being talked to like a cow."

"But it's true, I am a cow." The woman shrugged then thought a moment. "I mean, I *was* a cow. Hundreds of years ago... I think."

Umera wasn't quite sure what to make of the woman's announcement, but at least she spoke more coherently than the demon. Still, Umera was at a loss for words. Her mind blanked as she stood and silently watched the woman nod toward the forest.

"I used to be a milking cow. He changed me into a woman then stole me away. Isn't that romantic?"

"Wait! Y-you and him, together?"

Nodding, the woman untied the shirt from her waist and shook out the wrinkles. "We used to be lovers. He could be nasty sometimes but when you agree to it, it can be fun. But then I took something of his and he..." She stopped smiling and glanced downward. "He hurt me. He smashed my hand. Th-that's when I left."

Umera tried to process how a demon and human could be lovers, and how a cow could turn into a woman. She watched the strange woman with her large, dark brown eyes redress by slipping the shirt over her head. One of the woman's hands was different from the other. The twisted fingers pinched the fabric but lacked the grace and dexterity of her other hand.

"Couldn't find the Bisi, as much as I tried," the woman rambled. "But then I found this place." She looked around briefly. "People come here to die, I think, but my Master stops them."

"What you did back there," Umera interrupted, hoping to stop the woman's rambling, "saving me the way you did, that was very brave. Thank you, whoever you are."

The woman smiled. "I'm Mulga."

— 39 —

UMERA GAZED STEADILY at the woman, searching for any clues to her past life as an animal. She noticed Mulga's bony knees, wide forehead, and skin that sagged on the underside of her arms. Nothing about her reminded Umera of a cow except perhaps for the dark spot on her neck and her large, brown eyes which rarely blinked.

"So you're human?"

Mulga shrugged. "I'm more like a demon. Istok's magic makes me *ee-mortul*."

"Immortal?"

Nodding, Mulga tugged Umera's hand, leading her away from the glowing green haze until the air became clear again. As the strange air receded, the green glow appeared like smoke roiling inside a glass cage in the shape of a castle rampart. The wall receded in both directions into the forest.

"But I can't use magic like a demon." Mulga pulled Umera along through the forest. "Because I am magic. Does that make sense? I can't tell."

None of it made sense. The ideas of a forest inside a grove and a woman who was once a cow failed to uphold any reason or logic. She closed her eyes and tried to remember why she had come to this place.

Yensilva.

"I'm looking for my friend." She quickened her pace, surprised to find the ground level and clear of leaves, twigs, and stumps.

"Oh, did she come here to die?"

"No!" Umera cringed at such a morose thought. "Why would you ask that?"

"Because," Mulga sighed, "that's why people come here."

Anger never stuck to Yensilva. She mostly snapped at Umera when she was annoyed and then she'd tell a joke. Their argument, however, raised a fury the likes of which Umera had never experienced before. Yensilva lashed out in an unfamiliar way, and she hoped that no matter where Yensilva had gone, her friend was safe.

"Her name's Yensilva. Large girl, big muscles." She curled her biceps. "Always barking lots of rules."

Mulga's eyes lit up. "She's a dog?"

Stunned by the association, Umera was about to respond. She stopped herself and stifled a laugh when she realized Mulga was being serious.

"Ah, no." She coughed. "She's not a dog."

Mulga led her onto a dirt path which wound through tilled land. The ground split open with large pumpkins in some of the garden beds, while others brimmed with vines weighed down by plump grapes or tomatoes.

Patches of gardens flowed into one another, receding into large clearings containing huts, shanties, and barns. Trees skirted each clearing, and high above them, the forest canopy remained thick. She wondered how any vegetation could flourish beneath the shaded land of the forest canopy and yield an abundance of food. Thanks to Yensilva's constant instruction, Umera knew pumpkins and tomatoes needed direct sunlight to grow.

Being guided further along the path, Umera noted the small buildings huddled together, similar to the buildings in the Fashion District of Sondshor Market. Young people and old stood in doorways or at the fences to small yards, where plump cows stood, chewed, and mooed. Glancing sideways at her guide, Umera again searched for visual clues to Mulga's past life but was distracted by squeals of laughter.

Children ran toward them, a mass of waggling arms and smiling faces. Hands grasping for each other. Pushing, pulling. Umera froze as their mirth flowed around and in between her and Mulga.

Something cool and hard brushed against her flesh. Tingling shot up her arm. Pleasurable at first, the sensation eased her muscles and lulled her mind. She looked down at a young boy who clung to her arm and yammered about liking onions, white rocks, and the smell of metal. A girl with a long red braid scrunched her face and groaned, lamented about the onions, and told him she liked lilacs, caramel, and the color purple. When the boy blurted about how he hated lilacs,

Umera discovered the source of the vibration.

Wrapped tightly about the boy's wrist was a bracelet. Every time the fine, gold chain brushed her skin, a sense of ease overcame her. The boy pressed against her, the chain remaining in full contact with her arm. The sensation of well being began to vibrate. A tremor coursed through her arm and into her body. Jaws clenched, nausea mounting, she finally let out an anguished groan at the ache in her skull.

Mulga stepped back, her lower lip trembling. "Are you all right?"

She peeled the boy from Umera and shooed the children away. Coming back to herself, she watched the children recede into the pumpkin patch where each and every wrist glittered with a gold bracelet. Then she noticed that even the older people wore bracelets, everyone except Mulga.

"Where's your bracelet?"

Mulga grabbed her wrist, fingers gently rubbing her flesh. "Oh I can't wear any of my Master's charms. His magic hurts. It's because of Istok's magic in me." She nodded heavily and pointed at Umera's wrist. "But come, Kaleel will give you one if you want."

"Who?" She frowned as she recognized the name Istok had mentioned during his fit of seething.

"Kaleel? He's my Master."

A golden bracelet twinkled before her. Umera thought it strange how it reflected light in the shade of the porch. It dangled from a black talon pointed toward her. She knew she was meant to take the gift but was otherwise preoccupied by the appearance of her surroundings.

The demon reclined in a wicker chair on a wide porch, set beside the tall narrow door to a log cabin. Above the doorway, a maul hung on hooks. The double hammered head and the steel studs which ran the length of the dark wood had been polished and sparkled.

Beneath a canopy of orange flowering vines, Kaleel the Rex beckoned her to come closer. Unnerved by his torn ear, the thick scars marked his wrinkled flesh, and the belt of bone he wore around an emaciated waist, Umera wanted to run away. What made her stay were the demon's clear water blue eyes—intelligent, discerning, almost human.

"Why do you look the way you do?" She dreaded the question and silently berated her curiosity when Mulga, who stood at her side, let out a soft *uh-oh*.

Pinching the bracelet between talons, Kaleel lowered his arm onto the chair's armrest.

"Someone long ago," he began, "decided that the screeching wail and swiping claws of a feral cat were worth fearing." His voice rose from low in his chest and the tone was soft and lyrical.

"But cats purr too," she interjected, feeling suddenly at ease. "They chirp and nuzzle and rub themselves against you. They play with their tails. They can be quite charm... ing." And the demon was, she realized, very charming, despite having very little fur, paw-like hands, and a long, angular face.

Kaleel smirked.

"I like cats," she whispered.

Kaleel clutched his chest, covering his heart. She couldn't tell if his gesture was a sincere appreciation of her sentiment or if he mocked her. A glint from the bracelet caught her eye, and the demon held it out again.

Chewing the edge of her fingernail, she knew the bracelet was some form of magical shackle which kept everyone who wore it bound to the grove. Had the place been a nightmare of torment and anguish, where people were kept against their will, she would have easily declined the offer. Instead, she found herself longing for the familial home the grove offered.

Needing to understand the power of the bracelet, she accepted it. Her fingertips ran over the cool metal and began to tingle. The sensation radiated through her arms. She shuddered with delight as though she had been touched by a lover—Milos upon her thigh, Ibe along her neck—and the tingle intensified until it burned. Her skull vibrated and her stomach tightened. Pain flooded through her, excruciating and oddly familiar. Groaning, her fingers loosened and the bracelet fell to the porch.

"I can't," she gasped, grateful for how quickly her body released the pain and stopped trembling.

Mulga stooped to pick up the bracelet. Kaleel lunged forward and shooed her away. "Another product of Istok's?" he muttered. "Mmm, his ability's improved." He retrieved the gold chain from the porch and held it out again. "Are you certain? It's of the finest quality."

Umera nodded briskly, cringing at the trinket.

"I'm here to find a friend. Her name's Yensilva."

Kaleel sat backward and rolled the thin chain between his

fingers, brows furrowed. "No one here by that name, eh Mulga?"

Mulga shook her head.

Repulsed yet still fascinated, Umera pointed toward the bracelet. "H-how does it work?"

"It makes you forget." Kaleel brought the bracelet to his thin lips and kissed it. "Most things when they die leave behind something that stinks, eh?" Throwing his head back, he breathed deeply. "Some people, they forget to toss out the garbage. They cling to the rot for fear they might lose themselves, until it seeps into their souls. My charms melt away the memories, clean out the crap. And whoosh! There at the center of it all, shiny and precious—happiness."

Anger warmed Umera, fueling her words. "Did you do this to me? Take my memories away?"

Instead of an eyebrow, wrinkled flesh arched above his almond-shaped eyes. "Mind your mouth! I never take. I only give."

"But you must have—"

He leaned forward and snarled. "I'd be happy to make an exception and cut out that meaty wagger of yours. It's been a dog's age since I've eaten tongue stew."

Umera immediately fell silent. Her heart beat a faster rhythm.

As though picking up on her fear, Kaleel leaned back in his chair. His anger faded quickly. After a moment of silence, he sniffed.

"Calm yourself," he said, his eyes twinkling. "We've never met until now. I can't have taken your memories."

Sadness overcame her, simmering her temper. She struggled with her desire to remember while everyone in the grove had willingly forgotten. She needed to remember, no matter how dire or gruesome that past might be.

"If you can take memories away," she began, with a shaky breath, "can you return them as well?"

Kaleel smiled. He blinked a few times, amused by the question. "Only if I took them away to begin with."

Disappointed, Umera sagged.

"You see, these folk aren't the kind to understand that happiness is created with the same effort it takes to farm land." Where talon ended, wrinkled fingers began, and Kaleel gestured toward a patch of peppers. "We must cut away the decay to make room for growth, constantly dig up the land to discover what will grow. We must water and feed it all, sate ourselves with the yield and start all over again, else we die."

Sitting forward, he shook his head. "You must know, they came here to hang themselves from the trees. Either unable or perhaps too tired to clean their hearts, to free themselves of the mud and dung flung at them by others. Children too, orphaned by wars in a world where very few care. They have good reason to forget."

"But will they return to their homes?"

Shrugging, Kaleel peered over the porch railing into a cow field. "They can't go back to a world they can't remember. Some of them have been here far too long, the world's forgotten them. All the bad memories gone, all the good ones too. Here, their hearts and minds shine. Little suns making the forest flourish. Why would they want to go back to a world where everyone makes sport of casting each other into the shadows?"

In that moment, she understood. She saw how Yensilva struggled to ensure what few happy moments Umera experienced were stifled. Eating an apple. Talking to Crank. Admiring a spider. Growing her hair. All of it, always squashed in some way.

"You've noticed that too?"

Kaleel winked at her.

The cat demon again invited her to stay with them. Knowing another world resided beyond the grove, Umera graciously declined. Before she could explain herself, Kaleel spoke pleasantly, offering advice or perhaps a threat; she couldn't tell.

"If you send anyone to steal away my folk," he said, "I'll charm them too."

Mulga pulled Umera away from the porch, dragging her toward a spring fountain farther down the road. Water jetted from the center of a mound of volcanic rock that peaked at their waistlines. Leaning over, they both cupped their hands and captured the water as it fell back toward the ground.

"I need to find my friend." Umera splashed her face and wiped the excess water off with the hem of her shirt. "Please understand, she could be hurt or injured."

Licking her lips, Mulga stared into the woods. Her dark eyes blanked momentarily. She bowed her head, gingerly touched her withered hand.

"Isn't everyone hurt and injured?"

— 40 —

MULGA PEERED THROUGH the green haze, her eyes scanning the forest. "Stay close." She beckoned with her good hand.

Umera ducked down behind her, loathing to leave the protection the wall of green smoke provided. "Do you see him?" she whispered, searching the forest for anything that might be lurking in the shadows, waiting to pounce.

"Come." Mulga waved. "This way."

With a deep breath, Umera tried to calm her fear. A trembling set into her muscles as she ran behind Mulga through the smoky barrier. She gulped for air. Any time a branch snapped, she flinched. At the sight of the toppled fir tree and the gap between the saplings, she quickened her pace, fearful that, at any moment, a hand might reach out from behind a tree and drag her back into the darkness.

At the mouth of the opening, Mulga stopped. She looked around at the desert.

Clutching her side, Umera joined her. The spin of her anxiety slowed at the discovery of large footsteps in the sand. They receded from the opening and into the heart of the desert. With a final long haul of air, she caught her breath.

The world looked different. Less real, Umera realized. The clouds were too fluffy and white and seemed painted onto the sky. The wind felt empty as it whipped her shirt sleeves about. The desert shimmered like a mirage which she expected to dissolve into tendrils of smoke if she stared at it long enough.

"Thank you," she told Mulga. "For keeping me safe."

Mulga smiled. Inhaling deeply, she slipped off her shirt and wrapped it about her waist. She arched her naked chest toward the sun and after a deep stretch, turned back toward the gap. She bounded between the saplings, over the fir tree, and disappeared.

For the briefest of moments, Umera appreciated the open space of the desert until her mind suggested the possibility of the demon returning.

Digging her feet into the sand, she hastened toward Crank and made gentle tsking noises at him, urging him back toward grassy land and away from the grove, which was not what it seemed either. And now, with a scrutiny she hadn't possessed before, she wondered about the genuineness of the rest of the world.

Back at the farm, Umera led Crank into his stall where he snuffed in her hair and nickered.

"Oats and water you say?"

She filled his feeding bag and topped up the water in his small trough, sank onto the stool to chew on a green apple, and stared blankly across the barn.

Soft grunts and the occasional splash of water failed to break Umera's daze. The harsh cool light of morning shifted, and the lines of hay in the bails and the edges of rusted tools, even the knots in the wood planks of the barn wall, lost their detail, softened, and warmed.

By the warmth of the light, she knew it was late in the afternoon when she heard far away voices speaking to one another. She detected feminine and masculine tones blending together in their chorus of banter, and as they came closer to the farm, she stirred from her melancholy at the sound of her name.

She recognized the faces of neighboring farmers and their families when they found her in the barn, and with sadness, they reassured her she had searched long enough. Now she must join them, they told her, and the brawny men and women urged her toward the market, forced her into the rowdy revelry of Sunset House, where they all sat with honey mead before them.

A week had passed since the farmers banded together to search for Yensilva. Like so many search parties before, it lasted a few days before people returned to their daily responsibilities. Forever, they told her, people had always gone missing. Although it wasn't right, Umera knew the farmers were right; she had done more than anyone else. Quietly, she accepted her friend had gone.

Raising their glasses, they gave a lengthy toast in memory of Yensilva. Umera cringed only slightly at the foul taste after they downed the honey liquor. Afterward, they shared tales of their friend.

One farmer told of a time when Yensilva chased him as a boy and tackled him to the ground, where she sat on him until he agreed to be her boyfriend.

And another time, according to the farmer's wife, Yensilva set a bail on fire because the son of the ale maker promised her a kiss if she did.

Umera never questioned if any of what the farmers told her was true. The accuracy of the stories, she realized, wasn't nearly as important as how they kept the memory of Yensilva alive.

As they drank, she found it easier to fool them into thinking she was drinking along with them. Mostly sober, she felt the urge to dance. Despite the soft, slow ballad and the stiff, mechanical steps of couples bobbing along in rows, she stood at the edge of the dance floor alone, feet still. She began to sway. Her hips led, followed by her shoulders and arms. Flowing, undulating moves propelled her into a twirl and then another, until it seemed as if her feet didn't touch the ground.

Toes caught each other in mid-twirl and she stumbled, suddenly aware of other dancers laughing at her. Head held high, she pushed her way along the bar and ducked into a shadow. She ordered a cider and sipped it, realizing that in her attempt to hide, she found herself behind Milos.

He leaned against the bar in a freshly ironed white cotton shirt made brighter by the darkness of his skin. "Did you see that?"

Umera wasn't sure to whom he was talking until the woman next to him turned. Dressed in a long, narrow pink dress, her dark hair piled onto her head, Bethereel sipped at a glass of red wine.

"That was perhaps the most interesting thing I've seen since Sabien's show," she told Milos, her eyes searching the dance floor.

"That girl's never going to get a husband acting like she's trying to squirm out of a wet potato sack." With a long drawn out sigh, Milos smacked his lips and drank from his pint of ale. He tugged at the collar of his shirt, stood a little taller, and inched closer to Bethereel.

"I think she's brave," Bethereel said. She caressed the rim of the glass, scanning the crowds. "Being a little different can be fun."

"You're different." Milos laughed sharply. "Umera, she's just weird, not fun like you."

Umera felt an overwhelming urge to punch him again.

Milos coughed and Bethereel glanced at him.

"So how about it Bethi?" He nodded toward the stairwell. "You and me, have a little fun up—"

Before he could finish his question, Bethereel gasped. Pushing him aside, she rushed toward Umera. "There you are!"

Umera welcomed the firm embrace, letting it squeeze out her embarrassment and curb her growing anger toward Milos.

"Your dancing was truly..." Bethereel tilted her head slightly, her pale pink lips glistening. "...beautiful. The way you lifted into the air during the last twirl." Bethereel touched her chest. "It felt as if you were going to fly away. Is that what you intended people to feel?"

Blinking profusely, Umera finally found her voice. "M-my feet left the ground?"

"Not literally." Smiling widely, Bethereel's eyes lit up. "Although, for a moment there, I thought you might actually float away."

Umera felt her fingers begin to ache from clutching the mug of cider. Had she been listening to her senses, she would have put the glass down. Instead, she stood on tiptoe, leaned into Bethereel and kissed those soft lips that knew how to utter kind words.

Her weight shifted. She lost her balance, breaking their kiss with a soft smack. Cider sloshed down Bethereel's skirt, leaving behind a dark mark.

"Nooo," Umera lamented. Setting aside the mug on the bar, she tried to pat the wet stain with the hem of her work shirt.

Laughing, Bethereel grabbed her by the hand and led her past a sneering Milos and the rabble of Sunset House, out into the night.

Bethereel pulled Umera through the market toward that alleyway next to Elusis's shop. At the back of his building, she pushed Umera through a doorway and up a flight of stairs, where they both tumbled into a one room apartment that was long and tall.

"Elusis lets me stay here as long as I wear only his designs," Bethereel explained while stripping off the ale dampened clothes. "Everyday, I must go out and about, making sure everyone sees this dress or that pant suit, while he sits back and waits to see which style will become the next great trend." She laid the pink dress over the back of a chair next to an oak dining table and patted the fabric. "This is his latest design."

Umera's curiosity led her around the apartment. She noted the bricked-up doorways and the white washed walls. Around the apartment, forms were dressed in clothes she had seen Bethereel wear—the pale blue pant suit, the purple dress, and the long, red one too. She wandered all around until, at the very back, racks and more racks crammed with clothes impeded her journey.

"He keeps urging me to cut my hair in the latest style."

Spinning around, Umera wanted to scream at the suggestion. "Don't you dare!"

Bethereel was slipping out of a sheer undershirt. "But it's damp," she insisted, pulling it over her head and showing Ule. Her full breasts bounced a little as she balled the fabric and tossed it across the room.

"No," Umera said dreamily, watching as Bethereel leaned against the table and slipped out of her hosiery, one leg at a time. "I meant don't cut your hair."

Bethereel rolled her eyes and strolled across the room. "That'll never happen, don't you worry."

Her nudity caused a stirring within Umera.

"I need something of my own to play with."

Held captive by her beauty, she knew Bethereel was referring to her hair. However, the manner in which she unfastened the buttons of Umera's work shirt, made it seem she meant something else entirely.

The fabric of the shirt spilled away from her shoulders. The cool night air caused her to shiver slightly. Recovering her voice, she struggled to talk as her pants fell to the floor too.

"W-where have your basket purses gone?"

"Sold them." Bethereel flashed a smile. "I hear what the women want. If only the textile merchants would listen. Instead, they fashion styles to suit their own tastes."

"Uh-huh," Umera agreed to what little she heard Bethereel say.

"Do you really want to talk about purses?"

For all the clothes around them, Umera and Bethereel quickly discovered they preferred examining each other's nudity. Silent and curious, they circled one another, and when they grew tired of the dance, they chased one another around the racks of clothing.

Entwining of limbs and soft, warm kisses shifted Umera's focus onto their soft, yielding flesh. Memories of Milos's laughter, Yensilva's disappearance, Kaleel and his grove, all of the strangeness began to fall away until, in the final crescendo of arousal, even their bodies seemed to dissolve.

After the world slowly flew back into Umera's awareness, every ill comment made toward her, every glare or harsh glance, even the absence of the past in her mind, all seemed like mud clinging to her. For a few blissful moments, she had been free of the rubbish. Now, she realized, some of the rot which clung to her had nothing to do with her at all. What did belong to her felt old and useless, on the verge of disintegrating.

She slept peacefully that night.

Come morning, careful not to wake Bethereel, she rolled onto her back as far as the narrow cot would allow. The plaster wall pressed into her shoulder as she stared at the sloped ceiling of the apartment.

Through a series of tiny windows high on the wall, she glimpsed morning. Wispy clouds smudged the sky and were being torn apart by fine sprigs of light from the rising sun.

Clinging to the other side of the bed, Bethereel softly snored.

"I need to feed Crank," Umera whispered loudly, hoping to wake

Bethereel gently.

Snorting, Bethereel inhaled sharply and wiped her eyes. "Can't keep a horse hungry," she mumbled and rolled onto her other side, falling back to sleep.

— 41 —

THE SMELL OF old blood and fish wafted from the direction of the Food District into the alleyway. As the door to the building creaked shut behind her, Umera imagined the least smelly route home.

Cutting through the alleyways toward the Food District would certainly be quicker, but she hoped to avoid the assault on her nostrils. Turning down the alley which led to the front of the building and Elusis's shop, she knew her journey would be more pleasant if she cut through the Fashion and Wares Districts and made her way toward the junction near the smithy.

Halfway along the darkened alleyway, she noted two figures. One leaned against the railing of the porch, the other crossed the yard. At the mouth of the alleyway, they greeted with simple nods. When they turned toward one another, she noticed their familiar profiles and stopped.

She couldn't decide if Milos being hung-over or the unforgiving morning light was what made his face look wretched. As for Elusis, he looked well dressed as usual, wearing an impeccably tailored vest and navy slacks. The flask in his back pocket pulled the fabric tight.

"You should've seen them last night," Milos said, "celebrating while Yensi's still missing."

Grateful for the shadows, Umera ducked behind a stack of wooden crates before either men saw her. Their voices carried down the alleyway, and she heard the tone of disgust in Elusis's voice.

"Umera no doubt was there. The cad-swallower."

Numbed by the comment, she craned her head to peer around the crate. From their profiles, she discerned Milos smirking at his friend's rudeness and Elusis, eternally sour, puckered his lips.

"I've always wondered why she's stuck around. Now I know." Elusis tapped his foot. "She wants the farm. With Yensi gone, she probably expects she'll inherit it somehow."

"I bet she's faking the amnesia," Milos said. "You wait and see, she'll get her memory back once she's got the farm."

Nodding, Elusis sneered. "The girl's fooling herself."

Umera swiveled about and returned the way she had come, slipping around the back of the building, past the door to Bethereel's apartment, preferring the smell of fish to their hateful banter.

Mud, Umera thought. And she shook most of it off. At least Elusis was honest about his dislike for her, but Milos? He wasn't at all what he seemed, just like the grove.

She pushed through crowds of people milling about the vendors' booths and wagons. Instead of doubling back toward the Wares District along the road, she cut through the smithy's metal scrap yard hoping to avoid everyone.

She hunched over and slipped around a crate full of broken blades and hilts. She listened for the peel of hammer against anvil and heard only a low hiss from the forge. The wood on this side of the smithy house was lighter compared to the rest of the building, and she noticed what remained of joint braces where another building had been attached long ago.

In between the buildings, she followed the foot path and discovered an open window. She ducked beneath the window frame, and when she was nearly clear, she stopped at the sound of her name. She recognized the voice of the man with the fiery hair, the one everyone called Red yet she knew intimately as Ibe.

"Ul—Umera, whoever she is, she's not a very good Student. Too eager to please than apply herself." Silence followed and he spoke again. "She could show a little more imagination in the Lab, be a little more challenging during debates in the Lyceum. I didn't realize she was such a player, especially with the sex. Role playing works for her."

"Explain yourself!" The earthy growl of Avn rattled Umera's bones.

She shivered as his fury rippled through her. Although she couldn't see Ibe, she imagined his bright blue eyes wide and innocent when he asked, "Explain what?"

"Have you had sex with Umera during her amnesic phase?" A storm roiled in every word Avn uttered. His words simultaneously terrified and intrigued her for she didn't understand to what he was referring.

"I thought she was playing." Panic sharpened Ibe's words. His laughter was tremulous, uncertain.

The ensuing silence unnerved her, and when Avn did speak, his tone had turned cold.

"Did she at any time tell you she couldn't remember who she

was?"

"I don't know," Ibe snapped. "Maybe."

Avn's tone rose in pitch as he shouted, "Did she tell you she had amnesia?"

"Yes!" Ibe shouted back. "Okay, she did but—"

"It doesn't matter," Avn said. "It's non-consensual."

Something about Avn's urgency made Umera's heart beat faster. His words were assured, and they stirred a warmth inside which made her feel protected.

"Just so I'm clear about what you've accomplished since being here," Avn began. "You've called her by her real name?"

At the reference to her name, she squatted lower, ignoring the ache in her thighs as she leaned against the wall and listened intently for either of them to say what her real name might be.

"You've attempted to ascend with her," Avn continued. "And you've had sex with her, all after she clearly stated she had amnesia?"

Again, silence.

"You're a liability to this mission," Avn announced curtly.

"How?" Ibe challenged, his voice growing tense.

"By way of your arrogance."

Holding her breath, Umera pressed her back against the side of the house and slowly slid up until she could peer around the frame of the window. She watched Ibe lean precariously against the edge of a long table. Avn, who was perched on a stool, slowly stood. Veins on his neck popped as he approached Ibe.

"For non-consensual behavior and abusing your power of authority as a Mentor—"

Ibe shook his head in bemused wonder and stood upright. "What are you doing?"

"By the authority invested in me by our peers, I am imprisoning you."

Slowly, Ibe hugged himself. "A-are you serious?"

Avn snapped a hand toward him. Thick fingers locked onto his neck and dug in.

"No!" Ibe averted his gaze.

They each struggled against the other's strength, seeking dominion and control. Umera clutched at the side of the house, wishing she could find her own strength to run away. Riveted by the throes of their struggle, she watched, needing to know the outcome.

Ibe braced his hands against Avn's chest yet Avn proved stronger. They collided into the table, knocking lenses and books to the floor.

The stool tipped over and spun out of view. Avn clamped his other hand on the side of Ibe's face and forced their gazes to connect.

"No," Ibe grunted again. "I promise—"

Their eyes met. Ibe still struggled to push Avn away. One of his hands groped over Avn's eyes, tried to block his darkening irises.

Shivering, Ule felt her knees weaken as Ibe's body began to glow and become yellow light. Shielding her eyes from the brightness, she tried to understand how it was possible for Avn to grapple light as if it were solid. Then, like water, the light poured into Avn's eyes and he released his grip. After a few seconds, the light faded and nothing remained of Ibe.

Alone, quiet, Avn paced the room, the darkness in his irises returning to their usual green.

Umera final found her breath. Ducking and turning, she tripped over her own feet. Tumbling forward, she managed to stay upright as she sprinted along the footpath away from the house and the strange man inside.

Had she and Avn been friends, she might have felt betrayed for discovering he was more than just a smithy. Instead, she thought that perhaps Elusis had been right about the man all along—he wasn't to be trusted. And what about Ibe? He had displayed unusual skills himself, and he knew Avn, who had been associated with the powerful Grand Magnes Adinav, a magic maker. And she found herself dismissing the theory of them being demons in place of something else—They must be Mystics!

Emerging into the junction, she cast one last glance at the smithy, and slammed into the body of someone slight yet strong. She held on tightly to the man to keep herself from toppling over.

"You all right?"

She stepped back and shrank as the storyteller of strange desert tales held her still by the shoulders.

"You seem a bit rattled," Sabien said.

She expected anger or resentment in his tone for the way she had torn apart his stories during his show. Instead, he spoke gently, with genuine concern, giving her shoulders a slight squeeze.

"How well do you know Avn?"

Sabien balked at the question. "Very well. Better than anyone else, I would like to think."

Her heart raced as she struggled to understand what she had just witnessed in the smithy. "Don't you think his eyes are strange, the way they..." She searched for words. "They pull you in against your will?"

His lips slightly curled. "I rather like that about him."

She shook her head. "Nothing's ever what it seems, is it?"

He squinted in the morning light. "Reality can be incredibly harsh or terrifyingly beautiful." He paused to think a moment. "Or amazingly boring," he added. "It's probably why so many people prefer illusion. That's why I always use elaboration in my stories." He released her shoulders and stepped back. "And the more like reality illusion is, the better."

Saddening, Umera sighed. "That doesn't make any sense?"

Giving himself over to what she thought might be a smile, he patted her on the shoulder. "My feeling is it's not supposed to ever make sense. If it did, there'd be no need to ask questions, no desire for answers, then there wouldn't be any stories to tell."

Umera ran, not caring who she bumped into or what she tripped over. She wanted to go home.

Half way through the field of tall grass behind the farm, she froze. A tall figure lurked in the shadows between the house and the shower shack.

Strands of grass brushed against her forearms, making her flesh crawl. The world disappeared, as she focused on the cactus demon, strolling around the back of the house, dragging his fingers along the wall.

She heard the sharp scratches of his talons digging into wood and soft, sucking, mewling sounds as he called out to whoever might be home. Wondering if he had something to do with Yensilva's disappearance, Umera felt all sensation in her body diminish.

The soft rasp of her breath and an immovable pillar of determination within her racing heart preoccupied her awareness. Everything else, all of it—her hair and clothes, the cornstalks, what she thought about and even the way she felt in that moment—flowed. Always, all of these things, these aspects, they changed and would always change, except for what lay within the very core of her being.

Wrapped in fear, she felt a sense of self in its purest form, still and strong and unchangeable. The desire to protect her self overwhelmed her. She'd met the demon, not once but twice. On both occasions he tried to prick her with one of his spines. The first time she had been uncertain, the second time terrified. She had cared that she might be hurt, but not to the same degree she did now.

Now, she quaked at the prospect of dying at his touch, for he had made it clear that his intention was to kill her in some way. If she walked to the farm alone and unarmed, she would be choosing death. Now, she realized, she would rather fight, if she must, to ensure she lived.

The notion fortified her sense of self. Pride and love pervaded as she slowly, steadily, lowered herself into the grass, where she knelt and waited until the demon grew bored and wandered away toward the desert.

— 42 —

RISING FROM A freshly weeded potato patch, Umera's left knee cracked. The small of her back seized. Slowly she straightened, pushing through the pain in her hips, stretching her lower back muscles until they released. She looked across at the other garden beds, where vegetables fought for space amid invading weeds, and could hear a phantom Yensilva shrieking about losing the crops if they didn't keep on top of the weeding.

She was stunned at how quickly creepers, blowballs, and grass pervaded the soil in the days while she searched for Yensilva. Tending to the needs of the vegetables as well as the horse and the house made for long days. She had always known Yensilva was spectacular in her own way. How she managed the farm alone since the passing of her brother and father was both perplexing and impressive. She only wished Yensilva could have appreciated her own talents more.

Deep down, Umera knew she didn't have to do the work. She discovered she wanted to. She hoped that somehow she could appease Yensilva's spirit for their argument, protect her friend's family heritage, and prove that she was worthy of staying on the farm, which had become like a home.

She ambled toward the pump and leaned on the lever several times. Bending over, she ducked beneath the flowing stream and gasped as cold water spilled over her head. Shuddering, she stayed there, blinking through the water at her feet, where earth turned to mud and clung to her sandals.

Wiping water from her eyes, she stood at the sound of a slow, steady clop along the only dirt road accessing the farm. She stiffened as an old mare sauntered into the yard. Riding the complacent beast was Elusis. Despite his well kept short-sleeved shirt, red and beige striped vest, and black pants, his mouth was fixed in a long, drawn expression. He tilted his head and peered at her from beneath a wide brimmed, flat topped hat.

The mare stopped near the water pump and flared her nostrils. Umera wished Elusis shared the horse's disinterest as she glanced at the barn and the field beyond.

Anger glinted in his eyes, and she braced herself against his hatred. His gaze was fierce, as though he'd passed through a storm of grief to a place where he was entrenched in a firm, unalterable decision.

She shielded her eyes and struggled to clear the lump from her throat. "Is there any news?"

In the following silence, he grimaced. When he finally spoke, anguish tainted whatever harshness he could muster. "Yensi's gone. No doubt about that."

"Is there any reason she might've gone to Woedshor?" Umera thought of other areas to search, places farther away. "Does she have family or—"

Elusis raised his hand, motioning her to stop.

A shiver ran through her. She obeyed.

Leaning forward, eyes narrowed, he asked, "You still here then?"

She felt her heart quicken. Uncertainty about his meaning kept her silent.

"Figured you'd be gone by now," he said. "Half expected you to run off with anything you could sell." His lip twitched. After a sidelong glance and a lengthy exhale, he coughed sharply. "It's time you moved on."

"But this is my home—"

Elusis laughed. "*Your* home?"

He needn't say anymore. His few words told her the farm wasn't her home. It couldn't be, she wasn't family. She had no family, at least none that she could remember. Anxiety began a slow spin inside her chest.

"I know what needs to be done on the farm," she rambled, her throat constricting. "Yensi taught me everything. I know how to sell the produce, and maybe with a little help..." Pain pricked her neck when she tried to gulp the tension away. Her entire body ached. "I could manage the farm for you."

He snorted. Looking as if he wanted to say something, he decided to let the words pass unspoken and shook his head.

Blinded by the sun, she bowed her neck and watched phantom dark spots float over the ground. Tears welled in her eyes, but she wasn't sure what she wanted to cry about. The farm was Yensilva's life, not hers. Umera could be free to do as she pleased.

"You've till tomorrow afternoon to be gone."

Shifting in his seat, Elusis pulled on a reign and steered the mare into a sharp turn. "Take only what's yours and what food you can carry. Anything else is theft."

Angled away from the sun, the brim of Elusis's hat cast his face in dark shadow. Umera watched him. Despite his erect posture, she thought she saw his shoulders sag slightly, his hard eyes glisten. She doubted what she saw and decided she had been mistaken.

He flinched and spoke defensively. "I don't blame you, if that's what you think!"

She didn't believe him.

Elusis snapped the reigns once, and the mare turned in a graceful arc back toward the dirt road.

Umera stifled a scream of frustration. She knocked ripe tomatoes to the ground, stomped on them, and quickly regretted undermining the work which helped them grow. She finally found some satisfaction when she hurled a shovel, watched it spin handle over blade and disappear into the mess of dried corn stalks in the field.

"If it weren't for this damned amnesia, I wouldn't feel so, so… vulnerable."

Marching through the front door of the house, she searched the kitchen for a plate or a cup, anything she could smash into tiny pieces. She grabbed a clay bowl painted in mottled hues of yellow, and just as she was about to strike it against the edge of the counter, she stopped to pick at a chip in the glaze and admire the bowl's beauty. With a huff, she set it back down.

"You're free."

The voice was faint yet distinct, a whisper inside rising above hoarse bellows of powerlessness. The moment Elusis disappeared anxiety ignited inside, spinning into a storm of frustration, confusion, and uncertainty. Some how, some way, she had done or said something wrong, and she felt like she was being punished.

Fury threatened to overwhelm her again.

She heard the voice inside her again, louder and more

determined.

"Move on, it's time."

Move on to where, she wondered. Of everyone she had ever met, only two people had showed her any kindness—Avn and Bethereel. If she stayed with Bethereel, Elusis was certain to evict her. As for Avn, he must certainly be a Mystic, and she wanted nothing to do with him, even if he did remember her from the castle.

"Mud," Umera said softly.

Staring at her feet, she scrunched her dirty toes and watched the dried earth crack and crumble.

Anxiety began to diminish inside her. The voice returned.

"Sondshor Castle."

She knew what she needed to do—return to the place of her earliest memories.

Freeing herself from work clothes, she stripped until she was naked. In the middle of the kitchen she examined herself. Her flabby parts had shrunken and taken on the shape of deeply toned muscle. The ends of her hair brushed her shoulders. Standing tall, she strode out to the yard and into the shack beneath the rain tower. She showered until the basin emptied and the last bits of farm washed away.

Take only what's yours, Elusis had said.

Water dripped from Umera's hair as she contemplated her damp nudity. All that was hers had been torn down into kerchiefs, one with which Elusis blew his nose. She hunted through Yensilva's room for what remained of her old yellow dress and found a kerchief cleaned, pressed, and neatly folded inside a wooden jewelry box.

She glimpsed her friend's empty bed, the ends of the multicolored quilt still tucked neatly beneath the straw mattress. She sat on the edge of it and unfolded the soft cloth. The yellow fabric was the only reminder of Umera's past. Although she wanted to take it, she laid it on Yensilva's pillow and smoothed the edges until the creases disappeared.

She spoke to an imaginary Yensilva. "I'll use my sleeve, once I find one to wear."

Take only what's yours.

All that was hers was her body. Everything else had been given or loaned to her by Yensilva, a woman who had been pilfering the pockets of dead soldiers when they first met.

Bolting to her feet, Umera returned to her bedroom. Heart racing, she knew she was about to become no better than the thief Elusis wanted her to be, but she didn't care. She owed him nothing, she realized, as she started sorting through the contents of her bedroom.

"I'm taking only what I need," she promised herself.

And she knew what she needed would be a lot less than whatever Yensilva had stole from the dead.

Looking back over her shoulder, Umera snapped the reigns twice. She jabbed her heels into Crank's side for extra emphasis, her heart beating furiously for fear of a nearby farmer seeing her, pointing, and calling out *Thief!*

Crank willingly sped up to a fast trot, as though he understood he was no longer bound to the farm and adventure awaited him farther down the road. She felt a timidness in his gait, and she wondered if he knew he could move much faster if he wanted.

She had tried to say goodbye to him, but faltered at the fence to the field where she watched him fuss over a patch of long grass. Entirely by impulse, she led him back to the barn and fully saddled him. Only now did she question what might happen if Elusis reported her to the authorities.

The saddlebags bulged. She had packed a lot of necessities. Except for a lantern and a frying pan, which stuck out from beneath the flaps, she hadn't expected to steal anything as large as a horse or as difficult to hide. She longed for nightfall when they could not be seen so easily.

In silence, they camped at the edge of Woedshor, not too far from the road which led to the strange grove at the edge of the desert. From a small pouch filled with sils and keps, she retrieved the stone she had tripped on and examined the thick streaks of granite and fine lines of bright peach quartz. She mulled over a feeling of familiarity she felt about the rock. Oddly, it reminded her of Yensilva.

Come morning, they resumed their travels, cutting through Woedshor Forest. The ancient pines towered above them. Below, the bed of dried needles triggered Umera's memory of the first time she had traveled there, and she realized certain people and objects evoked feelings of familiarity for which she knew no explanation.

"The cactus demon definitely," she told Crank. "Avn and Ibe. That mummified Bisi nomad and the bird man from Sabien's

Exhibition. Even the smithy house, but..." She sniffed the pine scented air and squinted. "Without the forge and anvil. Somehow, they seem out of place, like they don't belong."

Making a list only confused her, so she stopped her mental exercise and focused on the journey. They camped in an open field on their second night away from the farm. She slept fitfully until thoughts of Bethereel drifted into her mind. She imagined they would meet again one day. With that comforting thought in mind, she slipped into a deep sleep.

For several days, they rode along a well worn dirt road which skirted the edge of Woedshor Forest and wound through a valley marked by rectangular fields of wheat and corn. Clusters of barns and houses eventually merged into a sprawl of smaller tilled fields that overtook the valley. Sondshor Market was tiny and spacious compared to the cramped, congested patches of vegetables surrounding the outer walls of the castle.

Passing the last of the larger farms, the dirt road turned into a wide lane of black flat stone. Huts, shacks, and more houses lined tilled fields which yielded the same vegetables she had once farmed. Carefully, she navigated Crank around pedestrians, carts, and other horses. As they were about to pass under a white stone gateway, a guard dressed in mail and breast plates stopped her.

The hairs on her arms prickled. Her heart pounded as she answered his questions. Where did she come from? The desert, she lied. What was her purpose visiting the area? She was searching for family that survived the war. This answer was mostly true, and she was surprised when the soldier returned to his post and waved her through.

Beyond the gate, stone walls receded in every direction. Buildings squeezed against each other making it difficult for her to distinguish storefront from house. In the distance, single level houses leaned against storage buildings which had been built onto over the years.

After centuries of being rebuilt into a mishmash of brickwork and a clash of old and new architectural design, Sondshor Castle erupted from the sprawl of shops, warehouses, and taverns, reminding her of a reclining gargantuan beast with the world clambering to suck at its teats.

Wooden scaffolding covered the tallest towers. Brace joints supported cracked archways. The shell of an old turret jutted high enough to reveal broken walls and scattered stones smothered by flowering vines. For a moment, an image of the tower intact flashed in her mind, and she added the building to her mental list of objects which seemed familiar.

For days she spoke to local merchants—bakers, butchers, tailors, smiths—listened to their stories. She told them about her amnesia, asked them if they had ever known her. When the locals couldn't help her, she wondered if she came from somewhere farther away. She began chatting with travelers, even the ones who couldn't speak the local languages.

Her reputation evolved quickly. Umera came to be known as the blond woman who spoke in tongues. Her services came with a warning: Beware her disagreeable horse!

From mediating contracts in different languages to acting as a guide for foreigners, she began to earn a meager income, enough to feed herself. As more and more time passed, she realized the likelihood of being arrested for stealing Crank diminished. Although her conscience eased up on the crime she had committed, she considered the possibility that one day her past might catch up with her and hoped she would discover her true identity before then.

— 43 —

RELAXING INTO HER new life in the city surrounding Sondshor Castle, she set out for breakfast at a local pub and thought she glimpsed a familiar face. Before she could properly identify it, it had vanished. A chill pervaded her for days afterward, for she felt as though invisible eyes watched her.

She waited for her arrest, wondered when an officer or some bounty hunter might jump out from the shadows. Then she saw him—Avn, the blacksmith. Alone, wielding his hooded leather jacket, armed with a full quiver and bow, he spoke with a butcher.

Questions spun through her mind: Why was he in this district? What was he looking for? Perhaps a person? Why did her heart beat furiously, a triple beat tempo she had come to know as an expression of fear? Had he seen her leave the alleyway that morning, after he had disintegrated Ibe with a glance, and come to explain himself? Or did he mean to silence her, to keep her from telling anyone what she saw?

Every month, now and again, she glimpsed Avn speaking with merchants. Uncertain of what his presence meant, she hid herself amongst the tables of wares. No matter where she ducked, whether it was next to a stack of folded fabric or a mountain of apples, his gaze always found her. Remembering what had become of Ibe, she shuddered every time, wanting to avoid those green eyes, to be as far away from the man as possible.

Avn would nod and recede into the crowd, leaving her frightened and confused by his aloofness. After every sighting, no matter who saw whom first, she fled. She flitted from one generous client's home to another, accepting room and board in lieu of wages. The constant change of homes helped keep her hidden, made her feel safe, until she overstayed her welcome.

Convinced that Avn showed no interest in making contact with her, she settled into the idea of seeking permanent shelter somewhere amongst the exuberant night houses and eccentric shops of the Eastgate District. Lured by a variety of distilled beverages and the cheap prices of food, she found lodging with two amiable young men in a rented room above a wood shop.

Both men worked in the theater. One had a thick chest with fine dark curls of hair across his chest and a permanent scowl, which he deepened when he played the part of a villain. The other was slight with caved shoulders and thinly plucked eyebrows, who played female parts exclusively.

They both took to her immediately, folding her into their lives as though she had been a long lost lover. Every night she nestled between them on a wide straw mattress. The proximity of their warm flesh comforted her until one early morning when sharp rapping upon the door woke them.

Jolting awake, Umera's heart knocked against her chest. Prying her friends' protective hands from her breasts and buttocks, she sat upright as the door swung inward. She gasped as two guards burst into the room.

Instinctively, she crossed her arms over her naked breasts, annoyed by their aggressive behavior. She hadn't murdered anyone. She was simply a thief. Yet they yanked her from the bed and pushed her toward an open wardrobe crammed with clothes and wigs.

Her roommates rose slowly from their ale-induced sleep, complaining about the noise. The burly one nearly lunged out of bed at the intruders until she warned him with a shake of her head. The other, clutched a blanket to his pale chest.

Shivering with rage, she glared at the guards who leered and smirked at her nudity. She shimmied into a teal cotton dress and orange leggings, ignoring the helplessness that over came her as she concealed herself from men who didn't deserve to see her that way.

The guards asked her questions, mostly about how long she had been in Eastgate District. She remained silent and even refused to answer her roommates, who begged and asked her to explain what terrible thing she had done.

Grateful for the cotton covering her flesh, Umera's vulnerability subsided. Avoiding the imploring looks of her roommates, who both remained in bed beneath a maroon quilted blanket, her eyes darted over each guard. Both had lost interest in leering at her once she had donned the short, drop-waisted dress.

The guard closest to her shifted toward his comrade. His back slightly turned, she saw a path open up before her—an opportunity for escape. In stocking feet she bolted toward the door. She made it only half way across the room before she felt herself shoved backward.

The brute force cued the dark haired roommate. He leapt to his feet, fists curled. His deep scowl and brazen nakedness caused one of the guards to flinch.

"No, no, no" she begged to her friend, hoping to prevent him from being hurt. Realizing she could no longer run from her past crime, she addressed the soldiers. "I'll go. Just let me put on some shoes."

Resigned to her fate, she reasoned that if she were to be arrested, tried, and imprisoned for thievery, she might as well look her best and bring only her best clothes. She slipped on a pair of slightly scuffed brown riding boots, and then began stuffing a few select dresses into her satchel, ignoring how it bulged and threatened to burst open along one seam. Before she could fling it over her shoulder, one of the guards snatched it and grumbled about her taking too long.

She combed her fingers through her long hair, kissed both of her friends goodbye, slipped through their clinging hands and ignored their calls as each soldier grabbed her by an arm and escorted her from the room, through the short hall, and down the stairs at the back of the wood shop.

Outside, the cool morning air stank of saw dust, hay, and manure. What was most disconcerting was the presence of two additional guards who waited in the quad.

"Four guards?" She snorted. "That's a bit much, don't you

think?"

None of the guards responded.

She felt a four guard escort seemed excessive for theft unless horses were more valuable than she thought.

"Crank!"

What would become of him? She couldn't in good conscience just forget about the beast. Turning toward the stable, she tried to pull herself free, but the guards' fingers dug in deep, holding her still.

"What'll happen to my horse? Someone'll take care of him, won't they?"

But Crank wasn't her horse, she realized. He would most likely be returned to his original owner—Elusis.

People stopped to stare at Umera being pulled along by the guards. She watched them watching her and felt an acute sense of aloneness crawl inside her. The distance between her and the world around her was tangible, and while she found the shift in her perception odd, she was grateful for the space it created.

The extra guards walked ahead of them, Crank in tow. He wore only his bit and reigns and reared his head repeatedly, making both men nervous.

She wondered if Elusis would know which oats to feed Crank or that he preferred an apple first thing in the morning and one late at night; the beast was fussy about his meals. Would Elusis make sure to ride him at least once a day? Or know to let him roam a little?

The east gate of the castle loomed high above them. To avoid thoughts of what punishment awaited her, she admired the delicate stone arch carvings of leaves and a six-winged bird. She examined the people milling about the first few courtyards within the inner castle.

High above, dirty and sweaty, men walked along scaffolding. They shouted orders at each other as the drumming of hammers reverberated off the stone walls. Below, officers barked orders at young, shirtless soldiers. Dressed in basic leggings, the soldiers glistened with sweat and fought fatigue as they repeated sprints, jumping jacks, push-ups, sit-ups, and other training drills to improve their strength and endurance.

Another world turned within the inner castle, a world which not just anyone could enter, and she was amazed at the number of people milling about the courtyards. Hammers pounded and soldiers shouted in unison, making it difficult to hear the discussions of austere men dressed in dark cloaks or what gossip the servants shared with one another as they strode past.

The noise drowned out Crank's snorts and whinnies. So when he reared up on his hind quarters, it seemed a silent act. He yanked himself free, the guards stumbling backward to avoid being struck by a hoof as the horse came back down on all fours and turned around.

Umera found Crank's attempt to escape back the way they had come exhilarating. At the sight of the slow yet exuberant trot he mustered, her heart sank. The guards, having gathered their wits, fumbled to recover control of his reigns.

"Run Crank!" She hopelessly called after him, noting the strange looks the guards gave her.

Umera expected to be pushed down cracked, unkempt steps into a dark, dirty prison cell. Instead, she was pulled up a wide, white stairwell with railings carved into tree trunks and a banister into a forest canopy.

She realized she was going to be tried immediately, punishment to no doubt follow thereafter. Shallow breathing overcame her, making every movement more difficult. Her legs felt heavy and stiff. Her eyes darted over every carved limb, knot, and leaf as she ascended and walked a long, wide hallway.

Desperately she clung to her last glimpses of life—sunlit stained glass windows arched in bas relief, black and white triangular floor tiles, the wiry grip of each soldier digging deeper into each arm. Statues washed in colorful paints stood between each window and on the opposite wall, a gallery of portraits watched her.

Each painting memorialized someone important: a conquering General, a powerful Mystic, and every single Magnisi for the past few centuries. Her eyes settled on the portrait of a funny looking man with wisps of dark hair about an aged, round face. The name plate read Magnes Fehran, and Umera found herself thinking an odd thought—his nose should be a little longer.

All of them, she realized, every single person in the portraits lining the hallway would be remembered, and she wondered how she could be remembered if she couldn't remember herself.

Passing through large double doors which spanned to the ceiling, she focused on what she did know about herself. She loved long hair, green apples, and dancing in painfully slow circles. She hated honey, shucking corn, and hangovers. She loved strength and independence, but mostly she loved clarity of mind and the pull on her heart when she followed her curiosity, and she was deeply and forever afflicted with questions.

Led into a receiving room, she admired the simple leafs carved along the dark wood of the throne. Elaborate reliefs of forest narratives were being restored to their original vibrancy on plastered walls. The guards urged her through yet another doorway, up a flight of stairs and down another hall into a turret room swathed in brilliant, colorful light.

She blinked at the tall stained glassed windows of trees and flowers. In the center of the room men crowded the perimeter of a round mahogany table. Among them she recognized a few familiar faces, men of importance who she remembered from Sondshor Market and occasionally saw in the Eastgate District. Guards stood at their stations along the walls as she was urged toward the far end of the room.

Across the table, a man hunched over a slightly charred parchment. Light brown hair curled around the gold crown set on his head. His short cropped beard was curly too. Fine scars marked his cheeks and bare arms. Umera suddenly wished Yensilva was here to see the newly appointed Magnes for herself. Despite the old wounds and a nose which looked to have been broken several times, even with a stern gaze, Magnes Lyan was undeniably handsome.

She tried not to struggle as he rose from the chair and motioned to the guards who accompanied her. He examined her with great scrutiny, then he bent over the table and selected a page from a pile of partially burnt parchments. He stared at it momentarily, shifting his thick callused fingers along the scorched edges of the paper.

"Rumor is you understand languages." His voice was loud and booming, a strong general's voice.

She gulped and nodded quickly.

"How many do you speak?"

Glancing up at him, she held his gaze and whispered, "All of them."

Magnes Lyan snorted. "That many?"

She nodded again.

He studied her briefly before focusing on the parchment he held. After a moment, he presented it to her. "Then read this."

Struck with fear, she remained still.

He shook the parchment at her. "On with it!"

Finding her reflexes, she accepted the partially destroyed document and began reading the translation out loud, something to do with herbs, minerals, and a scepter.

A murmur rose around the counsel table, Advisers speaking out at once: A ritual no doubt. Adinav's source of power. What became of the scepter?

"This," the Magnes gestured to the parchment, "is a language?"

She cleared her throat. "Not really."

A hush fell over the room.

"These symbol patterns are too precise and mechanical, too perfect," she explained. "Real language is organic, ambiguous... flawed."

Around the table, Advisers exchanged looks and whispered again: She's too young to be a Mystic. Perhaps she's gifted with sight. Adinav was gifted.

Umera caught her breath at being compared to the man who nearly destroyed the world.

The Magnes hushed them and stepped closer to her. "If not a language, then what is it?"

"Code," she replied. Her uneasiness slipped away as Magnes Lyan regarded her with awe.

"Can you determine ciphers too?"

Umera nodded eagerly. Forcing back a smile, she realized the guards had not dragged her to the castle to be tried and punished for the theft of a horse. No, they had escorted her. She had been summoned. She was to be employed by the Magnes.

Umera peered through the narrow window, watching young men—some of them practically boys—being drilled in hand to hand combat in the courtyard below. They trained in groups of ten, moving from one courtyard to the next, learning how to maneuver throughout the Inner Castle grounds. Their battle cries rattled the windows panes and reverberated off stone walls and turrets.

Across from her, she glimpsed the stain glass window of the Inner Sanctum looming over the courtyard. Blinking twice, she pulled away from the window and shook her head at the sensation of falling into that very same courtyard.

Life in the castle, she soon discovered, was just like many of the other places she had known—the farm, Sunset House, Kaleel's Grove.

Instead of Yensilva's rules, she followed the rules of the Arch Scribe, the Advisers, and Magnes Lyan. She endured the presence of the strange smithy, Avn, who occasionally returned to deliver custom weapons to the new Magnes. And she enjoyed late night festivities which surpassed anything she had experienced in Sunset or Eastgate.

"Another world inside a world," she mumbled, her thoughts drifting toward the tilled squares of land on the horizon. She longed for the quiet nights she once experienced on Yensilva's farm. Later, she promised herself, after supper in the kitchen, she would collect Crank from the stables and ride him in the fields beyond the northern rampart.

She rubbed her neck, listening to the bones pop and crunch at the base of her skull. The small of her back ached and she lightly massaged the muscles until they relaxed. She returned to the tiny, dark wooden desk inlaid with filigree patterns made of golden triangles. The room was filled with similar desks. At each one, someone sat working at their own assigned task, either sorting through parchments or restoring a book or binding a new one.

She translated, mostly the strange, fabricated codes Adinav created to conceal his work. She read about his rituals, military conquests, and business arrangements, staying alert for any clues about her past. If she had been a translator before, she reasoned, certainly something of her work must linger in the castle, and she made note of anything that might lead her to her old self.

Quill in hand, she resumed translating the encrypted and terribly boring passage from what remained of a partially burned journal:

Nothing more than a soft voice at first, I listened. She guided me and in my dreams, I found Her. Her world was dark and hard and beveled—a tomb until I arrived. She was elusive, difficult to understand at first, but Her words aren't the gibberish of madness. She knows more than all my Mystics combined. She understands what I have always known and the world pains Her just as it does me. She soothes me. She has made all the effort and the wait worthwhile.

— 44 —

"STOP FLINCHING SO much." Umera snapped one of Crank's reigns.

In a valley near the castle, the ground leveled out into wide fields spotted with small woods. Camped in groups over the fields, soldiers fought one another in various ways—hand to hand, swords, maces, spears.

"The soldiers are practicing at war. They need to be prepared should we be attacked by... someone, something?" She shook her head at the thought. She knew why they practiced fighting. "They know no other way to live," she told Crank.

Crank's hair rippled over his shoulder and along his flank. Patting his neck, she gaped at the strange metal contraption in the middle of a field.

The cylinder was the length of a man and about as wide too. Propped on an angle, the narrower end pointed upward slightly. The other end was sealed. A soldier stuffed debris into the opening then set fire to a long, thin rope. He cursed when the flame fizzled into smoke.

"Come on," Umera complained, urging the horse to move faster.

The clink of swords and the shouts of generals faded as they cleared a tiny wood. The next field was empty of military exercises. She breathed deeply as she relaxed as the noise of war play diminished. The castle was a constant bustle at all hours of the day and night, and her search through the past still had not uncovered anything. Riding Crank offered her a reprieve, and she welcomed the quiet.

Until a great cracking boomed through the air.

Her body jolted.

Crank whinnied, reeled onto his back legs.

Recovering her wits, she clutched the reigns and found herself slipping back in the saddle. She called out his name to calm the riled beast, clung to him as he stood on his hind legs. Holding her breath, she waited until he returned all four legs to the ground. When he did, he leapt into a full gallop.

Umera grunted when she slammed back into the saddle. Every gallop jolted into her spine. Wide eyed, she clambered to hold on as she felt herself slipping. Fear coursed through her and she didn't know what to do. Crank had never moved faster than a quick trot and she felt as if she would bounce from the saddle into the air.

Wildflowers, jagged stones, and smooth boulders whizzed past, and when she thought the ground seemed closer, warmth flooded the middle of her chest.

"You have a choice."

It wasn't a voice she heard so much as sensed somewhere inside her. Its tone and cadence sounded familiar.

"You could fall and hurt yourself and maybe even die. Or, you could stay on. It's your choice."

"Stay on, stay on," she pleaded, gasping every time she slammed against the saddle.

While she didn't really know what to do, she found her mind drifted from the wonky way Crank galloped, as if he didn't know how to use his legs, to the pain beating into the base of her spine.

Wrapping her hands tightly around the reigns, she leaned forward and pushed her behind into the air. Bracing her knees into a deep bend, she clamped her thighs against Crank's side and felt his muscles stretch and contract with every gallop.

The world brightened. Individual blades of grass became distinct. Hard edges rimmed everything, delineating cloud from sky, tree from forest, stone from ground. Everything seemed to separate and each object began to unravel into fine black threads.

Blinking away the illusion, she held onto Crank with all her strength, leaned forward a little more as he found more fluidity in his stride. Her fingers whitened as she waited for him to ride out his panic. When he showed no signs of stopping, she found her strength diminishing.

Her heart raced. Beneath her rose a feeling of strength that cradled her yet terrified her too, for she sensed a dark place—expansive, eternal. Somehow she knew the darkness caged an unbridled beast, and she gave herself over to it, to the presence and nature of the horse, hoping Crank would protect himself from danger.

She saw in herself the same darkness. Relaxing into the rhythm of his gait, her nerve endings fired off mixed signals. Terrified yet thrilled, she peered into the darkness and saw a part of herself as unalterable, unbreakable, and she let go of everything, including the world.

Her body counter-swayed to the rocking of Crank's long stride as his gallop turned into a graceful run. The darkness eclipsed the world until only bright light shimmered along the edge. In the center, she glimpsed a child weaving objects from glistening black threads.

And Umera recognized herself.

Heaving for air, every pore of her being inhaled. Elation whipped through her as fragments of memory returned. Places, faces, and events churned in her mind too slowly, and she urged them to come faster. Leaning forward even more, she snapped the reign.

Crank gave into her urging and raced the wind at his fullest stride.

Air whipped around them. Her fingers lost all feeling. Her hip muscles ached and her spine vibrated. None of it mattered as her memories coalesced, became whole. She remembered everything.

"I'm Ule." Her heart fluttered. "I'm Xiinisi."

The warmth in her chest blasted her with heat. The whistle of wind in her ear quieted. Crank slowed into a gallop, then a slow trot, but she still gripped the reigns tightly, her eyes wide, her body stiff.

Crank came to a halt. She slipped out of the saddle. Her feet touched the ground and her legs wobbled. They gave out beneath her and she collapsed into the tall quack grass.

"I'm Ule," she said again, sprawled on her back.

Crank towered over her, nostrils flaring with sharp blasts of breath. He tossed his head back, his muscles quivering.

She began giggling, the voice inside her too—a deep, unhindered, hysterical laughter which brought tears to her eyes.

Crank strained to look across the field. His eyes searched the wilderness. Always prone to a forward pull of the head and a heavy gaze toward the ground, he now stood erect, braced to run again.

Remembering her abilities as Xiinisi, Ule knew she could prod the strange turnings of a beast's mind or merge with its spirit, but she only had to look at Crank to understand that the workhorse had experienced freedom and wanted more.

"I told you you could run." She stood and stroked his nose several times. Silently, she began removing his saddle and reigns. "I'll miss you," she said softly and watched him back away.

He arched his neck and snorted one last time before galloping off toward the rise of the valley which led to the steppes of Woedshor.

Ule hobbled a few steps but her thighs resisted the movement. Looking around to make sure she was alone, she knelt on the ground and began plucking wildflowers. One by one she stuffed them in her mouth, chewed their bitter stalks and bland pedals until she felt enough energy had accumulated in her body to fuel accelerated healing.

Focusing on her thighs, she willed the tiny tears in the muscle to knit, for the muscles to relax and release any lactic acid, endured the phantom pain that followed. Once mended, she stood, stared at the castle in the distance, and remembered.

She had passed along cobblestone roads and under palisades, stayed in the chambers of many Magnisi. She had lived in the castle once before, for a very long time, bound in a ceaseless vibration which caused her great pain. While being a beacon of power to all who gazed upon her, she had been helpless encased in the head of a scepter.

"It's just a dream." The twinkle in Adinav's black eyes, as though each contained a universe, offered her hope. If all of it, every stone, tree, flower, and beast were a dream, it meant she could change it, she could break free.

"I don't know." Doubt still consumed her. She rolled onto her back on the bed, the blanket slipping from her naked body, and he rolled on top of her, also naked. Tucking her nose into the crook of his neck, she wrapped her arms around him. His flesh was cool, smelled crisp and smoky and something else that lingered beneath the other scents. No part of him seemed to emit heat.

"You know you can influence everything here." His lips settled on hers briefly. "All I need to do is make a little tear. Just a little one, and then I can help you go home."

"And you want to come with me?"

His youthfulness, the genuine sweetness about his curiosity and desire to explore, stirred her. He glanced away briefly, before those dark eyes settled on her again. "There's no place for me here."

"It will take time to understand the energies, to develop the skill."

"Oh, I'm a quick learner." He kissed her again. "Don't you believe in me?"

She tasted iron on his breath, something tangy which reminded her of sex, and the stink of bowel. And teaching him took time. How much, she couldn't tell. The sun and moon whipped across the sky so quickly, it was impossible to count the cycles.

Sitting upright, she looked across the room built of tile and tree. With a glance, a wall pulled apart, exposing the gardens beyond. She tore a hole in the sky, and beyond she saw a structure which she had forgotten about. It looked sore and angry, a visceral energy fluctuating rapidly.

In what remained of the sky, the sun and the moon chased one another and when they passed over the hole, their negative images reflected on the pulsing wall.

"I can't control those," she told him.

Sitting upright next to her, Adinav smiled. "They're not

important," he said. "Now that you've shown me how, let's see what we can change together."

In a flash, the world around them distorted. Tree trunks coiled back, withdrawing into a ground which receded into a space within that cocoon of energy. That energy began to break apart too, opening up onto another layer of sky. Everything within the dream began to unravel into tiny black threads.

She began to unravel.

Her fingers poured into black threads spilling into the tear. The threads began to turn, a tornado of tendrils picking up momentum. Her smoky body swirled with the force of its current, watching the dream world disintegrate and the sky of another world open up. Beyond she saw the pillars and pedestals of The Vault within her realm.

She wanted to go home.

Pleased, she watched the sky open and unravel more.

A second layer of emotion arose which obscured Ule's yearning within her dream. The panic which followed belonged to a waking Ule. "No, no, no..."

She bolted upright in her cot, slick with cold sweat. Her night clothes stuck to her as she shivered. The moon lit the tiny room with enough light for her to see the other cots, each stuffed into a corner of the room, where a fellow scribe snored or breathed heavily.

She waited for her panic to lessen. It didn't. The memories flooded her mind. Had Adinav found a way to their realm, the world of Elish would have ripped apart, at her hands. Another world, destroyed.

"Will I ever learn?" she moaned.

Pulling herself against the headboard, she folded her legs and hugged herself.

Learning was the inherent nature of her species, the purpose for their existence, and all she could do was repeat the same mistake over and over, never changing or evolving, the potential of her power still beyond reach.

The dream was accurate. Adinav had persuaded her. He seemed curious, he wanted to learn, and when her descriptions confused him, she showed him instead. She had misread his smiles as an expression of joy for learning. Now she saw them as a reflection of his amusement at how easily he manipulated her into doing what he could not do himself.

After a while, she yearned to return home. Only that mattered.

Had her deconstruction worked, she cringed at what might become of the Xiinisi realm had Adinav made it through too.

She dug her fists into her eyes, grateful that somehow the tear in the dream state she had inhabited had collapsed. She remembered a searing bright light had flooded through her being, obscuring her dream thoughts, that she had been frightened; beyond that, nothing more.

Aching, she doubled over, sobs wracking her body. She wept, dimly aware of lantern light flooding the room, of gentle inquiries and soft hands stroking her hair. The attempts to soothe her failed.

The amnesia may have hid part of her identity, but she had always followed her curiosity, been honest and open. These traits were eternal, like air within her lungs, and Adinav had exploited them. Whatever vulnerability she had once felt while ignorant of her identity seemed trite compared to the powerlessness of having those traits exploited.

Umera struggled for air as she began to understand the depth to which she had been subjugated by Adinav.

"I remember everything now," Ule said.

She sat, hands folded in her lap, trying not to be too self-conscious. Whispers floated over the walls within the Inner Sanctum. She blinked as bright greens and browns reflected onto her from the stained-glass window above. The wooden chair she sat in was hard and cold. Regardless of her discomfort in the situation, she needed to influence these men of power.

Magnes Lyan leaned forward in his chair. She appreciated his disinterest in formalities, the way he spoke with her casually. His steely eyes softened, as though he suddenly remembered he was dealing with a civilian and not a soldier, and he listened.

"Your amnesia has been cured?"

She nodded.

"And you know your real name?"

"Yes, it's Ule."

Magnes Lyan contemplated the name. "Yes, that name reflects you better than Umera."

"Thank you," she softly replied.

"And you knew Adinav personally?"

She nodded again.

"Then from what you know of him, please, tell us, how do we stop someone like him from ever coming into existence again?"

She felt the passion in the man. Lyan's conviction was like hers. Adinav had been responsible for a hundred years of war, the stripping away of resources, the decay of human spirit, the near destruction of the world, and she too wanted to prevent another man like him from gaining power, even if he had given her reprieve from pain and hope that she could escape her prison.

"I can tell you that he was... special," she said carefully. "The way Mystics are special with their sight. Instead of spending a lifetime cultivating the ability, he was already born with it."

Inhaling deeply, she looked around at eager, concerned faces. Some paled at what she suggested; others expressed outrage. Condemnations rose from the Advisers: How do we know she tells the truth? She's playing us on behalf of her old allegiance to Adinav. Tell the truth, traitor!

She remembered the Bisi, how they had turned on her so quickly, acting violently out of sheer ignorance, spurred by their fear, and she began shouting above the din.

"The chance of someone like Adinav coming into the world again is unlikely."

The Advisers slowly quieted, settling themselves. Annoyance flickered across their faces. Magnes Lyan chuckled.

"But not impossible," Ule softly added, hoping to subdue his mirth and his logical nature. "To stop someone else from striving for his potential, you must forget Adinav."

An uproar filled the Inner Sanctum. Magnes Lyan bellowed until a hush fell over the room. "How do you expect us to forget what he's done?"

"You won't, not what he's done or anything about the war. Just don't remember *him*," she insisted. "Destroy his journals, his letters, and all accounts of him. Portraits, statues, everything." She shook her head, knowing what she was asking involved altering a part of the world's immediate history. "Stories will always be told about him, you can't stop that, but without any fact, over time the stories will change him into something less real, less human."

With a deep breath, she stood. She approached Magnes Lyan and knelt before him. Gazing upward, she begged, "Please, you must make Adinav appear like a demon or some other monster, make him a myth as quickly as possible."

— 45 —

ULE RODE IN a carriage with two older men who dressed in the fashion of merchants—narrow cut pinstripe pants, form fitting vests, and signature crisp white shirts buttoned to the neck. They seemed tall, their heads brushing the top of the carriage at times, and their wide girths spread across the leather covered seats.

Squeezed next to one of them, she pressed against the window and stared out at the jagged and feathered canopy of Woedshor Forest. She imagined more efficient ways to quicken the slow return to Sondshor Market.

Shifting would allow her to move and pass through any object. She could travel half way around the world in less time than it would take to ride a horse at full speed—a phantom blurring the horizon. Or she could transform into a bird and fly there. Both methods, however, came with the risk of being discovered as something other than human, and she wouldn't risk it.

She recalled how the Bisi Nomads threw stones at her, called her a demon for something as unremarkable as floating in the air. And Istok, how he tried to cage her in a stone. After everything the world had been through—the war, Adinav, the demons—Ule decided any manifestation of her power might only cause more panic.

The carriage rocked, and she pretended to sleep while listening to snippets of the men's conversation. They spoke mostly of rumors and gossip from the castle, then Sondshor Market. At the mention of Elusis and how his drinking had escalated since the disappearance of his niece, Ule bolted awake.

The merchants recounted what they each had seen of the man, commenting casually on how Elusis had never been a fall down drunk or a slurred drunk. He was certainly nasty, and his insults had taken on a more bitter edge now that he was the last of his immediate family to be alive.

Always neatly dressed, the upscale textile merchant had begun losing customers because of his sharp tongue. And he had developed a new habit of passing out on the shop porch, collapsed in a chair with wide wooden arms which kept him propped up like a well preserved corpse, as one of his neighbors described him.

Ule fumbled in her pockets, pulled out a leather pouch, and fished around inside until her thumb ran over the smooth, round surface of the gray and peach stone. Fragments of memories churned in her mind, coalescing—she had stubbed her toe on an unusual rock at Elishevera; another on the stoop to the house; a black bird collapsed into granite in mid air and fell onto white sand below. Submutation, she realized.

By instinct, she smelled the rock. The merchant across from her cast a severe glance at the strangeness of her behavior.

"This is nothing," she told him. "A Mystic would probably lick it."

The merchants both chuckled at her comment, and their conversation steered onto the subject of those strange Mystics.

Cradling the stone, she projected her mind at it with tremendous force.

"Yensi?"

There was no response.

She remember how it felt to be transformed into something cold and rigid, how she felt trapped and cut off from the world. She imagined Yensilva frightened and lonely, in pain too, incapable of communication.

Her instincts took over. All she needed to do was descend into the rock and perhaps she could undo the magic. Anxiety seized her in that moment. Her lungs constricted and her body stiffened. For all her desire to help her friend, she froze as she considered the possibility of the demon's magic trapping her as it had once before, for a very long time.

Not again, she thought. Flushed by her cowardice, she pressed against the cool window and sank into a deepening rift of sadness at how many people had been changed and worn down into pebbles and eventually dust.

And she knew something had to be done about that demon.

The vibration shook through Avn's arm, rattled his mind into numbness, until dark thoughts and anxiety stirred and spun. He swung the hammer again.

Claaang— "Avn."

Claaang— "Avn!"

Claaang.

"Master!"

A voice cut through the peal of metal on metal. Resting the hammer, he regarded a young woman. Though he had watched over her progress at the castle and noted the changes in her physicality and confidence, she stood before him changed in some other way. As much as he stared and scrutinized her, what that significant change was eluded him.

She wore the traditional scribe's capelet, black and gray silks which hugged her upper torso and swooped down the back into a point at her waist. The stiff collar adorned with gold silk embroidered quills cradled her face. No longer subjected to long hours of labor beneath the sun, her paleness accentuated a delicateness to her features he hadn't noticed before.

Abandoning his tools, he wiped his hands on a rag and addressed her professionally. "What can I do for you today, Umera?"

Grabbing the skirt of her ocher silk dress, she folded it close to her legs and stepped around the anvil. Ash soiled the toes of her brown boots as she approached him, but she seemed not to care.

Close enough to smell her lilac perfume, Avn braced himself until he saw her eyes were pink and puffy. Sorrow and anger dominated her countenance. He detected a quiver in her lips.

She touched her breastbone and spoke softly. "Ule."

Her smile was weak. It faded quickly. "I'm—" Anger tightened her face and she looked down. "I'm sorry."

"Who did you say you are?"

She took a deep breath and glanced at him again. "Ule."

The double time pulse of his heart beat strongly. He felt it in his head. He had waited far too long to hear that name uttered from her lips, but he had to be sure. He grasped her by the chin, tilted her head back. Searching her eyes, he detected her self awareness had fully returned. A tremor wracked his body.

Her gaze faltered, pupils dilating. The mind connection which came with so much ease among their kind, which offered so much comfort, pained her. She winced and pulled herself free. He knew from past attempts at regaining her trust, if he insisted on making that connection, she would react in an almost violent way, and he couldn't risk her fleeing. She had at least tried for a few seconds, which was more than she had ever done since her release from Isolation.

Recovering her breath, Ule straightened her capelet. "I-I couldn't ascend," she said. "There's a barrier I can't get past, but now that you're here—" She forced back tears. "You can bring me back."

Scooping her into his arms, Avn squeezed her tightly, letting out a long sigh. She squirmed at first until he lowered his head. His mouth near her ear, he said, "It's not as simple as that."

When she finally gave into his embrace, he pulled away and

nodded toward the house. Shame, anger, and grief rolled off her in waves. She avoided his gaze. He recognized the primary impulse she struggled with—fight or flight—and he resisted the urge to shackle her down so nothing else could happen to her. "Let's discuss this inside."

Agreeing, she slipped past him and through the doorway. Removing her capelet, she sat on the stool next to the long table.

"I've been here before," she said, examining the disorderly shelves. "A long time ago, but I don't remember it all exactly."

Folding his arms across his chest, Avn leaned against the kitchen counter. "First tell me, how'd you get your memory back?"

"Crank."

"The horse?" Frowning, he clenched his hands and felt old scabs on his knuckles crack at the absurdity of her response. After all his research of rituals and rites, watching history unfold while she existed as a gemstone, observing the reversal of her submutation by a demon's sword, the restoration of her memory involved, of all things, a horse.

"He doesn't talk," she assured Avn. Her humor was sedate. She tried to smile again to lighten their conversation.

Scowling, he leaned forward and stomped the ground with his right foot. Anger erupted quickly. "I've been here over three hundred years, Ule!"

She recoiled at his outburst. A slow dawning came over her. "Is that how long I've been here?"

"A little longer." Avn calmed his rage. Frowning he added, "By a few years."

She shook her head. "So much time yet I remember so little. For a while there was pain, and fragments of the world. Mostly I was caught up in a wonderful dream then woke up in a nightmare. A battlefield. Before that was the desert and Elishevera—she's dead now—and the Bisi Nomads." She shivered. "And Istok."

Her cheeks flushed. Her lips pinched together on one side, as she tore open a money pouch and poured out a gray and peach stone. "He did this to Yensilva," she said, holding it up.

He took the stone from her and examined it. The granite felt smooth against his calluses. "It reminds me of her."

"I don't feel her presence." Ule said. "Do you?"

Returning the stone to her, he shook his head. "She's gone." He watched her disappointment. "We're Xiinisi," he explained. "It's in our ability to fluctuate between forms, not hers."

"I know that," she snapped.

"Except for a rare few here, most would die from being submutated, or supermutated for that matter."

Anger chiseled her cheekbones and the peak of her chin. "Istok!" she spat. "He murdered Yensilva and who knows how many—"

"We've other concerns at the moment," Avn interrupted her.

"Yensilva didn't deserve this. And Elusis..." Ule set the stone on the table and clenched her hands. Pressing fists into her lap, she sneered. "He may be a wretched man, but he's alone now."

Avn scooped a wide green bottle from the nearby shelf. He yanked the stopper free and tipped it. Clear liquor poured from the neck into a small glass, which he offered to her. She graciously accepted. Cradled in the palm of one hand, she traced the rim of the crinkle glass with her finger.

He watched the elegant flow of energy in her face as she contemplated ideas. Although she wouldn't let him read her mind, he was grateful her expressions were honest, simple, and transparent.

She drank the entire contents in one slow haul and set the glass aside on the table. A deep crimson flushed her cheeks. "Istok has to be stopped," she sputtered.

"You know the rules. You can't interfere," he warned her.

"Rules?" Her voice was sharp and harsh. She stood abruptly. "Demons aren't supposed to be in the Root Dimension. That doesn't abide by the rules, does it?"

Avn remained silent, uncertain how to respond.

Tilting her head, she asked, "What do you know about demons?"

He downed half the gin in his glass. The burn at the back of his throat stalled him for a response he didn't want to give. "Very little."

Frowning, she wrung her hands. "You must know something. You've been down here so long."

The remaining gin rolled down his throat with a steadily numbing burn.

"Maybe I can help you make sense of what you've seen," she said, inching toward him. "Show me. With your mind."

Nearly choking, Avn wiped his mouth. She meant what she said. All he'd ever wanted was her trust again and now she offered it to him.

Pouring another glass, he downed the gin in one swallow. "If I showed you what I've experienced about demons, you would see certain memories."

She shrugged. "Which memories?"

"What I've seen, what I've done to find you and protect you, they were the decisions I made. My choices," he said. "The circumstances were unique but my actions are still criminal."

She shivered.

"I won't burden you."

She gathered the empty glass from him and set it down on the counter. Placing her hands on his, he was struck by the softness of her skin and the strength of her grip when she squeezed his fingers. At the first twinge of his mind being prodded, he resisted.

"No!"

She recoiled again. Anger sparked in her eyes. In the silence that ensued, she strode back toward the table and grabbed the gray stone. Squeezing it again, she paused over a series of loupes mounted in a row to form a scope and flicked at them until they spiraled out of alignment.

He watched her think her private thoughts, come to some sort of decision, and turn back toward him. Her lip quivered as though trapped in a tug of war between anger and sadness.

"If you won't do anything about Istok, then I will," she said softly.

Then she vanished.

— 46 —

ULE RELEASED THE tension between her molecules. Her form shifted into a diaphanous state. She slipped swiftly through the wooden floor. Releasing more tension, she moved through the topsoil and more layers of coarse earth below, slowing as the stones grew larger and denser, until she stopped just above the regolith, where pushing through the layers of boulders would slow her down even more.

In mere seconds, any of the Masters could whip through lead and the densest of liquid energy found in cosmic plasma, but her skill was not as refined as theirs. Given her ability, traveling through the medium with the least resistance, the air seemed the obvious choice of escape. Instead of sky, she turned toward earth and hoped it would take Avn awhile to sense where she had gone.

Far below the topsoil, she stopped to determine her orientation and discovered large bricks and shards of painted pots packed in brown clay. Startled by the human head of a statue nearly her size, she examined its large black eyes, broad forehead lined with dotted scars, and a lower lip pierced and decorated with talons, claws, and bone slivers.

Avoiding the remnants of a past civilization, she slowed to veer around a ruin of collapsed rooms. She finally gained momentum passing through the lower shaft of a dug well, but when more ancient walls and marble stones threatened to slow her down, she propelled back toward the topsoil where the earth was less compact and dark with fine mica.

Within her mind, she felt his probing.

"Stop!"

He pressed in around her.

"You need to conserve your energy!"

She darted to the left, escaping the enfolding of his energy around hers. She saw wooden brackets and concrete for the foundation of a building in the market above them and streamed into a brick and mortar tunnel rank with dark liquid sludge. Recognizing she was directly beneath the Food District, she followed the sewer back toward the junction, where it began to bend toward the Wares District. She soared upward on a gradual incline. Breaking free of ground, she pushed through to air.

"You're making your body age faster. Mine as well."

"Then stop following me!"

Closing her mind to his, she recovered her molecular tension. Smokey tendrils formed into a small, spotted wild cat. She hit the ground in a flurry, crushing lush rattlesnake weed under her wide paws. Tiny white and purple flowers fluttered into the air, as the wild cat raced along the river bed toward the desert.

Avn found her quicker than she wanted. She darted up the side of the river bed into the long grass and morphed into another cat. For a second, she thought she had lost him, but she sensed him flowing through the grass alongside her. She shifted, seeping underground again until she poured into the roots of a tree. Rising through the core of the trunk into the branches, she rematerialized and burst into the sky as a falcon.

Reflected in a cloud, Avn waited for her there too.

Returning to the ground, she settled on the form of a sleek puma. No matter how fast her legs pumped or how much traction her claws provided, she remained only a few seconds ahead of her Master.

He called to her, begged her to stop, to leave the cactus demon be, but she ignored him, even when he ran alongside her as some loping lupine beast. Finally he vanished and she thought herself alone until she saw him reflected everywhere—in the sand, the boulders, and the tumbleweed.

His calmness degenerated into frustration and he thundered. "Will you ever learn?" Becoming human again, he materialized in a firm stance in the desert.

She barreled into his legs, cracking her forehead on his shin. Panting heavily, she arched her back, black fur gleaming beneath the sun. She hissed and spat. Peering over her shoulder, she skulked away in a wide circle.

Glowering, Avn spoke an ultimatum. "I'd imprison you like Ibe but I need you in human form."

Her cat form pulsed and bubbled. Muscles stretched and elongated. Fur receded and flesh lightened. She stood upright and completed the transformation back into human form, wearing the ocher silk dress, clutching the stone that was once Yensilva.

Catching her breath, she peered over her shoulder at him. His anger diffused into confusion and surprise, but she didn't care what had caused his mood to suddenly shift. She focused on her destination—the archway. Nearby a tree had been worn down into skeletal branches bleached white by the sun and worn smooth by sandstorms. An unsettling grief overcame her at the sight of the dead thing.

She squeezed the rock in her hand.

"It's no use meddling with this world." Avn matched her stride. "You know what happened the last time you did."

Stopping before the archway, he grabbed her wrist. "We're only supposed to guide, not interfere."

She flung herself from his grip with a grunt.

"Do you think you have the skill to kill a demon?" Avn snapped. "I'm not sure I do. What do you hope to accomplish?" Curling his hands into fists, he braced himself.

"I don't know!" She rolled the stone between her thumb and forefinger. "If it wasn't for him..." She huffed. "Satisfaction, maybe. Retribution."

"If you do this..."

"You'll what?" she challenged him. "Send me to Isolation again for violating your precious rules?"

"If he overpowers you, you'll be turned to stone again," Avn reminded her. His nostrils flared. A vein across his left temple popped. "If he overpowers me, we'll be trapped forever."

Weariness overcame him. "I can't offer you any more guidance."

She raised her hand, pulled her arm, and hurled the stone through the archway. The arc of trajectory was nearly imperceptible, the aim perfect. The stone passed through the center of the doorway, causing the air to shimmer, and disappeared into the hidden lair beyond.

The desert remained still and quiet.

"Get out here you sand scum!" Her shrill voice broke. Fury rippled through her body. She glared at the empty archway and waited. When the image of the desert beyond began to shimmer, she readied herself for what tore through. Small, gray, and slightly pink, she recognized the stone as it whipped through the air and struck her in the forehead.

Avn sucked in his breath when he heard the crack of stone against bone and Ule's sharp gasp at the impact. He watched her body stiffen then relax. A blood smeared welt began to swell on her forehead. Legs buckling beneath her, he grabbed her. Cradling her, he eased her backward onto the ground and set her lolling head gently against the sand.

She moaned again. Heavy eyelids fluttered. She touched the wound, and the gesture depleted her strength. Her arm collapsed across her chest and her eyes closed.

Strong odors flooded Avn's nostrils—freshly dug earth and rusted iron. The hairs on his neck bristled. Peering over his shoulder at the archway, the air stirred and rippled. Light folded around the demon as he emerged.

Black eyes swept the desert. The glint of a fierce, enduring anger locked onto the crumpled form of Ule. The demon tilted his head and mumbled, "I know her."

Still kneeling, Avn fought a rising dread.

Struck by recognition, Istok's eyes widened. "You're my gemstone." He tilted his head in the other direction, eyes roaming over her limp body. "After all this time, you don't look much different for a being that should be... dead." He smirked. "What are you?"

Avn had fought a war, killed many soldiers and creatures. He had defeated Istok in battle as well, even if he hadn't done it alone. The fear he felt then was overshadowed by what he felt now, as the longevity of their Xiinisi nature had been revealed. That Istok might determine him and Ule to be something other than human made Avn's skin crawl.

"While she sleeps," Istok pointed at her, "may I have a word?" He stepped forward, still smirking.

The forced cordiality of the demon sent a shiver down Avn's back. He bolted upright, bracing his feet and tightening his fists. Even at arm's length, the demon was too close for his liking.

"You and me, we hadn't met until that fateful day," Istok began, feigning a nostalgic tone. "Adinav had possessed me, and when I found myself liberated, to my surprise I discovered,"—a twitch distorted the demon's face as he leaned forward and yelled—"you'd cut off my fucking arm!"

Avn examined the scar that encircled Istok's forearm. The wound had healed thick and even, indicating he had made a clean cut. In a calm voice he declared, "I'll do it again if you'd like."

Lunging forward, he grabbed high on the demon's forearm, close to the elbow where the spines stopped. He gave the weakened muscles a sharp twist. Something within snapped.

Istok bellowed in anguish, tried to pull himself free.

Avn held on. He wrenched the arm a second time, and the ribbed green flesh partially tore open. Pale green fluid began seeping from the wound. He re-gripped the succulent flesh. Certain a final and third attempt would tear the arm entirely free, he geared up his strength.

A sharp blow struck the side of Avn's head. For a moment the world went dark. Falling backward, he shook himself back to his senses.

Istok's hands clamped down on both shoulders.

Bracing himself, Avn pushed both hands against the demon's chest. His heartbeat quickened as he increased his force and found the demon wouldn't yield. Nearby, he heard Ule softly groan.

Momentarily distracted, Avn felt himself being pushed backward and recalled the dead tree behind him. If he could get near enough, he knew he could use the trunk for leverage.

He barely felt the tapered branch enter him. The movement was swift and firm as the demon pushed him along the ever widening girth of wood. His stomach opened up, a lung deflated. Flesh ripped and tore until his chest no longer yielded and the branch became wedged tightly between the halves of his ribcage.

Istok stepped back and admired his work.

Weight gave into gravity as Avn's legs went numb and limp. His sternum held him upright regardless. He had been hurt before. Familiar with the slicing and skewering made by every kind of sword and knife, the pulverization of skull and ribs by hammers and boulders, the bubbling burn of hot oil on flesh, and the strange way poisons melt the nervous system, Avn separated his mind from body.

He had experienced death in many different ways too, and every time he waited till he was alone to regenerate. This time he couldn't wait. Ule needed protecting, even if it cost him another generation of life or revealed more about their kind to the demon—Istok had already seen too much.

Avn didn't disobey the laws of his kind very often, but he had broken a key one already, many, many times—the destruction of any sentient creation. He chose to fight in the war, over the course of many generations, for it was the only way to covertly undermine Adinav without altering the natural course of the world's history and evolution.

Avn was skilled among the Masters, he knew this. Very few knew how to destroy without upsetting the balance of the An energy. He dismantled dysmutations and poorly conceived worlds, which was regarded as a compassionate act when their creations suffered. Destroying fully functioning creations wasn't in his nature.

Stirring back to consciousness, Ule lifted an arm and rubbed her forehead.

Avn's head drooped forward. Weakness consumed his arms and shoulders. The sooner he died and regenerated, the quicker he could protect Ule.

— 47 —

A SPRAY OF sand doused Ule's face. Her eyelids fluttered, and she inhaled sharply as bright sunlight stung her eyes. Pushing past the throbbing in her head, she focused on the shuffle of feet nearby.

Something small whizzed by her face the way flies do. Smoke flooded the air and tickled her nostrils. Groaning, she rolled over onto her side and brushed sand from her cheeks.

More small objects whooshed by her. Bursts of smoke rose into the air. Squinting through the haze, she saw her Master driven backwards by the force of Istok, whose grip threatened to fold her Master's thick chest in half.

Glistening with sweat, muscles taut from grappling, Avn lunged forward, pressing his hands deeply into the demon's chest.

She closed her eyes against the harsh light and the violence.

Struggling to recover her scattered mind, she concentrated on the harsh grunts and heavy breaths exerted by man and demon.

A painful cry and sharp rasps of breath forced Ule awake, and she saw why the sounds of struggling had ceased. Shielding her eyes from the sun, she sat upright. Pain shot down her neck into her back. She peered upward. Blocking her view, the cactus demon plodded toward her.

"Avn?" Her voice cracked from the strain.

Squinting, Istok examined her. "You're the one from the farm, aren't you? You are! I see the resemblance now. All this time—"

She scrambled to her feet. Craning to look around the demon, she gasped at the sight of her Master impaled on the tree branch. Her stomach lurched. Calling out his name a second time, she choked.

"Give my regards to your friend." The demon shook his head as if he were trying to dislodge a memory. "What's her name?"

"Yensilva," she spat, glaring at him. "Tell her yourself, she's over there." She pointed her chin in the direction of the gray and peach stone, hoping to distract him.

Istok began to follow her line of gaze then stopped. "She was fun." He smiled. "The fearful ones usually are."

A part of her wanted to cry, another part wanted to rage until it prickled her skin. If it weren't for the demon, Avn wouldn't have needed to watch over her for so long; she wouldn't have become trapped; Yensilva, foolish Yensi, would still be alive, picking potatoes while she dreamed of fashioning dresses.

Istok stretched an arm above his head, letting the other with the re-opened wound hang limply at his side. He clearly did not see her as a threat for he arched his green chest and flexed his pup laden shoulders.

"I like talking with you," he said. "Preferably as a gemstone."

From the corner of her eye, Ule saw Avn's head bolt upright. Flooded with relief, she let out a breath as he fumbled over the red, slick spike jutting from his chest. With forceful yanks, he pulled himself along what looked like a fleshless dysmutated third arm.

Turning to see what had caught her attention, Istok huffed and narrowed his eyes. "Difficult to die that one is."

Avn continued inching along the branch, grunting with each pull until he was free.

"Reminds me of Lishev," Istok muttered.

At the mention of her old friend, grief crashed over Ule. Warm and salty, it lingered, making her mind spin. She gazed on the white tree with the bright red branch. Despite being weathered by the desert, bleached to the color of bone, the tree still remained wood. Elishevera, however, had become something else entirely. She had been transformed—submutated.

The hairs on her arms stood on end despite the heat. Her voice felt tiny and timid.

"What did you do to Elishevera?"

Istok pulled a spine from the back of his forearm and twirled it between his fingers. Suddenly, he jabbed at the air with it.

She flinched.

"Three pricks," he told her. "I expected her to turn into a stone like any other creature, but I discovered she was a little bit of everything—flesh and flora and mineral." He sighed.

"On the first try her glitter turned to dust, but she still lived. The second try, parts of her turned to bone, but the third try," he nodded at the memory, "once the last bits of her turned to stone, she was finally done. I could have pricked her a fourth time, turned her completely to dust, but there was fun to be had watching the Mystics and Priests mourn and squabble." He chuckled.

A hot, piercing anger engulfed Ule. She curled her hands into fists and when she spoke, her voice cracked. "Elishevera was beautiful, the heart of this world—"

"She was a fat pig!"

Struck by his outburst and bile, she trembled.

"She would've swallowed the world whole if it weren't for me putting an end to the libations," he ranted. "This world should thank—"

His silence was sudden. She found the slow melting of his anger into curiosity unnerving.

He tilted his head. "How can you know her ancient name?" Bending his good arm at the elbow, he directed the forearm toward her.

Instinct silenced all thought and emotion, propelling her into action. She lunged toward Avn, but the demon swiveled and shot the spine toward her. She stumbled, lost her balance, and pitched forward into the sand.

The whoosh of a second projectile passed overhead, and she buried her face in the sand, hoping for the best. Nearby, something heavy hit the ground.

"One down," Istok muttered.

Frantic, she searched the dust haze. When the air cleared, she found her Master glinting beneath the sunlight as a jagged chunk of cuprite.

"Avn?"

A shadow loomed over her. She rolled over and shuffled away from Istok.

"He's like you," he mumbled. "Or, you're like him, that's right, eh? Not Mystics. Not demons either. Something... else."

Tilting his head, Istok forced a smile. He plucked another spine from his forearm and rolled it between his fingers, back and forth.

Kicking up sand, she crawled backwards. Slate shards nicked the tender flesh of her palms. The growing distance between her and Avn riled her anxiety until she thought she would lose her breath.

She expected the demon to stoop and pick up the gemstone but his gaze was riveted on her. Carefully, he sucked at the tip of the red spine and rolled it over his lower green lip. She knew he wanted the first gemstone he had created too. He wanted both.

Caged, immobile, ineffectual, she had been valued for being possessed by others. Beyond touch yet still sensing a world just out of reach, her mind had collapsed into fantasy to soothe the misery of disconnection. The pain, the isolation—she couldn't experience it again.

She relied on her instincts as Istok advanced, his hand curling around the spine.

Wandering about the world without her memories had made her feel disconnected too. Yet, once she looked inward and discovered deeper facets which reflected constant aspects of her nature, she found herself connecting to something weighty, solid, and true. Like an anchor, whatever she discovered there kept her steady while everything else spun around her.

Bolting to her feet, she dove for the fragment of cuprite jutting from the sand.

Startled by the motion, Istok stumbled backward casting the spine into the trunk of the dead tree. It collapsed in a rain of ash and billowed into the air once it touched the ground.

Clutching the gemstone, Ule shifted her molecules and pushed down into the ground, where she streamed through the topsoil toward the archway. Near the portal, she emerged, took solid form, and snatched the gray and peach stone.

Shifting again, she streamed high into the sky above the archway and began to re-materialize. Smoky tendrils reformed into an eagle clutching a stone in each claw. A spine whistled at her. She swooped to avoid it. With a burst of flapping, she climbed higher into the sky.

Broken images of desert and sky danced together. The gleam of rippling sand distorted the fractured horizon until Avn adjusted his perception to accommodate the spherical scope of the world fully surrounding him.

In every direction, images of sky, land, and feathered bird bombarded him with information as he struggled against the stone prison. Bound within, he found himself unable to move beyond or between the crystal lattices of cuprite.

Above him, Ule's wings curved to hitch onto an air current and circled toward Sondshor Market. Within, a vibration began. Small at first, it increased until he recognized it as his own anxiety.

"You shouldn't have done that," he told her.

"Under the circumstances—"

"Breaking rules isn't my concern. I've broken many here," he said. "Istok already suspects we're something out of the ordinary."

A shrill squeal erupted from Ule. Pivoting in the sky, she swooped lower to the ground. "If it hadn't been for him," she seethed. "If he hadn't turned me into a gemstone, you wouldn't have had to endure a war or be turned into a gemstone too. None of this would've happened."

"You'd still be trapped, behind the barrier in the upper atmosphere," he reminded her. "Because Ibe failed to instruct you properly."

In the silence that ensued, he saw a sprawl of makeshift buildings flowing along one side of an ancient river bed dotted with footbridges. Sondshor Market fanned out creating a half circle—an odd, asymmetrical pattern.

During the many months that had passed since the final battle with Adinav, he sought to understand what had happened to undo the magic of the gemstone. Research and rituals failed to provide any insights. He had hoped to find documents accounting for demon culture, but like the Xiinisi, the inhabitants of Elish seemed to know little about their shadow halves.

"There's nothing for us in Sondshor."

Ule's chest rumbled as she warbled. "Where else then?"

What he knew for certain, of all the demons he had encountered, one in particular was by far the most effectual. "Turn back, toward

Woedshor. In the desert, there's a grove."

"Kaleel's grove?"

He noted the worry in her voice.

"I doubt he'll talk to me again," she said.

The vibration inside him spun a little quicker. The confines of the gemstone tightened.

"He'll want to when you show him me."

Descending through air currents, she glided down toward the ground. Nearing the grove, she swooped over the desert and saw a curious object stretched out in the sand.

Silently, she circled back through the air.

"What are you doing? Whoever that is must be dead."

"I recognize that vest," she said.

Landing at a distance from the body, Ule looked around in all directions. Nearby the grove shimmered. Before her, the body groaned. Quickly she rematerialized, returning to her humanoid form. She slipped both stones into the pocket of her ocher dress.

Being placed in the pocket cast a veil of yellow over Avn's perception, tinting the brightness of the world. He pushed his focus passed the dress fabric until he saw distinctly again.

Ule knelt next to the man. Again he was stunned by her strength as she turned the body over.

Elusis flopped over onto his back, revealing an empty whiskey flask he continued to clutch. His body reeked of the liquor, seeping from his pores in fumes. Sand pressed into his flesh and dusted his pin-striped vest. He hadn't shaved in days and his pallor was gray.

She shook him, forcing his eyelids to flutter, and they partially yielded to the touch of her fingertip. The whites of his eyes were bloodshot and jaundiced.

"What's he doing out here?" she wondered. Saddened, she sagged. "I can't leave him here." She grabbed hold of his arm and began to shake it.

Elusis awoke.

She shook him harder until he regained enough consciousness to eventually crawl and kneel, then stand. He ambled next to her, staggering every other step as he leaned on her shoulder.

"Do..." Elusis licked his dry lips. "Do I know you?"

"No," she lied. "My name's Ule. What's yours?"

"Elu... Elus..." He cleared his throat and waved at nothing in particular. "Ellie. She... she used to call me that. Ssshe can call me that again when I meet up with her."

Ule winced when he stepped on her open toed sandal. "Where are you meeting her?"

With great effort, he pointed to the grove. "Ssshe's gone before me. Thasss okay. I'll lie next to her sssoon. I'll lie next to all of my family in eternity."

"I'll take you," she told him, wiping at the sting of tears in her eyes.

He patted her shoulder and mumbled, "You're kind."

Too kind, Avn thought.

— 48 —

DRENCHED IN SWEAT, Ule swayed slightly on the soft grass before the porch of Kaleel's small home. Despite drinking a draught of water, her tongue still felt dry, mostly from her nerves being on edge. Fleeing from one demon to engage with another seemed futile to her, and she worried Kaleel would try to charm her, against her will.

Surprised to see her again, Kaleel joined her on the small patch of lawn. Leaning against the railing, he sucked on a long, tapered pipe. Puffs of smoke burst from his mouth and nostrils, sliding over his pale wrinkled face.

"Changed your mind about my offer?"

"No, I haven't." She waited for retaliation to her rejection, but the cat demon shrugged as he examined the chisel marks around the bowl of the smoking pipe.

Reaching into the pocket of her dress, she retrieved the jagged rock. "There's someone I'd like you to meet."

"Him?" Kaleel nodded at the figure sitting on the porch steps. "He's a right mess, eh? Mm, I've seen worse come here."

Ule knew Elusis looked terrible. The sun had baked his skin and some of the alcohol from his system, sobering him slightly as they walked the rest of the way to the grove. Once inside, several tumbles during their trek through the forest had torn his clothes and nicked his arms and cheeks.

He sat upright on the porch steps, Mulga at his side. His shirt was drenched with sweat. Cheeks flushed, he blinked profusely, smacking his lips at every haul of water Mulga offered him from a clay pitcher.

"Not him," Ule said. She held out her hand.

Kaleel leaned in to inspect the cuprite cradled in her palm. The salty, woodsy tobacco smoke swirled about him and began to cling to her as well. He rubbed the mouth piece of the pipe over an upper fang.

"I've seen something similar to this before," he mumbled.

Withdrawing her hand, she frowned.

"At the castle, where Adinav fell," he continued. Slyness curled the edges of his lips. His blue eyes glossed over and he began to nod. "During the final battle, Adinav's pet demon, armed with a war hammer, set out to destroy me. I chopped off his arm, stormed the Inner Sanctum, and cornered that heinous peacock. Oh, how the great Magnes squawked and quivered before me wielding a scepter as his only weapon—"

"That's not how I remember it!"

Wrinkled flesh arced across Kaleel's forehead as the voice of her Master projected into the air.

Ule braced herself, uncertain how Kaleel might react to the disembodied voice. To her surprise, he maintained a constant calm of objectivity.

From behind her, however, Elusis cried out frantically, "Who's that?"

Water splashed over the sides of the pitcher as Mulga set it on the steps next to her. "There, there," she cooed, softly patting his shoulder. Then she leapt to her feet, clambered down the steps, and rushed to Ule's side.

Ule tensed at the woman's proximity to her, who she recognized as Istok's lover from long ago, and began piecing together fragmented memories of Mulga and an enduring pain she associated with her.

"Oh, hello again," Mulga said to the stone. "I'm glad to hear you're well enough to talk now. I didn't mean to break you before."

Ule thought if she tried to explain that the gemstone was a different one, it might confuse Mulga, and so she remained quiet.

Finished with smoking, Kaleel tapped the pipe on the porch railing. Burnt tobacco tumbled from the bowl. With a sniff, he went to pat Mulga then stopped, his talons nearly touching her arm. Instead, he growled, low in his chest.

Unaffected by the aggressive sound, Mulga backed away.

He rested the pipe on the railing and inched forward for a closer look. Leaning over Ule's hand, his whiskers twitched and his nostrils flared with every sniff.

"Smells like Istok's work," he mumbled to the stone. "That you're alive says great things about you, but I don't know what you want from me."

"You can release him," Ule suggested.

Grinning, Kaleel chortled. "I brag a lot about the war, I admit, but I'm not *that* powerful."

"Your sword is." Avn's words were loud and firm. Nearby, two old men paused in conversation to stare in Ule's direction.

"She doesn't sound better," Mulga confided in Elusis as she used the remaining water from the pitcher to help him wash his hands. She spoke louder, addressing the stone. "Do you have a cough? Your voice sounds funny."

Struck by Mulga's genuine concern, Ule felt her anger cool. Old memories were being dampened by a recent one in which Mulga helped Ule escape from Istok and brought her to safety.

Attention fully occupied by the gemstone, Kaleel rubbed his chin. His tone was stern and cautious when he asked, "Tell me stranger, what do you know of my sword?"

"It's cast of metal from the lair of Areel, Mother of all Demons."

She wondered why Avn referred to one of the world's earliest errors when she had fixed it so long ago. Annoyed, she interrupted. "Areel isn't—"

Avn hushed her.

"A real demon?" Kaleel finished her sentence.

Surprised by his insight, Ule clenched the stone. Scanning the yard, she searched for all possible escapes just in case Kaleel was like Istok and wanted the gemstone for himself.

"I've been told this before," Kaleel mused. "By a smith who denied me a toast to our victory at Sunset."

"My apologies," Avn said. "I nearly died that day."

Again, wrinkles formed across the demon's face. Eyes wide, he nodded. "I always thought you should have died outside the Inner Sanctum, the way a smart man would after half his ribs were smashed to bits."

Dread struck Ule hard as she considered the nature of the injury Avn had endured in his struggle to keep her safe. He spoke nothing of what he had done or what had been done to him during the war, only that he had broken their laws but was willing to carry that burden. No matter how often she asked, he denied her any of the details, until now.

"Your sword can break this magic," Avn said.

Bowing his head, Kaleel scratched the back of his neck. "What's in it for me?"

"Since when do you snub the chance to undermine or annoy

Istok?" Avn laughed. "You have an opportunity to do both by freeing another of his victims."

Kaleel clicked his jaw while he thought. "Another? The other stone, was that a friend of yours?"

Stretching to full height, the cat demon towered over Ule.

She mustered all her strength to maintain her composure in his presence.

"No one survives my brother's pricks," Kaleel told the stone. "You should be dead... again!"

"Come, Kaleel," Avn began to cajole. "Aren't you at all curious about the power you wield?"

"Perhaps." Kaleel shrugged as he stared across the lawn. "Maybe a little."

Ule listened intently to every word spoken—and not spoken—between Avn and Kaleel, searching for some sort of leverage until Mulga's soft nattering to Elusis inspired an idea.

"Elusis!" She pointed at the slowly sobering merchant. The return of his discontent showed in the way his nose twitched into a sneer.

"He'll be as nasty as the whiskey he drinks once it wears off," she said. "You may want to slip him one of your bracelets, if you'd like."

Both surprise and delight softened Kaleel's expression. "You're giving him to me?"

"I don't agree with what you do here, but it's better than letting people kill themselves."

Lifting the cuprite higher into the air, she hoped her conviction would affect the demon.

"You can keep Elusis in exchange for releasing Avn," she offered.

Deep in thought, Kaleel squinted. A thin, bristly tongue dragged along his lower lip and wrapped around a fang. Sucking it back into his mouth, he slowly nodded. "I can agree to that arrangement."

From a black pouch mounted to his bone belt, he fished out a gold chain. As he was about to unfasten it, she stopped him.

"Release Avn first," she demanded. "Then you can charm Elusis."

She wasn't sure what to make of the cat demon's throaty chuckle or the leer he cast her. He pocketed the bracelet and climbed the wide porch steps, brushing past Mulga.

When he returned, he brandished the steel saber with an arched blade. Delicate fine lines embellished the flat steel, which diminished to a smooth, razor sharp edge. The subtle contradiction in the sword's gentle yet harsh design stunned Ule, as she wondered how something so beautiful had contributed to the visceral mess of war.

"Set me down in the grass," Avn instructed.

Uneasy about what might happen, Ule obeyed. She pushed the stone into the soft earth and stepped back.

Kaleel practiced a swing, raising the scepter high and stopping before it touched the gemstone. "Are you sure about this?"

"Absolutely," Avn answered.

Ule detected urgency in Avn's projected voice and wondered if he suffered the same increasing panic she had when she had been a stone.

Kaleel shuffled his paw like feet. He rested the tip of the saber on the gemstone. "Step back," he told her. "I seem to remember the impact as rather explosive."

Reluctantly, she distanced herself. She watched the stone to be sure Kaleel wouldn't attempt some slight of hand trickery and steal it.

Raising the saber high above his head, he swung down with full force. The blade struck the gemstone. The crack of metal against stone was followed by a thud as the blade veered into the earth.

"Mm, no, can't say that worked," Kaleel muttered, yanking the sword from the soil.

Ule listened for a response from Avn but heard only silence. Her legs began to tremble as she strained to hear past the loud pulse resounding in her head and Mulga's sudden chattering.

"She won't talk to you now." Mulga's discreet whisper to Kaleel was heard by everyone.

Images of being dashed against a floor reminded Ule of the sharp pain that resulted from the impact. It seared through her and around her for such a long time. About to lunge for the rock, she struggled to cry out for her Master until she heard his voice.

"There was blood." Slow and thoughtful, Avn spoke carefully. "It lit on fire."

Ule exhaled shakily.

"Yes, Istok's blood." Kaleel pointed the saber tip toward the stone. "From when I stabbed him. Do you want me to hunt him down now? I won't mind—"

"Wait!" Ule's thoughts spun. A memory kept replaying in her mind, one where she walked the path leading to Kaleel's home and found herself surrounded by children.

She pointed to Mulga, who smiled at the gesture and blinked her large brown eyes. Reluctant to distance herself further from Avn, Ule espied the fine scar encircling Mulga's left wrist.

"She can't wear your bracelets," she said. "You can't touch her, can you?"

"Not even for a second." Kaleel nodded. "It burns her."

"Maybe it's not Istok's blood you need," she said.

"If not the blood itself," Avn interrupted, "then perhaps what it contained caught fire."

Unwilling to leave her Master unattended, she waved at Mulga, urging her to come. After several moments of staring blankly, Mulga leapt to her feet and ran to Ule's side.

Ule addressed Kaleel, "You told Mulga she couldn't use magic because she was magic. Istok's magic."

Kaleel shook his head vehemently. "I won't gut her the way I did Istok. Never."

"We only need a little of her blood," Avn implored. "A small cut—"

"Istok's magic isn't just in her blood," Ule interrupted, "it's in her flesh as well."

Rearing backward, Kaleel sneered. "Do you expect me to cut off a body part?"

"No!" Exasperated, Ule pulled Mulga to her side. "Istok is in every part of her." Leaning forward, she spoke softly into Mulga's ear. "You won't feel a thing."

Ule began combing her fingers through Mulga's long dark hair. Loose strands gave way freely, weaving about her fingers. When she'd harvested enough, she crouched and carefully draped each hair over the gemstone. Once completed, she ushered Mulga back toward the porch.

With a shrug, Kaleel raised his scepter again and swung it down. Blade upon stone set off a deafening boom that rattled the porch and resounded through the forest.

Kaleel flew backward across the yard, the porch railing cracking beneath the force of his body.

High above, the forest canopy rippled and settled down again.

Regaining his stance, Kaleel stretched out his lower back and watched fragments of cuprite dance over the yard, aligning themselves to each other.

Ule watched too, shielding her eyes as they began to glow. Intense white light blinded her momentarily. The world rushed back into view along with Avn, sitting upright in the yard.

Remembering his wound, Ule rushed to his side prepared to help him heal, but the wound was mending rapidly along with his torn smith apron. Relieved, she fell against his chest and hugged him, grateful for his presence.

From the corner of her eye, she watched Kaleel give the saber to Mulga, who retreated quickly into the house and returned empty handed. The cat demon seemed both intrigued yet surprised by the transformation as he approached them.

"Friend!" Yet the tone in his voice felt neither friendly nor warm.

"Demon," Avn countered.

"I know what I am." Kaleel narrowed his eyes. "But what are you?"

As Ule embraced her Master, she felt the muscles in his back tense. His arms stiffened as he firmly grabbed her by the shoulders. He meant to separate them, but she refused to let go. Though her arms yielded a little and she loosened her grip, they remained wrapped about his waist, grateful to feel his warmth and the flow of energy molding his form.

"More powerful than a Mystic," Kaleel mused, "yet too human to be demon. You must be… Xiinisi?"

Stunned, Ule regarded the demon. "How—" But she stopped speaking when Avn's thick arm tightened around her, nearly squeezing the breath from her lungs.

"I've been around since…" Kaleel's almond shaped eyes rolled upward as he mentally counted. "…a long time. I remember the ancient demons, the first ones, telling stories about a race of world builders. Xiinisi. Am I saying it correctly?"

Ule shivered. Avn squeezed her slightly, enough to help settle her nerves. Neither of them responded.

"Your name is Avn," Kaleel pointed at her Master. "And you." He pointed at her. "Have you remembered who you are?"

She nodded briefly.

"Will you tell me?"

The demon had a gentle, charming tone.

Purposefully silent, she clung to Avn, her name about to spill from the tip of her tongue.

"I'm used to humans fearing me," Kaleel sang. "Have from the beginning of time. And now you two as well." He backed away from them, arms open wide. "No?" He fished the bracelet from the pocket in his leather trousers. "Do we still have an arrangement?"

Heavy hearted, she eyed Elusis. Whatever effect the alcohol had offered him was fading. Anger chiseled his face. Lips clenched, he forced his jaw out. Broken blood vessels reflected his grief. He wrung his hands then rubbed his eyeballs.

She had, for a brief time, the illusion of having lost her family while she endured amnesia. They were phantom parents and siblings, she realized, with a phantom feeling of disconnection.

Sitting before her, Elusis struggled with his reality, not with phantoms and fantasies. He was all that remained of his immediate family, and though she might never understand the nature of that particular type of grief, she had felt bereavement with the loss of Elishevera and Yensilva and from being removed from her kind.

"Yes," she told Kaleel. "We still have an arrangement." Squeezing Avn, she buried her face in the crook of his neck. "Please, we must go," she whispered, "before I change my mind."

— 49 —

EMERGING FROM BETWEEN bowed saplings, Avn crossed from grove into desert, where he saw Ule squint at the vast blue sky.

"Let's go home," she said.

He stood next to her, extending his mind. He felt her presence and pushed beyond until he detected another—faint, subtle, slippery. Like a breeze, a phantom presence flitted about just at the edge of his consciousness.

"I can't ascend," he reminded her and motioned to the sky. "Because of the barrier."

Nodding slowly, she gazed downward. Her voice sounded far away and a little sad when she spoke. "Ibe told me to make it. He seemed to think I could and I believed him because, and I feel silly now for thinking it, I loved him."

She circled around Avn. Her ocher dress snapped in all directions as the erratic wind pushed and pulled the light fabric. "It's only meant to contain the errors."

"It's containing everything," he told her. "Including us."

"Tell me how and I'll fix it."

"This isn't something to be taken lightly." He grabbed her by the shoulders and held her still. "Time's compressed down here compared to our realm. Should you undergo the Quietus here, your final death will trap both Ibe and I. Because we're older, it seems more likely we'll pass before you do, and you'll be alone again, cut off from our kind until you can figure out on your own how to breach the barrier." His words were harsh yet necessary. "Nod, if you understand."

Panic tinged her eyes. She nodded sadly.

"What's worse, the demons have retained a memory of us, and I..." Avn tried to fathom the possibility. "This has never happened before." Pulling her by the arm, he led her from the grove. "I need to train your focus and quickly."

Yielding to his wishes, she walked double time to match his stride. "W-why?"

"We're being watched." Avn scanned the horizon of dunes. "By the cactus demon, maybe Kaleel. I can't tell. Both of them have good reason to retain our powers. Let's keep moving. First, we must stock up on supplies." He pulled at the skirt of her ocher dress. "Find more appropriate clothes."

And he steered them toward Sondshor Market.

Ule watched the marvelous way the tendons and muscles in Avn's legs glided in tandem with one another as he climbed the gentle slope of a small dune. She understood why most of her kind maintained humanoid form in their realm and could never tire of its subtle, sophisticated grace.

They had been traveling for days, since their departure from Sondshor Market, where they purchased sacks and packed them with food, filled their canteens with water at the smithy, and scoured the market for appropriate desert gear.

He wore half-pants and a short tunic with long split sleeves, like the Northmen they'd seen in the Market. The fabric was a deep forest green, except for his turban, which was black. Slung across his broad shoulders were rolled up hides which they had purchased from a Woedshor hunter at the edge of the desert.

Avn stopped at the peak of the dune and turned his entire body toward her. Empty flasks strapped across his chest and at his belt clanked together. Through a veil of thin black cotton, which he used to cover most of his face, he shouted, "There's an oasis to the west."

She smiled at the opportunity to rest, to remove some layers of teal cotton fabric which were wrapped tightly about her body, creating a form fitting shift which stopped at her knees. She protected herself against the sun with black scarves draped across her bare neck and chest and wrapped around her arms. She also wore a black turban, appearing like a Northwoman.

She knew they only rested when the desert felt calm; as soon as Avn sensed something stir within his awareness, they moved again. Still, even with these precautions, sometimes he glimpsed shadows from the corner of his eye, and he urged her to continue on.

They had been traveling toward Elishevera. At night they conserved their energy by sleeping next to a small fire, and they never stayed in one place long enough to be seen by other travelers or detected by what followed them through the desert.

At first, she had been tempted to beg Avn to let them stop and began thinking of excuses: To drink some water, she first thought, but their water was nearly depleted. To empty the sand from her shoes, except they were open between the straps, allowing grains to pass through while the thick sole stopped her heels from being burned. Urgency drove Avn and she decided not interrupt his focus with fake excuses.

As soon as the fine sand was underfoot, he began teaching her immediately. He instructed her about barrier construction and dismantling. Most importantly, he showed her ways to hone her focus. Sharpening the mind began with sharpening visual focus which was accomplished by looking at points at farther distances then what she found comfortable, he explained.

The desert offered distant, unobstructed vistas, and within their current environment being an advantage to her training, she was certain to improve quickly. She practiced, and practiced more, pushing her skills only to discover her ability progressed slowly.

In the west, through the distortion of heat radiating from the sand, she recognized the sprawl of tents, wagons, and camels Avn pointed toward. The caravan looked the same as the last time she had seen it. Red canopies and soldiers bound in white had been untouched by the centuries, herself as well. Memories of being poked and stoned roused an old dread, which crawled from her mind and curled up inside her belly.

Ule wanted nothing to do with the Bisi.

She reminded herself that the Bes and the women she once met had died long ago. Sabien had proved that in his exhibition with the funeral box of the armless woman. The Bisi from the past could not hurt her again. This thought soothed the beast of dread, and it retreated back into her mind.

They resumed walking. She focused on the steady climb, on the dents left behind in the sand by Avn's sandals, on the overwhelming gratitude she had started feeling toward him for ensuring her safety and protection, for caring when she thought none of her kind did.

A blast of wind stung her cheeks.

"A storm's coming," she announced, glimpsing tumbleweeds. Tiny cactus pups rolled and bounced over the sand and her feet, prickling her exposed skin.

Eyes rolled upward, lashes fluttering, Ule sputtered. Her turban unwound, tumbling from her head. Her jaw clenched as another spasm shook through her body.

Clutching her tightly, Avn cradled her, comforted her while her nervous system began to collapse. As her breathing turned to rasping, he reviewed their previous activities for the day, searching for an answer.

She had successfully achieved microscopic vision of the back of a scorpion, viewing wriggling corpuscles within the mites adhered to its exoskeleton. Her mood elevated. She took the lead as they continued wandering just beyond the encampment surrounding the oasis.

Despite her accomplishment, she had been quiet and withdrawn. She stopped several times to pluck cactus pups that had stuck in the leather of her sandals. Every time she flicked her hand and sucked her fingers.

In her other hand, she still clutched the gray and peach stone, squeezing it tightly every few minutes, and he wondered why she held onto Yensilva.

He had pushed his mind into hers, just a little, expecting resistance. Instead he discovered her mind partially open and felt her anger waxing and waning. The tension of some struggle consumed her, and it peaked every time her gaze fell on the oasis in the distance. With every revolution, the struggle diminished and finally slipped away. Her fingers uncurled and let go of the stone. Sweat began to soak through her dress, and her breath grew heavy. She dropped to her knees struggling for air.

He had collapsed next to her, asking what was wrong. She began to spasm. He searched his awareness for another presence in the desert. The wind had picked up. Tumbleweed and debris rolled over the terrain. He detected nothing yet still felt uneasy.

Leaning over her, he examined her closer. Between parted lips, he discovered her tongue black and swollen. Her breath reeked of iron and decay, the cactus demon's signature magic scent.

He understood now what followed them in the desert—offshoots of the demon. Knowing Istok could cast poisonous remnants of himself throughout the world if he wished, Avn began to wonder and worry about what other lethal tricks the demon possessed.

He waited until Ule laid still, eyes half open, her body limp and lifeless and spilling from his arms.

Like a trickling effect, he observed her lean body mold into firmer muscle. She grew a little taller, darkened her skin. She pushed her yellow hair to a longer length. Her deathmorphing was slow, subtle, and familiar.

A whiff of ginger hung in the air as she regenerated and willed herself into a variation of her former body, and something about her magic scent intrigued him, for it had changed. The usual spicy sting was partially interrupted by the smell of something sweet and sharp.

Her breath returned and her body settled, yielding to Avn's embrace. She opened her eyes.

"Sorry about that," she whispered.

He held onto her. "I'm not. What I witnessed was... unusual."

"Wh-what did I do?" she croaked.

"You didn't dematerialize while you regenerated."

"I didn't?" Concerned, she touched his arm. "Is there something wrong with me?"

He shook his head wanting to shake away her self doubt. "No, it's just a rare skill. A few of the Masters can regenerate that way."

"Oh," she said weakly. "That is strange."

Avn smiled.

— 50 —

AVN STOOD CLOSE. Too close. The hairs on Ule's arms prickled beneath her veil sleeves yet she refused to back away. Stiffening, she let out a long breath and felt it bounce off his chest.

"Now you must learn to summon the meditative flame," he began. The rolls of hides on his back cast shadows across his face.

She had done this many times. All she needed was an object to anchor the flame, and she searched the sand until she found a shard of slate. She extended her arm, held the thin rock in the palm of her hand, and began to focus her intent.

He slapped the rock from her hand. It toppled onto the ground and split in two. "Not like that," he said.

"Why do you have to be so rough?!"

She regretted her words the moment she spoke them. When Avn stopped and peered over his shoulder, she froze.

"Is it him?"

"Maybe," he mumbled, urging her to move. They climbed to the crest of a dune and walked a mile before stopping again.

"Shall we go down into this gully?"

"No," he muttered, scanning the desert. He placed his fingertips on her breastbone in the center of her chest. "You need to summon the flame here. Now."

She gasped at his aggression, shifting the pack of their remaining food supplies slung across her back. Frowning, she listened to his instruction.

"The flame's a form which best reflects the nature of thought, it's... movement." He spoke carefully. "You'll feel that movement inside you, understand what it conveys. It won't burn, if that's what you're worried about. It might seem warm. The sensation is different for everyone."

He took her hand in his, turned her palm upward. "We begin here." His calloused fingers prickled her skin when he touched the center of her palm. "Summon the flame here the way you would with any object external to you."

She had used lanterns and dark black filaments in the Isolation Chamber and... something else. She searched her mind for other experiences, her gaze drifting across the desert. She imagined a grassy field, the wind whipping around her as though she was flying yet she remained close to the ground...

Avn squeezed her hand.

"Ow!"

"Stay focused," he growled.

"The voice," she snipped. "I'll hear it inside me?"

He nodded impatiently.

Delight pushed her annoyance aside. She understood. Instead of telling her Master, she would show him. Eyes glistening, she smiled deeply as she stepped backward and held out her hand. From her upturned palm, a tiny blue flame suddenly sprang from her flesh.

"Hello," the flame said to her. Then it bowed toward Avn and sang, "Oh, it's you little black bird. I see you became a man."

Avn snorted as though stunned by the immediate display of this ability. He was about to speak, when she stepped backward, motioning him to wait.

Without instruction, she focused on the flame and imagined it inside, deep within her solar plexus. The flame crawled toward her wrist, becoming a light blue aura licking along her arm until it sank beneath her flesh and withdrew inside.

Warmth radiated in her chest from the place Avn had indicated with his touch. Had she not experienced this sensation before, in a moment when she had held onto a bolting horse for fear of falling, pulling the meditative flame inside her might have taken a very long time to learn.

She sucked in her breath when Avn roughly gripped her by the back of the neck. He pulled her close to him. She shuffled clumsily in the sand, the weight of her pack pitching to one side. She sucked in her breath as Avn kissed her hard and long.

The meditative flame inside flickered away.

Stunned, she barely registered his eyes dancing all over her, the broad smile of satisfaction spreading across his scarred face.

A hand on either side of her face now, he searched her eyes. "Who taught you that?"

Nervously she touched her lips.

"Come on," he said, moving his hands to her shoulder and squeezed her. "Out with it! How did you learn to summon the flame internally?"

Smoothing out stray strands of hair, she found her scattered thoughts. She met his eyes briefly, tried to still a rising heat inside her. She cleared her throat, and finally replied, "I learned it from a horse."

Ule poked the fire with a branch, shifting embers into a small pile, and watched the tip blacken and crackle. The image of a much larger fire burned in her mind. Around it, women stomped the ground in wide circles, honoring and celebrating femininity.

"I channeled the An Energy once," she said. The word demon echoed in her mind. "I was dancing."

Warmth cascaded over her knee where Avn's fingers touched her. She was surprised at how cold she had become since the sun had set.

"Describe the movement."

"Sort of circular?"

She glimpsed his stern expression, saw something other than firelight flicker in his eyes. Sitting back, she wondered just how angry he must be with her for building this world, for trapping him, for being so damned flawed.

"Like this?" Starting low and lifting his arm, he inscribed a spiral in the air with his forefinger.

Nodding, she hugged herself. She pushed backward through her thoughts, passed the moment where she fled the Bisi encampment chased off by words and stones, her feet nearly dragging along the ground with fear.

"I had felt like I was floating," she recalled. "There was this bubbling inside, you know, a lightness that comes from excitement and joy."

Avn nodded.

"The world, well, it was like it was inside me," she continued. "Instead of me being inside the world." Images of entwined limbs and phantom moans flooded her mind. She smirked. "Don't know if it's the same experience being male. I suppose I should try that some time." Biting her lip, she thought briefly. "It's like this climbing, circling, rising feeling, then boom, you're floating."

"Ule?"

She caught her breath. "Yes?"

Squinting at her, he rubbed his beard. "Are you talking about sex or dancing?"

The question made her pause. She stared into the fire. "Both," she replied.

Afterward, he spoke very little. His mood turned pensive, and she couldn't help wondering if she had done or said something to upset him.

He focused on packing warm embers from their campfire into a small trench of sand which formed a large circle. Once filled, he imbued it with protection so they might rest properly yet be shielded from harm, if only for a few hours.

They spread hides over the sand within the circle until he paused and regarded her. "What is it?"

"Nothing," she nearly whispered, stunned by his abruptness.

"Speak your mind!"

She shivered at his tone. "Only... if you set Ibe free, he could assist you with my training or he could stand guard while I practice, anything to help relieve the pressure for you."

"Someone who expresses so little faith in your ability can't help you," he told her.

She was struck by the notion. Ibe had often doubted her ability. The realization stirred a deep irritation. She should have felt sad, but didn't. Whatever rejection she had once felt, long ago when she first descended into this world, had vanished.

Avn lay back on the hides. Eyes closed, he pinched the bridge of his nose. "He keeps raging, and I won't release him while he's like that. Not here. He'd only make our situation worse."

"Is he completely isolated?"

"No," he answered. "He sees, hears, and feels everything I do."

She curled next to Avn, resting her hand on his bicep. She nudged the tip of her cold nose against his shoulder. He neither turned away nor moved to embrace her, but she didn't mind.

Pulling a cotton wrap tightly over her mouth, she closed her eyes against a breeze which crept across the sand. She was simply grateful for what warmth she felt where their bodies touched, for the comfort of his presence.

Next to her, Avn shifted. His fingertips brushed her cheek, pulling away the cotton wrap from her mouth. Before she could complain, his lips smothered hers. She gave into his kissing willingly, felt the strength of his body as it pinned her to the ground.

A warm flush crept through her chest and up her neck, and when his lips parted, a curious sensation of melting came over her. He pulled away and she saw his eyes were darkened by tendrils of smoke pouring from her body into his. Partially solid, other parts of her dematerialized and slipped inside him, being pulled along by his will rather than hers.

"W-what are you doing?" Panicked, she clutched at the solidity of his arms and struggled for breath.

"Haven't you ever merged before?"

She shook her head frantically. "No," she gasped. "No one's wanted much to do with me since Isolation."

Within Avn, her energy spun around fine currents—a curious dance between them that both aroused and frightened her. His presence was unyielding and powerful.

"I assumed you..." He shook his head. "Give into the merging so that I can understand this sensation of movement you experience. It'll help me understand more quickly."

Knowing what he had done to protect her, all the generations he had lost being down in the world, she intrinsically trusted him. Abandoning her fear, she descended into his form, where all the fine currents pulled her toward his essence. At his very core, she gazed into the blazing light of a Master.

"Now recreate the sensation and movement," he said.

Terrified by the power she sensed in him, she mustered the courage to resurrect the strange spinning that ran from her stomach down into her groin.

Fear melted away. Loneliness evaporated. Tiny sparks of joy ignited as a result of the strange union. For the first time, she felt fully connected with another of her kind.

Finally, Avn released her, and she poured back into her form, rematerializing beside him. Catching her breath, she pressed into him again and kissed him.

"Rest now," he told her, peeling her arms from around his neck.

As she shielded her face again with the cotton wrap, restlessness overcame her. She understood now what she could become. The potential within waited to burst open. More than anything, in that moment, she wanted to become a Master.

— 51 —

POSSESS HER.

Avn fought the impulse, as he stood before her, shoulders braced, back rigid—on guard.

He had died again and again from the points of swords and the blows of maces, even the force of a dying Mystic's thought. Violent deaths bored into his heart, and still he fought all urge to take control of the world and every living thing in it.

Ule collapsed in the sand for the tenth time. She hugged herself, shuddering with rage. He was grateful she kept her gaze downcast for he worried she might see her disappointment and frustration reflected in him.

Helplessness came over him as he watched her struggle to master her skill and power. Her desire to learn had escalated, ever since their departure from the oasis, since their merging. She had become quiet again, introspective, unusually cooperative.

They had skirted the Bisi Nomads' camp, for he sensed a vengeful despair inside her. At the pond they refilled their canteens and flasks with water, and then headed toward Elishevera. Less than a day's journey, they mingled briefly with devotees, exchanging what little money they had for food and new sandals before returning to the desert. At a safe distance from the prehistoric creature, they continued to move about.

Within him, Ibe raged in fits, anger pulsing in hot, forceful waves meant to wear down Avn's strength. From one day to the next, Avn felt his reserve of energy diminish. Feeding on snakes, lizards, and what food they had bought from the devotees helped restore him, but the sustenance did not last long.

Possess her.

He had fought through battles, pushed through the wounds and a growing heaviness in his heart, and when no battles were left to be fought, he focused on the hammer and anvil; he found some sense of peace in that kind of creation. He'd even met a man that final day of war on the drenched and littered battlefields, who nursed Avn back to health, mended his broken bones and his broken spirit.

"Possess me." Ule sank to her knees before him. Sweat and dust stained her cheeks.

Avn thought of the nights he woke wracked with anguish. Returning memories of the men he murdered haunted his dreams—their eyes unbridled and empty, their final cries desperate and painful. Regardless of whether or not fighting in the war was the right decision, he loathed destroying sentient life. Alive, functioning, compromised by the will of Adinav, these men had been destined to die anyway, he told himself to justify the breaking of such a significant Xiinisi law.

He hadn't done anything truly wrong, under these circumstances. He was certain the Council would understand the decisions he had made. Guilt, the residual remorse that comes with making the choice to destroy perfectly formed creations, would remain with him no matter what punishment the Council did or didn't demand. The dead returned every night, in his mind—war cries and grunts, mania melting into the pain of fatal wounds, blood muddying the ground, reflecting the lives he had stabbed, crushed, and beaten.

If not for Sabien, he might have made foolish decisions, caving into the pressure of being trapped in this world. His gratitude toward the man overwhelmed him.

Sabien had never once asked Avn about the war, the reason for his nightly distress. Instead, Sabien helped ease his mind with simple pleasures—the comfort and release found in sharing impromptu tales and, of course, sexual pleasure.

"Channel your energy through me," Ule urged. "The world will recognize my signature and respond, but it'll be your power, your will."

Yes, possess her.

He questioned his urgency to return. He had murdered, that was by far his worst crime. He had possessed creatures too, without their consent—an abusive act; another crime. The certainty of punishment awaited him, as it should, but it would be lenient because of circumstance—the barrier, the unique phenomenon of demons wandering the Root Dimension. Avn wondered what the Council would have to say about them!

He needed to return. Because it was protocol. Because it was honorable. Because if he spent another moment in this world, after all this time, he might make a poor decision.

"I won't mind," she insisted.

Avn fought the impulse again. Even with her permission, it still felt wrong, for he had failed her as a teacher. He had failed Ibe too, he realized.

"No! You're stronger than you realize." He dug into an inside pocket of his leather apron and withdrew a folded piece of dark brown leather. Pulling back the edges revealed a yellowed lens. Gently, he handed her the skullcap.

"Tell me more about the nexus," he said. Withdrawing a green apple from an outside pocket of his apron, he fished around in other pockets searching for a knife.

"It's the portal which connects the Root Dimension with the Chthonic—"

"No, no," Avn stopped her. "Tell me about this specific nexus. From the accounts I've read, it was alive."

Ule wilted beneath the sun. "Oh, you mean Elishevera." Her face softened as she brushed her fingers over the ancient symbols tooled into the leather. "What does it matter? She's dead now."

"It matters." He frowned at her. "It's the last place of contact between the An Energy and the Root Dimension, where you stopped creating."

"The big old bellybutton of the world," she said as she gazed blankly into the sand.

Avn snorted at her odd humor. Fumbling through one last pocket, his fingers curled around a small knife and pulled it free.

"The An Energy's more accessible at the nexus than anywhere else in the world," he told her. "By proximity, being as close to Elishevera as possible, provides the least obstructed path to accessing the An energy."

Tilting her head back, she blinked lazily at him. "I didn't know that." She lifted the leather garment which had nearly blackened over time. "I also don't know what this is."

"It's a skullcap. It'll help amplify your focus." He cut a slice of apple and the whiff of the pulp reminded him of Ule's magic scent. "Put it on. The lens goes in front."

She backed away from him, removing her turban and replacing it with the skullcap. She swayed side to side at first, her head tilted slightly as though she listened for music. Raising her arms to one side of her body, she began to twirl in a large, sweeping circle, her arms stretched outward on either side. Suddenly she froze and ducked to the ground, peering at the edge of the dune behind him.

Avn tossed the partially eaten apple aside and glanced around them.

"I—" She caught her breath. "I swore I saw something."

Staring at the crest of the dune, Avn projected his mind and sensed other beings in the vicinity. Devotees milled about to the east near Elishevera, and over the next dune, a family camped. Then he sensed lone presences.

"It's difficult to distinguish him from the others," he whispered.

The sand next to Ule exploded into a cloud of dust. Lunging forward, Avn grappled her to the ground as another spine whistled past. He shifted both of them, propelling downward through the sandstone and stopping at a thick layer of shale far below the surface of the desert. Flowing along the shale, they traveled to the southern outskirts of Elishevera.

Rising from below, they emerged within an empty valley. Rematerializing, Avn scanned the crests of the surrounding dunes and once he was satisfied no one could see them, he nodded at Ule to begin again.

Arms outstretched again, the skullcap appearing black next to her tangled blond hair, she swung herself into a slow twirl, tightening and quickening with every spin. Drawing her arms closer to her body, her movement steadied into a consistent tempo of spinning which Avn found compelling and intriguing.

Breathing heavily, eyes rolled back until only the whites could be seen, she stood gasping for air, her arms spread wide.

"I—"

Prepared to flee again, his eyes darted around the valley. "What is it?"

"I have hold of the An Energy," she gasped.

At the mention of this, Avn's breath stopped. He trembled slightly. Excited and relieved, the fear of her losing her grip helped him recover his wits.

"What do I do? What do I do?"

"Find the barrier," he said calmly. "Ascend into it." He extended his hand when he saw how she trembled. Before he touched her, he stopped, worried he might break her concentration.

"Ignore the interstices. Focus on the lattices instead. Disengage the currents the way you would between any two elements. Do it slowly, one at a time. One molecule will do. We only need the slightest breach to slip through."

Her chest heaved from the effort of her concentration. Face tilted skyward, she swayed slightly and shifted, dissolving into the air.

The An Energy spiraled through Ule, feeling very different from its usual meandering and malleable behavior. Like riding Crank, she chose not to struggle against the motion. Instead, she yielded to its dynamic force.

The barrier was easy to find. Ascending, she moved deeper into the infrastructure of the atmosphere where lighter gases separated from the heavier ones. She detected the barrier, unseen to the eyes of anyone other than Xiinisi. She chose the nearest lattice. Three primary energies converged at the same point, a braid of thread-like currents which fluctuated in color.

Gaps formed in the lattice work as Ule severed the ribbons of primary energy by directing her will to imagine an absence. The loose ends snapped about like raw nerve endings pulsing with electricity, then faded into black filaments. Quickly they settled, humming low, blending into molecular space.

Sturdier than the flats, braided currents took patience to disassemble. One by one, she disengaged each thread-like current from the other. As they came away from the whole, they gyrated away in a flurry, color fading into black until they disintegrated.

She paused in the molecular space, appreciating the strange new dynamic of the An Energy. Breathing with every molecule, relaxing into the space, a fit of panic overcame her. Not understanding the source of the feeling, she quickly realized the fear and urgency belonged to Avn.

Swiftly, she descended back into the world, beginning to pull her molecules back together into solid form. Far below her, she examined the separate elements of what she saw. The cactus demon straddled Avn. Blood seeped from a cut on Avn's forehead. In the sand, a small knife glittered in the sun. At the center of the gully, limp and discarded, the forearm of the demon lay palm up, twine stitches pulled loose and broken.

Istok turned his healthy forearm toward Avn. "How dare you break my arm again!"

She shifted instead, sweeping through the air between them. As she approached solid form, the force of her re-materializing blasted Istok halfway across the gully.

"What are you?" Scrambling to his feet, Istok scraped the sand with his talons. "How do you do that?"

Glimpsing Avn's half-dazed state, she needed to somehow convince the demon to retreat from his attack. He'd already seen displays of their power, so mutating would be no surprise to him. What she mutated into might, if she chose the right form.

Her mind shot backward through time to the ancient world. At first she considered becoming Elishevera, but he had never been afraid of her. However, there was another whom the demons revered.

Slowly her body turned to smoke. Tendrils drifted toward the center of her as though being pulled through a rift in the air. Fine lightning rippled around her edges as she turned into sky tearing apart. Tiny at first, the tear grew until she spanned the valley.

A tiny gasp escaped Istok. "Areel!" He sank to his knees. Bowing his head, he sank a little lower and muttered, "Mother."

Ule felt the reserve of energy inside her deplete rapidly. She reduced the size of the rift. Usually she would enjoy the intriguing push and pull of her form slowly transforming. Instead, she blasted back into humanoid form, the violence of it making her tremble.

Startled, Istok peered up and glowered. "Trickery is for weaklings," he spat. "You must be a Mystic after all. I only know of one powerful enough to pull off such illusions. You must be descended from Fehran's Mystic, no doubt. Goyas would've been proud." Standing to full height, he huffed, regarding Avn lying helpless in the sand.

Leaping with long strides, Istok lessened the distance between him and her Master, who stirred slightly. Stunned by the demon's speed, Ule panicked. Instinct gripped her. She felt that place within, where something solid, unyielding, and worth protecting took over.

Drawing strength from her experiences, she remembered tilling farmland, speaking her mind to Yensilva, fighting demons, working for the Magnes, staying mounted upon a half-crazed horse, and all these times she had listened to that voice inside—its wants and needs, its advice. The world fell away. At the center of her being, calm grabbed her attention.

Ule remembered she was Xiinisi, a creator who had once destroyed her creations, who was willing to sit in Isolation another millennium to save her Master, no matter the punishment.

Strength swelled inside of her at the declaration of that sentiment. It coalesced and twisted tight, imbuing her physicality. Lunging forward, she reached for what had been abandoned in the sand and raced across the gully.

Istok stopped to examine the body of Avn. Raising his only good arm, he turned the spines toward the unconscious man. At first he aimed high then low, trying to decide on whether to target Avn's head or heart.

Ule prepared for battle. In a wide arc, she swung her weapon. It buried into the demon's back, striking him hard. The impact wrenched the weapon from her grip.

Istok flew forward, sprawling across the sand. He rolled over to face her.

She watched the glint of his black eyes disappear as they rolled upward into his head. Mouth gaping, he bellowed in outrage. Beyond glistening black teeth and tongue, she saw deep into his insides and witnessed his darkness, which was barren, she realized, like the desert.

Sand stuck to the light green blood which seeped from his half arm. He pushed himself to his feet and staggered forward. Reaching at first over his shoulder then low behind his back, he tried to grab hold of the weapon stuck there—his other arm. Finally, he grasped the limp wrist and began to pull.

"I-is that all you've got whore cow?!"

"Let's see," she shouted. "I could rip your other arm off and stick it somewhere else along your backside."

He sneered at her before spinning around.

She saw the severed arm embedded between his shoulder blades, stuck there like a burr. She shivered at the mournful moan rising from deep within Istok's chest and cringed at the sucking noises of the severed arm being peeled away from his back. Tiny red spines tore free from the arm, remaining deeply embedded in his ribbed green flesh. He appeared more cactus now than man-like when he turned again and stumbled toward her.

"Beat me with my own arm, how pathetic!" He laughed. "That perfectly good knife could have done more harm."

He pointed at a spot in the sand. She glimpsed the glint of the steel blade and tried not to doubt her instincts, that she had made the better decision, the more poetic choice, of choosing his severed arm as a weapon.

A strangled gargle erupted from Istok's throat. He clutched the torn arm to his chest. Eyes bulging, he jerked as though wracked with pain. He moaned again as fine sprigs of green light began to crawl over his body. The air where he stood began to distort and ripple. He fought the collapsing air with his good arm, but his arm folded in on itself—hand into forearm, forearm into underarm. His legs began folding too.

Straining against the pressure building around him, he managed to keep his head erect, grimacing from the effort, until it snapped forward and pressed into his neck. He screamed, until his mouth was engulfed by his chest.

The mass of deformed body collapsed into a pinprick of light and exploded in a blinding flash. Where Istok's chest had once been, a black object hovered momentarily and fell to the ground, spraying sand into the air.

Ule searched the ground as the dust settled and found the stone. Oval and polished smooth, it appeared black at first, until she tilted the smooth surface toward the sun and saw a dark green sheen. Running through the center was a fine, ghostly pinkish light that moved with her eyes.

"Ule."

At the sound of her Master's voice, she clambered to his side and helped him sit upright.

"Be careful." His voice croaked. With great effort, he licked his dry lips. "The demon—"

"Is dead." She held up the stone for Avn to see. "At least I think he is."

Weakly, he took a hold of the stone and began examining it. "It's large," he mused.

"Just like his ego."

Avn smiled weakly. "That's odd," he said, brushing his thumb over the moving pink light. "Usually with kornerupines, the color's a lighter shade of green, sometimes yellow. This pink, it reminds me of..." After a moment, he mumbled, "Sabien."

"Of what?"

"Love," Avn replied.

"What kind of love? A love to scare people?" she said. She sat next to Avn in the sand and eased the leather strap of a water canister from around his neck. "Oh, I know, a love of himself."

Still groggy, Avn chuckled. He drank deeply from the canister, prompting the cut on his forehead to heal a little bit.

"I had no energy left," he said sadly. "No way to restore my strength. All I could do was watch."

As his vigor returned, she brushed her fingers across his temple. Seething suddenly consumed her. Rage stole her breath. Confused, her eyes locked onto Avn's. She gasped as a temper flooded her with heat and ferocity, and that didn't originate with her. There was no one else around. Only him. "A-are you angry with me?"

He shook his head and raised the stone in his hand. "It's him. He's still alive in there."

Tentative, she leaned over the stone and asked, "Can you hear us?"

In the ensuing silence, a wave of rage seared through her and receded, and she understood—he heard them perfectly.

— 52 —

EXCEPT FOR EROSION along the peaks of the giant petals where devotees walked the most, Elishevera remained posed in the same sprawled posture beneath the desert sun. Three hundred years might as well have been three days, for the beast remained opalescent and unaffected by time. The same soft, stale breeze issued from the crevice at the center, and although a different generation of devotees flocked to the beast, they explored her the way their ancestors had before them.

Ule drew her knees into her chest, curling her toes against the warm, hard surface of the creature beneath her—flower beast, friend, the embodiment of the world's nexus. Though her pangs of grief still persisted, they weren't nearly as strong as when she first descended into the world.

Next to her, Avn sat cross legged, scrutinizing the area clustered with tents and shanties and teeming with travelers. He scanned the vast lily, and Ule couldn't help wondering if he disapproved of her choice to embody the nexus within a living creature.

"It's time to return," he said. Unfolding his legs, he stood. "I need to release Ibe to the Council, sort out what to do with this world, and with you."

"Technically," she said, standing as well, "Istok isn't dead, so I didn't destroy anything... right?"

Avn grunted, more to himself than her.

Concerned, she touched his arm. "Is Ibe raging again?"

Arching an eyebrow, he shook his head. "He's been strangely quiet ever since Istok cracked me in the skull." He hooked his hand about her elbow and guided her away from a trio of children tumbling and shrieking over each other.

"I'm sorry about Elishevera," he said. "She's an impressive nexus."

Ule warmed at the compliment. "I'm worried I'll forget her," she said. "If it weren't for..." The words stuck in her mouth. She wanted to say Istok, and she struggled with the word demon, but something about the accusation felt wrong to her now.

"Do you think her death prevented the demons from passing over into the Chthonic Dimension?"

Avn moved his hand to the small of her back, prodding her forward between barrels of water.

"No. Demons were corporeal long after the An Energy receded, while Elishevera still lived." He guided her toward the gentle decline of a petal, which would lead them down to the ground with the least amount of effort.

"What happened here," he continued, "is the result of something else entirely. I have to ask," he paused momentarily, squinting at the sun, "what was going through your mind when you made this world?"

She stepped over the charred remains of an old campfire. Reluctant at first, she finally allowed memories of Isolation to flit through her mind.

"I wanted to be near my kind," she began. "Hear the chatter of their mindspeak. As I got older, the desire to merge with another became strong but there was no one around. Had there been, I would've with anyone."

She side-stepped an old man. Eyes white with cataracts, he tutted at her when their shoulders brushed one another, but she didn't mind the brief contact.

"I wanted to tear down those ugly chamber walls. They were keeping everything I loved away from me." Staring blankly ahead, she shrugged. "I was young and I was lonely." She regarded Avn. "Anyone could have done the same in Isolation."

"Then let's go home."

Thoughts began crawling through her mind, as she and Avn squeezed between tents, side-stepped horses and camels, and breached the outer edge of the encampment. Distracted, she followed Avn out into the desert where they couldn't be seen. Her steps grew tentative.

"We'll ascend here," he said, stopping on the peak of a tall dune.

"I did this."

Her voice was faint. Her heart pounded. A strange combination of dread and assuredness overcame her as she considered how Istok had struck Elishevera with his spines. Her friend had succumbed to his magic, which shouldn't have existed in the Root Dimension had Ule not made one simple wish when she first began building the world.

"I made this happen, Avn," she said, her voice gaining strength.

He huffed and extended his hand toward her. "Come, we'll discuss this back in our realm."

Stepping forward, she ignored his hand.

"I'm not going," she said.

Swift and forceful, bitterness tainted her Master's mood.

Trembling, she bit her lower lip and waited for the blast of his words of fury. Instead he spoke, softly. "What do you mean?"

"I'm responsible for this world, for Elishevera, for you and Ibe being trapped, myself too. It's all my design, don't you see?" She glanced around her. "If I hadn't made all these errors, the world would've evolved naturally."

"The world is evolving naturally!" The green in his eyes darkened. His fingers clamped down around her arm. "As it should for what this world is. Now come."

"What if the demons… become human?" She wrenched herself free from his grasp. "What if they rise up and take over the world?"

"Then that's the world's evolution."

"What if more tears appear in the construction? What if… there's another Adinav?"

Her Master balked at the suggestion. Clenching his jaw, he remained quiet and listened.

"This world needs someone to watch over it." She inched forward, lessening the distance between them. "To monitor the demons and the Mystics and whoever else might try to make contact with us."

Mirth lit Avn's eyes yet he grimaced. "We stopped the practice of using Sentinels eons ago. If the worlds we create pose that serious of a threat, we can dismantle them without creating chaos or annihilating ourselves—"

"I'm not going," she insisted. Her voice softened.

"Enough with this!" He grabbed her by the wrist and dragged her toward the center of the valley. "Only Masters can become Sentinels. You don't have the skills."

Pulling herself free again, she stopped.

"I'll imprison you," he threatened casually.

"No, you won't!"

Avn faltered. Despair weighed him down. He fell to his knees in the sand and bowed his head.

She knelt in front of him, cradled his head in her hands.

"Not after everything you've done to keep me safe, you won't, now that I trust you."

Casting a glance over her shoulder, Ule frowned at the sight of her Master. He had started following her as she turned toward the heart of the desert. His pace was slow and tentative at first. Now, she realized, he had caught up with her.

Her dark skin itched with a mild burn. The cracked heels slipped around in her new sandals. Her hair fluttered about, bleached white, dry, and frizzy. She didn't care. Once she was far beyond the curious eyes of Elishevera's devotees and the suspicious glances of the Bisi Nomads, she planned to shift through the air and return to Sondshor. There she would resume her previous form, return to a life as translator for Magnes Lyan, and live the remainder of this generation as the woman people had come to know.

"Stop!" Avn matched her stride despite the thick sand which made walking difficult. "Let me release Ibe, then we can talk."

Something in his tone caused her skin to prickle. "Go back home," she insisted. "There's nothing you can say to change my mind."

"What if you become trapped again?" Breathless, he grabbed her about the waist and urged her to stop.

Reluctantly, she yielded to his embrace and turned to face him. "Istok's not a threat anymore," she argued.

"What if there's another demon powerful enough to hurt you?"

As much as she wanted to argue with him, she realized that was a possibility. "I'll be covert." With a sigh, she slipped through his arms. "Come visit once in a while."

Motioning for her to wait, Avn stepped back. Placing the palms of his hands on each temple, he focused intensely at the space in the air before him. His left pupil widened. At first, light trickled from the darkness. Then it began to pour out.

Coalescing into a mass, the light reflected the image of a man. With every flicker and pulse, the image solidified into a three dimensional form.

Ibe breathed rapidly, as though he had been holding his breath a long time. Fists slung low at his sides, he glared at Avn, his chest heaving. He smacked his lips, as though he were about to speak. Instead, he exhaled shakily, his expression sullen, angry, and disgusted.

Avn addressed Ibe. "You've committed crimes, minor compared to my own."

Ibe winced.

"I'll promise to be your advocate with the Council, urge them to show you leniency. I will accept the burden of the abuse of your authority over Ule as my own, but you need to help me return her to our realm by any means necessary."

Realizing her Master was willing to force her to ascend against her will, she trembled with mild rage. She addressed Ibe calmly and assuredly. "I don't consider what you did that terrible," she said, hoping to dissuade him. "Your intention was to help, right?"

Ibe remained reticent, his lips pressed firmly together. Something within him seemed diminished. The bright light she had always felt drawn to had dimmed.

"Ibe?" she called to him softly.

He glanced in her direction. Anguished eyes scanned her from head to toe. He wiped his mouth with the back of a trembling fist. Sneering, he threw back his head, cast his gaze toward the sun, and vanished.

In the afterward silence, his Ascension resonated as the answer to both of them.

"Looks like you're on your own," Ule said, realizing that her Master had hoped to influence his Student to break yet another Xiinisi law. "Good luck explaining that to our Council." She turned to walk away.

He grabbed her by the arm. "Once I go, I will not be coming back." His stern tone felt absolute.

Saddened by the thought of being on her own again, struggling to figure out the potential of her skills, she accepted her place and nodded to indicate she understood. "At least this time, the choice to be alone is mine to make."

— 53 —

INSIDE THE TENT, bright sunlight lit up the fluttering white canopy above. Displays of odd creatures and unusual objects were crammed together on tables and cabinets. Chatter blended into a comforting hum throughout the tent as townies milled about dressed in their finest garments. Farmers and farmhands wore soiled clothes from a long day's work in the fields.

Soft, cool fingers clutched at Ule's. She lightly squeezed them and turned toward the woman pressing against her arm.

Leaning forward, lavender scent drifted from Bethereel's flesh. "I'm to ask you," she said, peering through the short netting which draped from the top of her flat black hat over her eyes, "if you would like new clothes? One of the textile merchants wants to make you a more modern capelet."

Pinching the stiff collar about her neck, Ule pouted. "But this one's traditional for scribes."

Flattening the flared skirt of her brilliant purple dress, Bethereel shrugged. "I think he wants to have a hand at updating the look of that tradition."

"Come round, come round!" the voice boomed, interrupting Bethereel. She rolled her eyes.

"Come hear a tale of unrequited love!"

"Is there any other kind?" Bethereel whined.

At the call of the barker, the small crowd inside the tent squeezed together and pressed against a wooden table inlaid with bone fragments. In the center sat a crudely welded lead box, not much bigger than a human head.

"Long ago, when the world was very young, a demon like none other we've ever seen walked the world."

"Then how can we know about it?" Bethereel called out. "Did anyone even write back then? Where's your proof?"

Ule shied away from Bethereel and pushed herself deeper into the crowd.

"Here," Sabien arched an eyebrow at her. "We've a scribe amongst us." He pointed to the middle of the crowd. "Let's ask her?"

Ule cleared her throat. All eyes fell upon her. "Oh most definitely," she answered cooperatively. "At Sondshor Castle, there are parchments dating back to the Ancient World. People wrote back then." She paused a moment, before prompting the next turn in their conversation. "Is this the story about the cactus demon?"

The word cactus passed from one person to the next.

Sabien nodded dramatically, eyes swooping across the crowd. "Yes, indeed, but how could you know that?" His voice boomed throughout the tent.

Grateful for the shield her scribe's capelet provided as all eyes focused on her, she still couldn't get used to the scrutiny and shivered. She scanned the crowd. "I've read them. I've read all the stories from the Ancient World, and by far the most interesting are the ones I've read about a cactus demon."

Murmurs of excitement flooded the tent.

"Hush now," Sabien called out. Eyes wide, he mirrored the crowd's curiosity. He hovered near the table using a crate as a stage, one hand resting on the top of the lead box. "Listen closely. Let me tell you a demon's story." Turning slightly, he began.

"This demon wandered the world for centuries, finding nothing to inspire him, casting fear and mayhem, until one day he spied a beautiful woman the likes of which he had never seen before."

Pulling away from the crowd, Ule wandered amongst the displays and stopped at a loose flap at the side of the tent. She slipped through the concealed exit just as Sabien introduced the demon's desire.

"Her name was Mulga..."

She'd heard the stories many times now about the cactus demon. Although the story bored her, working up the crowd on Sabien's behalf always thrilled her.

Minutes later, a stirring at the tent flap caught her eye and she shifted to let Sabien through. He joined her in the shadows cast by the nearby store fronts.

"Has anything changed?" she asked him.

Pulling a pipe from his shirt pocket, he shook his head and leaned against a stack of crates. "I tell them how the rage from being rejected turned the demon into a rock."

Pipe in hand, long graceful fingers pretended to lift the top off the lead box, currently sheltered inside the tent. He continued his act, waving his hand over what would be inside: the dark green kornerupine on a pillowed bed of red satin.

"They feel the powerful anger from the stone. Sometimes, if they're sensitive enough, they swoon. When it becomes too much to bear, I finish." Sabien mimed replacing the lid on the box and concluded the act.

Frowning, he pulled a tinfoil pouch from the back pocket of his gray trousers. The edges of his face elongated as he focused on pinching just the correct amount of tobacco between thumb and forefinger. His shoulders collapsed slightly as he packed tobacco into the bowl.

"And the story, people are believing it?"

"It's a love story." He winked at her. "They're the most popular kind, especially when the love's denied." In the silence that passed, sadness settled over him. She barely heard him mumble, "Everyone can relate."

"It's a difficult artifact to display." He pressed the tobacco under his thumb, packing it down. "It's so small. The people at the back don't feel it. But under certain settings, it could be truly effective." He clamped the narrow end of the pipe between his teeth yet still managed to speak. "The pink line, it moves and in the right light, you'd think the stone was looking back at you. Really, it needs a separate booth where people can enter a few at a time to experience the full effect."

"Have you thought about a more permanent setup?"

"That would mean more money, hiring people—"

"You could have acts, sell merchandise too." She watched him mull over her ideas. "What about the smithy? Avn did leave it to you."

Shyness overcame Sabien. After staring at his toes for a considerable length of time, he peered at her. "No word from him, eh?"

She shook her head. "He wanted to return to his people in the south." Reinforcing the lie Avn had instructed her to tell Sabien to explain his disappearance, pressed her with pangs of guilt.

Sniffing, Sabien shrugged and puffed on his pipe, swirls of smoke gliding over his neck and head.

Movement in the shadows caused Ule to spasm, and she wondered if her nerves would ever settle down again. After nearly two months since fighting Istok in the desert, uncontrollable twitches still wracked her at the oddest times.

Frowning, Sabien swiveled his head toward the alehouse, where the figure of a man stepped forward.

"Sorry, Ule" a familiar voice said. "Didn't mean to scare you."

The man emerged into the light. Brown straight hair stopped at his shoulders. Clean-shaven, his features were almost boyish and nondistinct yet still handsome. He wore brown leather leggings, tall black riding boots, and a long tunic style jacket that she had seen worn around Sondshor Castle.

Her heart skipped a beat and her skin prickled from excitement.

If not for the familiarity of the man's presence and his green eyes, she might not have recognized her Master.

Her breath hitched slightly. She wanted to call out his name, but stopped herself when she realized he had returned in a different form. She needed to be discreet.

"Nav," he introduced himself more to Sabien then her. "I really enjoyed the show."

Hesitant at first, Sabien paused in his smoking. He pushed himself upright and shook the man's hand. The shake was brisk at first but slowed. Sabien tilted his head, reluctant to let go.

"Have we met?"

Their hands lingered.

Nav shrugged. "No, I don't think so. I'm new to the castle. Apprentice Mystic." Releasing his grip, he pointed at Ule. "Everyone complains of her. A favorite of the Magnes, she is. Can't walk anywhere without getting struck by her shadow."

Reunited not more than a few minutes, already Ule sensed her Master nudging at her mind, and she understood. They were intended to be strangers, for now, to let their conversation and encounter unfold naturally.

"Bethereel's waiting," she announced suddenly.

Sabien at least acknowledged her with a nod as she slipped away. Once she rounded the corner of the tent, she paused, peeked back the way she had come, and watched the two men.

"Nav, that's peculiar," Sabien said. "Is it short for something?" He slowly unfolded his body, standing tall again.

"Hmm, yeah, Navalis."

Nodding, Sabien smirked. "Short names. I hear they're a popular trend at the castle now."

Nav nodded again.

They exchanged good natured words which made Sabien smile shyly, even laugh a little. Avn, whom she would need to get used to calling Navalis, grew less reserved and more animated.

An intangible yet undeniable connection between them began to weave and bind. She likened them to two suns rising, setting each other ablaze.

And Ule basked in their warmth, allowing the light to burn into her eyes, unwilling to look away.

Made in the USA
Charleston, SC
14 March 2014